My Emerald Fire

Book Three

Elm Jed

To my Lemon,
Here's to conquering hills
and bringing men to their knees
wink

Content Warnings

This Book contains ON PAGE:
Self-harm, attempted self-harm, torture, gun & knife violence,
skillet violence, blood/gore, on page deaths, panic/anxiety attacks,
PTSD flashbacks, doors being broken down, motorcycle/vehicle
chases, attempted murder, attempted kidnapping.
Cliffhanger.

BDSM Aspect of the Book:
Fire play, rope play (shibari), sensation play, blindfolding, someone
calling "stop" to a scene, loose restraints,
cut out of rope, and anal play.
Honorifics and the "stoplight" method are used.

-Discussed-
Sexual assault, thoughts of suicide & self harm, forced
hospitalization, death/loss, homelessness, alcohol & drug abuse,
and domestic violence.

Prologue

Beware the Icy Heart

4 Years Ago

Fuckers are following me. I know they are.

I've learned to recognize the signs. I've gotten good at it the past year. Not really by choice, it was that or death. Or worse.

There's always something worse than death.

I round another corner, continuing the long route back to the shelter. I peek over my shoulder and see a man ducking behind a few people who are out in the cold. My hands grip into the tatters I call a jacket, quickly sidestepping into an alley and hiding behind a dumpster. It would've been easier to hide in Manhattan, plenty more people to disappear among, even as late as it is. Except Roger moved my drop point further inside Manhattan, and I can't take chances meandering around there. Usually it was safe to travel on foot, even with the longer distance.

Unless assholes are following me.

Cold metal presses at my back as I sink into a squat, further into the shadows. I wait.

My glasses fog up from my warm breath.

I give him time to look around and move on. Unless he decides to duck down this way. A stiff breeze comes, the alley almost becomes a wind tunnel as I huddle behind my wimpy scarf. The fogginess of my glasses worsens. It's fine, don't need to see to know if they're coming.

Freezing as I am and wanting to go back to the shelter where there's mediocre food, warmish blankets, and maybe a cot...I stay.

Minutes tick by and I begin to lose feeling in my fingers and toes.

I don't move.

Wait it out. Make sure he's gone. *Start memorizing his features, Sarah.* Blonde hair. Pasty skin. Average looking in size, not muscley like the bouncers at Gabriel's clubs. Or the runners some of the crime bosses seem to be hiring lately. Steve might be the only scrawny looking one out of them. Doesn't matter because he can still pack a punch.

My cheek muscle twitches. I carefully touch where the fading bruise is.

A few more minutes pass.

After a group of loud teenagers pass, along with more freezing wind, I carefully peek around the dumpster. All clear. I stand, continuing down the alley and take the few extra blocks to walk to the shelter.

What I wouldn't give to be on a clean couch watching a Nick Cage film, preferably with popcorn or pizza rolls. Fuck, I can't remember the last time I had those. Or sugary cereal. Or ice cream. Well, that's a depressing thought.

I hurriedly arrive at the shelter, stepping inside with a sigh of relief as I glance one last time over my shoulder. No one. Quickly, I wipe my glasses as the heat of the shelter hits me. After I close the door behind me, someone comes around the corner, a volunteer I don't recognize, and they stop me.

"We're out of beds," she says with a look of remorse.

The woman has her dark hair pulled into a bun, wearing a

heavy sweater and jeans with those fuzzy looking boots everyone seems to have.

"Are you sure?"

"I'm sorry, but it's late and cold so there was a bigger turnout tonight. Not to mention lack of donations lately, sorry, I'm rambling. I could make you some coffee? You can sit in the main room? But it's pretty crowded."

"I uh—"

"Hey, kiddo, you made it." A familiar rough voice comes from behind the woman.

Faintly, I grin at the older man. His usual terrible beanie is on his head, covering his curly blondish hair, and he's unshaven from the last time I saw him two days ago. His tattered Carhart jacket is open, revealing an old sweater covered in motor oil stains.

"Hey, Bobby," I whisper.

"Got a seat for you, come on." He pulls me under his arm as the woman tries to speak. "Already got a coffee for her. Thanks anyways, Linda."

I press closer, putting my arm around him while I chuckle under my breath. "You steal coffee from that shop again?"

"Who said anything about stealing?"

"You did last week."

"No, no that was *acquiring*. Besides poor coffee was left on the counter. All alone. No one to claim it." He playfully pouts.

"How terrible." I roll my eyes as I walk with him into the large room. It's filled to the brim with people trying to hide from the winter weather. Bobby weaves us through everyone until we get to a back corner, where a man with dark skin and locs waves his hand in greeting.

"Kept your seat, Bobby," he says, patting it. "Hiya, Sarah."

"Evening, Walter."

Bobby sits down and I somehow fit next to him, squeezing between the two men. Bobby sidles up next to another man who's asleep with their feet propped up on the bench. He holds up a coffee cup with the same logo from where he *acquired* from last time.

I raise a brow at him.

"Okay, *this* one was gifted to me. I paid for mine. Nice barista took pity on me after I asked for another coffee for my friend who was *supposed* to be here yesterday."

"Held up," I mumbled, taking the offered beverage and sip it with a slight moan. Not perfect, but yay for coffee and I haven't eaten for…okay, I don't remember. I'll grab a donut from an AA meeting down the street or something.

"What held you up?" Bobby asks. I shrug. "That, uh, boyfriend of yours again?"

"Not really a boyfriend right now," I whisper, keeping my attention on the coffee.

"Well given you're staying here, and not wherever he lives, I'd say he's not."

"Sounds like a motherfucker," Walter mutters, rubbing his hands together. "Letting you freeze out here with the rest of us?"

"What if I like the likes of y'all?" I retort.

He scoffs with amusement. "Need to recheck your judgement there."

"Aw come on, Walter, who wouldn't want to be around your adorable face?"

Walter smiles at me, patting my knee. "If I was twenty years younger, Sarah."

"She'd still reject you," Bobby chimes in.

All three of us chuckle low, huddling close when a strong wind makes the windows rattle. Even with the heat probably blasting, my fingers and toes are on the verge of frostbite.

Bobby and Walter start conversing as I lean back in hopes of feeling my feet again. Walter coughs heavily, whatever he got a few weeks ago not letting up. I try to ignore the harsh cough that worries me, almost falling asleep on Bobby's shoulder when there's a ticking warning along my spine. Anxiety travels over my skin. The paper cup is clutched in my hands as I drift my gaze over the space. I sink further between the two men.

The guy who was following me earlier is at the entrance. The woman who stopped me, Linda, is talking to him but he doesn't seem to be paying attention to her. His dark eyes scan the room, and I duck my head to allow my hat to cover most of my face. I lean forward, putting my elbows on my knees, which helps me hide behind Walter's burly frame.

Suddenly, Bobby puts his arm around me, bringing me in close. I go still, while Walter glances over his shoulder in suspicion. The man is still at the doorway, scanning the room before he finally relents and turns around. Linda shakes her head, moving to speak with one of the other volunteers.

"Wouldn't be the boyfriend, would it?" Walter asks.

"No," I rasp.

"Probably some creeper, eh, kiddo? Hard out here for some of us, maybe you should date Walter," Bobby mutters under his breath. We exchange a glance.

Walter chuckles, shaking his head as his cough starts up again.

"Why don't you get more hot water? Help that cough and add to the last of our coffee before it freezes?" Bobby suggests.

Walter grunts against his coughing, getting up to do so.

"Thanks," I mutter.

"Know who that was that time?" I shake my head. "You've been followed more often of late."

"Don't I know it." I finish the coffee, knowing I'm gonna need the caffeine. Bobby's arm falls from my shoulders as I stand. He stares up at me in worry. "I need to go."

"He's gone, kiddo. Better you stay here."

"Doesn't mean—"

"Stay the night. Dangerous out there right now with this weather. Disappear in the morning." Bobby's voice is rough as he stares up at me with pleading brown eyes.

Should've never told him.

Should've never almost involved him.

That was a close call, too close. Who knows who that man was working for. If it was Marchetti, and he realized his main drug runner's girlfriend has been hacking into their computer systems, I'm fucking dead.

Although, I'm almost sure I'm only being followed cause Steve told them to. He wants to know where I am, why I'm hanging around clubs not owned by Marchetti. He can't know I've been living on the streets. None of them can.

I've already cut out Leanne and Nancy for their safety; I can't risk Bobby or Walter's safety next. They've been too good to me the past couple of weeks. Too nice. Walter doesn't even know my involvement with the mafia. Neither deserved a fate caught up in the mob because of me. I've gotta keep them both safe.

"Bobby—"

"They won't do nothing with everyone here," he continues to argue softly. "You go back out there, you'll lose those fingers. Need them, right?"

I glance down at said frostbitten fingers, swallowing hard as I look at the entrance again.

Yeah, I do need them.

I sit back down next to him, and he pats my knee. "I'll wait til morning."

It's 3 AM when I leave with a heavy heart as they sleep, never returning to the same shelter or area again in fear of being tracked.

In my gut, I knew it was only a matter of time before they found me. I had to disappear.

The one regret I had—I never said goodbye.

Chapter 1

Monsters and Men

———

Leo

Leo's fist slams across the man's face, blood splattering into the air. Jameson punches the other, while Julio takes a shot at the back of the chained man's head. Leo steps back, glancing over his bloodied knuckles. Blood soaks through his shirt, spattered down his arms and hands. Jameson, Julio, and Isaac looking similarly the same. Owen remains off to the side, fiddling with a revolver. The two men are tied to chairs in only their underwear, wounds littering their bodies as bruises form. They spit up blood, choking back tears and crimson.

Evan, the man Leo punched last, mumbles, "*Please...sir...*"

"You don't get to talk to him without permission," Jameson answers, pressing against the broken bones in his shoulder.

The other, Greg, whimpers as he watches through swollen eyes as Jameson beats Evan more. Leo holds his hand up. Jameson stops, scowling at Evan.

"Needed to let off some steam," Isaac comments, stalking behind the men. They cower away from him. "Rough couple of weeks there. Good thing we have you to help."

Greg tries to speak, voice cracking, "P-please…what do-do you—"

Julio cuts him off, yanking back his head by his greasy blonde hair. "You think you deserve to know?"

The man whimpers again. "Whatever we did…we're sorry boss…we're—"

Evan grunts as Isaac punches his jaw.

Isaac waves his hand in the air, briefly looking over his bloodied knuckles. "Don't listen well there, do you?"

"Stop," Leo commands. He nods toward Owen, who walks over with a chair and places it in front of Leo. The mafia boss sits, leaning his elbows upon his knees. "I'm trying to conjure up a reason, why you two should even get a chance to explain your-selves. When I could just shoot you, be done with you."

They start to garble up a mess of words as Owen places the Colt Revolver into Leo's hands. The men strain against their chains as the Crew glowers at them. Leo spins the cylinder as Owen gives him four bullets. Unhurriedly, Leo begins to load the gun while the two men whimper.

"Fucking shut up or we'll gag you next," Julio warns, smacking one upside the head.

Leo juts his head, and all of them step back.

A dark threatening aura builds around the mafia boss as he speaks, his voice far too calm for the wrath laced with every word.

"Three years ago, you two were part of a "gang bang" with a particular woman, whom you left for dead." Both men go still. Evan flashes a look to Greg, who stares at Leo in horror. "You two should know my rules when it comes to such behavior. Acts as such have no tolerance with me, whether years ago or recently… you deserve punishment. Your comrades already met their fate."

Leo snaps the cylinder in place with a loud click. Greg starts to scream, "Ther-re's a reason! We—"

"I don't care," Leo says in an ominous tone, pointing the gun at Greg's groin.

"W-w-wait! We had orders!" Greg pleads.

Leo halts.

He glares at the man at the end of his barrel. Leo's eyes flash to Jameson, who meets his gaze before looking at the others. Isaac flicks his gaze to the two men and then to Leo. The other three never mentioned that. They didn't talk about being hired. Even after their dicks were cut off.

"Orders?" Leo asks in a cold tone as he leans back in his chair.

Greg gulps harshly. Both remain silent until Isaac kicks at their chairs. They whimper, swallowing harshly. Evan starts speaking, "Sh-she wouldn't f-fuck him. She wouldn't—"

"Who?" Jameson questions. "Who didn't she fuck?"

"P-p-please… he always sent—" Evan coughs up blood flying from his mouth.

"Answer the fucking question!" Isaac kicks at his chair.

"We p-promised—"

Leo aims and shoots Greg in the knee, causing the man to scream. He shrieks, answering finally, "Gabriel! Gabriel Marchetti gave the orders!"

A shadow falls over Leo as he goes extremely still. His veins become like ice as he stares at the man howling before him. Boiling fury beginning in his stomach.

Leonardo Luciano is deathly silent, standing without a word as he walks toward the man. He kicks his chair back, causing the bleeding, screaming man to fall unforgivingly against the ground with a thud. He then presses the hot barrel against the man's temple, causing him to whimper more.

"Are you telling the truth?" Leo asks in a very distant, composed tone.

"Y-yes. I swear…Gabriel, he…he ordered us. We had no choice."

"He told you it was for that *exact* reason? Not that she was a snitch? Or stole from him?"

The man's eyes go wide, shaking his head.

"She embarrassed him!" Evan pleads, as if he could save his counterpart or himself. "He...he ordered—"

"That meant spending over twelve hours torturing a woman because she wouldn't *fuck* my brother?" Leo sneers. "*That's* what she deserved?"

"Boss...we-we had no choice," Greg pleads against the gun to his head. "Gabriel would've killed—"

Leo pulls the trigger, blasting the man's head into the floor. Evan starts to sob, shaking so hard his chains rattle against his metal chair.

Leo stands fully, stalking toward Evan and cocks the gun to fire again. Evan begs, "No, please! Talk-talk to Gabriel! We had no choice!"

The air chills in the room. Leo's expression is cold and foreboding. None of his Crew moves, staying back as Leo presses the gun against the man's groin and pulls the trigger. He screams, thrashing against his restraints as tears stream down his face.

"I wonder..." Leo murmurs in a gravelly tone, "...did she plead like you are now? Did she bleed like you are?" He grabs a fistful of Evan's hair, yanking his head back as the man cries in pain. "Did you have no choice in how you broke her? How you *used* her body? Was there *no choice* in that?"

Leo traces the hot barrel over the man's cheek, and he cries even harder. Jameson takes a step toward Leo, but Isaac holds him back with a shake of his head. Owen remains still, while Julio steps further away from The Spartan.

Evan pleads as Leo snarls viciously in response, "*Beg me* to kill you."

Throat working, Evan whimpers as Leo presses the barrel against his temple. "Please...please don't—"

The gun goes off. Evan slumps over with a hole in his head as Leo lets go of him. Gun empty, Leo drops it to clatter against the reinforced floor. He stares down at the dead men, hands beginning tremble.

"How the fuck did we not know it was Gabriel who issued the orders?" Jameson asks.

"Or why…thought they attacked her because they found her link to the police," Owen says.

Leo orders with teeth bared, "Find every fucking person Gabriel gave such orders to. I want to know how may fucking women he killed without us knowing. Find me *every single one* who worked for him. Boss, captain, runner, club owners…I don't give a fuck. *Hand them over.*"

Isaac asks, "What if Gabriel finds out why—"

"I don't give a damn," Leo warns. "Find them."

Isaac nods once, walking out with Julio directly behind him without a word. Owen moves to Evan's lifeless body, kicking at his head. "Her fucking ex must've known the truth. He didn't know she worked with the police. It was just a fucked-up revenge rape for Gabriel."

"Did she say anything about Gabriel approaching her?" Jameson asks Leo quietly.

"No," Leo rasps, hands still shaking. "No."

"Maybe she doesn't remember," Owen suggests. "She mentioned being roofied and drugged at times, not to mention getting drunk…could've happened one of those nights."

"If she was roofied, how the hell did she fight him off?" Jameson asks. "Drugged or drunk for that matter? He's twice her fucking size."

Owen gives Jameson a stern look, glancing briefly at Leo before saying, "You saw what she did to that ballroom. She didn't survive hell without fighting. We can pretend every damn day she's Autumn Watson but…" he shakes his head as Leo meets his gaze, "…she's still Sarah Marie, the woman who infiltrated half the mob of New York."

The room is silent as Leo straightens himself. He loosens a long breath, trying to keep his anger in check as he orders Jameson, "Find Gabriel, keep him—"

The door slams open, Mila walking in with a phone to her ear. "We have a situation."

Autumn

I stare up at Steve as he points the Magnum at my head.

Old, familiar blue eyes fester with hate and ruin. I start to scoot back, but his slow rising grin makes me stop.

"Don't scream or make any noise," he threatens. "Otherwise, I'm gonna fucking shoot you and then I'm gonna fucking kill whoever comes through that door. Probably that old geezer of a woman, Nancy, right? Wouldn't want her to get hurt...would you?"

I frown up at him, flicking my gaze to the gun in his hands.

"Always the *bleeding* fucking heart, huh?"

My heart races as I scramble in my head for any escape.

Phone is in the bedroom, if I go for it, I'm dead.

I scream for Chesty or Animal, I'm dead.

Could fight him, but gun at head equals dead.

My muscles shake as I try to think. Something, anything to help me. I need that gun out of his hands first. His focus off of me... I need...

Forcing my breathing to sound panicked, my gaze flicks to the side.

"How did you get out?" I rasp in a frightened voice. "You were in max."

He scowls, moving forward to kick at my legs and then my stomach. I curl into myself, scooting further away from him as the pain burns through my torso.

"I *was* there cause of *you*. Supposed to be dead, Sarah, they told me you were *dead*," he growls, kicking for my head, but I dodge him barely. "Thankfully, a certain detective will do fucking anything to get what he wants. He'd do good in the mob. Tenacious. Underhanded. Picked the wrong career, I think."

My eyes widen, heart clattering in my chest. I creep further back toward the couch. "What?"

"Yeah, he's got it out for you, bitch," Steve taunts with a cocky flair. "Got me out with a deal that I'd give you over to him. Get the rest of whatever information he said you're hiding from him. Sounds like you *really* fucked him over good. What you do to piss him off?" He tilts his head in that condescending way he always did. "Beginner 101, Sarah, don't piss or shit on the hands who feed you."

I move further back. "He fucked *me* over first."

"Paybacks a bitch, baby doll," he sneers. "Said something else about me finding shit about this new mafia boss who replaced Gabriel. Said you're the link. The way in...*again*. Odd. What's with you and mob bosses? They just like your pussy that much? Is *that* who you were getting on your knees for? I mean, you were okay, but you were always better with your mouth shut and something shoved up your ass."

I spit at him, and he kicks me again. Pain flares through my body, causing me to groan against the pulsating throb.

He warns, "Watch it. Nancy would look awful in red."

I snap my mouth shut, grimacing as the pain lingers from my gut to my chest. My head throbs, pounding as I try to keep a clear head and move closer to the couch.

"If he wanted...wanted me, why are you—?"

"Here? Pfft," he waves it off, glancing around my apartment. "Come on, baby doll, you know how this works. Use that bitch ass brain of yours. Think I'm dumb enough to help him? He ain't got the immunity I need. Not to mention, not enough cash." I scoot another inch back, clutching my stomach as it churns. "That fucker is delusional if he thinks I'm just gonna hand you over to him. Mob is gonna pay a *shit ton* for you when they realize who you are. Hell, *Gabriel* would pay a shitload for your fucking body."

"Never," I sneer, continuing to move back. Almost there. "Police will—"

"No, they won't. I'll admit that detective was stupid enough to get me out, but not to *admit* he did. Making an illegal deal with ex-mob? A *murderer*? No. He was just desperate enough to think I'd help. Police never make fair deals, but you should know that... right?"

His face darkens, glowering with contempt.

My stomach twists in pain and fear, my chest collapsing in on itself as I move another inch back. Anxiety crawls up my spine, warring with my survival instincts that scream at me to get out.

Stay calm, Autumn. Come on...a little bit more.

Steve brandishes the weapon, pointing it at my head again. "So, tell me, what do I gotta pay, baby doll, for that pussy? What magic do you use to get these mob bosses to bend over backwards to taste it? Don't remember it being that good...better yet, what did Gabriel's *brother* pay for you?"

"I'm not your baby doll," I argue.

"Oh, yes you are. Cause if you don't belong to me, then you belong to Marchetti and whoever decides to fuck your—"

He goes to kick me again, but I slide back on the hardwood floor and reach beneath the couch. My hand quickly finds the hidden k-bar, yanking it out and throwing it at Steve's chest. I miss his heart, the blade landing into his shoulder instead. He lets out a loud howl, gun no longer pointed at my head, I rush him with a scream, "CHESTY!"

I crash into Steve, wrestling him to the ground as he tries to aim the gun at me, but I twist the knife deeper into his shoulder and he howls again. I'm able to grab his wrist, slamming it into the floor to make him drop the weapon. I swipe it away, getting up to kick him straight into his groin. Steve grabs for me as I scramble for the .22, but he yanks me back as he pulls the knife out of his shoulder. I'm flipped over and he brings the knife down. Just barely, I'm able to block it with a grunt. I punch where the knife struck him, causing him to tumble over as I use another maneuver Isaac taught me to flip him over. My foot kicks straight into his knee, distracting him as I grab the knife and slam it into his thigh.

He shouts as I get up, running for the kitchen. Steve knocks me down, almost dragging me over the hardwood floor. He punches my face and then again. Black spots pepper my vision as I fight back, kicking him as his hands go around my neck. I thrash against the weight of him, clutching at his wrists.

"You filthy bitch!" He screams, adding pressure to my throat. My vision gets blurry as I begin to choke. "They'll still fuck your limp body! Just like before!"

I let go of his wrists, reach down and grab his dick and twist... *hard*. He let's go immediately and screams as I hit him in the groin again. With a woozy, throbbing head I punch the wound in his shoulder, causing him to yell as I scramble for the kitchen. He gets up behind me as I grab the iron skillet on the stovetop.

There's a click from his gun, and I swing instinctively. The iron rings out as it makes contact with the gun as it fires, bullets hitting my cabinets instead of me. With all my might, I swing again and strike Steve across the head just as my front door slams open. Chesty and Animal enter with guns drawn as Steve thuds to the ground.

Gulping in oxygen, the skillet clangs against the floor as I drop it. Chesty comes over as Animal goes to Steve's body, keeping his gun trained on him.

Chesty grabs my shoulders. "You, okay?"

"Yeah," I groan, gulping down air. "But I officially want to move. Today."

He glances over my throat and then at the mess. "Don't blame you there."

"He's still breathing," Drew announces.

"Then make him stop," Waylon says as Drew already aims his gun for a clean execution.

"No!" I fall forward, gripping the counter with one hand as the other clutches my aching stomach. Oh, crud this hurts way worse than eating too much ice cream. Oh, how I wish it was the reason for this. "Roger got him out. Sent him…after me."

Waylon moves around me, grabs a cup and fills it with water. He hands it to me, and I take a few sips. It hurts to swallow, but the water is needed. As Waylon does this, Drew asks, "Caltz got him out?"

"Yeah. To get to Leo."

"Fucking cocksucker," Drew swears, pulling out his phone. "We couldn't even get this fucker out without drawing attention."

"Your ex-handler has some vendetta, huh?" Waylon mutters.

"Apparently like the rest of my exes." I take another drink, and Waylon raises a brow. "I need humor right now," I rasp. "My ex was hiding in my apartment, tried to kill me…*again.*"

I cough, rubbing my throat as it pulses with pain in tune with my throbbing headache.

"If Caltz got him out, means he's got some serious pull somewhere or favors," Waylon comments, rubbing his hand gently over my shoulder. "If Steve was willing to work for him—"

"He was gonna sell me to Gabriel, to the mob," I interrupt. Both freeze when the stairs creak.

Nan comes into view, who lets out a shriek with her hands flying to her mouth. She asks in horror, staring at Steve on the floor, "What happened?"

"Steve got out, tried to kill me," I answer with a hoarse voice. I drink the last of the water, making my stomach churn. "He knows too much."

"All more reason to finish him," Drew says. "Can't let him go, Autumn. None of us will have that. Caltz will come looking for him. Rest of the police may…but we can make it look like a mob hit. Old debts he never paid."

"Toss his body into a certain territory, maybe scare Caltz, too," Waylon adds.

"Can we not talk about this in front of Nan?" I ask as she continues to stare at Steve's unconscious body. "Nan." She looks up at me, hand clutching her chest. "Go downstairs. We'll take care of this. Go."

Still in a stupor, she nods and shakily goes down the stairs. She may have been involved with the mob years ago, but not like this. Finn maybe, but who knows how much he hid from her.

Drew and Waylon exchange a look. "We?"

"I was having a good fucking day, apart from Leo handling other *business*, but this bastard has already taken too much from me," I whisper, swallowing hard against the pain. I'm not certain why I'm so calm, even with the adrenaline wearing off. Maybe cause I'm not dead and just pissed off. "He broke into my apartment, attacked me, threatened to kill Nan…Leo promised I get to decide his fate."

"That would be?" Drew asks, putting his gun away and walks over to my hallway closet to pull out some rope. Did I buy that?

"He's got info. On Caltz. On Gabriel. On other people in other families and syndicates." My muscles shake, trembling with exhaustion. I move around the counter, glaring at Steve as Drew starts to basically hog tie him. "He worked closely with Gabriel, he'll know who may still be loyal to him, at least back then. Who to be weary of."

"You wanna use him for info?" Waylon asks.

Ire blossoms inside me. I remember what Steve did, outside of tonight, all of it flooding back. The man I once loved, so long ago, was far gone. A part of me tells me to push that anger away, shove it into a bottle and go be "happy" or some shit. I'm too angry. I'm too hurt.

"See how he likes being used," I rasp hoarsely.

"Autumn," Waylon warns.

"Give him to Leo." My gaze meets Waylon's. He holds my gaze for a moment before nodding once.

"Fine with me," Drew says, kicking Steve as he finishes the knots.

Waylon grabs my shoulder, turning me toward him. "You sure, sister? Give him that okay, you'll be going down a path that—"

"I already have. But I'm going with y'all this time."

He keeps his gaze level with mine. "We take you with us, there's no unseeing certain shit."

I flick my gaze to Drew, who's warm brown eyes meet mine with caution.

The Crew and Leo have tried these past few weeks to keep the wool over my eyes, shield me from what they do—a place I once swore I'd never return to. They've done their best to keep me away from the world that Leo has carefully kept controlled like a puppet. Except, last time, I didn't have a crucial key to survival.

I have to be a part of this. Roger is my problem and he's bringing the battle to my very home. I can't have them go against him on their own.

"Going into that meeting with him, I was told I was untouchable unless Leo basically says so, right? Does that still apply?"

"You're his old lady, so yeah," Drew answers.

"But I also sat in his damn chair, that places me as Leo's equal… correct?"

"Just about," Waylon murmurs.

"The *Forgotten Demons* will be there, too?"

"Always got your six, sister," Waylon responds. "In the *Italian Lily*, never gotta worry."

"Then I go."

They exchange a look, but then both nod.

It was time to pull the curtain aside, finally look upon what I've hidden from for years. Anxiety crawls up my spine, aching through my tired body. I shake it off, reminding myself of Leo's promises.

I'll *never* be used again. I flick my gaze down to Steve. Others I'll gladly put in my old place.

Chapter 2

Welcome to Hell

I hug Nan before leaving her with two bodyguards in her apartment. After a phone call made by Drew, two SUVs arrived with more men. Waylon assured me they were trusted people and she'll be moved to a safehouse. Whoever they are, they're part of the security detail outside the Crew, mainly mafia.

Steve is tossed into a car after his wounds were stapled together, keeping him from bleeding out. He's still knocked out by some drug that Drew gave him. I catch a glimpse of his gagged figure as they shut the door before Waylon ushers me into another car. Rudolf is in the driver's seat, while Waylon rides shotgun. Drew goes to the car that Steve was thrown into, and our little convoy pulls off as their cleaning crew arrives at the bookstore.

Night begins to engulf the city as we drive to the hotel.

I breathe in deeply, leaning back in the seat as I rub my head a little. I wince, feeling a bump and groan inwardly when I feel a cut on my lip. Flashing my gaze up, I catch a look at myself in the rearview mirror. Bruises are forming on my face and neck. I changed clothes, my bloodied ones handed over, probably to get rid of. Waylon checked my sight earlier, mentioning that I should be clear of having a concussion. My stomach revolts a little as I rub my hand over it, trying to ignore the aches sprouting across my body.

I got lucky. Could've been a lot worse.

"How you doin', sister?" Waylon asks.

"Fine." I concentrate on my breathing, even as my heart pounds. I've no idea what I'm walking into. Unsure how far Leo has already gotten with the other men. They could still be alive. Or in pieces already.

Anxiety ticks up my spine, telling me to run and I grasp the doorhandle to escape. Pieces of me recognize patterns from the past. Get out.

Not the same. I just need Leo.

A tear falls down my cheek, and I quickly wipe it away. Emotions churn, making my chest hurt as realization settles in that I almost died. Almost sold to the wrong side of the mob again. I try to recite *The Raven* under my breath, but it's hard to concentrate.

"Autumn," Waylon says.

"I'm fine. I'm fine."

"Breathe, *barchën*." Rudolf pulls the car down into the garage of the *Italian Lily*, weaving down into a private level. I look up, catching a glimpse of crinkles above his blue eyes in the rearview mirror. "Not alone."

I nod my head.

The car stops and Waylon lets me out with Rudy close behind. The big guy stops us, putting his hand on my shoulder as the other car parks. Steve is dragged out onto the pavement. He doesn't respond as two men pick him up. I glance over to see the private elevator, but then hear the freight elevator on the other side of the garage open its doors. Mila walks out.

"We taking the trash up?" Animal asks, folding his arms as she approaches our little group.

"Not yet, he said—" She stops, glancing me over with a scowl. "What the fuck is she doing here?"

"Wanted to come along," Chesty answers.

"You were instructed—"

"Don't have authority over me, Mila," Chesty practically growls. "Only two do and one of them is standing next to me."

Ringer folds his arms behind me, becoming a wall of menacing force.

Mila goes still. Her eyes slide to mine, and I tighten my jaw. Those steel grey eyes assess me, looking me over. All three men next to me stare her down as she flicks her gaze to them.

"Said you took him down, why is she covered in cuts and bruises?" She blatantly asks.

"Never said *we* did," Animal answers, then juts his head at me. "*She* did." He grunts at Chesty and Ringer. "Gonna work him over until the boss wants him."

Steve is propped up against the cement wall, blood dripping on the ground. Mila turns to me with a frown. "You shoot him?"

"No. Stabbed him twice. Then hit him with a skillet."

She quirks a brow, nods once, then heads for the elevator.

Chesty touches my shoulder, and I take that as our cue to follow. Animal walks away with Ringer directly behind him, veering for the three other men and Steve.

I hear some of the men talk, commenting on Steve's injuries. One of them whistles as I pass, "Damn, these hits aren't bad."

"Not too shabby," another says as Mila presses the elevator button.

"Keep your reviews to yourself," Ringer warns.

"Just complimenting the woman's skills." A guy with dark brown hair, faded cut on the sides replies. He glances over at me and smiles. It's not threatening or meant to be condescending, but something in my gut roils. "Should be proud of your handiwork. You did good, girl."

Cold runs up my spine. Inside something snaps at the words. Dark and possessive.

Chesty goes still beside me as I freeze as the elevator doors open. Animal snaps at the guy, "Shut your mouth, Mike!"

"Hey!" He holds his hands up in defense. "Being nice is—"

"Your name is Mike?" I ask suddenly, and everyone turns their attention to me. He stares at me, then nods. "Well then…*Mike*…I'd be very careful how you address me. I don't think your boss would take your *review* very well. You want me to ask him to find out?"

His eyes widen. Both Animal and Ringer step back, including the other two men at the stark coldness in my tone. I can feel Mila and Chesty watching, neither moving as they keep the doors open.

"Unless I give you *explicit* instructions to call me anything other than 'Miss Watson' or 'Ma'am' no other name comes out of your mouth for me. Are we clear? Or do you want your boss to be part of this little conversation…*Mike*?"

He visibly swallows. After a moment, he rasps, "No, Ma'am."

I quickly ease my expression, giving him one of my barista smiles, which causes *all* the men to look at me in shock. "Thank you. Remember to sanitize your hands after touching that shithead. Wouldn't want cooties."

I stride into the elevators with Mila and Chesty shortly behind. It's steel inside with bottom paneling made of wood. The doors close and we begin to ascend. My heart thunders in my chest as I take a long breath in to calm myself. My knees feel weak and shaky. Mila clears her throat as Chesty leans against the wall, not at all perturbed.

The elevator is silent, except for the pounding from my lingering headache.

"Very well…" Mila breaks the silence, our eyes meeting, "…you got balls, *Miss Watson*."

Chesty touches my shoulder as the doors finally open. There's a short hallway with grey walls and dark carpet. There's a couple of doors on the right, with a few more at the end of the hall. Mila strides towards one on the right, disappearing. My gaze can't seem to tear away from the door at the very end. Chesty says something, disappearing through the doorway where Mila went. I don't hear him. The roaring in my head too loud.

There's a pull in my chest, curiosity getting the better of me. It wrangles with my ticking anxiety up my spine. I don't know why I move forward to the door at the end of the hall. My limbs feel heavy as I'm not fully aware of what I'm doing, reaching for the doorhandle. It opens silently, but the shout behind me isn't.

"Autumn?" Chesty calls. "Autumn, don't!"

I don't listen, not heeding the warning in his voice.

I walk in and my gaze immediately finds the crimson that paints the floor, puddling beneath two bodies as the stench of death hits me. Stagnant blood and the remains of gunfire. I continue toward the two bodies, bound naked in chairs and covered in wounds. Dried blood and bruises riddle their skin. My chest shakes, along with my hands as I close the gap. Holes are in their heads, what's left of their brains spattered over the floor in a mess. My stomach convulses and my breathing stops as I look upon their gaping, shocked faces. Both stare with clouded vision and slack jaws.

Memories press forward as I try to shove them back, not wanting to remember, but seeing their faces again, shattered pieces of that night come pouring back.

I step back a little, time slowing as I realize the men before me are dead. Those distant memories, repressed over the past three years feel faint. More distant and faded. A mist seems to cover that horrible night as I stare at their lifeless bodies. My stomach clenches again, threatening to unfurl itself all over them, but I remain frozen as reality settles. A weight lifting off me.

The last of the five men who tortured and raped me are dead… gone. They're just bodies, heaped together like trash in a darkened corner.

"Autumn."

His voice comes through the terrifying stillness of my mind. I blink harshly, hearing footsteps and murmured voices.

"Dear Watson, look at me."

From that soft command, I do as Leo says and turn. He's only a few feet from me, and I'm met with the sight of his bloodied torso, crimson speckling his face and arms. His knuckles are torn. My gaze moves up, coming face to face with an ominous, menacing look that covers his gaze. He opens his mouth to give his usual response but stops as his jaw works. A sneer begins to form on his mouth as his gaze flicks over me. Leo's hands shake, flexing at his side. He's trembling. Not from fear…no, from the furious, murderous rage that I see clearly on his face.

Finally, I see the side that he and the *Forgotten Demons* warned me of.

Leonardo Durante Luciano, the mafia don of New York City, stands before me covered in blood and a wrathful aura. His hazel eyes burning like the fires of hell. While the men he killed lay bound behind me.

"Where is he?" Leo demands with a growl.

"Garage," Mila answers immediately.

Leo doesn't remove his searing gaze from me as he orders, "Bring him here. Chain him to a chair and lock the damn door." He steps towards me. "Find that damn detective. *Now.*"

Everyone leaves, including Jameson, at the orders not to be trifled with. Leo's jaw ticks as he stops just before me. I stare up at the man towering over me with a presence I've never felt before. I realize now, the snippets I'd gotten before barely scratched the surface.

The last few months flash from those moments. Deep down, an old part of me screams to get out. Save myself. That part of me recognizes the danger he possesses, apparent in the terrifying expression on his face. I realize why he became boss so easily, not just because of influence and money. It was the fear he could instill. *The Spartan.* A name he earned before replacing Gabriel…*why* he could replace him.

Suddenly, every shocked expression I've received from others clicks. To them, I should've faced his wrath, again and again. Defying his word and orders at times. Interrupting him. Talking so candidly. Laughing at him.

"He's a good man Miss Autumn…"

"Men like that—"

Leo brings his hand up slowly, stroking his fingers along my jaw gently. His touch is such a contrast to what his presence exposes, I'm almost taken aback. Old fears continue to prick at my skin, weary of his demeanor and screaming at the danger. Numbness begins to crawl over my skin, prepping to survive after the beatdown I've endured already tonight. His hand carefully cups my cheek and I remember his promise, washing away those fears.

"…your body will never be harmed by my hands, only protected."

His hand moves over my jaw, and I suddenly wince at the flash of pain. His scowl deepens, beginning to pull away, but I catch his hand to keep it where it is.

I trust him. Body screaming to run and cower, I don't listen. Survival to numb out, pushing it away. He'll never hurt me. He's Leo, *my* Leo.

Stepping forward, I lay my head against his bloodied shirt and fold my arms against the heat of his body. His breath hitches and he becomes stiff, but he wraps an arm around me protectively. His other hand strokes my head, and I wince again when he accidentally touches the bump on my head.

There's a growl in his chest. "Autumn—"

"He's yours. Use him. He knows people, those who worked for Gabriel. Drug runners and hidden routes and drop-offs. Use him as they used me."

His arm tightens around me, while the other clutches the back of my head gently.

The door opens, and Leo snaps his head to whoever opened the door. His arm keeps me possessively close to him. Another growl emanates from his chest, and he orders in a chilling tone, "Bring him in."

The sound of feet dragging and clanking chains echo in the room. Leo turns, keeping me from seeing who I know is being hauled in. Someone moves past toward the two dead men, and I hear more chains as locks are undone.

"Leave them," Leo orders. "He'll want company."

There's more shuffling as locks snap into place. Footsteps indicate people leaving, and I hear Steve groan. Leo begins to move us out of the room, still not allowing me to look at my ex-boyfriend being left with the stench of two lifeless bodies.

We're just out the door when I pull back from Leo, and he turns his attention to me. He starts to stop me, but I shake my head once. I clutch at his bloodied shirt as I step back to see Steve chained to a metal chair near the back of the room. He's waking up more, tugging at his restraints as he begins to take in his surroundings. His head comes up, looking up at the doorway where Leo and I stand. Horror, disgust, anger all line his expression.

For a moment, time stops, echoing through the surreal moment as I look upon him and see nothing left to save.

The door handle is cold in my hands. "Welcome to hell…baby doll."

I slam the door as he screams, *"Fucking bitch!"*

Chapter 3

Storybook Love

The peppermint tea is strong as I sip a bit of the hot beverage. I sit at the bar in Leo's top-floor office, where I had weeks ago when I returned from New Jersey. I glance over to Leo's desk, where he's looking over laptop screens next to Owen and Isaac with furrowed brows. Others talk in the office. A tense atmosphere encasing the place, even as I'm secluded from the rest. Rudy stands guard near the entrance of the bar, leaning against the wall.

After twenty minutes of Leo looking me over, convinced I wasn't too badly injured from my fight with Steve, I was sat at the bar. I'd forced a smile as he placed me in my spot, telling me to stay and inform him or the Crew if I needed anything. Rudy got me the tea, and since then I've just been sitting here for who knows how long watching Leo work with that cold, lethal expression.

Isaac let me know that Nan was at the safehouse, my apartment was cleaned and they're going through the security cameras, trying to figure out how Steve got into my apartment without getting flagged. Fucker knows how to lock pick and where I stage my cameras, that's how. As I watch them take care of the security breech that Steve caused, I can see the worry in their expressions. We've no idea if Steve already talked to Gabriel. If Roger knew when Steve would try to snatch me. Or if Steve talked to anyone else, preparing to sell me to the highest bidder. At least one fucker was locked up in a room, Roger on the other hand was not.

He's their biggest concern right now.

He got Steve out of prison. Even I don't know how he managed that. He's supposed to be on "hiatus" or some bullshit. Who helped him get Steve out?

Worry trickles up my spine, unsure who else knows I'm alive or that it was me who hacked into the mafia's computer systems years ago. Nerves yank at me. Leo's demeanor jars me a little, too.

I sit quietly, watching his movements and expressions more closely than I have before. The night I returned I'd been too tired to notice him at work. His posture is rigid and collected, filled with threat. His jaw muscles tense every few minutes, brow furrowing deeper than usual with an intense gaze. A gun sits on the desk next to him, just within reach. The bloodied shirt he wore is gone, replaced by a black long-sleeved shirt, hiding the tattoos that would've given him a more frightful look, I think. Even his voice is unfeeling. Severe.

Every little detail falls into the puzzle that is Leo when he's… this. The side of him he'd been trying to hide from me.

This was the mafia boss I had unknowingly been up against almost four years ago. The man that the police, FBI, and crime bosses couldn't touch. Why Roger had brought me in, thinking it'd been Gabriel, but it was him. The man who built a multi-million-dollar hotel empire from the ground up. The one who managed to take control of the mafia from the inside out, without his brother noticing. *He's* the one the police were scared of, not Gabriel. Although, his older brother has his own list of terrifying aspects.

My mind starts to spiral, attempting to make sense of the bubbling emotions inside, whilst trying to process what's happened in the past several hours. Instinct screams for me to run before I'm discarded, trickling along my skin to escape. My eyes flick towards the entrance a few times, remembering the hotel's layout. I did it once… I could—

No.

I'd left this world. I *knew* what power these people possessed. How they abused it. How they used people. It was cruel and mad. Steve's screams echo in my head, and my hands shake. I hold my head, breathing deep and struggle to hold onto Leo's promise. Every promise I gave him. That I'd stay. Mob boss. Biker. CEO. Monster…whatever title people gave him he wasn't that with me. Just a part of him. He was Leo. Just Leo…my Leo…I had to hold onto that.

"Upon…upon a midnight…" I whisper under my breath, chest constricting in panic. I rub my face and wince, gently touching my cut lip. I swallow hard, and my throat hurts. My mind flashes to Steve choking me. Hitting me. Not tonight, but years ago when I didn't fight back. When no one fought for me. When I was alone. What if that happens again?

I try to restart the poem but fail.

"Barchën?" Rudolf's voice reaches me, and I open my eyes to see him turned completely toward me. He glances over his shoulder, then comes closer with concern. "You alright there?"

I force a smile and nod.

"Want me to get the boss?"

I shake my head, peering past him as Leo talks with Jameson. "He needs to work. It's fine."

He purses his lips, seemingly not okay with that answer, but nods.

I turn from him, pulling my legs up and wrap my arms around them. I place my cheek against my knee, hoping for any of the oncoming panic to leave. Surprisingly, I wanted to go back to that dreary, grey penthouse and just wrap myself in something soft as I watch bad movies. I rock a little, hoping for the anxious thoughts to disappear. I know Dr. Maxwell said I needed to feel my emotions, but right now, I wanted to retreat into nothing, and hope memories don't return. Ever.

Tonight was a reminder of the mob I infiltrated. What I had endured. I knew I was protected; my security would be amplified after this, but I couldn't shake the terror. He got into my apartment. Past Nan and the security at the bookstore. He was in *my* room. I take another deep breath, willing the feelings to go away as I try to ignore the harsh voices in the next room. It wasn't working. All I wanted to do was cry.

"Son of a nutcracker," I murmur under my breath, pressing my forehead against my knees.

Doors open and close with low voices. Footsteps indicate someone coming close, and I lift my head as Leo approaches. He turns the chair for me to face him fully, cupping my cheek with a gentle reverence. I stare up into those hazel eyes which always calm me, not a trace of the man who was in that office minutes ago. They're now kind and warm as he softly strokes his thumb under my cut lip.

Tears that had been building up now escape, a few trickling down my face. Leo's expression changes as he lightly wipes the tears away. "Check in."

My mouth opens, ready to say *yellow*, but I stop.

He's out there, doing what he can to ensure my safety. He's dealing with business and people, besides just me. If I say anything other than green, he'll stop whatever he's doing to take care of me. Guilt starts to fester with the rest of the mangled emotions inside, ready to say green instead, but then I'd hate lying to him. I want to pretend that I'm fine, but deep down...fuck, I just want the afternoon back of us sitting peacefully together.

Everything was fine.

His brows furrow, and he says again, "Check in, dear Watson."

I swallow hard, knowing I can't lie, even if guilt wears on me. "Yellow."

"Why were you thinking of lying?" He strokes some of my hair back. I start to shake again. His gaze flicks over my closed off posture, moving his hand to my knee and rubbing it softly. "Talk to me, dear Watson."

I let out a trembling exhale, loosening my grip around my legs. "I'm scared."

"You're safe. He can't get to you."

"That's not…I mean…" my voice falters as I shake my head, trying to think of how to explain. His brows furrow more, showing that wrinkle on his forehead. It's different from the furrowing that he'd done in the other room. I smile faintly and reach up to touch it softly, causing him to stop. "…I trust you, but…tonight, it reminded me what I left. Tonight, it was like how it was…how brutal…how bloody…"

Leo stops rubbing my knee, pulling away completely as his expression falls slightly. A new panic flares as he starts to step away from me. I grab his hand before he can go far. Both my hands grip his, beginning to look over the scrapes along his knuckles. The deep lines across his palm and tiny calluses. The roughness from what he does outside the office and the riding through the years is there.

Leo's breathing slows as I bring his hand up, kissing his knuckles and place the palm of his hand against my cheek. He inhales sharply as I whisper, "I'm not scared of you, even if others are. It's the rest of the world that…that scares me. What if I'm left alone again? What if I keep causing trouble, not be enough, and be left? I don't want to be a burden, but I'm scared of being trapped again. I felt that fear tonight."

He moves his hand down to my neck, bringing up the other to do the same as he lifts my head gently to look at him. "You'll never be a burden, my dear Watson." I nod numbly. Leo brings his face closer like he's about to kiss me but stops almost a breath away from my lips. "You're truly not fearful of me?"

I stare into his eyes, finding the caring, possessive man I've come to love. Every part of him. Even the parts I didn't know or understand fully yet.

"I've seen you behind closed doors, and I know you'll never hurt me," I whisper. "I know what you're capable of, including how much you care about me."

His warm breath washes over my skin before he kisses me tenderly. The soft caress is gentle, filled with a veneration that I'm truly learning is reserved only for me. He breaks the kiss, murmuring against my lips, "I love you, my dear, dear Watson."

"I love you."

He eases my legs down, stepping between them to carefully embrace me. Leo kisses the top of my head, lightly rubbing his hand along my back, which makes the ticking anxiety begin to disappear. The breath I seem to have been struggling to find, comes to me as I wrap my arms around him. His hand continues to caress my back, helping me relax. The constriction around my chest vanishes as I finally untense my muscles. My body slumps entirely into his arms.

He says low against my ear, "Good girl."

A shiver runs down my spine, finally having a grasp of being content. I murmur against his chest, "Thank you."

Footsteps come up behind Leo, and he turns his head toward them. No words are spoken, but I can feel the slight change in his body. His hand continues to stroke my back as he talks. "There are more matters I have to finish tonight. Go down to the apartment, have some tea, and watch a Nick Cage movie. I'll join you as soon as I'm finished, I promise."

"Are you sure?" Part of the reason I stayed up here was because I knew it helped him if I was within his sight.

"You'll be safe, that's all that matters to me." He kisses my head. "You won't be alone, Autumn." I blink quickly and nod.

Leo helps me down from the chair, keeping a hand on my shoulder as he leads me away from the bar. Suddenly he orders, "Iron."

Owen comes over from Leo's desk, face passive as he flicks his gaze to me then back to Leo. "Yes, boss?"

"Go with her. You know your orders. We'll go over details tomorrow," Leo states. "Ringer, coordinate with Bond on new security details."

The big guy grunts, gives me a quick wink and heads over to the others surrounding Leo's large desk. Mila is among them with a bored expression, swiping through her digital pad. There are more people throughout the room I don't recognize.

Leo squeezes my shoulder gently, parting from me as I walk with Owen toward the main doors of the office. I keep my head down, feeling eyes on me and stay close to the wall with Owen directly beside me. There has to be more than a dozen people in here. Fuck I'm too exhausted and shaken to try putting on an air like I care.

All of a sudden, I hear the click of safety going off.

"I didn't give you permission to look at her." Leo's voice warns. The room goes still. Owen doesn't seem bothered as we approach the doors. "Devon, open the door."

I catch sight of said Devon who has long black hair tied into a braid and dark beard. His eyes don't meet mine as he opens the door for us. We pass through, and Devon closes it silently as Owen leads me to the elevator.

The elevator doors have barely shut when Owen asks, "You good?"

A nervous, exhausted laugh leaves me. "Mostly."

The rest of the ride down is quiet. Owen remains a steady presence next to me as we enter the apartment. I pause in the hallway, just before the kitchen and stare at the bare, grey walls. The emptiness suddenly feeling consuming.

"Autumn?" I shake my head, burying my face in my hands. I leave Leo's presence for a minute, and I want to fall apart again. Are you fucking kidding me?

Owen sets aside the device he had in his hand, quietly pulling me into his arms for a strong hug. Instinctively, I wrap my arms around him and accept the embrace.

"I'm…I'm…" I try to speak, but my throat begins to hurt again.

"Don't apologize, boss will hate it," he says in a low whisper. "Some fucker was hiding in your apartment, tried to kill you and threatened to sell you to mobsters. You then saw two tortured dead men, whether they deserved it or not, that shit isn't gonna give you daydreams. You don't have to be alright, Autumn."

Tears run down my face, and I nod against his chest.

I silently cry as Owen holds me right there in the hall. After a while, he says, "How about I start making us some tea? Not as great as Pretty Boy Bond is, but I'll do my best."

A soft chuckle leaves me. "Sure."

We break away. I numbly walk around the counter, aiming for the television room, but pause to look back at Owen.

"Why Iron Buffalo?" I abruptly ask.

He glances over his shoulder. "Surprised Chesty or Ringer didn't tell you."

I shake my head. "Supposed to be your story, right? Only you get to reveal?"

"Yeah, but sometimes they're nosey," he mutters with amusement. The kettle is placed on the stovetop, and then he starts walking to the small office as he talks.

"I was intel in the Army, but was always told I was made of steel or iron. Worked out a lot to keep from being beat up all my life, shit stays with you. First road name I got was Ironside. Never really liked it, and when I joined up with the *Forgotten Demons*, Chesty and Ringer were the ones who coined me Iron Buffalo."

Ah, that's why he thought they outed him.

"Why did they?"

He comes back with a laptop, placing it on the counter before coming over to stand in front of me. His hand dips under his shirt, pulling out the thick chain necklace I've seen before. Except, now I can see the dog tags that hang off it. He holds up the thinner one. "Mine from the service and…" he then holds up the thicker one that has multiple names etched in the middle, "…my ancestors who were soldiers."

I stare up at him. A small smile comes over his face, looking over the tags. "Chesty knew I joined the Army to get out of the hood, but also because I wanted to be like my great-great-grandfather, and uncles, family who fought for freedom. 1800s, black soldiers were coined as 'buffalo soldiers' and it carried on for decades. Even had a great-uncle who served in an infantry division in World War I that had a buffalo as part of their unit patch. Chesty's Marine Corps tradition loving ass decided I should keep on that lineage with my road name. I became Iron Buffalo, and I wear that shit with pride."

He puts the dog tags away.

"That's beautiful," I whisper.

He grins faintly. "What the buffalo soldiers did is considered a bit controversial and I know what I do…same damn thing. We do what we must to survive."

I bite my lower lip, letting it go quickly when pain pinches across.

"Thanks for telling me."

The kettle starts to slowly scream, and Owen walks over to take it off the stove. I head over to the stacks of DVDs that have been brought over from my apartment. I sift through the stacks, my hand coming upon the case of *Howard the Duck*. I stare down at the old case, wondering if I should put it in.

"What kind of tea?" Owen asks, and I jolt a little as I put the case down.

"Rose or peppermint is fine," I tell him.

I grab a different DVD and put it in before I head for the bedroom to change and quickly wash up. Not too long after, I'm sipping rose tea alongside Owen on the couch as *Princess Bride* plays. He types on the computer, working, but murmurs gladly, "Inconceivable."

I smile a little when Wesley and Buttercup argue on the hillside. My eyes flick over to Owen. "Hey, Iron Buffalo."

He grins with a bit of amusement. "Yeah?"

"If I asked something about Leo, could you answer? It won't about his road name, I swear."

He flicks his gaze to the two tumbling down the hill. "Depends on the question. MC stuff sure, mob…maybe."

"Fair." I shift in my seat, bringing my sock covered feet up under my body. "I know Leo didn't have many relationships before me, but was he always that…well…"

"Territorial? Possessive? Protective?"

I snort. "Well, since you covered all the bases. Yeah."

Owen puts the laptop down on the coffee table, stretching his arms a little before he grabs his tea. My attention is distracted a moment when Wesley and Buttercup enter the forest.

"Spartan's always been like that with those he cares about," he finally answers. "Won't say it often, but he does love and adore his younger brother. A lot. If he didn't, he wouldn't be a couple floors up conducting business right now. Or having me scan Matteo's fucking accounts." He mutters the last part as he sips his drink. "He'd take a bullet for any of the *Forgotten Demons*, and one time he did for Animal and Sombra."

"What?"

"About five years ago. Shit happens. Wasn't a bad wound." He waves it off like nothing. "Point is he's always been *passionate* in whatever he does, including being protective of his partner." I raise a brow. "Girlfriend seems too light a title for you."

I smirk, but it falls quickly. "Would you say the same about his anger?"

He shrugs. "Only dangerous when it's directed at you, which I doubt it ever will with you. You're the safest out of all of us."

"Okay look," I sigh. "People get angry at partners, girlfriends, lovers or whoever for whatever reason. It happens. So, pretty sure, one day he will be. I'm not that special that he won't—"

"Yeah, you are." I freeze. His dark brown eyes meet mine. "I knew you were the day you said his entire fucking name in that coffee shop, threatening him if he tried to do your job. You've told him off multiple times, to be honest, he needed it and it's almost made me smile every time. Rest of us would've gotten warned with a fist to the face by now. We function usually like most other MCs, but we know the reality of who holds the power and it's him. But you? You don't give a shit, never have that I've seen. That's a good thing."

"I don't want to overstep, especially with any of the Crew."

"You won't. You keep him in line, trust me. We meant it that we saw a change in him when you came around, he's more like the Leo we knew years ago. Before the blackmailing. For once, he's got someone he can whole-heartedly put his trust in."

"That's what I mean, what about the *Forgotten Demons*? You all have been together for a decade, if I mess that up—"

"Autumn." Owen reaches over, grabbing my shoulder gently. "We knew we'd have to continually earn that trust. That's true for bikers in general, gotta prove you're part of that club. Earn your patches. We know brothers fuck up sometimes. But you found something in him that we couldn't. He found someone to give his soul over to."

He squeezes my shoulder a little before letting go. I look away from him as Buttercup gets taken away by Humperdink. "You make us sound like a fairytale."

"Or just a storybook love." Owen pulls the laptop back onto his lap, seemingly going back to work.

If only it was that simple.

"Who you got left to learn their road name story?" Owen suddenly asks.

"Jameson and Julio...but I don't think I believe Leo's reasoning."

Owen goes to say something, but there's a noise at the entry. He quickly stands, leaving to meet whoever just entered. I know it's Leo the moment I hear his lowered voice. I remain seated as I continue half watching the movie, listening as Leo goes to the bedroom and then the bathroom. Owen comes back to grab his mug and laptop, gives me a nod, but pauses.

"You want your own laptop?" He asks.

I blink up at him. I haven't touched one in over three years. The idea of programming or having one makes my fingers twitch.

"Enigma and I can set it up, although I'm pretty sure you'd create better firewalls than us."

"Specialty was hacking and hijacking programs, not firewalls," I automatically respond. He smiles. "Sure."

"Get some sleep, Autumn."

"You, too."

Owen leaves, the door thudding shut behind him. Minutes tick by as Leo showers and I continue watching the movie. Leo enters the living room, glass clinks, and then he comes to sit down on the couch with me. He sets his glass on the table, situating me across his lap as he wraps an arm around me.

"No, Nick Cage?" He kisses my temple.

"Can't start one without you." I peek up at him with a faint smile.

His expression is soft. He flicks his gaze to the television screen. "This movie, I *do* actually like."

Although he's calm, there's a slight furrow across his brows.

"Leo, is—?"

"Tomorrow," he whispers, stroking my arm. "We'll discuss tomorrow. For now, it's just us, Autumn. Nothing else. Just us."

I settle further against him. "Okay."

We're quiet as Miracle Max comes on screen, and a small giggle escapes me at one of my favorite parts. I feel Leo look down at me, holding me closer as his hands absentmindedly caress my sides and legs. I let the atrocities and fear disappear with every stroke. Those horrible feelings are numbed as Leo's warmth engulfs me, protecting me as the TV light glows. Like it's any other night.

For a few moments, I almost believe it is.

Chapter 4

Americano Dreams and Nightmares

I jolt awake.

The ceiling looms above me as I gasp for air. The room is dim due to the early morning. I sit up rubbing my hand over my aching chest, swallowing hard against my sore throat. Leo sleeps soundly next to me, his calm breathing giving me something to concentrate on. After a few minutes, all that's left of the nightmare is cold sweat sticking to my skin.

Surprised that I slept at all, I get out of bed quietly to go to the bathroom. I wash off some of the sweat. Leo remains asleep as I leave the bedroom and go to the kitchen, grumbling as I start making coffee. The liquid bubbles and brews, filling the space with its robust smell. The first rays of sunlight peek through the horizon. Clock shows it barely 6 in the morning. As I pour myself a mug, I debate just sitting in the living room or maybe watching a movie, but venture back to the bedroom instead.

Quietly, I walk to the closet, brushing my fingers over the suits and shirts. Everything perfectly in its place. I move to the side that has slowly accumulated clothes I never asked for. All of it neatly organized by whoever the cleaning staff or personal shoppers are. Carefully sipping my drink, I leave the clothes alone and lean on the doorframe to watch Leo sleep. He's moved to his back, his chest rising with each quiet breath. Soft light from the morning peeks through the windows, cascading over the bare room.

My chest tightens a little, and I rub at it as I concentrate on the stark difference from yesterday. No blood. No screaming. No death. Suddenly, it's just gone. I try to wrap my mind around the tumultuous events of the past 24 hours. So much of what Leo and the Crew had been trying to hide from me crashed full force through their walls and mine. All because of my exes. Ex-boyfriend. Ex-handler.

Guilt starts gnawing at my insides and I clutch the mug close.

"They're not gonna leave you," I murmur to myself before the negative thoughts seep in.

I told Leo I could come back. I made that decision. At some point, the wool was gonna be ripped off my eyes, right? Someday this was going to happen, me being a part of this? Just gotta accept the good, the bad, and the horrible. The little moment he and I had on that bench would be achievable again, but it meant everything else would come first.

My mind flashes to last night to the blood covering Leo. The coldness in his voice. The threatening aura around him in that office. Memory then flicks to the garage, how I spoke to the man, Mike, and warned him with my own venom.

Huh, thought that part of me died with Sarah.

I scrunch my brows, wondering how I'm gonna fit into this world. Pinching my face together, wondering what roles those were, Leo begins to moan. Sounds of distress come from him as he grasps the sheets. I rush to him, putting the coffee down on the bedside table, and sit on the edge of the bed. He starts to mumble something as I place my hand against his cheek, wanting to wake him gently. The moment my palm touches his skin, he goes still. I stroke back his hair as his scowl begins to fade and his breathing becomes less strangled.

"You're okay," I whisper. "I'm here, Leo, you're okay."

One of his hands reach for me, clutching my shirt. Leo's eyes flutter open, fear and horror filling them. I give him a small smile, hoping to ease his worries. Leo pulls me down against his chest, wrapping his arms around me as he buries his face against my neck.

"Leo—"

"You were dead." He trembles, his voice shaky. "I didn't get to you...I didn't—"

"I'm okay. I'm okay." I hug him back tightly.

Minutes pass with us remaining in the silence together. Once I feel his trembling fade, I'm able to pull away and give him a brief kiss. I wince a little from the cut on my lip, somewhat sore. Leo stares up at me, stroking his hand through my hair and along my neck.

"Guess we both didn't escape the nightmares, huh?"

He flicks his gaze to the mug. "Is that why you're awake already?"

"Figured I'd start on the caffeine." I sit up, grab the mug, and hold it up. "Want some? It's got sugar in it though."

He takes the mug and sips it. He tries to hide his grimace, while I attempt to not giggle at him. Leo pokes my side, and said giggle escapes, which causes him to smile finally. "There she is."

I take back the coffee and playfully frown. "It's not that bad with sugar."

"For you," he counters, laying his head back.

I roll my eyes. "Fine, I'll pour you..." my voice trails off as an idea springs into my head, "...stay here."

I scramble off the bed, but Leo begins to get up, already not listening to my order. I scowl. "Stay." He raises a brow. "Fine, stay in the *bedroom* for like fifteen minutes, got it?"

"You're not making cereal again, are you?"

I smile mischievously. "Not today."

He stays behind as I make my way to the kitchen. I can't believe I never thought of doing this before. I glance over the fancy coffee maker and find the option to make espresso. Bingo. I quickly place the kettle on the stovetop, turning it on as I search through the cabinets and find a bag of espresso beans. There's movement in the bedroom, and I freeze, peeking over my shoulder. The bathroom door shuts. Quickly, I grind the beans and set up the machine. It's all a different technique than what I'm used to in the coffee shop, but I've got what I got.

At least he had fresh espresso beans.

I pull the kettle off the stove just as it starts screaming, and I hear the bathroom door open. The espresso finishes, and I get it into his usual mug and then pour the hot water next. It looks okay, but I use a spoon to taste it.

Good enough.

Leo walks out of the bedroom as I spin around. He's already dressed in slacks and an undershirt. I hide the mug behind me, and he stops, narrowing his eyes.

"What are you doing?" He steps closer.

"Close your eyes." He stops right next to the counter. Brows become fully furrowed in confusion, cocking his head a little. I almost laugh at the familiar curious look. "You can make breakfast but close your eyes first."

With a sigh, he does what I say. I grab the homemade Americano and walk it over to him, placing it into his hands. Once he has a hold of the mug, he opens his eyes. Leo's brow quirks, staring at the coffee in his hands and then to me. "I thought we decided you're not a brat, dear Watson."

I gape at him.

"This isn't a prank coffee, is it?"

I fold my arms over my chest. "Just drink it, mister."

He brings it up slowly to his mouth, sipping it cautiously. Bewilderment crosses his face before he looks to the coffee maker and then to the kettle.

"You made an Americano." His voice is soft.

I shrug, taking that as a win and begin to clean my small mess. "You always got them in the shop, but I never thought of making them here. Didn't cross my mind, I guess. Also never had a coffee maker where you can brew espresso, too. I know it's not quite the same, but—"

Leo suddenly spins me around, kissing me fervently as his hand clutches the nape of my neck and my side. I ignore the slight discomfort from my lip, gripping his shirt. His tongue moves gently over mine, and I can't help the sigh that I give in response. After the sensual, hot kiss he pulls away, and I grin up at him.

"Okay, my Americanos can't be *that* good," I laugh.

"Yes, they are."

"Never got that kind of tip at *Blue Java*."

"I'm against potential public indecency." I immediately giggle, bringing my hand up to cover my mouth. Leo catches my hand, kissing my wrist instead.

"So, um…" suddenly my thoughts are fuddled as his darkened eyes watch me, "…stick with coffee instead of cereal?"

"I do prefer your coffee-making skills over your…*other* breakfast endeavors, although I do find your attempts amusing and delightful." He steps back, letting go.

There's a fluttering down into my stomach, and I swallow hard as a knowing smile rises on his face. I break from his searing gaze as I grab my coffee and move out of his way so he can make breakfast.

"Barely seven and already using your charms on me," I mutter, and he chuckles as I sit in my usual spot. "Could just say you don't like the cereal."

He pulls out a pan and pot, turning on the stove and walks back over to grab his drink. He stands across from me as he sips the drink delicately. Jaw tensing, he puts the coffee down and sighs in defeat, "It wasn't…*that* bad."

I feign a gasp with an over-the-top gesture. "Are you *admitting* you liked the marshmallow goodness?"

"Not what I said."

"Fine, but I want it in writing that you didn't hate it." I look around the counter for a notepad or something that's been left behind. Oh, come on Owen!

Leo comes around the counter, catches my chin with a playful, wicked look in his eye.

The flinch is involuntary.

A pinch of pain races over my jaw, down my neck reminding me of what I went through only just yesterday.

The amusement in his gaze vanishes, his hand quickly letting go as if he touched fire. I go to tell him he didn't hurt me, but Leo kisses my forehead, making me remain quiet. Silently, he goes back to making breakfast, focusing wholly on that task.

I touch where his hand was, wincing again. The penthouse is quiet aside from pans and utensils knocking together as Leo makes scrambled eggs, oatmeal, and hash browns. Concern crawls up my spine, so to keep busy I go change into some leggings, some random blue shirt, and a long sweater. I sit back down, and Leo is still quiet as he cooks.

Knew any form of normalcy would fade. Then again this *is* our normal now, isn't?

Crud muffins. I hate it.

He puts my plate down, and then his before he comes around and sits next to me in his usual spot. I stare at the food as he points at it. "If that's too difficult to eat, I'll make you something else."

He gave me very soft looking scrambled eggs and oatmeal. If I can't eat this, I'm gonna be stuck with smoothies for a week.

As I pick up my spoon, Leo reaches over and places his hand over mine. "I didn't mean to become shut off, Autumn. It wasn't your fault, but I thought I hurt you."

"I know and you didn't," I sigh. "Was really hoping the happy bubble wouldn't burst yet. Even through breakfast."

"It's still early, we can stay inside it a bit longer."

I take my spoon, digging it into the cinnamon apple oatmeal. "Let's be honest, Leo, every time we say we aren't gonna talk shop during breakfast…we do. It's a pattern at this point."

I absentmindedly fling my spoon in emphasis, and a glob of oatmeal lands on the counter. Are you fucking kidding me?

Leo grabs a napkin, swiftly cleaning it up as I meet his gaze with an embarrassed smile. He only gives me a kind expression. "It does appear to be our discussion time, doesn't it?"

"We're the mob version of *The Talk* or *Good Morning America*, but no awful segments or overrated bands to listen to. Or awkward interviews."

"That's what Jameson, Isaac, and Owen are for."

I snort at his little jab.

We end up eating in silence, which only makes me nervous. The silence from Leo is both telling and not. There's something else. He seems rigid. And in my gut, something tells me more happened last night than just Steve breaking into my apartment.

I eat what I can, making him another Americano and placing it in front of him. I sit back in my spot, loosening a breath as I push what's left of my breakfast aside, and ask, "What happened in that room, Leo?"

He stares at the counter, clenching his fist. "Check in first."

"Green." I flick my eyes to the muscles tensing down his neck. "You?"

"Green."

"Don't lie." His head snaps to me. Anguish in his hazel gaze.

A beat goes by before he explains.

"I don't want to place you in a predicament that may cause a flashback." The food I just ate feels like lead. "I understand I cannot control every aspect when it comes to our relationship, but I will do what I think is best for you and your health. Except, I'm torn in not telling you whole truths."

I gently take his hand, threading his fingers in mine. "I don't want you to feel like you have to hide things from me. Especially due to a fear of something neither of us have control of."

"I'm trying to protect you."

"I know, Leo, but remember that my flashbacks or panic attacks are not your fault or your responsibility to manage. They're mine. And I want you to talk to me." I squeeze his hand. "Help me understand what's going on."

"There are atrocities and aspects of this world I can't...won't share with you."

"Leo, I've seen it, perhaps worse."

"Then I will do whatever is necessary for you to *never* witness it again." He holds my hand firmly. "You shouldn't be subjected to it—"

"Neither should you," I counter.

"Autumn."

"Maybe you grew up in this, dealt with it longer, along with the Crew...you all know how to handle it better than me, fine I'll agree. But neither of us deserve to be subjected to the horrors or dangers of it. And I don't want you to go through that alone."

I run my hand through my hair, wincing when I accidentally touch the bump on my head. Leo goes to grab that hand, too, but I hold it up for him to wait.

"I've seen plenty of dead bodies and those tortured, not just me," I whisper. Leo goes still as I meet his hard gaze. "Seeing those dead men didn't really scare me, shocked me, sure...including when you found me in there, but I wasn't scared. These past few weeks, I think I was pretending with myself that coming back to the mob wasn't that bad. Kind of distracted with other stuff, but perhaps, both of us, hoped I never would see certain aspects. Except...that's not reality, I'm not sure it ever will be."

We're silent, our hands gripping one another's.

"Can you accept that?" He asks quietly.

I stare at the hand holding mine, knowing it's the only thing I need to hold onto. As long as I have this, no matter how terrified I become I could do this, I just can't lose him.

"Yes," I answer. "Can you?"

The desperation in his clutch shifts to his eyes. His jaw muscles tensing as he scowls, tearing his gaze away from mine. Gonna take that as no or struggling to say yes.

"Leo, the last time I was in this world, I was fucking alone. In the past, I would've never risked being broken again," I say in a calm voice, placing his hand in both of mine, and then stroke my thumb over his knuckles. "Even if at moments I think I'm alone, I'm not, but you and *The Forgotten Demons* have come through for me. *You* still came through for me. I'm scared of what's to come, yes, and fighting a lot of instincts I taught myself to survive, but I can do that differently now. I can use new tools to survive this *with* you. We've gotta do this together. That's what partners do."

Pretty sure I'm starting to sound like Dr. Maxwell. Probably a good thing that the therapy is working.

The furrow in his brows deepens, concentrating hard as he glares at his breakfast plate. I bring his hand up, kissing his knuckles this time and feel his body become less rigid. The deep lines disappear from his face as he finally looks over at me.

"Here I believed you were the one teaching me I wasn't alone," he whispers.

"Tomato, tomato." I shrug lightly.

Leo loosens a long exhale.

"I am against it, but you're right. We may need to do this together, even if I don't like it. There are still some things I cannot say or show you."

"How about a balance then? Compromise of a new level in the Crew, with girlfriend benefits."

"Girlfriend benefits?"

"Unless you'll get upset with me telling you what to do." I smile innocently, and he snorts. "See? Benefits."

"I will tell you what I believe is need-to-know information pertaining to you," he says. "There's no need for you to know every little working detail. The Crew trusts me in a similar manner, I hope you'll do the same."

I nod, sipping my coffee as I notice the inflection of his voice is changing. It's shifting into his business tone, the collected one. "I'll trust you, but if I ask a question about something, I'll want an answer. I'd rather know, even if it's bad. I just don't want white lies."

His jaw tightens, brows pinching together again. He finally nods in agreement, "Very well, my dear Watson."

"When it comes to the…bloodier…side of things…" my voice trails away, caution covering Leo's expression, "…I'll steer clear of it. I won't enter a room if you tell me not to. Last night, I was dazed and…I shouldn't have gone into that room after Chesty told me to stop. I apologize."

You'd think I'd have learned by now not to enter rooms I shouldn't. Alas, here we are.

Leo cocks his head at me, fingers drumming the counter for a moment before he stands and starts to put dishes in the dishwasher. Gears are definitely turning in his head, enough for him to feel like he needs to move. I wait until he closes the dishwasher, leaning over the counter with a tight grip.

"What *did* go through your head when you saw them?"

I blink at him, speechless for a moment. Not the question I was expecting.

I know what I felt, but the guilt in feeling it weighs on my shoulders. A lot of emotions had gone through me when I entered that room, including nausea. Reminding myself he won't think horribly of me, I answer, "Relief."

His eyes snap to me. "Relief?"

"Just like how I felt when you told me you killed the others," I murmur. "All I felt was relief. Weight lifted off my shoulders. I finally felt heard and…a peace I hadn't felt in years. Maybe that makes me a horrible human being, but I don't care. Knowing they'll never hurt me or anyone else, I felt relief."

"What about seeing me like that? What I'm capable of? Knowing I'm no different—"

"You're completely different." My voice is harsh, causing Leo to straighten. "Yes, you killed those men, but you're precise in what you do. You'd *never* do this to me or another innocent person." I point at my face where bruises lie. "You wouldn't wait in a woman's apartment to attack her, or on the streets randomly because you have to fulfill your ego. Or do what those men did to me and others. I don't care how angry you get, and how that makes people wary to be around you…*you* are not the monster. I've met them. I should know."

Leo stares at me, jaw grinding away as one of his hands' flexes at his sides. Different emotions flit over his face. Even regret. Is that why he's been so rigid and quiet?

He begins to pace, stalking out of the kitchen and into the living room. My heart begins to pound, not liking the restlessness that surrounds him. Does he think I hate him for doing it? That I blame him for what happened or…?

"Leo, do you feel guilty for killing them?"

"No." His tone is sharp.

"Then what happened last night? Why do you keep shutting down on me?" He shakes his head, facing away from me as he runs his hand through his hair. I remain seated, unsure what else to do, but say again. "Leo, please talk to me."

"There's something I know I have to tell you, that you need to know."

"But you don't want to tell me?" He nods, still facing away from me. "Is it why you're worried about me having a flashback?" He nods again.

So much for a quiet morning.

My chest aches, not liking where this is going. What could possibly be worse than me being attacked by my ex-boyfriend last night?

"You said at the estate that I can't control everything," he says suddenly, and anxiety begins to prickle across my skin. "That I can't take blame for what happened to you, but this… if it's true, then I am partially at fault. I should've been able to prevent it."

"What are you talking about?" My voice becomes shaky as I stand, taking a step toward him.

"They admitted what happened, why they were hired. It wasn't Steve who brought them to you."

I stop. Frozen.

No. Roger said it was Steve. He found out I'd spoken with the police and wanted to teach me a lesson. They had said it that night. *"Teach her a lesson."*

"No, no. Maybe they were lying, you can get the truth from Steve—"

"Men like that don't lie before they die," he argues, turning to face me. "The truth always comes out, whether to throw another to the wolves and save their own ass or just pure cowardice."

"But…but no one else knew what I'd done. I would've been told if I was *really* fucking compromised, and if I had been, fuck that means someone knows now that I'm—"

"You hadn't been compromised." Leo's voice is soft. Too soft.

A dark, warning slithers down my spine, threatening to pull me under. Maybe he'd been right to try avoiding a flashback. But it's too late now.

"Why else were they sent if not because I was undercover?"

"Do you remember anything the night before the assault? A club or venue you visited? Anything the week before?"

My mind begins to spiral, grasping at the past. A headache begins to form, and I rub at my temple as all I get is darkness. I've spent years repressing the past, those nights. Fragments come back encased with bright lights, smell of Marlboro, cheap alcohol, and wet cement. A vice grips my lungs as I remember the stale smell.

Fear grasps at my spine. The word is on my tongue, but I can't seem to get it out.

Leo is abruptly in front of me, cradling my head as his thumbs move over my cheeks. I clutch at his shirt. "You're safe. Only memories. You're safe," he murmurs.

I nod my head, fighting against the oncoming panic and slow realization that what I knew is about to shatter. It's like I'm back in the interrogation room again, surrounded by grey walls and crumpled newspapers. *"You lied to me!"*

The anxiety worsens as I glance to the side and see the wall color.

"Autumn—"

"Who?" I rasp. "Who sent them?"

His grasp tightens, making me look up into torture-filled eyes. Finally, he replies in a strained voice, "Gabriel."

My breathing stops.

"Not because of the police." I feel sick. "You wouldn't… wouldn't fuck him. You apparently refused him publicly, embarrassing him. He sent them to send a message. You weren't the first."

Slowly, I step back from Leo. He lets go, face crumbling. I try to comprehend what he's telling me.

"Because…because I wouldn't fuck him?" I choke out.

"Autumn." Leo grabs my arms. "I should've known what he was doing. I had people tracking him and he must've known I was to hide who he'd been hiring. I should've known and stopped him. I'm sorry, Autumn…I'm sorry…"

"No." I shake my head. Thunder pounds in my head, making my stomach convulse and hands tremble. "No."

"We're looking into how many women he went after. You were the last, but not the first. I'm going through every phone call, text message, and all video footage, *anything* to tell us who else he hired." Everything starts to go numb as I feel my mouth water, my jaw suddenly flexing as my throat tightens. "I'm not giving him another chance, Autumn. He's finished once I get my hands on him. I'll talk to Matteo—"

I can't hold it in anymore.

I tear away from his hands, rushing to the kitchen sink as the vomit begins to climb. I barely make it to the sink as my breakfast and coffee come back up, splattering into the sink. My throat burns, stomach clenching as I hurl with a horrible force. Leo is quickly behind me, leaning over to turn the water on and rub his hand over my back. A warm washcloth presses lightly against my throat, and then over my head as I continue to puke until I'm dry heaving.

"Breathe, sweetheart," Leo whispers, his voice struggling to remain calm. His hand dips under my shirt and sweater, bringing it in contact with my skin. The roughness and warmth a small semblance of relief against my spine. My body finally stops trying to evacuate everything, but my mind spins.

Roger lied. Again. He *had* to have known. That's why he was willing to put me back undercover. He *knew*, the bastard knew I hadn't been compromised. No one knew it was me.

Sarah didn't have to die.

Three years I thought they were after me. I gave up everything.

I didn't have to die.

My knees buckle and I can't keep myself up anymore. The floor slams into my knees before Leo can fully catch me. The entirety of my body seems to go numb, a throbbing ache following behind. The roaring thoughts stop, eddying out as my knuckles turn white gripping onto the counter above me.

"You screwed up!" "You failed me first."

The last remnants of what I knew were truth are shattered. I stare at the dark cabinet as the foundation of what I had built this new life out of disintegrates. Everything I'd done to do "the right thing" feels as if it's been vaporized.

In a daze, I whisper so very quietly, "Have the lambs stopped screaming?"

"Autumn?"

I wrap my arms around Leo's neck, clutching him with what strength I have left. He murmurs something in my ear, but I don't hear him. Inside, I'm promising a merciless vow.

If it's the last thing I do, Roger and Gabriel will regret the night they killed Sarah Marie.

Chapter 5

To Help and To Hold

I feel like hell.

I lean on the counter, stirring honey into my tea in hopes to settle my stomach and make the pain in my throat leave. All of the Crew are scattered throughout the apartment, most with liquor in their hands. Although I know Leo wanted to lock the door, and keep everyone out after this morning, there were a few problems we had to take care of.

For one, my ex who is chained in Leo's… "loud discussion room."

Two, Gabriel may end up being a bigger problem than we thought.

Three, Roger is *definitely* a bigger threat than we thought.

All this meant that taking a "day off" wasn't really in the cards just yet. Even if I hadn't upchucked breakfast, I didn't feel like visiting his top-floor office. So, we brought the *Demons* to us. Trying to ignore the discomfort that flutters over my body, I focus on the men's conversation.

"Checked the system, and apparently the pendejo was let out on parole for good behavior," Julio says, leaning back on the couch.

"Not sure who that detective knows, but he got someone to sign off for the state parole board to release him."

"Judge, maybe? Someone who knows how to slip it through?" Animal asks, situating himself at the end of the couch next to Julio.

"Possibly, but even our contacts couldn't do that," Owen answers. He sits at the counter across from me, laptop already open. "Someone owed that detective big time."

"Or made one hell of a deal," Julio comments.

Rudolf grunts from the bedroom doorway that he leans on.

"See it more of an opportunity to get rid of him, pin his death on someone to make others scramble," Chesty comments, sipping his whiskey. He flicks a look to me. "After we get what we need that is."

Maybe that's what I needed to feel better—seeing my abusive, manipulative ex be beat into a pulp. My stomach churns, and I clutch my mug at the thought. Okay, maybe not.

I clear my throat softly, not really ever wanting to see him again.

Isaac catches my eye from the other side of the couch. He raises a brow, and I try to give him a reassuring smile.

"He had a phone on him, we get anything on it?" Jameson asks from next to the fireplace, Leo on the other side. Both have a crystal glass of one of Leo's expensive scotches.

"Not yet," Julio answers. "But maybe we'll find text chains, planned meet-ups with the detective, or phone numbers to trace."

"Roger wouldn't do that," I say automatically, and all eight of them turn to me.

I clear my throat again, flicking my gaze towards Leo's stern expression. My attention goes back to Owen and Julio. "Roger never used cellphones, he lost too many contacts that way from them being tapped. Never put in enough effort to get encrypted ones. Only phones that were encrypted, well…"

"You did it," Julio answers. I nod.

"How else did he swap information with you?" Isaac asks.

"Paperwork. Back to the basics."

"Such as?" Owen asks, tilting his head at me with curiosity. Leo scowls at all three. I notice Jameson grumble something under his breath to him. It prompts Leo to frown at him next.

After this morning, I don't blame Leo not wanting me to be a part of this, but I can help. I know how Roger operates. I could be useful after all the mayhem that my past caused in the last 24 hours.

"You ever see the show *Alias*?" A few nod their heads as I tap my fingers on my mug. "Similar concept. Roger devised a plan that at four specific payphones, at certain times I'd check in with him. Give him notice I was alive. Through coded messages over the phone, I'd relay if I had intel and we'd devise a meet-up. At first, it was doing the hand off directly to Roger, then to another officer, and then finally I just had a drop point."

"And if you didn't check in on time?" Rudolf asks.

I shrugged. "Assumed I was dead. Usually gave me an extra 48 hours, just in case, before he would report I was deceased."

"You remember which payphones?" Owen asks. I recite off the coordinates for them, not by street, making Isaac and Animal's brows rise. Those coordinates were practically branded into my memory. Leo's intense gaze sears into me, while a couple of the others shift a little. After a few minutes, Owen hums and looks over his shoulder at Julio and Isaac. "All of them are still operational."

"Then we can tap into them," Julio says with a smile. "You just helped us find a couple needles in a haystack, *hermana*."

"You'll have to piggyback on some old systems, but you could—"

"Trace phone numbers and then collect their calling lists," Julio finishes, and I straighten with excitement.

"Could also triangulate where the calls were going to the most often, you'll just have to catch someone using the payphone."

"Oh, we're a bit better than that." Julio grins. "Well, I am."

"Sure, but you're not me," I tease, causing Owen and Isaac to grin. "I could give you—"

"That's enough," Leo interrupts, voice strict.

"Leo, if this helps—"

"I told you I'm not going to use you like they did. Not now, not ever. Enigma, Bond, and Iron can take care of it."

My jaw tightens as my heart sinks a little. The excitement I felt dies, battling to listen to Leo's "request" or arguing to assist more. No one moves, watching us cautiously. I want to defy him, be useful again, especially in something I'd once excelled at. But I wanted to respect his wishes as much as he's respected mine.

If I checked in with him right now, I know what his answer would be.

I loosen a breath, struggling to put faith in the others' skills to use what I've already given. I nod.

Confusion crosses Leo's expression, the lines above his brows more evident as he straightens. Even the others appear shocked.

Oh, come on, I'm not *that* argumentative. Am I?

"What? I can compromise, too." I snort, grabbing my mug and acting like I'm ignoring them as I sip my tea.

"We'll still see if there's anything on the cell," Julio restarts the conversation. "But no tracking devices are on it. We're safe there."

"Would've thought it did," Chesty murmurs.

"Too unreliable." It takes me a second to realize it was me who had spoken.

Leo's jaw works as he holds his glass tight. Yeah, he is definitely hating this. Just stay calm, don't have a panic attack, or puke in the sink and he may stop scowling.

"The clubs cut out most signal, and if you made a show of trying to get it to work, well, it put a target on your back. Too risky. Especially if someone grabbed the phone, didn't have any fancy buttons," I say.

Isaac smirks at the comment.

Jameson asks, "Did you ever make contact in—"

"Don't." Leo's warning is cold.

"Fuck sakes, she can answer—"

"No."

"You're being unreasonable," Jameson growls at him. Leo practically growls back. "Leo."

"Jameson."

Rudolf steps further away, while the others shift in their seats. They exchange glances with each other. I'm not sure about MC protocol, but something tells me mafia is about to overrule whatever those two are about to throwdown.

"Leo." I set my mug down. "Leo, look at me." His head snaps to me. "I'm fine, but how about—"

"I will not—"

"Let me finish," I say with a harsh tone. The Crew goes still. "Please."

Those harsh eyes could scorch someone, but he nods.

For a split second, I debate whether having this conversation in front of the others. On a gut feeling, I gesture toward the dining room we never use. He places his glass down, following me into the room and closes the door. Almost as soon as we're alone, Leo's stony, severe demeanor lessens.

I take a steadying breath before saying, "I know you don't want to involve me with anything regarding the mob, even before our talk this morning. It's why I want you to use Steve; squeeze anything out of him. In the end, kill him, get rid of him. Pretty sure none of us will sleep soundly until he's gone. That and keeping him chained upstairs won't last forever."

I fold my arms over my chest, but quickly drop them not wanting to seem defensive. Leo's irate façade falls a bit more.

"Even with whatever information he gives you, it may not be enough. You're not extracting information from me. I am *freely* giving it over to you. If it gets too much, like this morning…" I swallow hard, wringing my hands a little as Leo tracks the movement, "…I will tell you. Okay?"

His hands flex at his side. He then finally admits in a distant tone, "I don't like it."

"Neither do I, but let me help you, Leo." Something shifts over his expression, almost remorseful. "I don't want to always be on the sidelines. I want to be a partner, your partner. This isn't going to be easy. And you're going to need to stop trying to make what happened this morning...*not* happen."

"Autumn, you became sick." I step back, now folding my arms over my chest. "I'm trying to not let *that* happen."

"I'm not weak," I blurt out suddenly.

"That's not what I said. But that reaction—"

"The day you find out your boyfriend's brother tried to rape you, but hired five men to do it for him instead, practically killing you, *then* you can tell me how to react."

Leo goes rigid, eyes widening at my outburst.

Shit, this is not what I wanted. I'm not angry with him, not really. He's just being Leo—overly worried and protective.

I rub my hand over my face, taking a few long breaths. Footsteps come forward and Leo grabs my hand gently.

"I'm sorry," he whispers. "I'm struggling, Autumn. I don't want to become like those men who abused you. I don't want you near them. You've been through enough since we came back to the city."

My heart sinks. Flashes of the past few weeks come quickly. Him waking up to my screams, watching me in that interrogation room, walking in with a k-bar at my wrists, coming back to me destroying the ballroom. Suddenly, I'm wondering how harrowing it is to watch someone you love in agony. And you can't do anything, except just...be there.

I grip his hands and whisper, "I'll let them know out there what they need, and then I'll step back. If it gets too much, just say 'red' and we'll take a break."

Leo's face falls completely. His hand reaches for the nape of my neck, stroking his thumb over my skin as I watch him closely. He relaxes, the rigidness vanishing. I feel myself become less rigid, too. Whether the struggling hurt in his eyes is from guilt or another thing digging at him, I just want it gone from his eyes.

"That's my job to ask you," he answers quietly

"Two-way street here, mister."

Hazel eyes flick to my mouth, and I nod once. He gently kisses me, holding my head firmly with tender affection. We pull away from the other and I say, "Besides I'll always have a privilege that none of those other *Demons* have."

"What would that be?"

I smirk, "Fuzzy socks."

He chuckles softly, placing a brief kiss on my cheek. "Very true, my dear Watson."

Leo keeps his hand in mine, opening the door and walking back out to the others. I go to separate from Leo for my tea, expecting him to go back to the fireplace, but once I grab my mug, he pulls me back to him. He leans against the other counter, keeping an arm around my middle.

Jameson eyes us, sipping from his drink.

"Do we even wanna know?" Animal calls over.

Both Leo and I reply, "No."

"Double trouble," Chesty laughs.

My gaze catches Owen's, who smirks.

"Shall we continue? We've got other business to attend to later as well." Jameson restarts the conversation.

Julio leans back in his seat and says, "So about those payphones."

***

It's chilly, not quite a winter wind that blows, but the temperature is headed that way. I bundle up more under the blanket, settling further into the chair. I sit out on the balcony after spending the last hour or so with the Crew. Once Leo deemed they had enough, Julio and Owen assured me that what I gave would be valuable. The conversation began to drift to Gabriel and Roger, although a part of me wants to know more, I left the room.

The noise of the heater somewhat drowns out their voices from inside. Doesn't matter, I don't think I really want to know. Yet, a dark feeling at the pit of my stomach is telling me to do more. I shouldn't be doing nothing out here. Be useful, give more than what I've already given. Guilt continues to nag me, prickling some of my anxiety as I shift in my seat.

I stare out at the city, wishing it would all be over. Gabriel to just be gone. Roger far away and to stay away. The rest of the mob could cease to exist and Steve…that piece may be over before I know it.

They'll all be dead. Every single man who assaulted me that night. I still feel relief, but with Steve, I'm not sure. Something hollow is left behind.

The door opens, voices disappearing with vanishing footsteps. Leo comes out to the balcony, the door shutting behind him as he approaches the railing. The expression on his face is neutral, void of emotion as he looks out to the hazy skyline.

"Any other meetings today?" I ask.

"No. I'm having everything canceled for the next two days. Jameson isn't happy about it, but board members or investors can fuck off." He clears his throat, gripping the railing. "I won't be able to concentrate until that fucker is bleeding, broken, and no longer breathing."

"When are you…going to interrogate him?"

"In 48 hours."

I blink at Leo as his jaw tenses, eyes flicking over the city scape.

"Poetic," I murmur as I wrap my arms a bit tighter around my legs.

Suddenly, I'm *very* aware that Steve is a couple floors up, chained in a room with two dead men. The itching at the back of my spine is something I can't quite ignore now, an unease seeping through me. Doesn't matter if he is locked up, the anxiety won't relent. Maybe it isn't just Leo who won't be able to concentrate.

Fuck, I actually miss my job at *Blue Java*.

"Autumn?" I blink quickly. Leo watches me carefully.

"Sorry, was thinking. Kind of."

"About?"

"Could just shove him over the building side. Quick and easy. Knowing my luck though, he may fucking survive," I try to joke.

Leo comes over and I scoot over for him to sit in the chair with me. He sidles up next to me, pulling the blanket over us both as his arm pulls me in close. It tightens when another breeze causes me to shiver.

"He's not getting away this time, Autumn."

"Hard to believe that, you know?" I murmur. "He's been a part of my life for so long, for almost a decade, and haunted a good portion of it. He's only a part of all this, but it's difficult to come to terms that you're right. With everything else, trying to find the next steps, this one is pretty simple. Seems a little *too* easy."

"Wouldn't exactly call what happened last night, easy."

I shrug. "Maybe cause I'm just used to that behavior. Trying to kill me. Sell me. Taunt…" my voice trails off, remembering something Steve said.

"What's with you and mob bosses? They just like your pussy that much?"

Son of fucking biscuit, he wasn't just talking about Leo…but Gabriel, too.

"Do you want one last word beforehand?" Leo asks suddenly.

"I don't know honestly." Probably would just end up screaming at him. Not sure how helpful that will be, but could be cathartic.

"Whether yes or no, you'll have that option before we start on him."

I nod my head numbly, resting it against his shoulder. "Until then?"

"Whatever you want."

Problem is, don't know what I want. And the feeling of helplessness doesn't help, while watching the others take care of issues as I'm just here. Sure, I gave them some phone booth coordinates or whatever, but there was *more* I could do.

"I could show you when I was undercover—"

"No, Autumn. We discussed this," he sighs. "You've given enough."

"I don't want that time in my life to go wasted," I argue

suddenly. "Yes, I gave you some names, coordinates, and such, but there's more. Maybe—"

"You've already given enough," he repeats.

"Not really."

"It was what *you* did three years ago that put me in this position of power. Why do you keep bringing this up today? Did Steve say something that spurred on your relentless need to throw yourself back into the mob?"

"No."

"Then what is it? We agreed on how to handle this going forward, but why aren't you adhering to it?"

I clutch my head suddenly, gripping my hair. "Because I *need* to help you and the Crew. I care about you all and don't want you getting into the mess *I* created years ago. There's already so much on your plate, I don't want to continue being this…this *person* you have to always protect. I just need to help. *Please*, I want to be useful."

My hands drop, breathing heavily. His brows furrow heavily, eyes searching my face. There's an ache in my chest, building as my stomach becomes like lead. The deep-seated guilt rips at me as I recall begging Roger to let me be helpful. To keep my friends safe. How I begged Steve years ago.

Shit, am I steering towards old ways again? Was Dr. Wilson right about me falling into old habits? Anxiety suddenly wars in me, screaming that I'm falling. I've been around this mobster world for less than 24 hours and already I'm collapsing back into old, destructive habits again. Fuck. Shit.

Panic begins to build.

"Autumn, the night you came back I gave you a promise. I would never use you like them. You're worth more than intel. Trust in me and the Crew to do our jobs. If there's anything imperative we need to know, then we'll discuss about you being involved. *This* is why I didn't want you talking. Not just because of the flashbacks."

I avert my gaze. My chin quivering, wanting to break down

again.

"Look at me, dear Watson," he commands softly. Slowly, I do as she says. "Good girl." I almost whimper at the words as he strokes my hair back, his other hand caressing down my side. "Breathe with me."

Apparently, I had been holding my breath.

I inhale a long breath with him, and then exhale. We do this a couple of times as he gently cradles my face in his hand.

"There's nothing for you to prove. You're not broken or worthless. I understand you want to help me, but not like this. Not like before." He strokes the side my face, careful not to touch the bruises. "I am where I am today, partially because of you and what you achieved undercover. Not the police. Not my brothers. Not the other crime bosses. I won't take anymore from you, please do not ask me to take more. What I am doing is almost in repayment of what you've already provided me."

Leo kisses my forehead lightly.

"If I could, I'd keep you far away from this world. Protect you from its horrors and take away your pain, but I can't. As you said, we have to do this together, but there needs to be a balance and not a scoring system." Leo tips my head back a little. "Someone once told me that sharing parts of ourselves doesn't mean there's a complete give or take."

My face falls as Leo retells what I told him from that first date.

"I think that can include this, as well," he continues. "You've adjusted, very quickly, to abrupt changes. You're still adjusting, changing lifestyles, and not just because of the mafia. I am doing all of this Autumn, because I *want* to. You are the most wonderful, good that has ever happened to me. I will give you everything with want of nothing in return but your love. I do truly mean that."

He kisses my forehead again, then presses his lips against mine softly. The anxiety gradually washes away as I slip my hand up around his neck, clutching at his hair. Leo then whispers against my lips, "My dear, wonderful Watson."

Another breeze rustles over the balcony. Leo tucks my head

under his chin. His warmth engulfing me as I clutch him close.

His hand caresses down my back, and slowly back up again. "You can walk away. I'll help you walk away, Autumn," he murmurs against my ear.

Even with the gentleness in his tone, my body locks up. Pure fear chilling me to my bones at the supposed implication in those words.

"Not from me, dear Watson," he adds quickly. "You came back, and I have every intention of doing what I can to keep you."

Oh, thank fuck, but crud muffins preface that beforehand. All that talk of love, but I still have a fear of him leaving me behind.

"I mean from the mafia. You don't need to have any part of it. We talked about you knowing some things, but you have no obligation to be involved. None. Myself and the rest have done this long enough, we know what we're doing. You can walk away."

"Leo."

"Not to pretend it's not happening or faking like it's not a large part of what I am, but to have that distance from it. You don't need to be a part of it." I stare out past the balcony railing. The cloudy skies that cover the city. "Just think about it."

I nod and he pulls the blanket more over us. His hand continues to stroke my back in that tender, loving manner of his. It's barely afternoon, and already it feels like too long of a day. My head wants to spin with a thousand thoughts. I do my best to shove them away, attempting to hold onto this quiet moment that we've tried to have since this morning.

"I love you, Leo," I whisper. "I just don't know what to do. And I think I really am just scared."

His arms tighten around me, pressing his face against my hair and breathing deeply.

"I love you and I'm here, my dear Watson. We'll figure it out."

We hold onto each other as the city's sounds echo below. The clouds becoming darker in the distance, closing in. Much like the shadows that I feel creeping towards me.

I'm just not certain if they're from my past or the present.

Chapter 6

Feel the Rain

I stare at the door.

Bricks have seemed to pile in my chest. My eyes can't peel away from the door, remembering the bodies and blood. They were dragged out yesterday. It feels like an eternity since I last stood here.

For the past day and half, Leo and I remained cooped up in the apartment. We watched enough Nick Cage films to last him a lifetime; me for about a month. Maybe. I felt like I could breathe again. Until the final hour struck.

I should be able to walk in, tell him off, that he's going to die a pitiful death. Scream and swear at him for the pain he's caused for almost a decade. Simple. He can't hurt me. He can't touch me.

I can't move.

Still staring at the door, I wring my hands. Was I weak if I didn't? Words are jumbled on what to say, but else *was* there to say? It won't change what happened. What he did. I know what he'll do with his name calling, taunting, pleading, and will say it was my fault. I know what's through that door, and I don't know if it was worth it.

Was I coward if I walked away?

My breathing goes still. *Was I coward if I walked away?*

A hand touches my shoulder, and I jump, turning to see Leo. He's wearing a dark tank top, jeans, and boots. A shoulder holster is draped over him, holding two revolvers. The rest of the Crew are a little way down the hall, wearing similar attire.

Oh, goodie, it'll be a group bonding experience.

"Check in," Leo murmurs, eyes grazing over my features.

I face the door again, chest tightening as I begin to feel sick. I should be able to confront him. One last time. I'm about to tell him green, but I can almost taste bile.

I can't do this.

No, I don't *want* to do this.

"Red," I rasp. Leo turns me away from the door as I begin to shake my head, shutting my eyes tight. "I don't want...want to see, I don't—"

"It's alright." He grasps my face gently, and then kisses my forehead as I loosen a shaky breath. "Walk away, it's okay."

His words pierce through me. Is it okay?

"I don't want to be coward," I admit earnestly.

"You're not." He tugs me against his chest, moving his hand over my back. "If you're done, then you're done, Autumn. We'll take care of the rest."

"I'll help you walk away."

I swallow hard and nod. "I'll stay in your office, until...until you're done."

"Mila," Leo calls out, and a door opens. "Stay with her. If she needs anything, give it to her or call Chiari."

"Yes, sir."

He strokes his hand up my spine, coming to the nape of my neck and holding me still for a moment. "I love you."

"I love you," I whisper back.

Finally, I open my eyes and look up at him. I give him a faint smile, and then a brief kiss. He lets go as I walk past toward the office door. I pass the others, all of them giving me a singular nod. Lastly, I come to Isaac who holds the door open for me.

"You owe him nothing," he says softly, and I stop to look at him. He gives me a half smile. "He doesn't deserve to see you one last time. Just one last shadow to stop running from."

I smirk at him, and he winks. I take his hand, squeezing it briefly before I walk into the large office as Isaac shuts the door with a loud click.

<hr>

Leo

O nce every member of the *Forgotten Demons* is in the chilled room, Owen shuts the door. It stinks of the dead and dried blood, even with the temperature having been lowered. Steve is gagged with a ball gag, shivering against his metal restraints. He breathes slowly, not quite asleep, not quite awake. He's had enough water and food to keep him coherent for this final step in his journey. Leo comes around in front of him, glimpsing down at the chair and the puddle underneath. Drool drips around the gag as Steve slowly raises his head up to look at the mafia boss before him.

"How does it feel to sit in your own piss?" Leo asks, nodding once at Rudolf to bring a chair over. "Locked up for 48 hours? Forced to smell and hear things you don't want?"

Julio and Drew roll out a canvas filled with tools across a small table that was brought in. Jameson and Isaac move to the other side of the room, along with Owen. Leo takes the chair from Rudolf, flipping it around to straddle and lean forward onto the back. He nods at Waylon, who pulls out a lighter, flicking it as Drew pours a thick liquid into a cup.

"Here's how this will go," Leo instructs as Steve sluggishly moves his attention from one member to the next. "You'll answer every question we ask, depending on the answer, it'll determine what kind of marking you'll take into hell with you."

Leo pulls out his revolver, handing it over to Jameson who spins the cylinder and snaps it shut. The action causes Steve to flinch.

"First question," Jameson starts. "Your favorite color purple?"

He mumbles against the gag, more drool sliding down his chin. Leo doesn't take his eyes off Steve as Jameson aims and shoots Steve's shin without warning. Steve's muffled cries are ignored by everyone in the room.

"Must be orange," Waylon comments.

"I was betting yellow," Owen mumbles.

Steve's eyes are blown wide, moving to Leo with terror in them. Leo's own flare with a foreboding wrath, yet his expression is eerily calm.

"Starting to realize this is the end?" Leo asks. Steve trembles violently, the chains rattling around him. Leo leans forward, pulling the other gun out of his holster and cocking his head to the side. "Finally learning the rumors are true? It's not Gabriel you should've been scared of?"

Waylon comes up behind Steve, who jolts and thrashes as Waylon flicks the lighter again near the man's ear. Drew comes up beside Waylon, grabbing Steve's hair and yanks his head back.

"Next question, who starred in in the movie *Shrek*?" Owen asks.

Steve mutters against his gag.

"I think he guessed wrong," Julio comments.

Drew keeps his head pulled back as Waylon flicks the lighter and trails the flames under Steve's jaw and to his earlobe. The man screams, sputtering against the gag as he tries to move away from the flames.

"Not so tough now, huh?" Waylon asks.

The flames punch out as Steve breathes heavily and tries to wrench his hands tied behind his back free. All it does is cause the chains to clatter.

"Drench his lap," Leo instructs, and both men step back as Julio grabs the cup and unceremoniously pours it on Steve's lap. The man thrashes.

Isaac strikes a match, walking over to Steve who watches him with wide, horrified eyes. "Where you're going, you won't need your cock."

Isaac begins to bring the match down, Steve screaming against his restraints and tries to mumble something against the gag.

"Stop." Leo's command halts Isaac. He flicks out the match instead, stepping back quietly.

Cold fury unleashes through Leo's veins. His vision warps for a few moments as he stares at the man who haunted Autumn for years. Agony clenching his heart for every moment he witnessed.

The cuts on her legs.

Night terrors.

Her puking into the sink.

Guilt and fear in her eyes.

Every moment of her attempted self-destruction.

All of it because of him.

Leo stands, walks over to Steve and crouches to be eye level with him.

"You chose the wrong brother to fuck over," Leo speaks in a chilling, damning voice. "Should've had the smarts to run when that detective let you loose. Not go after the woman, the only person, who had a say in your fate. Because maybe, *just* maybe, she would've given you a chance to live." Steve's eyes widen. "But no, she chose a different fate for you."

Leo juts his head toward where the table sits. Steve following with his gaze.

"You're going to tell us every single thing you know about Gabriel, his operations, every person you worked for, what drugs you shoved up your nostrils, how you planned to contact Gabriel, and whatever hell else we demand of you. The more honest you are, the less you'll already be cooked, ready to go for our friends in hell."

He then takes his hand, pressing his thumb against the bullet wound in Steve's shin. The man yells and whimpers against his gag, mumbling in pain.

"You *will* be begging for mercy," Leo states. "You *will* die tonight. And she will *never* have to fear you chasing her again."

Steve garbles and cries against the gag as Leo digs into the bullet hole, before finally pulling away. He stands fully and looks down at Steve with disdain. Leo turns his gaze to Isaac.

"Start with his fucking hands."

Julio grabs a lighter, tossing it to Isaac. Rudolf undoes one of Steve's bound hands, wrenching it to the side and away from the man's torso. Steve attempts to fight him, but he's no match for the wrestling giant.

Leo grabs his chair, pulling it back and turns it around to sit and lean back to watch.

It would be a miracle for Steve to last longer than an hour, but he will. They'll get what they need for him, use him like she wanted them, too.

Leo watches the man, who screams against his gag, feeling nothing. Whatever would be left of him, will be a warning to anyone who ever dares to even try touching Autumn. For those who already have…

…this was only the start.

<hr>

Autumn

Four hours.

I check the clock again. Yup, only been five minutes since I last looked at it.

It's raining, has been for the last three hours. Once again, I get up and walk over to the large window of Leo's office. The rain drizzles down the glass, illuminated by the lights of the city as evening ascends. I fold my arms over my chest to get my hand to stop tapping against my leg.

Chiari has delivered tea to me three times now. Each a different blend she's recommended from the hotel's main kitchen. Mila has been the only one in the room with me, tapping away on her laptop or on her phone. I've tried to stay busy with reading, but the romance with the Scottish Highlander who lives in the hills just ain't cutting it.

Perhaps deciding to stay in a singular room until they were done wasn't the best of ideas. I wasn't sure how I'd handle being alone in the apartment though. I called Nan, checking in that she made it back to the bookstore safe. Pretty sure she only escalated my anxiety with some of her comments about the situation. I decided to wait to tell Leanne what happened, texting her only to say I wasn't feeling the greatest and staying with Leo.

She knows something's wrong. I just didn't want to tell her over the phone *"Hey! Guess who gave a surprise visit and tried to kill me?"*

My finger begins to tap my forearm, and I eye Leo's chair. Wonder how quickly Mila will have a heart attack if I decide to spin in it. Maybe she'll want to race. I glimpse over at her sitting on the couch. Poker-faced and still typing. Don't think she'd be game.

Instead, I sit in his chair, no spinning, and roll up to his desk. My fingers drum on the wood, lightly pushing at folders that Jameson left behind.

Mila clears her throat loudly. I find her watching me suspiciously.

I pull my hands away from the folders. She goes back to her laptop.

"So…" I begin slowly after a few more silent minutes have passed, "…how long have you worked for Leo?"

She continues staring at her screen. "That's confidential."

Well, at least she spoke.

I lean back in the chair, swiveling lightly. The rain comes down harder, pattering along the glass. It's only beginning of November, yet it rains like its April.

"You have a…hobby outside of work?" I ask, trying again at small talk.

"A few."

Once two long minutes pass of no explanation, I realize she isn't going to elaborate. "What are they?"

"My job, Miss Watson, is to provide security, nothing more. Per

Mr. Luciano's orders. Unless, given direct instructions from him, there's no reason for you to know my personal life."

Well, at least she's succinct.

I get out of Leo's chair, walking back to the couch across from hers and sit down. My mug is still warm as I pick it up, sipping the hibiscus tea. Before the silence tries to drown me again, I put the mug down. "I just want to know who you are, Mila. I've gotten to know the other—"

"They are a special exception," she interrupts. "Part of an allegiance, that myself and many others are *not* a part of. Rules that Mr. Luciano decided upon. Perhaps you have a significant role in his life, but I still only take my orders from him. Not you. This includes no private information."

Private life stays private. Forgot about that note.

"Not ordering you, Mila."

"Obviously."

I sigh deeply, trying not to press my fingers into my eyes. Whether she likes me or not, this is distracting me, thankfully. So, like the looney I am, I keep talking.

"If you don't like me, just say it. Don't play games with me though, I had to endure that for weeks at *Blue Java* because a twenty-something doesn't understand boundaries."

Somehow that gets her attention, finally looking up. Her dark grey eyes meet mine. I freeze at the stark expression. In a collected tone, she responds, "I'm not stupid enough to say I don't like you. One word to my boss and what's happening to your ex would be similar to my fate. Thus, why you didn't tell him about *Mike* downstairs."

Oof, touché.

"He's not *that* controlling." My attempt of a defense is met with a raised a brow. "Someone trying to hurt me versus saying you don't like me, is not the same."

"Not to him." Touché number two.

"Fine, but like Mike...I wouldn't tell him." The exasperated deadpan look on her face almost makes me laugh. "I'm not saying any of this to *make* you like me, well, maybe…or more like I'd like to understand why or what I did."

"I never said I didn't like you."

"Your enthusiasm needs a revamp. May I suggest a Disney film?"

"Again. My job is security, not to be…buddies with you."

"See, that's why I don't think you like me." She scoffs, going back to her computer. The laptop remains more interesting than me, so I decide to let it go.

I grab my mug, getting up to pace around the office a little before I come back to Leo's desk again. I clutch the tea to my chest, trailing a finger over one of the folders.

"It's cause I'm a coward, huh? Always running?" I voice my thoughts out loud. "Should've stayed. Should've grabbed the folders." The typing of her keyboard stops. "Should've confronted Steve, cause that's what you're supposed to do as a survivor, right? Get the last word in. Face the monsters. Tell them off. Maybe I am just a coward…with all of them."

I turn around, catching the reflection of myself on the window. For a few moments, I see Sarah Marie. Long blonde hair that hung past my shoulders, copper-wired glasses I always wore. Thin, but not the kind of skinny people crave, the kind where people worry. My skin had always seemed pasty, discolored and wrong from the lack of nutrition for most of my early twenties. Not just with Steve, but before, too. My attempt to survive college and work towards a masters that I never achieved. Leaving home. Escaping to New York. All that time I spent hiding and running. Could it really just be over once he's gone? That chunk of my life?

"What do you do when your monster dies?" I whisper as my vision comes back to the present. The short reddish-brown hair, no glasses, not as pale, and finally weight on my body. No bruises. But the largest difference I see is in my eyes. There's no distant look in them. A longing to keep running.

"You're not a coward," Mila says, and I almost jolt, remembering I'm not alone. I turn towards her.

"Sure, about that? Isn't it cowardice to run away?"

"Sometimes it's for the best," she says, looking back down to the computer. "Besides, you came back, which goes to show you have a lot more guts than most men I've met. Much like how parents will for their children, it's best to let others slay the monster under your bed."

"Speaking from experience?"

She flicks her gaze up toward me. "There's a reason many of us are loyal to Mr. Luciano. He's very good at slaying the monsters under our beds. Including some of mine."

I stare at her in disbelief. More than I ever thought I'd get from her and then there's the comment about Leo. I flick my eyes toward the side office door.

Okay, maybe I'm not a coward. Just someone who's having a hard time taking the next step in healing. It isn't forgetting, but not letting the pain control you.

I place the mug carefully on Leo's desk. My chest tightens slightly as an odd feeling creeps up my spine, refusing to adjust to the idea of walking away. The sheer fear of it. Guilt. Shame. Worthless.

Mind beginning to whirl, I decide I can't take it much longer in here. It's going on five hours now, and I need…I need…

"I'm going down to the ballrooms," I say, heading for the door.

Mila swiftly stands, beating me to the door to stop me. "Boss said—"

"He said anything I needed to give it."

"And the ballrooms are that?"

"Yes." Mila is a good foot taller than me. She stares down with a frown, narrowing her gaze. I give an exasperated sigh. "It's just the ballroom floor." She doesn't move and still frowns. "I don't like grey walls," I whisper.

She purses her lips, looking over at the side office door. Finally, she steps aside and opens the door, walks to the elevator, and pushes the button to go down. Quickly, she points at a spot in front of the elevator. "Stay here."

I do so as Mila walks back into the office, picks up her phone and grabs another device. Is that a pager? She then brings the phone to her ear, talking low as the elevator doors open. I step on with her close behind. Mila inputs the code to go down and hangs up the phone. I rock on my feet as we move. What feels like almost forever, we arrive. The doors open to people bustling around in the hall. Two of the ballrooms are open. People are dressed in suits and floral dresses, meandering in the brightly lit hallway. I quickly get out, weaving through the throng and aiming to go check if any of the other ballrooms weren't being used. The only one open is the *Orchid Ballroom*. Mila grumbles something behind me as I sneak in, none of the other guests really paying attention as they sip their drinks.

The *Orchid Ballroom* is completely bare. No tables or chairs. No stage. No dancefloor.

I wander into the room, moving my gaze up to the chandeliers that are dimmed, intricate designs on the carpet, and the beige colored walls with gold trim. I breathe easier. It's warmer in here, even if it's a gigantic open space.

Mila remains at the doors. I stop once I get to the middle of the room, tilting my head back to stare up at the largest chandelier. I keep staring, hoping the scenery change will help the anxiety at the base of my spine. The heavy tightness around my chest.

"You can't just walk away! You made a choice—"

A lump forms in my throat.

"Do the right thing. Prove that you—"

Mila says something, but her words don't register as I stare down at the ground next.

"If you want to get out, then you have to die."

I shake my head, pressing my palm against my head. Mila says something again, and I inhale a sharp breath and turn my attention to her.

There's a phone to her ear. She's gesturing to walk back through the door, and I think she's telling me we have to go back upstairs.

Her words aren't registering. There's a quiet roaring in my head, anxious, old emotions crawling over me.

Run. They're occupied. Run.

I walk towards her, numbly leaving the ballroom and into the sea of people. Glittering dresses, satin, champagne, and laughter. It all eddies out as I step through them to the elevator.

Run. The instinct, learned for so long, yells at me again.

The public elevator opens, people streaming out, and I glance over my shoulder. Mila is a bit behind, still on her phone and there's people separating us. She turns away, glimpsing back at two guys who are speaking loudly over the crowds.

Without thought, I get onto the public elevator and press the *close-doors* button. Mila turns, eyes going wide and starts running for the door. Déjà vu hits me as the doors shut before she gets to me. Calmly, I press the button for the basement.

"Sarah, get back here! You have a duty —!"

I take a long breath in again, flicking my gaze up to the security camera.

Once the elevator dings and the doors open, I swiftly begin walking for the loading dock. My steps are quick as I pass people, skirting past them and then pass an office door. It opens directly behind me, and I start jogging when a man calls out, "Miss Watson? Miss Watson!"

I run down a hall, turning a corner quickly and pass more of the evening workers for the hotel. The voice calls my name again, but I continue until I get to the final door and fling it open.

Rain pours from the sky, splashing into puddles that have begun to grow on the pavement. The overhang keeps the rain from hitting the dock where I stand as I look up at the dark sky, and a streak of lightning flashes. Behind me the door slams open, and the same man who was calling my name, says again, "Miss Watson."

He doesn't stop me as my feet carry me down the steps and out into the heavy rain. Closing my eyes, I lift my head up and feel it wash over me. I listen for the crashing of thunder. The metal that pings with every drop. The honking of traffic.

"You'll never see the outside again…"

Within moments, I'm drenched. Finally, I can breathe.

Bringing my head down, I look down the backway, devoid of any delivery trucks. My feet begin moving on their own accord, walking away from the hotel and towards the road where car horns blare. The rain pounds against the pavement, lightening flashing in the sky again. I walk without hiding, not dodging behind trash, or checking over my shoulder. I just walk through the rain oddly composed as the storm blows around me.

"Autumn!" A voice calls out through the darkness. "My dear Watson!" Closer, but I continue walking. "Sarah."

I stop as the thunder rumbles against the city noise.

Water drips from my fingertips. I've almost made it to the street.

Slowly, I turn toward the voice.

Leo stands only a few feet from me, drenched. He changed. The black tank and jeans are gone, replaced by slacks and a white button-up. All his tattoos are visible. The soaked white shirt not hiding anything inked upon his body, while his chest rises heavily against the downpour. His hair plastered across his forehead.

"Is it done?" I ask in a rasp. Unsure if he'll hear me.

He nods.

"Did you kill him?"

Hazel eyes sear into mine as he slowly nods his head. My breath hitches.

"He's gone, but it wasn't me who did it."

Shock should've filtered through my senses, but it doesn't. Steve is dead.

Leo steps towards me as I remain planted in my spot. I abruptly say, "I wasn't running."

"I know." He strokes back the wet strands of hair across my face.

"I needed to know I didn't have to," I say against the rain. "To not feel trapped."

We remain standing there in the pouring rain. Neither of us moving, and I wait for him to pull me towards the hotel. To yank me back to safety. Out of the storm. He doesn't. Leo stands there in the rain with me, shoes filling with water and becoming soaked to the bone as we do. He doesn't force me to move. He remains.

I place my hand against his chest and feel the pounding of his heart. He places his hand over mine. The rain washes away the last of the blood on his hands. I stare as the trickles of crimson fade.

"Help me walk away," I say, looking up at him. "I think you're right. I need to leave it behind me. I'm done running."

No furrowed brow. No confusion. Nothing of the mask that Leo wears. Calm is all there is on his face. He simply nods.

I reach up with my other hand to the nape of his neck, pulling him down with trembling hands. Leo kisses me in the storm, finally settling the anxiety that ticks at my spine. I hold onto him as the wind blows and more lightning flashes across the sky. Inside, I'm serene. Finally, I feel peaceful as the decision to step back lightens the weight on my shoulders, the urge to run disappears. I kiss him harder, needing his touch. He wraps his arms around me, kissing me intensely. He then shifts to pick me up into a bridal carry.

"Let's get you inside, dear Watson."

I lay my head against his shoulder as he walks us back to the *Italian Lily*.

Chapter 7

Be My Guest...

Isaac had taken Steve's life.

It seemed fitting that my current "shadow" killed one that had followed me for so long.

I didn't ask for specifics when Leo carried me into the hotel all the way up to the apartment. Jameson, Chesty, and Rudolf met us in the foyer to speak with Leo about something. An odd burnt smell drifted from their clothes.

The next week felt like a blur.

Things were set into motion, calculated to be in our favor. The two men's bodies were cut to pieces. One sent down the coast of New Jersey, another outside of Staten Island. Steve's body was discreetly placed inside a crime boss' territory Leo had been having issues with lately, also within Roger's jurisdiction. Steve and the two men had been tortured in a specific manner, all three deliberate to mimic two different enforcers within the mob. Somehow, Julio and Isaac had gotten the enforcers' fingerprints, placing them everywhere, misleading the police. The captain from Roger's precinct "caught" one three days after the body was dumped, after an anonymous tip provided evidence of others the enforcer killed. He was awarded, too. Roger on the other hand was still suspended.

The others believed he got the message. I wasn't so sure, but kept my mouth shut in an attempt at walking away. Among other attempts to remove myself from the details, I saw Leanne and Trix. Leanne the day Steve's body was found, finally telling her the truth. Wasn't the most fun of conversations, but hey, he's at least dead. Nan settled back into routine but mentioned going on a long vacation soon for the holidays. I don't think either of us feel safe in the bookstore anymore. Even with extra security, it'll take a while to not flinch when a floorboard creaks. As for Nan...pretty sure the whole mob stuff is getting to her, too. Of course, she won't say anything.

I sit with Dr. Maxwell across from me. Second session this week. Chesty, Isaac, and Leo all suggested I see him more frequently. I agreed. There was something still gnawing at me I couldn't put my finger on.

"Still no nightmares?" He asks, sipping his usual cup of tea.

"Nope. Still haven't since the night I was attacked. Some trouble falling asleep, difficulty concentrating, and random loss of appetite, but that's it."

"Natural responses. You're recalibrating as your brain tries to make sense of the situation." He sets his mug down, crossing his legs and folding his hands together. "This newer dynamic with you and Mr. Luciano, are you struggling with it?"

"Meaning?"

"Some light was shown upon the shadowy side of things again, but now you're stepping back more deliberately. It being a more conscious decision to place that boundary, has it been difficult doing so?"

I lean onto my knees. "I think I'm just trying to wrap my head around how I fit in. And I worry about not being part of that with him, but I feel somewhat...torn."

He remains quiet, giving me a small nod and smile to continue.

I clear my throat.

"The others, the Crew, they all have their place. Each with their own important part to play, they're able to prove that they belong.

They're good at what they do, providing and working towards a goal. For me, I don't really have a place. I thought maybe I could provide intel, help the Crew with Roger and such, but I guess not. They have it handled. Don't really need me. I just seem to always end up doing nothing or not enough it seems. Like I'm always a few steps behind. I'm trying to figure out how I fit, where I can contribute."

"What are you doing in your off time?"

"Work some hours at the bookstore, working on bikes, learning to ride, and spending time with Leo when he's done with…stuff." He quirks a brow, and I chuckle under my breath. "Best way to explain everything that can encompass what he does. He works *a lot*."

He nods his head. "Do you perhaps feel behind because of the amount of work he does?"

I shrug.

"There's no requirement of how much work people must do to be praiseworthy. Mr. Luciano has a significant amount that requires more time than most. You don't need to match it. Or do what he does." He tilts his head to the side. A thoughtful look coming over his face. "It's his decision to do so, and I doubt he'd ask the same of you."

"I get that, and I've grown used to the hours he works, it's just that…that…" I sigh, pushing some of my hair back, feeling the guilt gnaw again, "…I feel like I need to do *more*, not just work."

"Why?" I stare down at my hands. Shame begins to pile on with the guilt. After not speaking for over a minute, Dr. Maxwell finally says, "You mentioned worry, where does that come from?"

"I don't know."

"I think you do, but you're afraid to say it out loud." I lift my gaze to his. "Don't think, Autumn. Feel and speak it into the open. Let's get it out into the air with what you're grappling with."

I take a long breath in, my leg beginning to bounce as I lean back into the couch and wring my hands a little.

"Take all the time you need," he reassures me as I try to stop my hands from shaking. Apparently, the guilt and shame run deep.

Finally, I answer, "I don't want him to leave me. I feel guilty for not working, specifically for…him. To not be useful like the others. And maybe, that I really am just a burden. These past few weeks I've been…a lot."

"Do you feel like you need to earn your spot at the table?"

"I had to when I was undercover. Growing up. Even in college. You have to work to be there, be useful. Computer forensics was what I was good at it. I could use that again like I had been for the police, but …he wants me away from the mafia. I agree. Yet, I can't help having this guilt. I don't want to be trouble, useless, or deemed…expendable. I know we talked about some of this, but…"

My voice trails away as I blink back tears. I rub my face and then at my chest, anxiety building.

"Breathe, Autumn. Keep talking, get it out."

"I don't want Leo to blame himself for what…what Gabriel did, but I blame *me*. No matter how many times he tells me I've done enough, all…all I've seem to be this past month is trouble. What… what happens when it's too much? When *I'm* too much? With… nothing to show I can be helpful?"

"Autumn, your worth is not tied solely in being an asset to him."

"I know, I *should* know that, but I can't shake the feeling that me walking away from the mafia while Leo continues with it…he won't need me anymore."

I sniffle, grabbing a tissue and wiping at my nose as my leg continues to bounce. I wrap my arms around my stomach.

"Autumn," Dr. Maxwell says, bringing my attention back to him. "I want to try something to help you manage these thoughts, but I want your permission first."

"What is it?"

He settles into his seat. "I'd like Mr. Luciano to join us for our session."

My eyes widen. "You…are you suggesting couples therapy?"

Son of a nutcracker, is that where Leo and I have come to? We're not even engaged or married yet.

"Not necessarily. I'd like to hear from him, his perspective. It may help me understand a couple of things, and perhaps yourself as well. Alright if we try?"

I glance at the clock, not wanting to interrupt Leo's day. Or piss off Jameson by doing so. Eh, could always make Jameson whatever coffee he wants later as an apology.

I nod my head, and Dr. Maxwell smiles. He heads over to the door and has a quick conversation with Isaac. In the past week, Isaac seemed to have gone from part-time bodyguard to full-time. My personal James Bond has rarely left my side whenever I go anywhere.

I slump back on the couch, wondering what Dr. Maxwell has up his sleeve. Couples therapy may be a thing for us. We're not exactly a normal couple. What's normal at this point though?

I shake my head as Dr. Maxwell sits back down in his usual spot. He smiles as he grabs his mug. "He'll be down in a few minutes."

"Five bucks he checks in," I murmur, standing and walking over to Leo's liquor cabinet.

"You think he will even though you're in a safe environment?"

"Oh, yeah." I pour a small drink for Leo, and then place the glass on a coaster near my mug but pause before sitting. "Would it be okay if he drank? He doesn't really do tea and I don't have an espresso machine in here."

"He's just a guest, and it *is* his office," he smirks. "And building."

"Don't worry. I'll be sure he doesn't party too hard."

He grins when there's a knock at the door. Leo doesn't wait for an invitation, entering like he does own the place. He instantly puts his hand out to shake with Dr. Maxwell, who stands to greet him.

"Dr. Maxwell. I was told you wanted to see me," Leo greets.

"Yes, good afternoon, Mr. Luciano. It's an honor to finally meet you." He shakes his hand, then gestures to the open seat next to me. "I appreciate you coming on such short notice."

"No issue at all." Leo's tone is collected, keeping an easy air about him. I turn slightly as Leo unbuttons his suit jacket and sits down. His gaze finds mine, and touches my shoulder. "Check in."

I don't look at my therapist, knowing he owes me five bucks, and smile. "Green."

He leans over to kiss my cheek, then sits back, glancing at the drink I set out. He hides his small smirk, reaching for it as he places a hand on my thigh gently and the bouncing stops. Relief floods down my leg to my aching foot.

I notice Dr. Maxwell watch the encounter with a thoughtful expression.

"Mr. Luciano, I'll preface that nothing is wrong. I had a thought and wanted to explore it further. Autumn has already given permission for you to be here, but I'll do my best not to keep you."

"However long you need, doctor." Leo sets his drink down. "And please, call me Leonardo."

Wonder how long before Dr. Maxwell gets the upgrade to "friend" level.

"Very well." Dr. Maxwell shifts in his seat, folding his hands on his lap. "Is there a reason you felt the need to implement the stoplight method just now?"

Leo stiffens. I mostly can only feel it from the hand on my leg, but I can sense his walls immediately go up. He stares at the doctor, jaw tightening as his brow begins to furrow. I'm about to assuage him when Dr. Maxwell speaks first.

"Everything said in here will not be repeated outside that door, Leonardo," he assures him. "Autumn and I have spoken in great length, including some of the BDSM tactics you've implemented to aid in your relationship. Which, I must say, I commend you for. I think it's helped her greatly. But, with that being said, I'm not your personal therapist, so if I cross a line you must tell me. I want your perspective and a few insights, that's all."

I place my hand over Leo's, stroking my thumb over his skin. His grip loosens on my thigh. The rigidness of his body following suit. He glances over to me, and I give him an encouraging smile.

Leo clears his throat and then explains. "Autumn doesn't always relay how she feels about situations she's in. Even in environments she'd be considered safe, there are still triggers of hers that can be brought forward from simple phrases or tasks. She'll hide her true feelings behind smiles, jokes, or other manners. And given that she's in a therapy session, I think it's only wise to check in, since she's in a space that could very well bring forth one of those triggers."

Dr. Maxwell hums. "If she had said yellow then?"

"I'd ask you to leave."

"Red?"

"I'd demand you to leave."

The doctor nods his head, then looks at me with an easy smile. "Good thing you said green, then."

His amused expression and the *very* Leo response makes me giggle suddenly, and I throw my free hand over my mouth instinctively. Leo allows himself to smile faintly as he removes my hand from my mouth. I whisper. "Was a very *you* answer."

"Is that so, dear Watson?" I nod, biting back a smile.

Of course, Leo would threaten my therapist after just meeting him practically five minutes ago. Honestly, if he hadn't, I may have been concerned. Leo kisses my hand, looking at me like it's just us two in the room.

"Where did the nickname come from?" Dr. Maxwell asks, breaking the small moment. I see a flicker of annoyance flash over Leo's expression, his jaw muscles tensing. I roll my eyes then look over at Dr. Maxwell, signaling Leo to answer him.

The man accepts an invite into the session, and then gets annoyed when the inviter wants to talk. He must've been in one boring meeting before this.

"A few weeks after we met," Leo answers, leisurely sitting back. "I'd spent a good deal at the coffee shop she worked in, although we had amicable conversations, she was cautious about giving me her number. I understood, and was patient, but she did tell me her last name. The 'dear' part came naturally, and I enjoyed having a name for her that no one else uses."

"You cared for her well-being."

"Immensely."

"Would you say you fell in love with her quickly?" I blink at the doc, unsure what he's getting at as Leo doesn't look at all surprised by the question.

"Yes," Leo answers.

"What was it that first attracted you to her?"

Yup, no clue where he's going with this. Is he trying to prove something to me? I thought he was going to bring up the guilt stuff, not Leo's feelings for me and why.

Leo's hand gently caresses my leg, bringing my attention over to him. He meets my gaze with an affectionate look.

"I could be romantic, say it was her laughter or smile," Leo begins. "Or her attempting to help a stranger from having coffee dumped on them. Her efforts at small talk with a very, niche Batman joke. The little wave she gave me while mopping when she could've ignored me. Little things. Simple acts of kindness. There was one quality about her that always brought me back."

"That would be?"

Those hazel eyes shimmer, a very slow and deliberate smile forming. "I finally wanted to smile."

He reaches over to stroke his thumb over my cheek, wiping away a fallen tear. I blink in surprise. Leo returns his attention to the doctor.

"She's important to you," Dr. Maxwell states.

"Extremely."

He hums, grabbing his tea and taking a sip. None of us say anything as he sets it back down, crossing his foot over another and settles into his chair. I feel Leo begin to tense, but his hand on my thigh remains gentle.

"Autumn has made it clear in our sessions that she highly respects you," Dr. Maxwell says, breaking the silence. "She trusts you, but her past can make it difficult at times to hold onto that trust. Am I safe to assume that is one of the other reasons you use the stoplight method? The moment she safe words, in any situation, you adhere to it, cementing more of that trust?"

Leo narrows his eyes at him for a moment, and then answers, "Yes."

"Something you knew from the very beginning, her trust is valuable, such as when you listened to her when she first refused you her phone number." Leo nods. "You want her to trust you."

"I'm not sure what you are implying—"

"What are the two things she asked for at the beginning stages of your relationship?" I catch my breath as Dr. Maxwell interrupts Leo, who's hand goes still on my thigh. I flick my gaze in worry toward Leo as that mask of his falls into place—stony and abrasive.

Dr. Maxwell doesn't even flinch.

Chesty didn't get me a therapist with just a backbone, he found someone with a spine of steel.

"Communication and honesty," Leo answers. "We've had roadblocks from time to time, like any couple I presume, but I've striven to give that to her whenever I can."

"Why?"

Leo becomes more rigid. Please don't let me lose another therapist. Dr. Maxwell gives him an easy smile. "I have a point to this, I assure you, Leonardo."

Leo clears his throat. "They're important to her."

"Do you know why?"

"Something tells me, *you're* about to inform me of the why." Suddenly both men smirk.

Dr. Maxwell turns his attention to me. "Autumn, why are communication and honesty important to you?"

I blink, confused from the small shift. "They're...key parts of relationships."

"That's you analyzing," he tells me. "Why are they important to *you*?"

I scrunch my brows, trying to decipher what he's getting at. I do what he says, stop analyzing of "what should be" and what I feel instead. Slowly, as I keep my gaze with Dr. Maxwell's, understanding clicks. Fuck.

I've been scared the entire time.

He must see the realization, because he leans forward a little and gives me a reassuring expression. "You haven't told Leonardo why, have you?" I shake my head. "Not the mask of you *think* and *know* about relationships, but what you need and why?"

My nerves kick up, anxiety beginning to make my hands shake. Leo and I have talked so much, yet I don't think I ever explained any of the deep-rooted stuff. Guess I wasn't as vulnerable as I thought.

Leo shifts in his seat, keeping his hand upon my leg. Breath gets caught in my chest as I stare at Dr. Maxwell.

"Autumn, don't think as I ask you some questions. Just feel, as we've done before, and remember you're safe to speak and be honest. No repercussions."

My heart thunders in my chest. "Okay."

"Are you fearful of Leo leaving you?" The tightness worsens, not wanting to admit it with him right next to me. "Don't think."

"Yes."

"Why?"

"Because others left me." I can't look at Leo, unsure how he's looking at me now.

"Why do you think they left?"

"Because I was replaceable. I wasn't enough," I rasp, and he nods for me to continue. "My family didn't want me. Never showed up at my funeral. Friends disappeared when it got rough. Police forgot about me after I gave them their intel. Roger replaced me. Coffee shop fired me, without a bat of an eye. Empty promises, lies...they just left me."

"Why do you need communication and honesty?" He asks again.

"To know if I need to be ready to be alone again," I murmur, staring at the ground. "If I'll be replaced again or if...there's something I can do that's worth staying for."

Out of the corner of my eye, I see Dr. Maxwell shake his head once at Leo. He asks, "Did Leo sound like someone who'd find you replaceable?"

I blink past some tears, shaking my head. "No," I answer earnestly.

"Do you find him replaceable?"

"No." The word comes out faster that time.

"Does he need to prove to you that he isn't?"

"No."

"Do you expect repayment from anything you've done for him? Small or large?"

"No."

"If I asked Leonardo similar questions, what do you think his answer would be?" My throat constricts as my jaw works, trying to stave off the lingering panic attack. "Deep breaths, Autumn, you're doing great. Be honest with yourself."

I close my eyes concentrating. "He'd say the same."

"I brought Leonardo down to hear his perspective, but also to give you both some clarity before you move forward with this new arrangement of you being less involved with Leonardo's...job." I bring my gaze up to meet the doctor's. "I agree it may be best for you to step back, until we reach some easier management of your trauma responses. We will get there, but until then other parts may rear their head. Sometimes it's hard to separate the reality of the present from that of the past. What's happening is not just guilt of being a burden, but you may be punishing yourself for achieving that communication and honesty when you hadn't in the past."

"Punishing myself?"

"You found happiness, and don't believe you deserve the kindness that Leonardo has given, such as the option to step back from the mob again." My face falls as a haze of tears fill my eyes. "Those past relationships were abusive, requiring you to fight, earn, and work for decency that should've been freely given. They were not healthy. Good relationships rely on growth with each other, respect for another, communication, and never needing to *prove* they deserve to be in. It is a *given*. Someone should care about you without strings attached. You, Autumn, deserve to feel safe without the consequences of owing someone."

I inhale sharply, trying to force the tears away. Slowly, I turn my head toward Leo, who's watching me intently. The lines above his brows are gone, gaze gentle.

"What I want you to work on, outside of this office," Dr. Maxwell continues. "Anytime those feelings centered around the need to prove your love, guilt of not being enough, or feeling replaceable, tell him. You trust him to tell you the truth, trust yourself to do so as well."

"Communication," I murmur.

"Yes." He smiles. "With new adjustments brings new bumps to overcome. When we find new freedoms, sometimes we realize what we'd neglected due to surviving instead of focusing on thriving."

"Kinda rhymed there."

"I'm behind on my poetry." He winks. I smile as he pulls out a notepad and writes down something. "Speaking of, I have some books I'd like you to try reading. May provide you with another insight on relationships."

"Sure, and thanks."

He turns to Leo, and says, "Thank you for joining us, Leonardo, I appreciate your cooperation. I think that's good enough for today."

"Thank you, doctor."

"I'll talk to Isaac about the next session," I chime in as all three of us stand.

Leo shakes his hand once as I walk around the couch to show Dr. Maxwell the door. He pauses, handing me the small sheet of paper. He touches my shoulder, and whispers, "It may help you understand him more, and how power exchanges can be helpful to let go."

My eyes widen, flicking my gaze to the book titles about BDSM. Alrighty then.

With a nod, I close the door behind him and join Leo at the couch. We're both quiet for a few minutes. Thought I was done with the self-punishment phase, but here we are.

"So…" I start, rubbing my hand over my face briefly, "…we're both scared of being alone essentially, quite the fucking pair."

"Or perfect pair." I snort. Leo rubs his hand over the nape of my neck. I close my eyes leaning into his touch. "I'm not leaving you, dear Watson. That's not why I suggested you step back."

I sigh, "I know Leo, I do…it's just—"

"Autumn." He gently turns my head to face him, eyes peering into mine. "I know you do, but it won't hurt for you to hear it from me. As shown by Dr. Maxwell."

"What did you think of him?"

A brief look of concentration comes over him and he replies, "Seems trustworthy. He's confident."

"Like someone else I know," I tease slightly.

He smiles as he pulls me closer, lips meeting mine. I hum against the contact, falling into his embrace as he kisses me. I cuddle into his side when we break the kiss, sighing as the last of the shakes leave me.

"What meeting were you in?"

"Buying a couple of apartment complexes in Chicago. After Isaac called, I upped the offer and walked out."

I snort. "What meetings are left today?"

"I have another in two hours…to tell a board of directors about these new apartment complexes in Chicago, I may have overpaid for."

"Do they have *any* say or control?"

"As much as I allow them to think." He kisses my temple. "This particular board is more of a formality."

"Well, you left your meeting early and therapy also ended early, wanna go toilet paper your competition? My treat."

Leo chuckles, standing up and helping me stand next. "How about a coffee, instead?"

Chapter 8

Coffee Lover

We stand across the street from *Blue Java Cafe*.

"You've gotta be kidding me," I grumble.

"They have good coffee," Leo retorts.

"Yeah, I should know, I worked there." Also drank enough coffee to fuel a rocket ship. "Why here and not the hotel?"

I haven't even been to the hotel's café yet.

"Are you scared?" He smirks. I'm half tempted to push him into the street. Guilt suddenly gone. "You were close to a barista there, Mabel, correct?"

"Yeah." I look at the shop, noticing her behind the counter. It's mostly empty inside, not surprising being late afternoon. I meant to contact her, especially after the interrogation, but been a bit preoccupied. And frankly, forgot.

"I know you're not the petty type." I eye him. "But I wonder how they'd react seeing me with you publicly. It'd be quite unfortunate if a certain ex-coworker heard about your relationship status."

I stop myself from smiling. "That is underhanded and sneaky." I grab his hand. "Let's go."

He chuckles as we stroll through the crosswalk. His fingers wrap around mine, warming them against the chill. Winter is showing its first signs. Even as I press closer to Leo for his warmth, it's not much needed with the new clothes he's gotten me. I miss my thrifted jean jacket but will admit the peacoat I'm wearing is far warmer than the jacket I once owned. It also matches his. Leo wraps his arm around my shoulders, leading us across the street. I glance over my shoulder, noticing Isaac already in the other coffee shop he used to sit in along with Animal.

"Is Isaac still doing things outside of being bodyguard?"

Leo follows my gaze, side stepping a businessman as we reach the sidewalk. "A few, but he's in charge of your personal security now. He asked for it."

"Really?"

He nods once, not elaborating. I glance back again, deciding it's not my place to pry for now.

It's going to take me a bit to stay uninvolved, especially when there's elephants in the room like Gabriel and Roger that are hard to ignore. I can't quite shake wondering what Leo wants to do with his older brother, because I sure fucking don't. Reactionary response is to bury him in cement. Secondary, I remember he's still Leo's brother and Matteo's. There are family politics at play, other- wise Leo would've wiped Gabriel from this earth years ago after what happened with Matteo. What those politics are…I'm not sure I want to learn them.

I shake my head, clearing it to focus on getting coffee.

Leo opens the door, and I feel a bit nostalgic and misplaced. I peek over the counter to see Mabel in a turquoise sweater with dangling silver earrings. She's even started to grow some of her hair out.

"Afternoon, what can—" she stops when she sees me, then lets out a soft shriek. "Autumn!"

"Hi." I don't stop my smile and laughter as Mabel quickly comes around the counter and I meet her halfway to hug her. She sputters in shock, clutching me. A few people look our way but go on about their business.

"Please tell me you've come back to work," Mabel pleads,

pulling back to grip my shoulders. She scrunches her face. "Nah, you look happy. Keep your peace."

I laugh harder, tugging her back into a hug. I hadn't realized how much I'd missed her until she saw me. After a minute, I finally let go and say, "Thought to get some coffee."

"Hey, you better be visiting for me, too."

"Of course." I flick my gaze to the back. "Who else is here?"

"Don't worry, hurricane barbie doesn't work the same shifts as me." I narrow my eyes at her, and she shrugs. "Warned Yuki I'd quit if I was scheduled with her. New girl is in the back."

"Does she have moon shoes?" I joke.

"No, which *you* were supposed to share." She taps my shoulder.

"Forgot, sorry." I glimpse at her hands and quirk a brow.

"It is winter! Don't give me that look." I dig into my bag, pushing past the book and cloth napkins I think I may have stolen from *Giglio Giardino*. Finally, I find the lotion and hand it over. She gasps in relief, squirts some, and lathers her hands up then her forearms. "Still the best coworker."

I snort and just give her the bottle. "Keep it here, since you'll need it more than me."

"Thanks." She starts to say something else, but then freezes as she looks behind me. I turn, noticing Leo quietly watching us. Mabel brings her wide eyes back to me, and whispers, "Shut up, are you...*girl*."

"Mabel, you remember Leo?" I gesture for him to come forward. He steps up beside me and she practically gapes at him.

"It's a pleasure to see you again, Mabel," Leo says in that usual business tone.

"Likewise." She flicks her gaze to me, and I give her a look to wait. "Want some drinks?"

We nod, and she quickly goes behind the counter. Leo passes me a look, and I shrug, acting nonchalant. I go to the register with him close behind. "What's your specialty of late?"

"Dirty chai with a smidge of cinnamon and toffee."

"I'll take that, and then a medium Americano." I catch Leo's little smirk.

"Oh, I haven't forgotten his order, how could I?" She says, scrunching her nose in a cute way. "You don't forget certain... *customers.*"

Mable turns away to start the drinks. Leo leans close to whisper, "Is there something I should know?"

"What? Nooo..." I look at him with mischief, and he smiles. Suddenly his phone begins to ring, and said smile is quickly gone as he pulls it out with a scowl.

"Almost an hour, that's a record," I comment.

He grunts under his breath, pulling out his wallet and hands me cash for the drinks as he answers the phone. "This better relate to the paperwork from earlier."

He walks toward the table near the corner window. I move my attention back to the register, finding Mabel with a wide grin and sparkling eyes.

"Are you two like, together, *together*?" She types in the order.

"Yeah, we're official. Practically already moved into his place." The hotel that is.

She giggles, dancing in her spot. "Yes! Oh, you got the better end of the stick. Finally! Please tell me I can rub this in Bailey's face."

As much as I'd like that, I shake my head. "Done with that, Mabel. Moved on. Sucked how everything happened, but I'm happier now. Apart from missing you that is." I glance over my shoulder to Leo. I smile a little, screw it I can be petty. "Or you could just mention you saw us. Then text me her reaction."

"That's my girl." She laughs. "Eight-fifty by the way."

"Giving me a discount?" She shrugs and I chuckle. I look at the cash in my hand, rolling my eyes. I give her the ten for the drinks, and then place the fifty-dollar bill into the tip jar.

"Oh, how I missed that," Mabel sighs, handing me back the change. I place that into the jar as well. "And you, of course. Drinks will be right up."

I nod, heading down to the pick-up counter to let her work. I lean against the wall, watching Mabel take some orders and see the new barista join her. She's got blonde hair, pulled back into a French braid, and is wearing a dark green sweater. She's young with freckles on her cheeks. Relief washes over me when I see her help Mabel easily, glad she has someone who's competent to work with. I overhear Mabel say her name, Cassie, and note that for the future.

Maybe I could come back.

Leo hangs up the phone and begins to head toward me. I smile, but it falters when a tall brunette with beige skin and a tight sweater approaches him. Her smile is bright, greeting him and stopping him in his tracks. A tightness develops in my chest, and I quickly avert my gaze as my stomach twists. What is it with this coffee shop and people flirting with him? Was it something in the air?

I shouldn't be jealous or worried, but suddenly I'm feeling grateful for rarely going out in public with him. That stupid sickening feeling of being replaced comes back and I want to groan out loud. Oh, look almost an hour before any anxiety. Son of a nutcracker.

"Drinks up." Mabel's voice pierces through my anxious thoughts, and I look up with a forced smile. She flicks her gaze to the side. "Kind of missed that scowling look of his."

I look over at Leo, noticing his stark, stony expression as the woman talks to him. His unamused darkened gaze flash to mine. Leo holds his hand up, causing the woman to quiet and begins walking around her.

Mabel chuckles under her breath as the woman gasps at Leo. The door opens, bringing in a whole new group of customers. Mabel touches my hand briefly, which makes me wrench my gaze away from Leo. "Gotta get back to work. Don't be a stranger, Autumn."

"Yeah. Still owe you drinks," I respond.

"Yup!"

I reach for the coffee when two arms wrap around my middle from behind. I barely stop the yelp that comes out of me as I jolt from the contact. Leo whispers against my ear, "Don't drop them, dear Watson."

"Don't scare me, mister," I say breathlessly.

"Apologies." He kisses my neck before stepping back and grabs his drink. I flick my gaze as I take mine, seeing the woman glaring at me as she steps into the line. I loosen a shaky breath. Seriously, is there something in the coffee that makes women want to claw another's eyes out in here?

"Autumn, look at me," Leo orders softly. I do so, finding his serious expression. He cups my face, bringing his close to mine. "I only see you."

"Sorry, anxiety again," I mumble.

He maneuvers us out of the way as people begin to linger near the pick-up station. His hand moving down to my hip. "How can I help remedy that?"

Leo's voice is low and rough, contrasting against the gentle touch. Heat pools in my stomach, my chest tightening for a different reason than before. My breathing picks up, staring into those eyes that flick down to my mouth.

"I've got an idea, but don't you have a meeting?" I ask hoarsely, holding my dirty chai close.

"Something more important came up." He immediately begins leading me out of the shop. His hand remains at the small of my back, keeping me close as we walk out. Leo whispers into my ear, "Check in."

"Green."

His hand moves to the nape of my neck, squeezing gently. "Good girl."

Leo locks the door behind us as I put our drinks on the kitchen counter. I don't hold back my nervous giggles as he tosses his coat off. The counter presses into my back as Leo stalks toward me. He takes his phone out, turning it off before he tosses it on the other counter. My breath becomes heavy as he towers over me, tracing a finger down my jaw.

His hands glide over me, removing my coat and cardigan, and then tearing his suit jacket off next. "If we get interrupted again, I may rip their heads off."

My eyes widen a moment. The man is on a mission.

He grabs my ass, lifting me against his chest as I wrap my legs around his waist.

"I need to make something very clear with you, my dear Watson," he speaks in a rough voice. I go still in his arms as he carries me into the bedroom, shutting the door with his foot. Yup, all precautions in place. "Understand I am not upset of any sort, but I *need* to crush whatever anxieties or worries of yours to dust. I seem to get through to you with declarations and…showing you."

I swallow hard, butterflies flying around in my stomach. Leo places me down onto my feet in the middle of the room. He cups my face, kissing me with an affectionate tenderness that makes me weak in the knees. I grip his arms for support.

"Listen to me, my dear Watson. Listen, *very* closely. Understood?" I nod my head. "Good girl."

His hands slide down, grabs the hem of my shirt and pulls it off. He removes his shirt next, agonizingly slow, while his heated gaze stays upon mine. The clothes drop to the floor unceremoniously as he removes his pants and then mine. Both of us soon standing, what feels like a sauna, in only our underwear.

My eyes travel over his body, following the intricate lines of the tattoos as they fall into the other. Flames, thorns, wires tumbling together in a colorful array as they're covered in smoke, joined by phrases of Latin and more. Each dark spiral, twist, and connection I concentrate on, until he begins to circle me. Leo's fingers stroke lightly over my skin, making my breath hitch as I watch him from the corner of my eye. He hums, trailing those fingers down my spine and back up to the base of my neck.

"Check in," he murmurs.

"Green."

"I cannot rid every anxiety or fear from you with a snap of my fingers, even if every fiber of my being wants to." His voice is a dark sensual, loving tone. I close my eyes, focusing on his touch and voice, finding peace in them. "But I will use every waking moment of mine to remind you of my feelings whenever they show their ugly heads. One…is that I love you more than my own life and would *willingly* crawl on my knees through hell for you."

My eyes snap open. Leo stands before me, tracing fingers down my neck to my clavicle. His hooded gaze is observant, chest rising with a heaviness that matches my own. Trembling begins in my arms, and I concentrate in hopes to stop it. Leo takes my hands, placing them against his chest. My fingers splay out over the tattoos, the heat of his skin ensnaring me.

"Two…is that I will only *ever* have eyes for you. No one else."

I swallow hard as he lets go of my hands. His own travels up my arms as he comes in close, moving them down my sides as he begins to kneel before me. Leo stares up at me in adoration and reverence that makes every thought in my head vanish. He grips my hips, caressing his thumbs over my skin, while I try to keep from making a soft noise. My breath catches as he leans forward to place a kiss on my stomach, hips, and chest.

Hazel eyes lift to mine. Oh, fuck me.

"Third…is that I belong solely to you. Every part of me." He places a hand over mine, directly over his heart. My chin starts to quiver. "I am yours, Autumn Watson. There is no chance of me ever leaving your light because it owns me. Do you understand?" I inhale sharply, gripping my fingers into his skin. "Do you, my dear Watson?"

"Yes," I rasp.

"Remember that if *anyone* including yourself questions that. You never have to earn your place beside me because you've already conquered me."

He leans forward, dragging his hands down the back of my

legs, moving them around as he goes slowly over my scars. The ones left behind from when I ran from him.

I want to cry, kiss him, and fall further into the chasm he's created. I'm consumed by his touch and the voice that makes everything feel safe. He's right about me listening when he does this; using every sense to show me. His touch. His voice. Him on his knees.

He loves me.

Something snaps inside me, causing my skin to tighten and almost burn. I move my hands to the sides of his face, tilting his head back. Oh, fuck me. Held within my hands is the face of a man who looks up at me with such worship and love that it could break me. My throat tightens, swallowing back a sob. It's the trust in his eyes.

"I love you." It's all I'm able to get out at first. He smiles faintly. "I love you, please…take me to bed."

"Very well, dear Watson." He wraps his arms around my legs. I stifle a yelp as he stands, almost falling over his shoulder.

He lays me down, making quick work to remove my bra. He caresses my sides, hovering over me as he leans down to kiss me. His tongue strokes over my bottom lip and I open, tasting him as I arch my back, wanting to feel more of him.

"Check in," he says against my lips.

"Emerald."

He chuckles, tracing his tongue along my jaw. "Haven't even started yet."

"Your foreplay is that good."

He kisses my neck, voice vibrating against my skin. "Good girl."

I whimper at the endearment, wanting him to call me that again and again. My body tingles as he continues to slide his hands over my skin. They slip under the hem of my underwear, and I raise my hips for him to take them off. Every muscle relaxes as I lay underneath him.

"What do you want?" He asks, nipping at my ear. I groan, not really knowing what I want apart from just him. I want him to keep touching me like I'm priceless or feel his mouth against my skin.

Touch. I wanted his touch upon every inch of me.

"Tell me, sweetheart," he says.

"Touch me," I finally gasp. "I don't know how else to say it, but…touch me."

"Like this?" He strokes the back of his hand against my ribs. I hum, nodding quickly. "Very well, put your hands above your head and don't move."

I snap open my eyes. He gives me a small smile as I do as instructed. He kisses my forehead before getting off the bed. I lay there quietly, watching him lock the bedroom door. I chuckle as he smirks.

"Extra, extra precaution?" I ask as he goes to the closet.

"For others' safety."

He disappears and comes back out with a black tie. I freeze. Uncertainty slithers up from the back of my mind as he comes back to the bed. He kneels beside me, holding up the tie. "I won't tie you up, I know it's a hard limit for you. Instead, you'll keep your hands in place without anything to keep you there. It'll take more restraint from you, understood?"

I go to nod my head, until he quirks a brow. I giggle, "Yes."

"Good girl." I bite my lower lip. He chuckles next, kissing the side of my mouth swiftly. "Next, I'm going to place this over your eyes. Not tied. At any point it's too much, take it off. You don't need my permission. It'll help conceal that sense, alright?"

"Yes."

"I won't be frequently checking in, so be sure to tell me if you move anywhere past green. Understood?"

"Yes. Yellow and red are my safe words."

His smile broadens, placing the tie over my eyes which puts me into controlled darkness. The back of his hand caresses down my neck. "Good girl. Pay attention to my touch and voice."

"Uh-huh," I whimper, already partially distracted.

His hands glide down my body, one stopping at my breast to

begin massaging my skin. I hum as he presses and circles around my nipple. His other hand moves down toward the apex of my thighs, opening my legs a bit more with silent command. His tongue surprises me, trailing down the center of my chest and back up to lick the nipple his thumb isn't circling. My breath hitches as his tongue flicks it, trying not to laugh at the light sensation. I bite back another giggle as he does it again.

"Make all the noise you want," he tells me, stroking a finger through my sex and pressing slightly. "You're gorgeous when you do."

He continues to caress my skin, moving over my body as if he's studying every part of it. More of my body relaxes into the bed, becoming loose and languid. He moves off the bed suddenly, and I hear something click open. The bed dips again, Leo moves his fingers down below, now slicked with lube. I hum as he inserts a finger, using the other hand to caress my torso before grabbing my hip. I moan when his tongue slides down my neck and toward my chest, swirling his tongue over sensitive areas as his hand works me below. Leo goes at a slow, sensual pace.

When he adds another finger, my breath catches. Hot breath washes over me as I arch my back, resisting the urge to grab at him. I let out a long moan, squeezing my eyes shut, struggling to keep my arms above my head. They shake as I fight to keep from grabbing him as he continues the wonderful torturous touch over my skin.

"Leo," I plead, lifting my hips to drive his fingers deeper.

"Concentrate on every sensation you feel." He kisses my shoulder. "All of it meant to bring you pleasure."

He keeps speaking with loving affection as he presses his thumb against my clit. I breathe heavier, hips moving on their own accord as his fingers pump into me. He continues to massage my breasts roughly, squeezing them before he presses down along my stomach. My head tilts back as my body quakes beneath him. The tie slips off and I shut my eyes. I struggle against the instinct to put the tie back or grab him.

Every tiny thing that tries to pull me away is washed away by the overpowering sensations. I go through my head of every word he said, envisioning him looking up at me with hands clutching his face. On his knees for me.

A shudder travels through my body.

I can feel myself climb closer to orgasm, the crest of it nearing. He presses and circles his thumb more, hooking his fingers downward. I whimper, thrusting my hips up.

"Who do I belong to?" He asks abruptly. Fuck, I'm supposed to answer. He's making me multi-task right now? His breath brushes over my ear. "Who do I belong to, Autumn?"

"Me," I whimper, the orgasm rushes closer as the base of my spine tightens, legs shaking.

"Good girl." He kisses the underside of my jaw, squeezes my breast, and thrusts three fingers into me. It undoes me as I let out a soft scream, body going tense as I come and then go limp.

I let out a sigh, melting into the bed as Leo kisses me gently. He pulls his fingers out of me, stepping off the bed and taking the tie with him. I open my eyes as he comes back without underwear on.

"Check in."

"I take it back, *now* it's emerald." He laughs softly, nuzzling his face against my neck. "I can move my hands?"

"Yes." I wrap my arms around his neck, then thread my fingers through his hair. Bliss makes my mind hazy. I bring him closer so I can kiss him, tasting his sweetness. I moan from the contact. He pulls back, placing a kiss on my nose.

I muster as much confidence as I can and ask, "What do you want?"

He raises his brows, flicking his eyes down my body. "You."

"More specific, mister." He looks at me with amusement. I swallow hard and ask again, but a bit more quietly. "What do you want?"

He tilts his head slightly. A slow smile rising. "To try a new position."

My brows raise next. "That's all?"

He brings his face in close, murmuring against my lips. "Yes, dear Watson, but I may be a bit rough."

"Okay."

Leo kisses me hard suddenly, stealing my breath away. I gasp at the force of it as he moves a hand to grip my hair. He tilts my head back, giving him space to abruptly end the kiss and suck upon my neck instead. I clutch at his back, pleasure spiking at the sudden change of approach.

He lets go of my hair, grabbing my hips and flipping me to my side. His hand roves over my ass and down my thigh, positioning himself over my legs. Leo maneuvers my bottom leg between his legs, bending the top one against his stomach. Once again, Leo is on his knees for me, but this time he seems like a giant above me. I clutch at the sheets, staring up at the man who handles me roughly, yet still tenderly.

His hand continues to caress my thigh and over my ass, moving down until he probes a finger inside me. I gasp, still sensitive from the latest orgasm. He presses two fingers into me, and then three again as I moan at the intrusion. With a brusque movement, he removes his fingers and I feel him enter me with his dick. My breath catches as he lifts my leg a little, thrusting in short movements until he's fully seated. He stays there, pinning my leg with my shin against his lower torso.

"Check in, sweetheart."

"Green."

"I'm going to be rougher than usual."

"Okay," I say, clutching the blanket.

Leo pulls back, gripping onto my thigh as he bends my leg further, completely making me immobile as he plunges back into me. A gasp leaves me as my body sparks from the thrust. He doesn't give me much time to adjust to the new rhythm and position, quickly pulling out and doing it again. His hips piston against mine and already my legs begin to shake.

From this side position, it feels like he's rubbing my g-spot, hitting nerves I don't always feel during sex. It's tighter than usual as his cock slides into me. I moan loudly into the blankets as Leo continues the harsh onslaught, pounding into me. His hand clutches at my upper thigh, sliding down to my ass and tightening his grasp. I choke out a breath at the sudden pain, but it feels numbed as Leo fucks me.

For a moment, panic blinks at the far reaches of my mind. The roughness of him and the hard grip he has on me. I concentrate on the pleasure that builds from his cock thrusting inside, brushing against my inner walls. I turn my attention up to Leo, watching as sweat begins to form on his forehead and glistens on his chest.

Leo grunts before his eyes snap to mine, his hips beginning to slow their pace. He bends over me, one hand on my thigh and the other landing near my head. I grab at his wrist as he clutches my leg, keeping me still as he fucks me at the steep angle. I let out a soft scream, digging my nails into his forearm as ecstasy rushes over my skin. My muscles tighten when Leo growls near my ear.

Oh, fuck me.

"Leo," I plead.

His body snaps up as he takes hold of my bent leg, moving it to wrap behind his back. I scream as he adjusts, pushing into me. With the swift angle change and his fingers biting into my skin, I come hard. My entire body goes tense as sparks fly up my spine, causing me to arch my back, pushing him deep as he gives one last final thrust with a grunt. He breathes heavily, panting as he brings his hands down on either side of my body to keep from falling on top of me.

I blink, unsure what just happened, but holy fuck was that good.

I swallow past the dryness in my mouth, and ask, "Check in?"

He kisses my shoulder, then says breathlessly, "Peridot."

I giggle, making him grunt as he pulls out to lay beside me. "Another gem?"

"You already took emerald."

"We can share," I say between giggles. He spoons me, placing tender kisses along my neck. We lay there, trying to catch our breath when I hear a faint buzzing of a phone from the other room. "Have you skipped this many meetings before?"

"Not before you," he murmurs, giving no indications of letting go. "Since I'm probably receiving an annoying, long discussion about it…we should continue ignoring work."

"Oh, *we*?"

"Do you want to cuddle alone?" I shake my head. "Then it's we."

I smile, snuggling closer against his body as his arms tighten. "Teamwork makes the dream work," I sigh.

Chapter 9

Hallmark Holiday

Leo

His hand passes over his pocket again. Leo loosens a sharp exhale, trying to concentrate on the data in front of him and contracts attached. Once certain he's read it over twenty times at this point, he tosses them back into their folder and across his desk.

"Distracted?" Jameson asks, handing a folder to Owen.

Leo eyes him, not daring to give away his thoughts. Thankfully, a knock at the door saves him from giving a curt retort.

"Come in," he calls, leaning back in his chair.

Isaac enters with Rudolf, who remains by the doors, whilst Isaac approaches the desk. "You wanted to see me before we left?"

Leo pulls out a cream-colored envelope decorated in gold lettering from his desk drawer. He pushes it across the desk to Isaac, who raises a brow and chances a look at Jameson and Owen. They also give a look of surprise.

"Give this to Autumn, no earlier than 4:30," he instructs. "If she has any questions, I'll be there soon to answer them."

Jameson walks over and scoffs. "You're *actually* going."

Rudolf clears his throat as Owen steps closer with a raised brow.

Busy bodies, Leo thinks.

"Not earth-shattering that I attend social events," Leo says, standing up to adjust his suit jacket.

Isaac's blue eyes narrow, until Leo's expression hardens suddenly with a scowl. Isaac takes the invitation off Leo's desk, putting it inside his jacket. "I should remind you, she's not going to like the crowd."

"Then I'll remind you that she won't leave my side the entire night, and some of you get to play prince as well." Jameson grumbles, making Leo frown at him. "There's an invitation for you, too, *Mr. Vasquez.*"

"Don't start," Jameson mutters.

"Figured with your worries of late and Carrie's about publicity, it may be good in the long run."

Jameson glares at him as Isaac tries to hide his smirk, Rudolf out right grins, and Owen clears his throat.

"Don't make it sound like I agree with her," Jameson retorts. "On *anything*, but I'll go if you are. Make sure you behave."

Leo snorts. Isaac shakes his head, leaving the office along with Rudolf.

"We'll talk about those shipments after the meeting," Leo tells Owen, who's getting ready to leave.

Owen pauses before stepping out. "By the way, I'll have Autumn's computer ready in a couple days. Enigma wanted to add some extra malware protection."

"Computer?" Leo furrows his brows. Owen nods his head, waiting for any resistance. Leo clears his throat. "She agreed to one?"

"Yeah, maybe get back to the outside world a bit again."

"Right." Leo shoves away a feeling of unease. He nods once at Owen who takes the hint and leaves.

"She sure does rip that mask off of you, even when she's not here," Jameson comments as he grabs the folders Leo tossed aside.

Leo gives him a bored expression. "What does that mean?" His best friend only smirks. "Weren't you insistent about attending these meetings?"

"Wouldn't have needed to if you hadn't pulled a Ferris Bueller the past couple days."

Leo scoffs at him, heading for the door. "Nothing blew up, don't get your panties twisted."

"Coming from the one who's worked like he couldn't breathe without it for over a decade." Jameson's comment makes Leo stop. "Could be jealous it was her to get you to realize it, but I'll take the win, maybe finally get some more riding in."

"Itching there, Sombra?"

"Always." Jameson shoves the paperwork back into Leo's hands. "Whatever is on your mind with her, work it out or at least don't keep giving me the problem companies."

Leo's heart constricts a little, but keeps his demeanor composed. Jameson still flicks his gaze over him with caution.

"You two are fine...right?" Jameson asks.

"Course." A silent beat passes between them. "Something on *your* mind?"

"Just wondering if it really is a good idea to keep her secluded from mafia dealings." Leo's expression darkens greatly, causing Jameson to cock his head at him a little. "Last time you hid it from her, it didn't go well."

"*This* time she knows."

"Not everything."

"That's the point."

"If you say so, Spartan." Jameson lifts his hands in surrender, walking toward the doors. "I'll stay on the sidelines."

Leo snorts at him. "For what? Two days?"

"A record for me." Jameson gestures toward the hall. "Can we go take care of the board members *you* pissed off by blue-balling them twice?"

Leo strolls toward the doors, adjusting his cuffs. "Perhaps I'll remind them that some people are replaceable, including them."

———

Autumn

"We gotta go back, take Leo with us, of course, just to see her face."

I take the books from Leanne.

"As wonderful as it sounds to be that petty, I don't want to use him like a show pony." I roll my eyes.

"That's not what I said," she counters. She takes a few cookbooks from the stack, pointing at my chest. "I'm *saying*, let's get coffee, smile and leave. Ignore her and be happy. Best revenge is being happy in front of your enemies."

"Is that what the kids are being taught nowadays?"

"Only middle schoolers. Elementary is still learning how to share." Her tone is sarcastic.

It's mid-afternoon. I've been working in the bookstore the past few days, staying busy clearing off shelves for new ones to be placed in. There'll be a few other small renovations due to Steve's break-in, as instructed by Jameson mostly. Such as a new back door, locks, reinforced bullet-proof windows for the front, and let's not get started on the security cameras. Most of December the store will be closed for renovations, allowing Nan to leave for Georgia for the holidays, coming back in the New Year. She wanted a vacation, but I could see the uncertainty in her eyes around the store.

Steve broke into our home, *her* home. So, the Crew is doing what they can to make it feel safe again.

Leanne gives the cookbooks back. She had a half day at work, came by to help. She didn't ask about Steve, but I could see her trepidation when I told her about the bookstore's renovations. Time to move on and I desperately wanted to.

"When does Leo finish work?" Leanne asks. I quirk a brow at her. "You two sound busy the past couple days."

I roll my eyes at her again, poking her side. "Shush."

She laughs, following me around another empty shelving unit.

"Look, I'm just saying I'd love for anyone to play hooky for me." Her tone sounds a bit sadder.

I crouch down to organize a shelf, looking up at her. "Thought stuff was going well between you and Jim? Didn't you have something planned for Christmas and such?"

She purses her lips. "He was offered a position in St. Louis." I gape at her. "And he took it."

"Oh, nutcrackers, sorry, hun."

"Don't be." She waves her hand in the air. "Only been seeing each other for a couple months at most. Doesn't make sense for him to stay. He's already left." I keep my mouth shut. Leanne crouches next to me. "I'd rather wait for the one who *would* stay."

"Does that mean you're still going home for Thanksgiving?" She nods. "Well, tell your mom I say hi, and remind your sister that wine is not an appetizer."

Leanne snorts. "My sister still thinks you're a prude."

"I refuse wine one time." We both start giggling, helping ease the brief gloomy moment.

We move down to another shelf, her helping me check books off, moving on to the gardening section. I glance over at the fantasy section. Oof, *that* section will take a while.

"Hey, any idea who Alex Randolph is?" Leanne asks. I look over my shoulder at her.

"Chef, I think, they died a few years ago. Why?"

She holds up a cookbook, flipping through the pages. "Found some fun recipes, might get this for my mom. Although I'm surprised you knew that."

I shrug. "Nan like's their stuff. When she's not making her original recipes, it's usually theirs."

"Does the rest of her family know?" Leanne smiles.

"Promised to take it to my grave." I smile back. "You going right back to yours for the winter break?"

"Probably. I'll be here for like two weeks and then gone again. You staying?"

"Yeah, but not like *here*." I gesture to upstairs.

"Can't believe you've already moved in with him."

"It's been a few months." Chaotic and more so, but that's beside the point. There wasn't much to move in anyways, especially when you split your stuff between two penthouses essentially. Beginning to understand why Leo got me more clothes. "And hopefully I'll be busy, cause we both know this time of year never seems great for me."

"I know, hun." She comes up, rubbing my shoulder softly. "Thankfully, he'll be around. You could always hang out with Trix, too."

"She's gonna be in Boston and then D.C." Leanne raises her brows. "Remember? She's trying to strike that deal with those investors for the centers?"

"They're actually flying her out?" I nod. "Fingers crossed, then."

Leanne then grabs my shoulders, making me blink. "Maybe Leo will reveal he owns a Christmas tree farm, and you'll start making pottery!"

"We both know I'm only great at making random shaped paper-weights."

"Your final project is still on my desk." I start laughing remembering the hunk of clay I tried to paint in a rainbow. Bless Leanne for still using it. We're laughing when Isaac comes around the aisle with an amused expression.

"Looking for cookbooks?" I ask.

"I believe the one who needs lessons is you, Miss Autumn, not me."

"*Ouch*, that hurt *me*," Leanne comments, holding her chest and giggling.

"Bodyguards with sass," I mutter. "Pretty Boy." He eyes me, and I smirk. "What's up?"

He reaches into his suit jacket, pulling out an envelope. "I was instructed to give you this."

"Anyone ever tell you your accent is sexy?" Leanne wiggles her eyes at Isaac, who gives her a slow smile and blushes slightly.

"No hitting on my shadow," I chide.

"I tell him all the time," Nan chimes in, poking her head around the corner, flicking her gaze to the envelope in my hands.

That's more suspicious than the accent comment.

"To answer your question, yes, Miss Kelley."

"I'm gonna go distract myself with shiny gold lettering as you two discuss accents." I wave my hand at them, turning away to open it. I pause when I see it's addressed to Leo and not me. Ominous.

I glance over my shoulder and see all three watching me. "Whatever happened to privacy?" I mutter, tearing it open.

"Just curious," Nan answers.

"Same," Leanne adds.

I pull out the card. It's an invitation for Leo and guest to attend a charity gala in a week. Apparently, a long-time annual event that happens near Thanksgiving. I continue reading, almost dropping the card as I stare down at the venue.

The Rainbow Room at the Rockefeller Center.

My jaw drops. This isn't some party, it's one of *the* parties for only the elite of New York City. I continue staring at the card, heart thundering, almost convincing myself this isn't real until I grip the thick paper. Yup, it's real. I stare at Isaac, no words forming. Leanne leans over, gasps, and *her* jaw drops.

"Rockefeller Center?" I rasp, holding up the card.

"Oh! How marvelous!" Nan exclaims.

"This is amazing!" Leanne says.

Never in my life have I ever thought *I'd* attend a gala, let alone it being in the freaking Rainbow Room! It's up there with the Russian Tea Room; you look at it from a distance while wearing converse.

Leanne grabs the card. "Didn't take Leo for being one to attend these fancy things. Thought he was a recluse."

"He doesn't normally attend," Isaac informs. "He thought to make an exception this year."

Something shifts over his gaze, already I know why. Leo *wants* to take me to a gala, an event probably filled with millionaires, businesspeople, and probably politicians. Mafia boss or not, he still owns a great deal of real estate throughout the city, not to mention being a hotel mogul. Okay, maybe I really do forget who I'm dating. Right now, oh, I am remembering.

"New dress time!" Leanne exclaims.

"I can't afford shoes that would be appropriate for this event." I point at the card. Or underwear.

"Oh, pish, I'm certain Leonardo has plans to dress you up himself. He better if he hopes to take you," Nan comments.

I feel myself begin to hyperventilate. We've gone out to some nice restaurants, but nothing like this. Each time I've felt out of place. I'm not the woman who goes to these things; I'm the one who holds the tray of champagne. Could I honestly go to this and *not* look like a fish out of water? As I'm rambling in my head, I start pacing the back of the store.

Mafia shit was easier to deal with. I can yell or throw frying pans at people.

Nan chuckles. "Oh, nothing to get worked up over, dear. You'll get to see the city like you've never seen before."

"It'll be fun," Leanne tries to reassure me. "Even with all those people." She mumbles back to Isaac. "She won't be alone, right?"

"Correct."

Why am I freaking out about this? Not like it wasn't going to happen at some point. Maybe I'm still trying to wrap my head around some things. I've no idea how to act around these people other than asking, "do you want sugar with that?" Terrible thinking, but it's been my reality for 28 years.

"Hun, breathe, you can be excited about this," Leanne tries to soothe me. "I'll go shopping with you! We can bring Trix before she leaves, and we can do a girl day. Although only a week out and near a holiday, finding the right dress may be hard, not much time for alterations."

I pause to look at Isaac. "He's going to buy everything, isn't he?"

"We both know the answer to that, Miss Autumn."

I let out a groan, hanging my head back as I rub my hands over my face, pacing once more. "I said no more clothes, but pretty sure *Old Navy* or *Macy's* won't do the trick. I don't even know *what* stores to go to."

"I'll take care of everything." Leo's voice jolts me.

I yelp, stumbling over my feet, which catch over a stack of books, and fall on my ass. I slump against the floor, groaning in defeat. Leo is instantly there with a gentle smirk. "Still falling for me."

"Aren't you funny," I retort, closing my eyes as I lay my head down. "I trip over books, get coffee spilled on me, and have a panic attack over a dang invitation. Sure, you want to introduce me to high society?"

Leo hovers over me, placing his hands beside my head to lean down and kiss me gently on the forehead. "I'm quite certain, dear Watson."

"Couldn't give a heads up?"

"Not how surprises work."

"Oh, well you *definitely* surprised me, mister Americano."

His amused expression vanishes, replaced by concern. "Do you really not want to go?"

"No, that's not, hold on." I sit up, and he grabs my hand to help me stand. I glance through the shelves, seeing the others with their inquisitive eyes. Isaac at least tries to look distracted, the other two begin whispering with each other. I sigh, grabbing Leo's hand and pull him behind me to the back hallway and close the door to the bookstore for some privacy. Worry lines his features, along with furrowed brow.

I steady my breath. "I overreacted."

"Autumn, no, you didn't—"

"Wait, wait." I hold my hands up, then lean forward to tap my forehead against his chest. Somehow that helps me think. "It's not that I don't *want* to go. It sounds nice. Maybe even fun. It's just a lot to take in cause it's not something I'm used to or ever thought I'd attend."

"You knew about my lifestyle and what it may entail, Autumn."

"Yeah, I did, but the mobster stuff kinda made me forget about the hotel empire stuff." I lean back with a sassy smile. His face relaxes a little. "Of course, I want to go with you, but please don't feel like you have to go to this because of me."

Leo cups my face, stroking his thumb under my lip. "I want to spend time with you. To give you a wonderful time, lavish you with gifts, and have a night with no responsibilities. If it's the money you're worried about—"

"Oh, stopped worrying about that weeks ago, amazingly." I pat his chest. His smile grows before he leans down to kiss me softly. I wrap my arms around his torso, feeling calmer as he finishes the kiss.

"I have one condition," I say against his lips.

"That would be?"

"Okay, a couple. One, I get to choose the dress. And two, you don't get to see it until the night of." He raises his brows. "Look, if I'm doing this princess shtick, I'm going all out. And the Crew will *definitely* help me achieve that. Especially, Animal, Rudy, and Iron Buffalo, who are Disney princesses at heart."

Leo snorts a laugh, making me smile. "Very well, but I'll choose the stores, pay for everything, and no matter what…" he brings his face close to mine, "…no looking at the price tag."

"Do I get to donate some of the other clothes you've gotten me, after?"

He eyes me a little, and then relents. "Fine."

"Sorry for panicking. You were trying to be sweet and stuff."

He shakes his head, tugging me into a hug.

"Don't apologize for being truthful," he murmurs, threading his fingers through my hair. I hold him tightly, adjusting to move my arms, but he suddenly moves back. He opens the door to the bookstore. "I already have appointments set up and you can take Leanne or whoever with you."

Guess I'm going to learn how far Leo will go to spoil me.

Chapter 10

Yes to the Dress

I look up at the dazzling sign of the gown shop. Trix hugs me, grinning with excitement. "This is gonna be great."

I give her a worried look.

She rubs my back a little. "Because you got me and Leanne."

We stand a few feet from the entrance of the store, where Leo apparently made an appointment a couple days before I got the invite. They also do jewelry and shoes. My own one-stop-and-done. I loved him for knowing me.

Isaac's off to the side of the sidewalk, on the phone as he keeps an eye on us.

"Any idea what you're looking for?" Trix tilts her head. The silver chains that adorn her violet scarf sparkle against the sun. It's cold out, the sunlight not doing much for warmth. Leanne better hurry up.

"Like the color?" I ask.

"Oh, really don't know much about fashion, huh?"

"Nah."

"Yup, that's why you have us. Okay, what are some things you *don't* want? Like lace or colors?"

"Uh, nothing too revealing, small heels, not a lace person, and no floral colors. Pastels don't look good on me."

"Thankfully, it's late autumn, so avoiding those colors won't be a problem." I give her a confused look. She laughs lightly. "Certain color palettes are more presentable during different seasons. Pastels normally don't work during this time of year."

"Noted."

I hear a shout over the crowd coming towards us, and I see Leanne practically skip through the crowd. She lands hard against me, giggling as I hug her back. "Oh, it's been too long!"

I laugh at her. "It's been a day!"

"Too long!" She bemoans, pulling back with a grin. She hugs Trix and then blows a kiss to Isaac. "Hey, sexy."

He gives her a smirk, almost blushing again.

We walk into the shop, and are met with the fanciest clothing store I've ever been in. Chandeliers hang from the ceiling, every-thing is a cream white with blue and lavender accents, decorated with brilliant flowers and gems. Gowns are on display, mounted on marble surrounded by luxurious seating. This must be what brides feel like when they walk into Kleinfeld.

A woman stands at the front desk, wearing a dark suit. She has loose black curls and red lips. She gives us a bright smile, flicking her gaze over us. "How may I help you today?"

"I have an appointment." I glance back at Isaac, upon realizing I don't know if it's under Leo's name or mine. He takes the cue, strolling past as he adjusts his coat.

"Good afternoon, Melanie," he greets. "There should be an appointment under the name Leonardo Luciano for Autumn Watson." Melanie, with name tag, types up something on her computer and her eyes widen. "The appointment should include full complimentary service and private fitting room."

"Yes, of course! A pleasure to have you with us today. I'll take you to meet your stylist." Melanie gestures down a bright hallway.

Trix winks at me, taking the lead with Leanne close behind. I fall back a little to whisper to Isaac, "Thank you. I was fully ready for a *Pretty Woman* moment."

"Not with me around, Miss Autumn."

We follow Melanie through some seating areas, where people mill about. Everything is in satin and cream. Maybe I did land in Kleinfeld. We arrive at a small archway, entering a private seating area with a platform and mirrors. There's a curtain to change behind, tables with wine, treats, jewelry, and shoes. Melanie leaves as we take our coats off, and Isaac situates himself on a chair next to the entrance.

"Faaaancy," Trix comments, looking around and picking up a piece of cheese.

I hang my coat up, staring at everything. I miss the 50 Cent thrift store.

Leanne gives me a side hug. "Here to have fun, indulge in your boyfriend's…" I give her a look, "…kindness."

Trix brings over a couple glasses of wine, handing one to Leanne. "We'll find something that's gonna make his jaw drop," Trix says with a wink.

"Exactly!" They clink their glasses. "And we'll take care of this wine for you."

"My heroes," I chuckle.

A young woman in similar black attire to Melanie walks in with dark red hair, bright green eyes, and a cheery voice bordering on fake. "Hi, I'm Jen. Pleasure to meet you all."

We give introductions, then she asks me about the event I'm attending. Her face lights up as she talks about the store, proudly stating they're dressing others attending the event. Shortly after, Jen leaves to look for what to begin with, suggesting I look through some myself. My anxiety spikes at the prospect of going through that many expensive gowns. Leanne and Trix quietly tell me to stay and that they'll go look instead.

I sit on one of the small couches. Isaac comes over to sit beside me. "You alright?"

"Yeah, just a lot," I whisper.

"You have good friends to help."

"Other than Leo, they're the ones who know what I'll like or not. Help me say no, too."

We both settle back, quiet in the lavish room. My gaze comes upon the flowers on the table beside us, and I lean over to smell them. I smile, scooting closer to look at the petals. They look like orchids, but I'm not positive. My fingers trail the soft petals gently. Memory flicks to my first date with Leo, and then the first time at the hotel apartment. He always seemed to catch me smelling flowers. The anxiety that ticks up my spine fades as I stare at the petals. Should really stop to smell the flowers more often.

"Here are some first picks," Jen says, entering the room and holding an array of colorful gowns. I stand up straight, Isaac slowly following me. "These will look fabulous. All eyes will be on you."

I follow her into the changing space. Isaac gives me an encouraging nod as the curtain closes. Jen helps me into the first dress, talking about my style. She tells me not to worry about length or alterations, orders are already in to take care of that. I think about talking about something else, but she seems too focused on her task. I let her do her thing, finally she opens the curtain, which reveals Leanne and Trix sitting on the couch where Isaac and I were. Their jaws drop. I get up on the platform and turn toward a mirror.

Holy cabooses Batman.

The dress is a deep blue, glittering with an overlay of sheer fabric. It's strapless with chains of diamonds dangling from the top hem down to the waistline. It's called a mermaid cut, so the skirt flares out near the bottom. I blink, unable to tear my eyes away from the sparkles.

"Well, hello Anastasia," Leanne comments, leaning back with a large grin.

"That color looks great on you." Trix gets up for a closer look, touching the small gems. "Wow, that's a lot."

"Swarovski." Jen smiles broadly. "Your shoulders look amazing, and the flare out gives you a bit more height."

I nod, unable to speak as I concentrate on breathing. Trix meets my gaze in the mirror, and murmurs, "How do *you* feel?"

I stroke the fabric around my torso, feeling a bit more vulnerable and showier without sleeves or straps. I give her a look and she nods, glimpsing at Leanne who says, "Maybe mermaid isn't for you."

With a tight smile, Jen ushers me back into the changing room. Once the dress is off, I take a deep breath and close my eyes. Although it looked good, I didn't feel great. After another measured breath, I open my eyes and try on the next dress.

Then another. And then another. And another.

Before long, ten dresses have come and gone. All of them quietly declined by me or by my friends. It's like a marathon of gowns.

I stand quietly on the platform, once again, Jen gone to look for other gowns she thinks will work. Leanne and Trix left too, determined to find one. Feels impossible at this point. Every dress I've tried was either too revealing, lacey, low cleavage, or didn't feel right. And now, I stand in a satin emerald dress with off-the-shoulder capped sleeves. The hem over my breasts is pretty low, and there's a slit that almost reaches my hip. I rub my arms a little, not liking how much skin is showing.

A shaky breath leaves me as I murmur the first few lines of *The Raven*, hoping to keep calm.

"We can take a break, Miss Autumn. We have all afternoon." I startle, turning to find Isaac standing beside the platform. He smiles softly.

"Except, now I'm a bit determined to find a freaking dress that isn't going to give me a panic attack." I glare at the mirrors. "Thought it was only supposed to be this hard for wedding dresses."

"Could be your practice run," he jokes.

"What if I just went in jeans?"

"He wouldn't mind, we both know that."

"Until I embarrass the crap out of him."

"Miss Autumn," Isaac speaks delicately, grabbing my hand to help me down from the platform. "Concentrate on what you want, not others. Don't try to be anyone else, especially at events like this one. Believe me when I say you'll never embarrass him as long as you are yourself."

I let out a sigh, looking at my reflection. All the dresses felt like something I *should* be, this role of the woman on the prestigious Leonardo Luciano's arm. I can't help thinking about the looks or gestures I've already gotten. I want to ignore them, but it's hard.

"I miss that bar Snake Eyes owns," I whisper. "It feels more natural being in places like that."

"You're not alone feeling that."

I look at Isaac in the mirror, noticing the stillness around him. His blue eyes meet mine. Although he's his usual calm self, there's a more protective demeanor about him. Almost rigid. He kind of has been for the past couple weeks. Ever since…

As I turn around, I flick my gaze to the entrance. I clear my throat; figuring I might as well broach the subject finally.

"I don't need to know why you were the one who did it, pulled the trigger I guess," I whisper, and Isaac stiffens. "Didn't think we really needed to talk about it, but…thank you. Not just for…you know, but also being a friend, even if we had a rocky start." He quirks a brow. "I'm thankful for you being around."

His posture softens. "My pleasure, Miss Autumn."

"Pretty sure you're my favorite out of the *Forgotten Demons*, so don't tell them. Rudy may get upset," I tease.

"Oh, I know not to cross you, Miss Autumn, only a fool would." He smiles. Isaac steps forward, then very gently places a kiss on my head. I don't hold back my grin. "You're my favorite, too."

He steps back, blue eyes glistening with light tears. Oh, damn, he's gonna make me cry and we haven't even found a gown.

"By the way," I start, smacking his shoulder as I clear my throat.

"You haven't finished teaching me how to make a proper cup of tea."

"Nor introduced proper biscuits."

"Those too!"

"There have been a bit more pressing matters."

"Did you just admit there are more important things than tea?" I feign a gasp, clutching my nonexistent pearls. He grins and I give him one back.

Jen walks back in, strappy dresses in hand. Isaac gives me a wink before stopping her. He begins to look through the gowns for any that I may not like, and she starts to argue with him. His voice drops suddenly, and she looks somewhat offended, until Trix and Leanne come back in. They have a gown in their arms, holding it up with excitement.

I end up back in the changing room with Leanne. Once their pick is on, I swivel a little and feel the brushing of the fabric against my skin. We walk out and she helps me onto the platform. I thank everything above and below that Leanne is my best friend.

The dress is a deep sapphire blue. It has long sheer sleeves, encrusted with bright gems up to the shoulder. The top dips, but not too low as diamonds continue down the velvet bodice that hugs my figure. The dark velvet material flares out at my hips, cascading with more gemstones with a layer of black that blends with the blue. I turn and see the open back to show some skin. A giggle escapes me as I twirl and feel the rustling of fabrics. It fits perfectly, a bit long, but I could dance in this. I twirl a little, watching the dress move around me.

"Oh, am I *good*," Leanne says.

"You're fantastic," I say. "Wanna be my stylist?"

She scrunches her nose with a shrug.

There's a gasp, and I turn to see Trix gaping. She lets out an excited squeal jogging over to lift the skirt. I laugh with her as she inspects the dress, conversing with Leanne.

Jen gives us a smile, and I tell her this is the dress, and she seems a bit relieved that I chose one. We go over shoes next, and I land on a pair of low heels. Apparently, Leanne grabbed a couture dress or something, and the seamstress that comes out is particular about alterations. It'll be done in time, but thankfully the dress fits me like a glove already.

I touch the velvet bodice, almost calming.

I can do this. Just be me. Easy enough. Right?

Chapter 11

My Lovely Lady

I glare at my reflection. Fuck eyeliner, dude.

Rummaging through the bag of make-up Leanne got me, I yank out a wipe, cleaning my eyes of the small mess. I start over, deciding on lighter touches. Thank goodness I had the smarts to go to the salon at the *Italian Lily* for my hair, next time I may have them do the rest. Hair was perfect and poised, now if I could get my face on the freaking program.

I've had butterflies in my stomach all week. The dress was hanging up in my closet, hidden in its garment bag from Leo. He decided we'd leave from the penthouse, staying here after and for the rest of the week into Thanksgiving.

There's a light knock on the bathroom door, and I call out, "Come in at your own risk!"

Leo comes in and I stare at him through the mirror. He's wearing a three-piece black tuxedo trimmed in satin with matching bowtie and silver cufflinks. His dark hair is swept back and he's clean shaven. It's a compliment to faint, right?

"Not that disastrous," he comments, but I'm still staring. He furrows his brows, breaking the spell. I'm supposed to put *him* into shock, not the other way around! No fair.

"You weren't here earlier when I fought the eyeliner, by the way, it won. None tonight." I press on some blush, then go into the bag for some lipstick. I grimace, hoping it doesn't rub off.

I startle when I realize Leo is directly behind me. He gently places his hands on my shoulders, dragging them down my arms. I'm only wearing a robe and underwear, meant to protect me from my artistic skills. He bends low to press his lips against my neck, and then behind my ear.

"You're lovely no matter what you wear," he whispers.

"Thanks." I grin at him through the mirror. His eyes meet mine, smoldering. It takes everything not to clear my throat as heat blossoms inside. My breath hitches when he kisses my neck again, squeezing my arms gently. "Careful, mister, I still gotta finish."

"How much time do you need?"

"20-15 minutes. Promise. You should head downstairs."

He stands fully, tilting his head. "Telling me what to do, dear Watson?"

"Yup. Cause you'll distract me."

"How so?" The mischief in his voice is telling.

I point at the door with a raised brow. "Deal was surprising you, so downstairs you go. Or I'll tell Chesty or Animal to escort you."

"Still my apartment *and* building." He struggles to keep back his smile.

"Yeah, yeah, big bad boss and owns stuff, good for you," I chuckle, turning toward him and preparing to push him out. An odd emotion passes over his face, but quickly vanishes and steps back with hands up in surrender.

"As you wish, I'll see you downstairs." He walks out closing the door behind him.

Okay, that was kinda weird. Maybe he's nervous, too. I laugh to myself. Leo? Nervous? No.

I finish my make-up, using a lip stain that Trix suggested, then put on silver earrings. I walk out of the bathroom, going out to the hall to peek around the corner to see Chesty and Animal standing at the kitchen island. Both have drinks, murmuring. I'm about to step back into the bedroom, when I overhear Animal say, "Never thought I'd see him like this."

"He just wants it to be perfect," Chesty says.

"True there."

Hm, maybe this is a pretty big night for us both. Jameson mentioned this would be good publicity for the hotels. Could be the whole limelight thing again.

I close the bedroom door quietly, heading to the closet and unzip the garment bag. I smile at the dazzling fabric of my dress hidden inside before I put it on. It fits perfectly with the length of it barely brushing over the ground. Easy to walk and twirl in. Carefully I get my shoes on and pause in front of the full-length mirror in the closet.

Looking good there, Watson.

Satisfied, I take a deep breath and grab the blue velvety wrap and stroll out to the living room. Low whistles greet me as I appear, spinning to show off the gown to the guys.

"Like it?" I ask, spinning again.

"Prettiest one out of us all," Animal comments.

I turn around and point towards the back. "Can you make sure I'm all zipped up?"

Chesty comes over, fiddling a little with the back, and then pats my shoulder. "All set and ready to rule."

"Thank you, although I will say, I do miss wearing leathers." I fold the wrap up in my arms.

"You and me both, sister," Chesty says. "Should do a club shindig, maybe finally get you out on the open road."

"That's the dream," I sigh.

"On the way to being one of us," Animal chuckles, nodding toward the door.

Chesty takes my wrap, keeping it folded over his arm. Butterflies rise in my stomach as we head to the elevator. My hands shake a little when we reach the lobby.

Xavier, the main doorman and security for the building, is there in his usual spot behind the desk. He's in his late fifties with a full head of grey hair, stubble along his jaw, and a perfectly tailored suit that compliments his dark ochre skin. He grins, warm brown eyes crinkling in the corners. I hold my arms out, showing off the dress.

"Miss Watson, I declare, you look absolutely stunning," he says in his raspy voice.

I've gotten to know the older man the last few weeks, learning about his upbringing out west and then the south. His wife passed away some years back from cancer, while his children live out in Colorado. He came to the city for a woman, relationship ended, but he stayed.

"Thank you." I curtesy. "Where's Leo?"

"On a phone call outside, told me to tell you to wait here for him."

"If Sombra gave him…" Animal grumbles under his breath, heading towards the doors. I giggle as Chesty and I exchange a look. He hands me my wrap back, following Animal outside.

I look at Xavier and ask, "Did Leo seem nervous to you?"

"Mr. Luciano?" He frowns briefly, then shakes his head. "The boss is rarely nervous, but then again he's been showing more emotions of late, especially around you Miss Watson."

"So, I've been told," I mumble. Shaking off the weird jitters, I give Xavier a grin. "Want to see the dress in action?"

He comes around the desk to take my wrap and holds out a hand to pull me toward the marbled lobby floor. "The stage is yours."

Laughing lightly, I take his hand for him to spin me across the floor, allowing the full effect of the skirt to flutter. I hold my arms out, twirling as I look down and see it sparkle. Elation travels through my body as I hang my head back with a sigh. On the verge of getting dizzy, I stop and shake my head with a wild grin. Xavier grins back, nodding past me.

I spin to find Leo staring at me. He's completely frozen at the entrance; mouth open as his gaze travels down my body. Passionate heat is within his gaze, mixed with shock. I'm used to seeing surprise on his face, but this time it's like he's been struck by lightning. Awe fills his eyes as they find mine.

Finally, he walks forward. I hold my hands before me as he stops inches away from me. His hand lightly strokes the underside of my jaw, raising my chin to look at him. Such soft tenderness in his gaze.

I whisper, "Hi."

Leo smiles, gliding his hand to the nape of my neck as he kisses me tenderly. My breath hitches at the gentleness, grabbing his arms to keep from collapsing. Desire travels from him to me, and vice versa. As the moment passes, Leo pulls away and whispers, "You are absolutely breathtakingly, beautiful, my dear Watson."

Blinking rapidly to keep the tears away, I swallow hard. He steps back, gesturing to Xavier for my wrap, who hands it over diligently. Leo places it over my shoulders, then leads me out into the brisk, late-autumn night.

***

Paparazzi wasn't on my bingo card.

I stay close to Leo as pictures are snapped of people entering the Rockefeller Center. Leo, Jameson, and Rudy block them from getting photos of us, my wrap at some point handed off to Isaac. Only Leo, Jameson, and I are going to the gala, the others on standby for emergencies.

I squeeze Leo's hand as we ascend to the Rainbow Room, reciting *The Raven* in my head. He leans down, brushing his lips against my ear. "Check in."

"Nervous green." I tentatively smile.

He lifts my left hand, kissing and holding it there a moment. Jameson clears his throat, causing Leo to slide his gaze toward him. The elevator doors open suddenly, cutting off whatever those two were about to get into.

An extravagant glow pours over us. My breath is stolen away as Leo places my arm in his, leading me into the fray. I'm surrounded by bright colors of marvelous splendor; flowers everywhere decorated with satin and jewels. Leo's strict, stoic mask is put into place, his posture tall as we travel through the crowd.

My gaze flits from person to person, noticing expensive jewelry and gowns they wear to perfection. People laugh holding drinks as waiters travel by with champagne and hors d'oeuvres. There's a twist in my stomach, an overwhelming feeling hitting me at the sheer luxury. An itch is at the back of my mind, telling me I don't belong here and hide. I cling to Leo's arm. His other hand brushes over my arm, stroking toward my hand and I relax. We make it to the main room, and I gasp at the large chandelier along with the gorgeous setup for the gala. People continue talking above the soft orchestra music, which is being played live on the other side, gentle and sweet.

I continue staring at the decorations, not paying attention to those vying for Leo's. A large smile crosses my face when I see the marvelous sight of New York City outside, bright lights against the darkness of the night sky. Yup, a new way to see the city. It's somehow a tad different than from the hotel's view.

"And who may this be?" Someone asks, and my attention moves to a woman in front of us. She wears a gold gown with a plunging neckline. Her long brown hair cascades past her shoulders, which compliments her light skin and dark make-up. Her eyes graze down my body with a tight smile.

"This is my date, Autumn," Leo introduces me. "Autumn, this Ivana, who owns a few publishing companies in New York, although she's more known for her charity work."

She flits her hand at him, smiling as her gaze shifts slowly over his chest. "We all must do our part to help this city. I'm simply doing mine. I've heard you are as well."

I clear my throat, then ask, "Which charity work?"

Ivana drags her gaze over Leo again, answering, "The homeless. It's dastardly and *so* upsetting seeing them out in the cold, nowhere to go."

It's like someone's punched me in the gut as she continues talking. Maybe it's the tone in her voice or how she keeps looking at Leo, but the sickening twist in my stomach worsens. I tune her out, remembering it wasn't too long ago that I'd been one of those in the cold. Wet sweater, tattered scarf, and some blanket I found in the dumpster. Socks were the best to keep your hands warm it seemed.

Huh, haven't truly thought about those nights without it just being a passing thought.

Leo suddenly turns us away from her. "We'll talk another time, Ivana. Please excuse us."

"I'll have an open seat next to me—"

Leo guides us through the crowd, him ignoring people as they try to catch his attention. It's then I notice the sweetly smiling women giving displeased looks only to me. Great. I'd like to go back to being oblivious due to shiny objects and flowers, please.

"Check in," he murmurs against my ear. My arm tightens around his as I swallow hard. "Do not hide from me." I only shake my head in response, suddenly losing the ability to talk.

Leo stops us near one of the windows, away from prying eyes and ears. He moves in front of me, shielding my vision from the party as he gently raises my chin to look up at him.

"Talk to me, dear Watson."

I focus on his touch, inhaling a few long breaths before answering. "She said homeless, and I...remembered. I don't usually care, but the way she said it, I don't know. Struck a chord."

His brows furrow, frowning deeply as he strokes my cheek gently. "You're no less than them."

"I know, really, I do." I clear my throat, hoping to shake off the nerves. "Sometimes I just forget I was there, you know? Like, *oh right that was me once*." His brows somehow scrunch further, and I smile softly, reaching up to touch the worry line. He softens. "After so much change, sometimes you forget things. Maybe it was due to...well, being homeless and poor at one point seemed like the least of my worries. I know I've mentioned it, but it...it was easier than the other stuff. Simpler, maybe. And now I don't know if I'm making sense."

Leo wraps an arm around my waist, bringing me close so that I place my hands against his chest. He speaks quietly, "At times, I forget I was that 17-year-old working at the lowest of hotels. Nothing to my name, living in a tent just outside the property. All Jameson and I had were our bikes, one good suit, and enough money to not starve. Even when we caught that first break, it wasn't a lot. But sometimes, I forget, too." He kisses my temple, while his hand skims down my side and up my spine, bare hand touching my skin. "Do not feel guilty for how far you've come or where you were, but be proud of yourself that you got to this point."

I nod, tilting my head back to look at him and say earnestly, "I don't feel like I belong here."

"You belong next to me, only that matters." He takes my hand, kissing my knuckles gently. I can't help but smile at his attentive affection.

"This place really is lovely," I whisper, flicking my gaze out toward the city skyline.

"Plenty of flowers to inspect?"

"If I disappear, it's cause I'm checking out the roses in the corner." We laugh quietly.

It's announced that dinner will be served soon. Leo takes my arm again, leading us to our table. I'm relieved to see Jameson sitting with us, who's next to an older gentleman. I sit between Leo and him, with Leo on my left holding my hand beneath the table. An older woman is on Leo's other side, Grace. She's poised with black hair pulled into a bun, wearing a simpler black gown adorned with diamond jewelry everywhere. She attempts to speak with Leo, who gives her a few words and short nods. The others around the table are a mixture of tuxedos, jewels, and perfectly styled hair.

Dinner goes smoothly. Near the end, a waiter comes by, and I grab my glass to hand it to him, trying to help him from reaching over. One of the women across from me practically flares her nostrils, but I ignore her and thank him before he leaves.

Jameson smirks, and whispers in my ear, "Isaac may have forgotten some pointers. No talking to the staff and allow them to do everything."

I quirk a brow at him. He does it back. I lean in closer and whisper, "Then I guess I'm the pariah for the evening."

The man next to Jameson catches his attention, leaving me on my lonesome to poke around at my fish. Conversations flutter around me, the entire room filled with voices as the orchestra plays. Most of the dinner I spend listening to the lovely music. Discussions on stock markets, overseas exchange rates, and real estate I don't fancy much. Also, why talk about all that at a party? Have any of them watched television? Read a book that didn't articulate the rise and fall of market shares? Or that *one* weekend in the Hamptons.

"What do you think, Autumn?" I blink, finding a couple gazes on me. I glance over at Leo, who's impassive face is harder to read than usual.

One of the men, Jared, chuckles low. "Oh, it seems we've disrupted your daydreaming."

"Is our conversation boring you?" Evelyn, next to him, says while bringing her glass to her pursed lips.

"No." I clear my throat. "I just don't know much of the subject to discuss."

"What *do* you do, then?" Evelyn asks, swirling her drink. Leo's hand trails down my leg, squeezing above my knee through the skirt.

Not knowing how else to answer, I say, "I work in a bookstore."

"Oh, that's quaint," Meredith says, who sits on the other side of Jared. "How long have you owned the store?"

"I don't."

"Oh, well then, still quaint," she muses.

"Is that how you met Leonardo?" Evelyn asks suddenly, eyeing me with a questioning gleam. "In that *little* bookstore?"

Isaac's etiquette rules said nothing about hitting anyone.

My jaw tightens, unsure what to say. I'm not embarrassed that I was a barista or that I don't own a business. I loved my jobs, made good friends, sometimes enemies, but I did love them. Except, now I'm torn between being ridiculed or standing my ground for those decisions.

"Story for another time," Leo interjects calmly.

"Ignore, Evelyn," Grace says abruptly, and I look at her. "She just wants new gossip. And you're new."

Before Evelyn can object to Grace, the waiters come to offer more drinks. I decline, while others receive theirs.

"Don't care for wine?" Meredith asks. "I'm sure they can bring champagne instead."

"I'm fine with water," I answer.

"Oh, but it's divine!" She insists, waving at the waiter to pour me a drink anyways. "The best is being catered, and you should *indulge* while here with Leonardo."

"She's fine," Leo interrupts, nodding at the waiter to leave. Meredith shuts her mouth, glancing between us. His hand strokes my leg.

"Quite the catch you've found, Leonardo," Evelyn murmurs from behind her glass. "Wherever did you find this peculiar girl? Did her plain wholesomeness appeal to you? It's like watching *My Fair Lady* in real life."

Suddenly, I miss Ivana.

Shame digs at me as I try to keep my face neutral. I don't want to feel embarrassed, but it's like being surrounded by wolves. With mafia shit, at least I can hit them over the head with a skillet.

"Not all of us gain relationships through bought time and assets, Evelyn, as you should know," Leo speaks unexpectedly, his tone almost threatening. Evelyn stares at him as he leans back in his seat, practically owning the whole table. His hand glides up my arm to the nape of my neck, landing there softly as he strokes his thumb upon my skin.

"What I meant—"

"Some of us treat our relationships with respect and honor, although I hear that's not a certain quality you've had in your more recent relationships. So, perhaps, the only one here with that peculiar storyline, using people as *projects* would be you. Where is your *newest* husband tonight, I wonder?"

A quietness rushes over the table. Jameson sighs, picking up his drink. Evelyn's mouth works, sitting her drink down heavily as she tries to compose herself. She straightens, giving more of that air of arrogance.

She argues, "Hardly not the most proper conversation to have here, don't you think? We are here to—"

"But the conversation of belittling Autumn's livelihood and drink choices are? I'd say with that being the course of action you've taken all evening, then this topic is certainly appropriate. Otherwise, I'd have to title you as a hypocrite, but outside this conversation I'd say it wouldn't be very far from the truth…would it?" Her eyes widen, seething, but it quickly vanishes when Leo's strictness gains an edge of deeper warning. "Of the many roles I play, I am far from Henry Higgins as *you* should remember."

Evelyn goes extremely still. If Leo wasn't gently stroking my skin to keep me and him calm at this point, I'd believe he was planning on her not leaving this building alive. Then again, night is still young.

Luck is on her side as the lights shift, and then the stage becomes more well-lit. Everyone around our table is brought out of their trance when someone begins a speech about charities or whatever. I'm *definitely* not paying attention.

Evelyn turns away, along with the others. Only Grace is smirking, while Jameson shakes his head. Leo frowns in Evelyn's direction, concentrating as he keeps his hold against my nape. I place my hand on his leg, and slowly he turns to me.

I didn't need him to embarrass and practically threaten the woman, but it's comforting to have someone in your corner. The shame bubbling inside has subsided, and I loosen a breath.

"Thanks," I murmur.

The only change on his face is the softening of his gaze. "Of course, dear Watson."

Chapter 12

Emerald Dreams

People mingle, leaving to grab cocktails while Leo and I remain in our seats. A short auction was announced for different charities. Ivana was up there at some point, discussing her "work" for the homeless. I frown. Each subject discussed sounds the same: aloof and disconnected, almost like it's a game. A part of me is appreciative that they're trying to help people, while the other part wanted to drop-kick them. Jameson stands, pausing to whisper something in Leo's ear, who nods shortly with a scowl. Jameson then nods at me, disappearing into the crowd.

I turn to Leo and whisper, "Do any of them know your, *moonlighting* gig?"

He raises a brow. "Is that what we're calling it now?"

"It's that or I ask the band to play *I'm Shipping Up to Boston*."

"I'm not Irish."

"Apologies, *The Godfather* theme."

A small smirk comes over him, but disappears as he adjusts in his seat and puts his other hand in his pocket. A focused look comes over him as he answers, "A handful, but none were sitting with us. I won't allow it."

"Not even Jared?"

"He tried to swindle me out of some property," he says succinctly, sipping from his wine glass. "So, I caused two of his company stocks to plummet."

Oh, so he's cutthroat in other areas. Not surprising.

"So, uh, the whole…well, your strict mannerisms really aren't just cause of the moonlighting gig?"

He turns himself a bit more towards me. "It works for both *gigs* to obtain what I want, which includes my need for control or telling someone to shut up."

"Shark week every day then?"

"Usually, but most of them are just asshole dolphins."

I sputter a laugh, quickly trying to quiet it with my hand. Leo pulls it away, which only makes my giggles worsen as I put my head against his shoulder. The laughing fit doesn't relent, until I realize I'm wearing foundation. Yelping softly, I pull away and stare at the bit of tan powder on his tuxedo.

"Shit, son of a nutcracker," I mutter, grabbing a napkin to lick it, and then gently wipe away the makeup on his shoulder. He remains still as I scowl at my mistake, mumbling under my breath, "Fucksticks and dang powder stuff."

I relax when I see I've gotten it all off, tossing the napkin onto the table. Don't care if it's not the right thing to do. Leo watches me with a perplexed expression. I pause, staring at him unsure why he's looking at me like that. I wasn't about to leave him with my "forehead stamp."

A tender, warm look comes over him as he takes my hand. "I have something to show you."

"Better not be flowers, cause they bought them all." I stand up alongside him.

"Not quite." He hooks his arm through mine, guiding us through the crowd as the lights cause the dazzling decorations to illuminate. Fake candles turn on, flickering against the flowers. I catch a glimpse of Jameson, who smiles while raising his glass and turns away. People attempt to stop us, but Leo waves them away until we finally reach the elevator.

"Are we leaving?" I ask.

"No, just going a floor up." I scrunch my brows as the doors open. We get on, traveling up another floor and Leo loosens a long breath. I glance at him, confused even more when the doors open to an empty hallway. I peek to the right and see a ballroom, decorated with lilies and tables with lace.

"Okay, I was kidding about the flowers. Are we supposed to be up here?" It's quiet with no one in sight. "Cause this seems like it's for something else."

"It is." He gives me a gentle squeeze, gesturing toward the other direction to windowed doorways.

I follow him and he opens the doors, revealing a patio covered in sheer white drapery. My eyes follow the row of candles along the side, distracting me from not seeing what's directly in front of me. When I do, I freeze and grip Leo's arm as I stare at the rooftop garden before me. The lawn spreads out over the building, lined with shrubbery and lights which glow with the city in the background. I let go of Leo, holding my skirt up as I step forward to see more of the cathedral right next to us, St. Patrick's Cathedral. Holy shit we're on the rooftop garden of the Rockefeller Center.

A giggle comes out of me as I head up the short steps, looking around at the greenery that doesn't seem to fit within the steel and glass of the city. Lanterns with their warm amber light contrast against the stonework. My heels sink slightly into the ground, not yet brown or frozen from the oncoming winter. I'd take this over the Rainbow Room any day, not to mention it's only us.

I turn back to Leo, who stands at the edge of the grass with his hands in his pockets as he watches me silently. I gesture around us, beginning to feel chilly, but ignore it. "Leo, I know you have a lot of pull, but are we really allowed up here?"

"Yes, because I reserved it for the entire night."

I blink. "Why?"

"I wanted to give you a night to remember, but knew you'd have gotten suspicious if we came straight here. The gala was the perfect excuse without you wondering what I was up to."

"Oh, I'm always wondering what you're up to," I chuckle, holding my hands in front of myself. "If you wanted to dance, mister, all you had to do is ask. The *Italian Lily's* ballrooms are perfect."

His smile is tender. He comes toward me, taking my hands carefully. "Except I have something else I wanted to ask you."

There's a tightness in my chest, nerves traveling over my skin. My heart thunders, pounding in my ears. I stare up at him, hands beginning to shake. Leo kisses my left hand, eyes meeting mine. Wait…

"I have told you that I belong solely to you," he speaks in a loving tone that makes my throat constrict. "You have been the most precious person to have entered my life. There are days I'm not sure how you're possible or why you kept taking chances on me when all the odds were against my favor. Yet, somehow…you came back. You kept coming back to me. I fully intend to make sure you'll always stay by my side."

His hands cradle my face as I clutch onto his jacket. My chin quivers. "Leo."

"I love you beyond my own life and soul. For I am sure you are the reason I made it this far. Your courageous nature, loving heart, and your brilliant view of life. You are a wonder of the world, Autumn Watson, and the light in my darkness." Leo kisses me with reverence. A tear rolls down my cheek as I kiss him back ardently.

He suddenly pulls away to place his forehead against mine. "I thank every ancestor of mine, God, or angelic force that you waved at me through that window. And am grateful for the kindness of a woman, who smiled at me with foam around her finger." I giggle a little. "There she is."

Leo steps back, reaching into his pocket as he begins to kneel. I quickly grab his arms, keeping him standing.

"I'm gonna end up fainting or hyperventilating if you do the kneeling thing now," I say quickly, trying not to yell.

He smiles, eyes shining with amusement. He brings forth a small velvet pouch from his pocket and I look at him confused. "You'd have noticed a box."

I sputter a laugh, then almost choke when he pulls out a ring. It's silver with small diamonds running around the band with an elegant emerald sitting on top. I cover my mouth, gasping as every thought blanks out. My body trembles as I stare at the ring in his hand, finally meeting his eyes with tears in mine.

"My dear Watson," he whispers, taking my left hand and kissing it gently. "Will you do me the greatest honor and allow me to belong to you every aspect, to formally and officially become your husband? To be my wife?"

Tears stream down my face as I struggle to breathe. I swallow hard, trying to talk and finally answer, "Yes…yes, always yes."

Leo crushes his lips against mine, holding me flush against his body. I shiver as a breeze blows over us, throwing my arms around his neck. He hardens the kiss, gripping me with passion. I smile against his lips as he picks me up, spinning us and causing my skirt to flutter in the breeze. He places me down, kissing my cheeks as I laugh and shake from excitement.

"Thank fuck," he murmurs.

"You were worried I was gonna say no?"

He hugs me close, pressing his face into my hair. "Maybe that it was too soon. Too much commitment, but I just want you in every capacity, Autumn. To be yours in every sense."

"As long as I'm yours in every capacity."

He kisses my neck. "Always, my dear, dear Watson."

Leo finally takes my hand, smiling as he slides the ring onto my finger. I hold my hand out, turning to see it with the background of the church behind it. I'm still shaking pretty badly, but from nervous excitement. I turn, grab his tuxedo and tug him back to kiss me again. He chuckles at my enthusiasm and embraces me, kissing me with the same glorious fervor. After what seems like forever, I break the kiss to stare up into his hazel gaze. There's a shine over them, lined with his own tears.

"*You* are the most beautiful thing to happen to me," I declare, stroking my hands up his chest. "I never want to go back to the time before you, because your heart is the most precious to me. I don't care what happens. I love you, Leonardo Durante Luciano… my wonderful, mister Americano."

He wipes away tears from my face as I do the same for him. This time when we kiss it's filled with tender adoration and love. I thread my fingers through his hair, humming blissfully. Nothing exists but us.

Another cold breeze passes, and I shiver against his hold. He breaks the kiss, swiftly lifting me into his arms and I laugh as he carries me back to the building.

"Leo!" I giggle. I hold onto his shoulders, grinning at him as he carries me under the patio drapery. I reach for the doors for him, when they suddenly open revealing *The Forgotten Demons* all dressed in suits and bowties.

I screech in excitement as they all cheer once I raise my hand to show off the ring. They all give their congratulations as Leo places me onto my feet. Each of them I give a hug, whilst smacking those for being in on this, especially Jameson.

We move toward the small ballroom area. I realize now why it's decorated with lilies and other little pieces that remind me of Leo's and my first date. I go to say something to him, but music begins to play, and Leo takes my hand.

"Time to show off that dress!" Julio shouts.

I can't stop grinning as Leo leads me to the dancefloor, getting us into frame and then asks, "Care for a dance, dear Watson?"

"Still not playing by the rules, huh?"

He shakes his head and nods at Animal and Julio. The music changes and I instantly recognize the song. I narrow my eyes at him as he begins to twirl us across the dance floor. *Faithfully* echoes through the space. I hear some of the Crew making cute noises, glancing over to see some of them trying to hide their tears. I roll my eyes at the tough bikers, but soon become lost in the dance.

Leo twirls me, bringing me close as he picks me up, spinning us and speaking the lyrics, "I'm forever yours."

"Faithfully," I sing back, smiling larger than life.

Chapter 13

My Love, My Darling

I open my eyes to a shadowed bedroom. I rub them, clearing my throat as something inside me tugs. I sit up fully, noticing it's not even 6, which explains the darkness.

Leo rustles beside me, moving to his side and I can just make out his sleeping face. He hums as I trace my fingers down his jaw gently, smiling as a peaceful warmth fills me. I stroke my hand over his hair, entranced by his handsome face, but soon quietly get off the bed to let him sleep. I stretch a little when I notice the ring sitting on the bedside table.

My engagement ring.

Oh, right. I'm engaged. To Leo.

I'm engaged.

Reality crashes back and I cover my mouth from accidentally laughing, screaming or both. Last night floods back from Leo proposing, the Crew celebrating with us and dancing late into the night, and then coming back to the penthouse where Leo and I celebrated on our own. I glance at my dress on the floor, Leo's tuxedo is thrown about the place and there's handprints on the closet mirror.

I peek over at Leo, silently grabbing the ring and then my robe, and sneak out of the bedroom. I sprint down the small hall to the upstairs I've rarely gone to, and race into the office, closing the door. I put the ring on the desk and stare at it.

I wait. No panic attack. No creeping anxiety. No hyperventilating.

I'm actually pretty calm. Huh.

I pace a little, glancing around briefly at the... I guess, study given the amount of law books, ledgers, and other books lining the mahogany shelves. I'm soon distracted by wondering if I *should* be having a panic attack or whatever, but then wave that thought away.

Happy. I'm happy.

Finally, I pick up the ring and slide it onto my finger. It's perfect. Size and everything, and I'm not gonna ask how he knew.

I start squealing in delight, dancing in place. Once my little dance party is over, I head back down to the kitchen and start up some coffee, along with prepping the espresso machine. When Leo realized I could make Americanos again, he had another machine bought for the penthouse.

Looking at the emerald ring on my hand, my gaze flits to the rest of the penthouse. Much like the apartment at the hotel, it's pretty bare. We haven't really discussed where we'd live mostly, but it'll more likely be split between the two places. Maybe I could convince him to redecorate the place.

"Still needs macaroni art or movie posters," I mumble.

I head over to the windows, opening the long curtains to let in the first glimpses of dawn. A small hum comes out of me as I walk around, poking at bare shelves and spinning around on the wooden floor. I've been here only a handful of times. Once to drop off some of my movies, some of my clothes, and this week getting ready for the gala.

The coffee finishes and I grab a mug, continuing my wondering and musing around the spacious place. I decide to go back up the stairs, glancing at the office again and then peeking into the guest bedroom which is modern with white walls. The gym has a few different machines and weights, along with a mirrored wall. You'd never know this second floor was up here. Sighing, I go back down the stairs as boredom sets in and I debate rearranging my movies or watching one. Kind of feeling *Conan the Barbarian* or *The Adventures of Buckaroo Bonzai Across the 8ᵗʰ Dimension*. I scrunch my face, unsure if they're here or at the hotel.

I walk back to the windows, leaning my forehead against them and look at the long balcony outside. I could turn on the outdoor heaters and get some morning reading in. Still debating my options, I scoot on the floors again as I approach the kitchen counter. I put my coffee mug down, find my phone, and quietly go back into the bedroom to grab the Bluetooth headphones Julio got me. I scroll through some music, finding a playlist.

The first piano keys play as I slide across the living room. I start dancing, sliding and holding onto the furniture to help me move. Giggles erupt from me as I slip over the hard surface and get up on the couch. Bob Seger sings about old souls and today's music, while I start shaking my hips and jumping on the cushions.

The music plays loudly in my ears as I mumble the words to myself, hopping from one cushion to the next, playing air guitar, and jumping down with a flourish. I do a few more crazy moves, popping back up on the couch and jamming out. The song finishes, and another favorite begins. I run to the kitchen, grabbing a spatula to sing with. My socks slide over the floor as I dance around the kitchen counter, lost in my own dance party.

"Take me home—" I sing, running and sliding before I hop back onto the couch. "Tonight!"

I do a jump spin, coming back to face the kitchen and find Leo leaning against the counter with crossed arms and a grin. I screech, dropping my "microphone" and falling onto the couch. I'm out of breath, panting from my dancing, and groan. I can't believe I got caught. AGAIN. Well, this time I didn't trip over anything.

I slip the headphones off, then hide my face behind my hands a little and peek through my fingers. Leo is still there. He cocks his head, still smiling. Oh, good. He's fine with this kind of wake-up call.

I mumble through my hands, "Morning."

"Good morning." He walks toward me. "Did you put something in the coffee?"

"Apart from sugar?"

"I don't remember you being *this* energetic in the morning." He pauses at the end of the couch, quirking a brow.

I try to think of a smart reply, moving my hands down when I feel the bump of the engagement ring. I blink rapidly at it. Hm, maybe *that's* why.

Swiftly, I get up and launch myself into his arms. He grunts softly, easily catching me as I wrap my legs around his hips. I grab his face, kissing him with a crushing force and he meets me with the same energy. I hold onto him tightly, pulling away with a large smile.

The smiles drops when I glance behind me. "It's okay that I was jumping on the couches?"

"Plural?"

"I needed the space."

He chuckles, walking us over to the kitchen. "Yes, and it's *our* couches."

"Not even engaged for 24 hours and already starting on *our* stuff."

"I'm warming you up." He kisses my cheek as he sits me on the counter. He stays between my legs, stroking his hand down my cheek and neck. "Next will be real estate."

"You're getting the short end of the stick, cause all I got is movies, books, frozen pizza, and cereal. And you only *kinda* like the cereal."

"But I get you," he whispers, kissing the underside of my jaw and I close my eyes. "Which is all I'll ever need."

I hum as he caresses the back of his hand down my chest, stroking my skin under the robe. He kisses my neck again. The heat of his breath causing a shiver down my spine, while his other hand grips the nape of my neck and gently tugs my hair to tilt my head back. He continues to softly caress me as I grip the counter.

"Leo," I groan.

"Yes, dear Watson?"

"I want to make you coffee and breakfast and you're deterring said plan."

"Was the dancing part of said plan?"

I pull away enough for his lips to leave my skin. "How much did you see?"

He smirks. "Addition of the spatula."

"Oh, and here I thought it'd be more embarrassing."

"It was wonderful." I give him an unconvinced look. He grins kissing me again. "Please dance and slide through this place however much you want."

"Just you wait, we'll have a rematch on the sock derby," I warn him with a grin. "Now sit. Stop distracting me."

He does as he's told. Thank goodness.

I make him his Americano first, sliding it toward him across the island counter. He narrows his gaze. "What are you making for breakfast?"

"Are you worried there, mister?"

"Depends on what you have planned." He brings the mug to his lips.

"You know you're gonna need to put more trust into this 'formal' engagement," I tease, grabbing a pan and setting it on the counter. I pull out a carton of eggs, bread, butter, and some salt. I pause, staring at the knobs for the stovetop, trying to remember which is which. Thankfully, I turn on the correct one, and then go about cracking eggs into a bowl. I then stir them with a fork, adding some salt and then pour the eggs into the sizzling pan. I notice Leo watching me with curiosity. "What?"

"I honestly thought you were going to make cereal," he answers.

I bite my bottom lip, shrugging as I put the bread into the

toaster. "I may have been learning some tips from Isaac and Chesty."

"You have?"

I avert my gaze away and say quietly, "I wanted to cook for you again since that disaster at the estate. And, uh, been learning a bit more appreciation for food lately."

His mug clacks against the counter, distracting me a moment before I go to work on the eggs. They're not turning out how I was hoping. Hardening too fast. Crud muffins. The toast pops up, and I turn away to grab it, but realize too late I should've waited. I come back to the eggs which have begun to burn.

"Shit, fuck," I mutter.

Damn the eggs almost look worse than the pancakes I tried to make Leo. I want to cry, frustrated with myself. I should stick to pizza rolls and dancing on couches.

I'm too busy tossing the eggs onto a plate, debating starting over, that I don't notice Leo get up and come around to step beside me. I startle, almost dropping the pan. He places his hand over mine, and says gently, "It's okay. Let me help."

I look over at him feeling relief when I see those hazel eyes. They're filled with sweet affection.

"It wasn't gonna be much, thought I could at least do eggs," I say.

"Used to burn mine, too."

He goes to the fridge, coming back with milk. I step away, but he catches my arm and places me back in front of the counter, standing behind me. It takes me a moment to register what he's doing as he helps lead my hands to cracking the eggs, whisking them, adding the milk, and whisking them again. He continues to help guide me, adjusting the stovetop temperature and pulling out a different skillet.

"Are you pulling a *Ghost* on me?" I ask, looking over my shoulder at him.

He smiles warmly. "I appreciate you wanting to cook for me, but I think I'd rather cook *with* you, my dear Watson."

I allow him to guide my hands carefully to pour the eggs into the skillet, feeling his chest against my back as a grounding force. The quiet is peaceful as Leo helps me cook the eggs perfectly, sliding them onto the plates along with new toast. We pause once finished, him still directly behind me, arms wrapped around my waist.

"Good girl," he murmurs. I lean back into his body and smile.

Chapter 14

Burning Promises

We went from *Ghost* in the kitchen to *Ghost Rider* in the television room.

Earlier we watched *Valley Girl* and *The Wicker Man*, which didn't help my case on how great Nick Cage movies are apparently. If this one doesn't help, *National Treasure* is next. No one can dislike that one.

I grin as Cage's face becomes a flaming skull. I reach for a chip to munch on as Leo shifts next to me, peeking over to see his brows furrowed in thought. For a moment, I think he's trying to decipher the CGI effects, but then I notice his eyes don't seem to be focused on the screen. No one thinks that much while watching this film.

I grab another chip, holding it out to him. "Chip for your thoughts?"

"I believe the saying is a penny."

"My wallet is in the other room."

He gives me half a smile, taking the chip. "I'm not sure if you want to talk about it yet," he starts, scowling at the screen as Cage whoops someone's ass. "But...do you know what you want for a wedding?"

Not at all what I was expecting to hear. I reach over for the remote and pause the movie. He gives me a look. "Didn't feel like proper background noise for the conversation," I explain, and he exhales sharply. "Guess this would be the typical discussion for engaged people, huh? Except most women have a scrapbook of what they want."

"I'm assuming you don't?" He smirks.

"I'd have a scrapbook of him…" I point to the frozen Cage on screen, "…before that."

I bring my legs in close, thinking if I've ever really thought about it. Nothing comes forward. No images of a "perfect" dress, venue, cakes, or even flowers. I hum with a scowl.

"Never really thought about it. I mean, marriage kinda, but not the ceremony," I say as he strokes my back. "Not a subject I've dreamed about. I went from crappy childhood to one bad relation-ship to the next, just surviving…so never been a priority. Last three years, well, focused more on healing." I shrug, pretty passive about the subject. "If there's something you want, I'm open to ideas, mister."

He frowns. "I haven't thought about it either. Never thought it would be possible for me, but then my coffee spilled on you."

"Those two cups of coffee really changed the course of our lives, huh?" I smile, looking down at the emerald shimmering against the warm light of the room. I lean back with a sigh as Leo places his arm around my shoulders. "Well, if we've got no idea of…well, theme, would next question be when do we?"

"When do we?"

"Get married. Say the vows. Toss flowers at people." His brows shoot up. I'm beginning to think I'm *very* ill-prepared for this engagement stuff already. Already slacking on the scrapbook. "Or is that *not* the next question?"

He clears his throat. "Have you told anyone we're engaged, yet?"

"Nan is already in Georgia, Leanne left yesterday morning, and Trix is traveling, too. I'd feel better telling them in person. They may be miffed that I waited, but it feels like an in-person announcement. Be a good surprise to come back to. What about you?"

He gives me a look. Right. Those he'd tell were there last night, apart from Matteo, I guess. Anyone else will find out when he sees fit, which could be weeks or months.

"Well, guess we can just wait to plan it," I say, plopping my chin on my knees. "Some people wait, right? You're hiring the wedding planner though, I ain't got that kind of money. Or the patience to tell people where to sit or stand."

Leo chuckles. "Of course, but a wedding planner may only be needed if we require seating arrangements or other things."

"Would we need that?" I'm *truly* realizing how much of the future Leo and I haven't talked about. Then again weddings aren't a hot topic when discussing mafia secrets and disposing of bodies.

"I think I'd rather have a small wedding, nothing extravagant, but…" my voice falls away, mind working on overtime. Worry begins to crawl up my spine. Would it even be safe to have a public wedding? Being the center of attention? Who would the guests be? I have no idea how the mob could play into this decision or Leo's brothers. What about other family he has left? Not to mention him being a hotel mogul, would there be expectations of a fancy wedding? Oh, fuck would there be paparazzi like last night?

"Autumn." His voice tugs at me as my thoughts spiral. I close my eyes, shaking my head and feeling dizzy. "Autumn." I rub my head harshly, hating the unease clinging to me. "Look at me, dear Watson." I do as he says, finding his warm gaze. "Good girl. Breathe."

He massages the back of my head and I take a deep breath. After a few moments of concentrated breathing, I ask, "Would it even be safe to have a 'formal' wedding?" Leo goes still. "Between your brothers or maybe police snooping again, would it be smart to? Or should we wait it all out?"

"I can't say that any of it will be settled anytime soon," he answers on a harsh exhale. "Nor can I say it will ever. We'll have security, take every precaution, and could have it somewhere that can dissuade people from potentially crashing."

"Look, I may not know what I want, but I kinda don't want to pick a time or place for *that* reason," I mumble.

"I'll give you whatever wedding you want, Autumn. I'll make it happen."

"I don't know if it's something I want," I say, and his hand goes still against my back. "Meaning the ceremony part not the marriage part, that I do want."

Leo relaxes, pulling me against his side for him to lay his head against mine. "All I want is to call you my wife and know that I'm yours."

"Same," I murmur. We're quiet, sitting on the couch as I stare at the frozen picture of *Ghost Rider*. "Why can't this be simple?"

"Because our lives are not simple. One of the few times I wish it was, dear Watson. But if we both don't know, then we'll wait."

Why can't we just say "I do" and move on?

It's obvious neither of us want a big wedding, not just because of the dangers that could come with it. Even with a small wedding, it could be months or a year or two before it happens. Who knows how many protocols we'd have to set up just to make sure no one slips. Perhaps, we could do it at the estate, wait for the others to come back. Ugh, but that still requires planning or telling Trix what Leo does or breeching security for taking any of my friends up there. That's gonna be a long security discussion with everyone. So long engagement it is then until we figure out how to do the ceremony.

Waiting isn't necessarily bad, but I really didn't want to. Maybe it's because I almost died a few weeks ago. I knew deep down this was forever. It also felt unfair that we'd have to wait for others or to avoid prying busy bodies.

"You know," I say my next thoughts out loud. "Wouldn't mind going down to the courthouse." Leo stops, meeting my gaze with confusion. "Seriously, Leo, I don't want any of that wedding stuff, honestly. I know what I don't want, and it includes a white dress."

"We want the same then."

"You don't want a white dress either? Good, would've clashed and I'd make you change," I tease. "What about jeans instead?"

"With boots?"

"Yeah, duh. And *those* can match."

"Very simple and seems more appropriate for us. Although, I won't complain about last night because you were ravishing."

"So were you." I kiss his cheek. We sit silently, staring at the television as it sinks in. "Did we just agree to elope?"

He leans back, scrunching his brows together. "We did."

Another silent beat.

"Why don't we?" I ask, shifting my legs under me and begin rambling. "Neither of us care about the ceremony part, let's admit that. I like flowers, but not to spend hours on picking bouquets or having someone decide on geraniums or tulips. I've found out recently I don't really like dress shopping, shocking, I know. We could try having it at the estate, but that's probably a security breech to invite people. Maybe the hotel, but press will be *everywhere*, anywhere we go really. And having a public wedding will only give you and the Crew worry lines from the extra stress, cause you'll have to vet *everyone* who's involved. There'll never be a right time either, something will always come up. We don't like parties, we don't like crowds, and we both hate being the center of attention. That's all a wedding is. So...let's not do it. Who says we have to?"

Leo stares at me, brows deeply furrowed in concentration. "You're serious."

"I love you. I just want to be with you. That's it. I know I'm being very unromantic, given everything you did last night, but honestly, Leo—"

Lips crash against mine. My breath hitches as I wrap my arms around his neck, kissing him fervently. He cradles my head, tracing his tongue over my bottom lip as I open to taste him more. A small moan escapes me. He ends the kiss with a heavy breath.

"I love you, dear Watson, and you saying you just want to be with me is romantic enough. You're right, I don't want any of that shit. Let alone another reason for people to pry into my private life."

I smile, kissing him quickly. "Okay, then again…when do we?"

"When would you want to?"

"I mean, we got time before the new year," I tease, and his expression turns serious. "I'm slightly joking."

Leo's quiet, standing suddenly and walks out of the room and then comes back. He starts pacing. Him losing his composure is a rare thing, and right now confusing.

"Okay, I'm totally joking then, doesn't need to be that quick."

"Autumn, I'd have a judge come up here right now to marry you." Oh, good, we're on the same page of irrational, fuck it leaps today. Perfect pair. Dr. Maxwell would be so proud of this communication.

"Okay, then why the pacing?"

"No one will be happy if we did. Nor will they agree with an elopement or quick marriage after months of only knowing each other."

My turn for confusion. "Who won't?"

"Nancy? Your friends? Can you honestly tell me they'd be fine with us eloping?"

"They know I hate crowds and attention. Probably be mad at first, but we could have our own little reception after. And *you* told Leanne and Trix you don't give a fuck about anyone's opinions concerning our relationship. Elopement is kind of that. This is about us, not them."

Leo snorts, but continues to pace.

Yeah, I don't think that's who he's worried about. "What else is there?" I ask, and he doesn't answer. "Talk to me, Leo."

He stops and I can practically see his emotions tearing through him. I watch him silently as he comes back to sit beside me, placing a hand on my leg. "I need to explain something to you, that *does* involve of when we do the deed as it were. I'd planned to discuss it with you after deciding wedding details, but it seems it's best to discuss it now."

I give him my full attention. "Okay."

He squeezes my leg lightly and some of my worry eases, but it simmers low. The ticking at the bottom of my spine doesn't help either.

"I had a plan," he starts. Of course, he does, probably has several. "I want to marry you because I love you. Marriage is an avenue for me to keep you safer, give protection in several ways I can't now. Do know these next reasons aren't *why* I want to marry you, but additives. Do you understand?"

I nod, but he quirks a brow. I smirk, "Yes."

"Becoming my wife tells many you're untouchable. You've encountered fractions of what that entails at times. No one will touch you, and if they try, I'll have every right to destroy them without much consequence. In the mafia, it is an unspoken rule that wives are to be untouched. Those who break it, suffer for it." He pauses, watching me carefully and I nod my head slowly, understanding. "Outside of the mafia, it'll be easier to protect you from the police or anyone questioning you again. I hold power in the judicial system but being married means *legally* I'll be able to protect you, including anything involving a hospital."

My mind flicks back to the women's center and precinct. Finally, the hospital and my hand absentmindedly trails over my lower stomach.

"Even if…if I sign a DNR?" I ask quietly.

He clears his throat, but answers, "Yes."

I shove away the guilt of putting him in that position, but the fear from years ago lingers. Slight relief comes next, knowing he'd protect my wishes. I whisper, "Thank you."

Leo takes my hand, kissing my wrist to entice my gaze to meet his. Understanding passes between us before he continues.

"Lastly, I want fail-safes in place for if anything ever happens to me, which includes when we marry, you'll have full authority and control over every single one of my assets. Equal co-owner. Anything that doesn't belong to Jameson or the Crew, will be yours. Especially any businesses connected to my family…including the mafia."

My heart thunders in my chest while my hands begin to shake. What?

I try to wrap my head around what he just said. I don't want his money. Leo's a multi-millionaire, who owns businesses outside of the hotel franchise *and* the mob. That kind of money and power just handed over to me is…holy shit. I've been fine with it all because it's *his* money, whatever he wants to spend it on. I've barely ever had more than a thousand dollars in my account at once.

"Check in."

"Yellow," I rasp, staring at the ground.

He cups my face, trying to get me to look at him. "I trust you, Autumn. I always have."

"Weren't kidding about the real estate sharing, huh?" I hope humor will help me think through this rationally and not panic. Cause I'm on the verge of panicking.

I stare at the engagement ring on my finger.

"Autumn, look at me," he instructs gently. Slowly, I do as he says, and he smiles softly. "You won't be in charge of anything. You'll just have a card with your name on it, and whatever you want you won't need my permission for anything. I don't want that kind of control over you."

"Just gonna end up buying books and movies."

"Then I'll buy you a library to put them in."

"Really know how to woo me, huh?"

"I'll include fuzzy socks and skirts to twirl in."

I purse my lips. "What about my own Harley?"

"You'd have to learn how to ride first," he says a bit seriously.

I force a grin, not giving away the *one* surprise I'll have for him. "Well, yeah. Gotta graduate from bitch pad and backpack."

He chuckles, stroking strands of my hair back. "Check in."

"Green."

He sits more upright, explaining further. "Those businesses

will be in my control and Jameson's, unless something happens to me. I want to be sure you'll be taken care of. Due to what I want to do with my companies, estates, and accounts with you, that's where a problem arises. My lawyers will want a very, *very* lengthy prenup or clauses in case you run away with everything or only allow you certain access. Even Jameson will want something of the kind, his position has always been to secure my finances and businesses. He will approach it in that manner and see you as an added liability."

"You've already talked to him?"

He nods solemnly. "Every time he's asked if I was insane. Even if he and the Crew trust you, that's another level of responsibility and faith to place in you. Giving you that much power worries him because it will also cause turmoil in the mafia."

"Like if someone will use me against you?"

"Yes," he answers bluntly. "Without needing my permission to access my accounts, someone could use you to. Or the matter of the family businesses I inherited only can be shared with family, per a clause my grandfather instated. There are a few other stipulations my grandmother had within her will before she died, concerning the Luciano fortune. Right now, only myself or Gabriel may fully inherit or hand off assets to our families, which includes wives."

"Why not Matteo?"

"He does not have Luciano or Salvadori blood," he states. My brows raise, unsure what he means. Then it hits me. Matteo is his half-brother, he's talking about his mother's side of the family. We haven't talked much about family, but I know most are still in Italy.

"You can't...you can't sign anything over to the Crew," I murmur. "If you disappear, everything goes to Gabriel."

"I've tried to negotiate with Renato, my uncle, the past two years to allow Matteo to be a successor, but he's refused at every turn." I nod slowly. Leo grips my hands. "Again, this isn't why, Autumn. You having financial control will help me safeguard you."

"Let me guess, they're not gonna be happy with an elopement either?"

"Or having a woman they've never met have access to such a fortune."

"Then how about not signing me onto any of that? Give me a stipend or whatever."

"Because I won't allow you to become homeless again," he states, and I blink at him. Leo kisses my hands, letting out a long breath. "I've worked, bled, and fought for all of it. It is *mine* to decide what to do with it. I have earned that right. And I want *you* to be a part of it."

I kiss his knuckles next, clutching his hand as my mind whirls. "Really trusting me with your empire, huh?"

"Not an empire," he murmurs.

"We'll see about that after I see the paperwork." I pause and then frown. "It's gonna look like one of those terms and conditions things, isn't it?"

"Most likely."

"Ick," I groan, getting off the couch grumbling. Leo remains seated, giving me space to think and to grab a tub of mint chocolate chip ice cream. I pace in the living room across from him, plunging my spoon into the frozen dessert. "Okay, I'm going to agree to signing whatever you tell me to."

His brows raise.

"You've been thinking about this for a while, I take it, which means you've given it more thought than me at the moment. All points you've given are valid. I also know you think very, *very* critically about your businesses. I trust you," I say, eating some of the ice cream.

He nods for me to continue.

I pace, eating bits of ice cream to help me think. "We've decided neither of us want a wedding, small or large, for several reasons. And safe to assume we also don't want to wait years to do so." I pause to look at him and he nods in agreement, and I continue pacing. "We want to elope, but may need to go through hordes of lawyers, Jameson, the Crew, probably board members of certain companies, and who else knows to even get *approval* of marriage it seems. We could take our time, get that paperwork together and you convince them I'm not trying to play runaway bride, but then we'd both be stress-filled, anxious balls of humans until that's done. If ever, which is probably…never. Even though we basically have strong codependency to never screw over the other, don't tell my therapist I said that."

I plop the spoon into the tub, pulling a large scoop to suck on.

"You may want to add Dr. Maxwell to that list of people."

I scowl at him with the spoon in my mouth, and then say, "The one thing I'm sure I want, not anxious or having a panic attack over is the one damn thing I have to convince *others* that it's a sane thing to want."

Oh, good that barely made sense even out loud.

I pause eating ice cream, looking at the ring on my finger.

"Autumn?"

"We could wait, figure out how to make it work in our favor, but what if something happens to either of us until then?" I wave the spoon between us. "I don't want to think about it…but if while we're trying to convince others to agree, we're fucked. Well, I'm fucked. You're the one who owns my old building. But hey, gotta have that prenup." Leo remains quiet. Okay, I understand the pacing and losing one's composure. What should be a decision between us, just became a business venture. "This is bullshit."

I sit on the couch with him, spooning out more ice cream, and offer him a bite. He takes the offer, but doesn't look as thrilled with my flavor choice. I take another bite and ask, "I miss anything?"

"They *will* want a prenup, which will cause many arguments when I refuse it."

"Could just do it to appease them."

"It's the principle of the matter," he says, leaning back. "They'll know they'll have that deciding power over my estates."

"This is gonna sound cliché, but you're the boss."

"I am, but those whom I employ want to safeguard what I own. They are tenacious to keep *their* money and properties." I roll my eyes, course it's really about *them* and fear of losing money. "Not to mention Jameson will give me lecture upon lecture for handling business or to not piss off board members or lawyers or what's left of my family."

There's something poignant about becoming the one to inherit a fortune once meant for Gabriel Marchetti. Karma at its finest.

"When did marriage have all these political strings attached to it?"

"Always has for my family," Leo mutters, gesturing for another bite of ice cream. I give some over, and he grimaces again. I smile at him, using my thumb to wipe away a little under his lip. His expression is adorable as he watches me lick the ice cream off my thumb.

"Guess we're gonna have a long engagement then," I mutter around my thumb, and getting another spoonful of ice cream. "We should start on our power points for counterarguments. I'll take Nan, you take Jameson."

Suddenly he asks, "Would you marry me today if we could?"

I look at him with surprise and spoon in mouth. I pull it out, setting the ice cream on the coffee table. "If it was possible, yes. Meant every word so far."

"I have a proposition for you." He takes my hand.

"That's ominous."

He kisses my knuckles, eyes darkening with a sudden determination. "You're right. I am the boss. And I won't allow anyone else to tell me what to do, except for you, my dear Watson."

Yup, definitely ominous.

I stare at the stack of paperwork with a fountain pen beside it on the long conference table. I try to ignore it, pacing next to the windows. It's early evening, the sun having just set. I hug myself, looking out at the skyscrapers.

Anxiety ticks at the back of my neck. I turn around to find no one. I shake my head, knowing it's only spiking because of the documents on the table. Flashes of signing the deal with Roger come back. Signing over what I created, the information I gathered, and giving away what was left of my life. That small interrogation room where I'd been beaten down and tired.

Leo would never hurt me like that. He'd take care of me, that's what this was, him making sure I never have to be in that position again. People are going to be furious when they realize the truth. Leo will probably get the ass-chewing of the century from Jameson. Apparently, he didn't *have* to have anyone present to giving me access to his…stuff. Estates, assets, properties, wealth or whatever. Leo, being a man in need of control, had already created an iron-clad legal document to grant me access to everything. Not to mention, sole power of attorney and vice versa.

His idea was simple: we get married without telling anyone and he signs me into his empire. He found a lawyer not part of his team, hiring him to draw up the paperwork and remain quiet. Guy isn't gonna talk with the amount of money Leo is paying him, that's for sure. And then a judge already under his thumb to officiate the marriage. Here I thought I was the romantic one.

We'll pretend to be engaged until the time came to tell the truth. If anything happened to Leo, I'd be safe and will inherit his family's estate and businesses. If anyone came for me, he'd have the power to protect me legally and illegally, and so would I. I'd be his failsafe, too. I'm not sure which is more ludicrous; that we decided to get married after less than 24 hours of being engaged or that we're hiding it from *everyone*.

Talk about couple's exercises.

The door opens, and I spin as Leo enters the room, shutting the door behind him. He's wearing jeans, boots, and a plain black sweater. We match. Seemed dumb to wear white. Our leather jackets are draped over some chairs.

He walks over, placing a hand on my shoulder. "Check in."

I bite my bottom lip, glancing at the paperwork. He went over every detail with me, what certain jargon I needed to know and any limitations I'd have. There were some parts we'd have to face later when people learned the truth, but I'd rather not think about that now. Guilt and nerves turmoil inside, reality and the past blending together.

None of this seemed as jarring back in the apartment when Leo explained his plan. The phone call to the Crew to say we'd be out and wanted privacy. The subway ride and other little things I do to evade bodyguards to make it to the law firm up in the Bronx. It was odd seeing Leo in the subway with me, just a snippet of normalcy for a moment.

I murmur, "Green."

"Autumn—"

"I love you." His sweater is grabbed in my hands as I put my forehead against his chest. He drapes his arms around me, shielding me. "I understand why all of this. I'm not backing down, just some old fears…scared."

"No matter what, my dear Watson, you will always have me. I will always come for you, protect you, and love you in all ways possible."

I nod against his chest when the door opens. Leo snaps his head to the intruder, basically snarling, "I told you to wait."

"Apologies, sir." The lawyer quickly shuts the door.

I start laughing softly against his chest. "How about not threatening the one who's helping?"

I step back, still gripping his sweater as he looks down at me with that scowl of his. I kiss him briefly, and his expression softens only slightly. Finally, he lets the lawyer in.

The next half hour is spent going through the paperwork and signing, down to the nitty gritty. Everything Leo owns, I now own. There won't be a public statement anywhere that this occurred, but it'll be like a quiet liquidation or whatever legal term. Only if someone peers into it, they'll notice 'wife', my name, has been added to complete ownership and access. I can enter any space Leo owns, use any bank account, or even sell one of his companies without his permission if I wanted to.

Once everything is signed, the judge is in the room with us and is signing the marriage certificate, the lawyer and secretary are our witnesses. Before I know it, he's asking, "Do you take this man as your husband?"

My chest is tight. I stare up into those hazel eyes. For some reason, a memory flashes across my mind. Not the first time we met. Not the first date. Not the bike rides or even last night. I remember the look of relief on his face the night I returned to New York. The ragged man before me, who had taken a chance on us… to try.

"I do," I answer, tightening my hand around his.

The judge asks Leo, "Do you take this woman as your wife?"

Leo whispers, "I do."

The judge says something about power invested and state of New York, but I don't really hear him. All I see, feel, and hear is Leo as he cradles my head and kisses me. I clutch him with trembling hands as he holds firm, keeping me steady as I melt into our first kiss as a married couple.

Chapter 15

So...This Is Love

"You know the weirdest thing about all this?" I ask Leo.

"What?"

"You wearing jeans unironically in public, and not a Harley in sight." I gesture around us.

We left the lawyer's office over an hour ago, now not far from his penthouse building. We'd taken some of my "maneuvers" to make sure we weren't followed, ending up at a small sandwich shop. After the long day, it felt appropriate. Pretty sure the Crew thinks we're on the other side of Manhattan.

"Gonna eat your fries?" I ask, pointing at his basket.

He pushes it towards me with a smirk. I'd already finished mine and my Rueben. Leo had ordered a pastrami sandwich. The man may be particular with food, but deep down he's a true New Yorker.

I chew on a fry, glancing around the small shop. We're seated in a corner away from the thrall of college students who didn't go home for the holiday. Most are huddled around their tables, talking as they eat. I smile at them, flicking my gaze to the door. There's still some unease coiled in me; that old familiar feeling of looking over my shoulder. I constantly check the entrance, feeling a bit more on edge than usual.

"You alright?" Leo asks. I bring my attention to him as he watches me with concern. "You've been quiet."

"Just thinking." He raises his brows, leaning closer to place his hand on my leg. Instead of admitting the prick at my neck, I blurt out the first thing that comes to mind. "Do I have to change my name? When we go public."

He grins faintly. "Only if you want to."

I grab another fry, humming to myself. Then, while munching on said fry, I say, "I know *my* name is relatively new, but I've grown attached to it. Then again, Autumn Watson Luciano doesn't sound too bad."

"No, it doesn't."

"Are we crazy?" I abruptly ask. "Like what we just did definitely isn't what anyone else would do."

"Reminder that I don't play by the rules." I roll my eyes at him. "When has anything we've done been like how others have?"

"Touché."

"We're in a world where anything sane never survives long," he murmurs, flicking his gaze toward the entrance. "Best to keep others on their toes."

Isn't wrong there.

I huff, snagging another fry and chewing it slowly. "I know I've been saying this a lot lately, but I think I'm just scared. Everything has just been so…new," I admit, poking at the fries now. "Worries keep ticking at the back of my mind, cause it's unknown territory and…" I sigh, leaning back in my chair, "…marrying you wasn't a mistake, cause it was going to happen no matter what in my mind, but I'm just afraid to lose you. You've made sure I never have to sleep on the streets again, but I'm more afraid of sleeping alone."

Leo takes my hand, tugging it gently to bring me over to sit on his lap. I wrap my arms around his shoulders as he places his hand on my hip. He whispers, "I'm not leaving you."

Leo starts to speak in another language, Italian I think,

murmuring against my head. I've no idea what he's saying, but it sounds beautiful. I start to giggle, laughing against his shoulder at the idea that he could recite the menu in Italian, and I'd probably think it's romantic.

"Are you laughing at me?"

"No," I attempt to stifle my laughter. He tries to pull me away from him, but I'm too busy trying to hide my grin. Leo suddenly presses his face against my neck, kissing it tenderly. I pull away to see his mischievous face.

"There she is." He strokes my cheek. "Should I speak other languages to make you laugh more often, then?"

"Of course, you speak more languages." He starts to speak Spanish, and then quickly changes to German. I catch snippets of words from being around Rudy and Julio. I place my hand over his mouth to make him stop. "Show off."

Suddenly, Leo picks me up and stands as I let out a soft yelp. The two workers at the shop, look up and one of them, an older gentleman, begins to chuckle. I wave at them as Leo nods briefly to them, carrying me out into the cold night. The temperature dropped drastically today, bringing ice and snow. I'm thankful I didn't end up frozen on top of the Rockefeller Center yesterday evening.

"Gonna put me down?" I ask.

"What if I don't want to?" He kisses my head, and whispers, "Siete bellisima, come al solito."

Oh, a girl could get used to this.

I keep my arms wrapped around his shoulders. "Marriage has somehow made you more swoony."

"Swoony?"

"Yup."

"I'll take it." He finally places me down. I keep hold of his arm, staring up at the sky as snowflakes fall. They drift through the night lights. There's a thin layer of snow on the ground, people already slipping on the sidewalk. Leo puts his arm through mine as we stroll down the block. I inhale deeply, letting the cold air refresh my lungs. The sounds of the city meld together, bringing a small bit of familiar peace.

We arrive at a crosswalk near the park. Leo pauses, and he asks, "Already played hooky all day, want to take a longer walk?"

"I may still get anxiety from grass," I grumble. It's been weeks. Not since the last panic attack have I been here. It looks peaceful across the way with snow falling lightly and paths illuminated by the lamplight. It honestly looks like a Hallmark movie poster.

"If you do, then we'll leave," he says. "You'll be safe."

"Oh, I know I'm always safe with you." *Mister Mafia Boss*, I think. "Aren't we already pushing it though? You never go anywhere without someone nearby."

"We'll be fine." He adjusts his leather jacket, and I catch a glimpse of the 9-millimeter tucked away. He has two knives hidden in his boot, and another at his belt. Definitely set.

I glance up at him, finding his gentle hazel gaze. Time alone as a newly married couple, without anyone interfering, sounded nice. Just a quiet walk in the park. Smiling, I nod. He kisses my hand, and then proceeds to walk us toward the park entrance.

More snow falls. I hold onto Leo, using him for balance as I tilt my head back to gaze at the light reflecting against the glittering flakes. White begins to overtake the park, creating a beautiful effect over the place. Guess it's gonna be a white Thanksgiving.

"Well, good news, the grass is covered by snow, so I think you're safe," Leo muses. I gasp, slightly pushing him in jest. He chuckles as I stick my tongue out, and then attempt to catch the tiny flakes.

We continue walking through the snow, winding down some paths. I'm hopeful for no panic attacks as a few people pass us. After some time in silence, Leo asks, "Given we were married in unusual circumstances, is there anything you *do* want?"

"I'm pretty good." I peer up at him, his face not showing he's convinced. "You're gonna need to try harder than that for me to spend your money, mister." He grunts, and I sigh, "*Our* money."

He continues to scowl, jaw working as he contemplates my answer. I laugh a little. "Seriously, Leo, I'm…well, wait."

He stops. "Are you admitting—?"

"Careful, I may suggest thrifting." He smirks and has us walking again, while gesturing for me to continue. "We could redo the hotel apartment and…penthouse."

"Such as?" Get rid of the fucking grey for one.

I clear my throat, not wanting him to know how much I detest the paint on the walls. "Nothing with the structures, but interior decorating. Add a plant or two. Different paint job."

"Would the ideas you've given before be what you're suggesting?"

I stop us now, pinching my brows together in confusion. After a moment, I finally realize what he's referring to and begin laughing. "Maybe…not entirely. I was a bit loopy in that interrogation room, so those ideas…let's call them backup."

Leo wraps his arm over my shoulders, pulling me in close as we start walking once again. "Then what ideas do you have now?"

For the rest of the walk through the park I go into each detail I've had about the two places. Leo listens intently to every suggestion, most of them based on the estate's décor and the *Italian Lily*. The snow falls quietly around us as we approach the park exit. We're walking in silence for the last bit when there's a prick at the back of my neck.

My body goes on high alert, almost going rigid as my footsteps falter from the abrupt change in my body. Leo looks at me oddly, and I wave it off as I gesture to the snow. He holds me closer, in attempt to keep me steady no doubt as we get closer to the street.

I peek over my shoulder and don't see anyone. It doesn't ease the panic rising up my spine, the old familiar feeling rushing over my skin. I focus on breathing, swallowing hard as we make it to the entrance and head down the sidewalk toward Leo's building. The prickling worsens, shrieking at me to run. It doesn't relent as more people cross our path as we head across the street. The bright lights and sounds of the city surrounding us more, the snow barely muffling it.

We're fine. It's just because we were in the park, and you have anxiety with grass.

I swallow hard again as we approach our building's block. Some of the pedestrian traffic becomes lighter, almost vanishing as we pass a small street. Leo begins to slow his pace, and says in a low voice, "When I tell you, run for our building. Don't look back. Get inside."

My heart thunders in my chest as if bricks have smashed against my lungs. "Leo…"

We reach the corner of the next block. *"Run, Autumn."*

His command punches through me. Leo lets go of me, reaching for his gun as I bolt. Snow crunches under his feet as he turns, something snapping. I sprint, hearing people scream as shots ring out behind me and shouting. It echoes against the buildings. I want to turn around as another shot echoes, but somehow follow his instruction and keep running. I skid around the last corner, and see Xavier standing outside.

"Xavier!" I scream and he turns. "There's someone—"

Suddenly, a body slams into me, almost picking me up. I shriek, panic coursing through my body as Xavier runs towards me.

"It's me, Miss Autumn!" Isaac yells over the noise, outside and within my head.

"Isaac…Leo…there's—" I struggle to talk as he practically carries me into the building's lobby. There's more shouting, tires screeching, and sirens. "Leo…"

Isaac attempts to grab my attention, but I can't stop staring at the snowy night as lights flash by, melding across my vision as more cars pull up. Everything is a blur as my heart pounds into my head. The roaring in my head won't stop.

There were gunshots.

Horror consumes me. I want to scream. I want to run back outside, but Isaac keeps me from leaving. "Miss Autumn, stay here. I can't—"

"Leo's out there!" I finally start yelling. "He told me to run! He—"

My chest concaves, struggling against Isaac's arms to get back outside. I should've turned around. I should've told him something was wrong. Why didn't I listen? I should've fucking told him!

We were happy. We'd spent time together like any couple on a date night; walking in the snow and talking about decorating. How could it switch so quickly? One night, one *damn night*. My mind races, terrified of where Leo is.

We've only been married for hours.

"Miss Autumn," Isaac says softly, tugging at me to look at him. Familiar blue eyes, which are calm, but they aren't hazel. Not the ones I need. "He'll be fine. I'm sure—"

"Mr. Luciano is alright," Xavier says suddenly, walking into the lobby. "They've apprehended the assailants, but more police are on their way."

Police? FUCK.

Owen and Chesty enter the lobby next, snow blowing in with them.

"Where is he?" I gasp. Neither answer me fast enough, causing my heart to squeeze. *"Where the fuck is he?"*

"Autumn, he's okay," Owen answers, holding his hands up with worry etched on his face. "He took care of the men, and they're being—"

"Men? Multiple?"

"You were being followed," Chesty answers. My chest hurts and it's hard to catch enough air to breathe. It's difficult to hear any of them. I'm not even sure how much time has passed. Has it been minutes? An hour?

Isaac places his hand on my shoulder, his voice sounding distant, "We're handling it, don't worry…"

I begin to feel dizzy, panic driving through every vein. My mind flits back to every time I'd been followed, stalked, and chased. Those dark feelings that shadowed me everywhere; to warn me of danger. I should've listened to my fucking instincts. I got too comfortable.

Hide. Run.

My stomach twists as I feel like I want to puke.

The doors whoosh open, bringing shouting. Jameson's voice cuts through the rest, yelling about safety as a beeping sound goes off. There are more people, even someone in a police uniform. More voices I don't recognize. Until I hear Leo, pinpointing where he is in the mass. Everything else becomes a blur as I start to run forward. Isaac tries to keep me back, but I yank my arm viciously out of his hold as I push past the others. Leo's gaze finds me, ignoring Jameson as he rushes forward.

A sob escapes me as he embraces me, clutching him as I struggle to breathe. His arms tremble, shuddering as he cradles my head against his chest. There's still yelling around us and lights flashing outside. The cacophony is deafening, and I wince when something drops, sounding like gunfire.

"I'm okay," he whispers roughly, burying his face in my hair. "You did exactly what I told you. Good girl." He kisses my hair, rasping, "Good girl."

I cry harder, throat tightening and jaw hurting at the terrifying thought of never hearing him call me that again. Leo holds me tighter to his chest as if he's trying to shield me from the crowd. He goes rigid suddenly, head lifting as he says in a booming, dark tone, *"Silence."*

All noise stops abruptly.

"If it continues to sound like a damn zoo in here, I will gladly lock myself and her in the penthouse until New Year's, are we clear?"

I hiccup a little trying to get myself to stop crying. Except, the tears won't stop. Over and over again I hear the crunch of the snow under his feet and the gunshots. Him telling me to run.

"Give me ten fucking minutes with my…fiancé," Leo orders. "Do your damn jobs in the meantime." His voice is lethal as he starts to move us toward the elevator. There're footsteps near us, and Leo's head snaps to the person, almost snarling, *"No."*

It becomes so quiet, you could hear a pin drop.

He gestures at them, guiding me out of the crowd and to the elevators. I try to concentrate on breathing when he stops us. He brings his hands to my face, holding me gently as he lifts my head to finally look at him. Weariness, lined with anger and frustration cover his face. I can practically see him battling to remain calm as his thumbs caress my skin to help *me* calm.

"Check in," he whispers.

I peek at the crowd gathered in the lobby, but Leo steps closer to block them out, invading my space to keep my attention only on him. One of his hands slides to the back of my neck, massaging my skin as I swallow hard.

Finally, I murmur as more tears fall, "Red."

He kisses my forehead and I close my eyes, trying to concentrate on him being here. He's not dead. He's fine. We're fine…we're fine…

Yet, my heart won't stop racing and the tightness around my lungs won't loosen. I can't stop shaking. The panic not leaving me.

"I don't want to be away from you, but I need to handle the last of this. I also don't want you down here. Will you be alright in the penthouse?" I nod once. "Isaac and Waylon will be with you. I'll be with you as soon as I'm done."

I open my eyes as some of the shakiness begins to subside. I answer quietly, "Okay."

He nods once, kissing my forehead. Letting me go as he punches the elevator button and calls out, "Bond! Chesty!"

Leo steps back as I hug myself close, staring at the ground as I enter the elevator with the other two. My gaze moves up at the doors close, catching sight of Leo's scowl before he turns away.

"You're both okay, sister," Chesty says, rubbing my shoulders a little. My chin quivers as I nod. Suddenly, he brings me into his arms as I start to cry again.

Face/Off plays on the screen. I hoped it would calm me, but not really. Chesty's been in the kitchen on the phone, his muffled voice barely carrying into the television room. Isaac sits in another chair, silent since we've arrived up to Leo's…our penthouse.

I hold my knees closer, swallowing against my rough throat. As the evening has worn on, numbness has begun to settle in; that dark chasm churns inside me with the fear of losing Leo and frustration for not listening to my instincts.

My hands rub together, one of my fingers bumping over the engagement ring. I stare down at the emerald that catches the light, inhaling sharply.

All those times before I'd been the one in danger. Just me. I hadn't wanted to die as I scrambled for a reason to live, but it was just…me. Tonight, it'd been Leo who'd been in danger. Left behind. He'd been legitimately in danger where I could've lost him. Hours after saying "I do", his plan would've been brought into action of me inheriting everything.

"I'd rather be homeless again," I murmur to myself.

"Miss Autumn?"

I shake my head, while clearing my throat loudly. "Nothing. Just…mumbling out loud."

He hums at my response, but my mind keeps spinning.

I don't regret marrying Leo or signing those papers in secret, but the heaviness on my shoulders worsens every passing moment. The responsibility it bears. I wouldn't truly be alone if he died, but the thought of living without him…

Fuck, I feel like puking again.

Tears trickle down my face.

Doors slam suddenly, followed by loud voices. I go to stand, but Isaac gets up and gestures for me to stay. "Wait, here. Please."

He disappears, partially closing the door as the voices get louder. Most are muffled, but I can hear Jameson chastise Leo for disappearing, along with Drew. Police getting involved. Owen chimes in next about there may not be a next time. Leo argues with them as I begin rocking in my seat. Isaac intervenes, then Waylon, then Julio. All their voices overlapping, practically yelling at Leo for being stubborn and that he should explain where we were. Why we're supposed to have security. What if they'd been hired by Gabriel? Another crime boss?

The shaking begins again. It worsens along my arms as my stomach twists. The voices of the Crew blending in with those forming in my head. *Fuck...no, not again.*

"Stop," I plead in whisper. Breaking glass. Yelling. "Stop."

Someone raises their voice. My body shakes violently now. I can't tell who's who. Is it Steve yelling? Roger? The last few weeks pile back on me. Horrid memories of blood, gunshots, the rain, and knife near my throat. Tonight, the anxiety crawling over my skin, married in secret, the crunch of snow.

Walk away. You can never *walk away.*

I clutch my head, stumbling off the couch and tripping over the coffee table. I land hard on my knees, fingers gripping into my hair as I feel like I'm drowning. The roaring shoving me under as panic builds, making it harder to breathe. My chest tightens as fear wrecks through me when that little sliver of a thought comes back, *break the glass, use it on your—*

"No," I grunt through my teeth, slamming my knuckles into the ground. The compulsion to grab something sharp, break anything yanks at me again. I shake my head, trying to will away the thoughts. The floor slams into my fist again. Again, the pain jolts through my arm.

Relief. I just want fucking relief. Make it stop. I want it to stop... I want...

"*Leo!*" The scream rips from my throat.

I slam my fists into the hardwood floor. The pain rushing against the howling in my head. I keep doing it. Anything, *anything* to make the agony stop. My fists are raised to do it again when someone grabs my arms and yanks me against their body.

"Sweetheart, stop." Leo's voice carries through the darkness.

"*Red*," I choke out, thrashing against his embrace. I continue to repeat the word, screaming it. The word echoes as I sob uncontrollably, wanting the pain the stop. Guilt and shame riding the wave next as my screams don't relent, losing control of my body as I fight Leo's tight hold that pins my arms against his chest.

"I've got you," he says against my head. "I'm right here, dear Watson. I'm right here…I've got you…"

I continue screaming into his chest, unrelenting as I had been in the ballroom as everything crumbled inside. Leo keeps his arms around me as I feel myself breaking again. And the words I desperately want to cry out, to admit, but can't ring in my head.

Don't make me a widow!

Chapter 16

Our Dark Wells

My throat hurts. I moan a little from the dull ache throughout my body.

"You're okay," Leo murmurs.

I blink harshly, finding myself in bed with Leo sitting beside me. He strokes my hair gently. I shudder a breath, slowly sitting up as I hold my head. I try to remember what happened until it slams back into me. I stare at Leo with guilt and embarrassment.

"Leo, I'm sorry—"

"Stop," he gently instructs. "Don't apologize for having a panic attack, a bad one. Especially since it was me and the Crew who caused it."

My mouth works, not yet ready to form words as I look at him helplessly. Leo quickly pulls me toward him, wrapping my legs around his waist as I fold against his chest.

"We should've kept our cool, Autumn. We know your past, and yet we acted out like assholes, yelling at each other like it was bar fight. I'm sorry."

"It's not your fault. Everyone was just upset."

"Let me take the responsibility this time, Autumn," he whispers. "I fucked up."

We sit there in silence as I take a few grounding breaths, already wanting coffee and to watch *Reefer Madness* before having to admit more of my inner thoughts. Guilt coils in my gut. Unable to keep the terrible thoughts to myself, I whisper, "I thought you were dead."

Leo goes still.

"I ran, kept running…" I continue, "…but heard those gunshots and thought the worst. Even seeing you, holding you, wasn't enough. All I could think was how I'd…I'd married you hours before and almost lost you. How much I'd rather be homeless again than be left with your fortune alone."

"Autumn—"

"I was so angry with myself." I grip his shirt. "Angry that I knew someone was following us. I fucking *felt it* like I had for years, and I should've warned you. It's my fault you were—"

"Autumn." Leo cups my face, but I close my eyes. "Look at me, dear Watson." I shake my head, chin quivering. He sighs softly, and then whispers, "Please look at me, my dear wife."

My eyes open at the new endearment.

"I knew someone was following us," he says and my breath catches. "I didn't want to alarm you, not knowing how many there were, but needed us closer to home. None of it was your fault. You did *exactly* what I told you, which kept me focused on handling those men. I'm not leaving you anytime soon, my dear Watson." He brings his forehead against mine. "I was terrified of losing you, too."

Relief floods me. My arms go around his neck, burying my face into his shoulder. "Fuck, I'm sorry if I scared you."

He kisses my temple. "I love you unconditionally, even the parts that you worry I'll hate. I am yours, and you are mine. In every capacity. Yes…you scared me, but do not apologize for a reaction you can barely control. I understand you do not *want* to hurt yourself, but it is a compulsion that happens when you're overwhelmed and panicked. It's also been a long month."

I hug him tighter. We stay in silence as he rubs my back, while I listen to his heartbeat. I hadn't realized I'd been shaking again. It's only minutes, but it seems like forever as I melt into his hold, finally my muscles untensing completely. Once I do, Leo breathes out a long exhale.

"I love you unconditionally, too...my dear husband." The words are soft from my lips. I lean back, my gaze finding those calm hazel eyes. Tenderly, I kiss him for that reprieve he brings. I move my hands down, bumping them against his shoulder and I wince.

Leo breaks the kiss, bringing my hands down between us to look over the light scrapes and bruising on my knuckles. I don't remember hitting the floor *that* hard.

"You didn't bloody them, fortunately, and you can move them. But I want you to take it easy for the next week." I nod numbly. "I'm not angry with you, Autumn."

I exhale sharply, thankful that he said it first. Fuck, I feel like a wreck again and just plain exhausted.

"I know healing isn't linear," I say. "But I was really, *really* hoping these panic attacks or flashbacks wouldn't be as bad. Have a bit more control."

"You will manage them better in the future."

"Didn't feel like I made any progress last night."

"You have."

"Sure, about that?" I raise my hands. "Couple of weeks, already hurt myself again."

"You did something different than before."

I pinch my brows at him. "Apart from you not walking in on a knife against my wrist or throwing furniture, what changed?"

"You called for me." Confusion still hasn't left my expression. "In the past, you didn't ask for help. You've never called out for me or others. You suffered in silence." He holds my hands up. "You knew you were going to hurt yourself, but called for help."

"But...I still did. Hurt myself." Where's he going with this?

He holds my hands gently, stroking his thumb gingerly over my wrist. Leo surprises me with an analogy. "Your panic attacks are like hanging from a rope that goes into a deep well. Sometimes, you may feel like you're deeper in the well than other times, but it's always dark beneath you. Before, you've clawed your way out without saying anything, bloodying your hands." He holds mine up. "Other times you've let go and fallen into the well until someone came to lift you from the darkness. But this time, even though losing your grip on the rope, you asked for help. You screamed for someone to find you in the well this time, not falling in without a sound. And one day, you'll be able to pull yourself out without bloodying your knuckles."

I stare at him. Truth in every little detail, pinpointing what it feels like. A little too on the nose. "You learned that for yourself, didn't you?"

"You're not the only one with an intuitive therapist who's spot on."

"I didn't know you had panic attacks or something like that."

"A few, I think I'd be insane if I didn't for what my work entails," he murmurs. "They're not like yours, but I doubt that well changes much from person to person."

"Yeah." I let out a sharp exhale, smiling faintly with a new appreciation that blossoms. Guess it wasn't just from being a Dom that he recognized the signs. I'm grateful for him in many ways, but his patience and understanding will always take top spot. Even if a tiny part of me hates that he understands on a personal level. "Thank you, Leo."

He strokes my cheek, then murmurs, "My dear wife."

"Something tells me *that* is gonna be your favorite endearment for me now," I smirk.

He smiles, maneuvering to lay me down on the bed as he blankets me with his body and warmth. He kisses me affectionately, lovingly caressing my skin as I shiver against his touch. Leo says against my lips, "But you'll always be my dear Watson."

I thread my fingers through his hair. A tingling sensation of safety, relief, and warmth makes me shudder. Suddenly, Leo pulls away and says, "You need to eat."

I fall back to act dramatic, which causes him to chuckle. Not that I was fully expecting sex, given the small headache and hands throbbing, but a make-out session sounded nice.

"Being responsible again," I mutter.

"It's my job," he says against my ear, nipping at my earlobe before getting off the bed.

I sit up, leaning back into my elbows and glance at the time. It's half past eight in the morning. And then I realize it's Thursday. We made no plans for the holiday, and after last night, something tells me Leo is gonna be occupied.

Before I can ask, Leo comes back out of the bathroom and says, "Don't go out there naked."

I scrunch my face together. "When have I *ever* done that?"

"The estate."

"I flash you *one* time." He raises a brow. "And *you're* the one who's opened the door naked." He smirks, but only slightly. "Fine, but it better not be because you have the entire day catered or whatever."

"Not all of it." Figures. "The Crew will be here for dinner. Practically had to kick them out because they wouldn't leave last night."

"They didn't go...have plans..." my words trail away when I remember the lack of family they have outside of the MC. Right, they probably spend the holidays together or just don't celebrate them.

"Unless you want me to kick them out."

"No, no." I get off the bed, waving off the idea. "I've never been one for holidays, but it would seem mean to kick them out." I start heading for the closet, but stop and ask, "Did you...tell them what we did?"

"No." Leo comes over, stroking my hair back. "All they know is that we wanted time alone, that's it. They may apologize to you when they arrive, be sure to let them."

"I'm not mad at any of you," I sigh, rubbing my chest lightly. "There's no reason—"

"Autumn," he interrupts. "They may not know we're married but being engaged is enough for them to behave differently. It's out of respect not just for you as my partner, but potential of you co-owning everything they work for. And there's our own biker code, when it comes to respecting women, especially someone's old lady. Let's be frank, last night, they disrespected you in your own home. There's no excuse for what happened last night and the aftermath of how it was handled. Their duty is to protect you and last night will be seen as a failure to their moral code we follow as a club."

All the *Forgotten Demons* hold their values close. If they didn't, they wouldn't have helped Leo take out my ex, the men who brutalized me, or be willing to go after Gabriel. Aside from that, whether I like it or not, the ring on my finger means I'll be treated slightly different now. The responsibility for me has shifted, become more dire.

"Advice on handling that next step?"

"Do what you feel is right."

"Oh, gee helpful," I mutter, rolling my eyes as I head into the closet to change.

"You're a smart and compassionate woman, Autumn. How your relationship with them evolves is up to you, not me. Been doing a good job on your own already." I pause before pulling some leggings on, finding him leaning against the closet doorway.

"Meaning?"

"You had them wrapped around your finger before I ever introduced you," he smirks. "Only you could get Ringer to lay in grass and look at clouds."

Not sure if such shenanigans will work again, but maybe. I continue getting dressed as he disappears. Maybe Leo's been going to therapy more regularly again. He's always understanding, but this feels different. Maybe it's marriage.

Leo goes to take a shower as I head out into the living room. It's almost eerily quiet, the morning sun streaming through the windows as I enter the kitchen. I start brewing some coffee and espresso, putting the kettle on to make Leo's Americano. There's a knock at the door. Ah, reason one to not be naked.

I go answer, finding the only person who'd arrive this early in the morning on a holiday without a death wish. "Hey, Jameson."

He stands before me in slacks and a green sweater. Those brown, golden eyes of his flick over my face as he puts his hands in his pockets.

"Apologies for last night. We all should've handled it more professionally," he says as way of greeting.

"Not mad at any of y'all, but I forgive you and the rest of the Crew."

He nods, pursing his lips and brushes past me. I blink at the abrupt behavior, but I shake it off as I close the door and meet him in the kitchen. He looks over at the hallway to the bedroom. "He up?"

"Taking a shower. Want a coffee?"

"Sure."

I start pouring him a cup, pulling out some cream and sugar to place on the island. I lean back against the other counter, watching him stiffly pour cream into his coffee. I'm reminded of the diner and the uneasy atmosphere. He's got shit on his mind again, and I doubt I want it festering.

"You've got 5-10 minutes before he comes out," I say finally, breaking the silent tension. I'm in for a hard talking to. Might as well get it over with and hope he doesn't figure out what we did. "So...get it out."

Quietly, Jameson puts the spoon down on the counter. He only takes a moment before he snaps his gaze to mine. "Whose idea was it to leave without a bodyguard or security?"

"Mine," I answer automatically. Leo and I haven't discussed our alibi, but he did say go with what I felt was right.

"Figured," he mutters.

Suddenly, that decision doesn't feel right. "Excuse me?"

"I said that you've changed him for the better in multiple ways," he begins in a low voice. "Myself and the rest can see it and thank fuck. But that doesn't include you influencing him to do things that are dangerous and irresponsible. There's a reason he doesn't travel alone. *Ever.*"

I try to act nonchalant, grabbing my coffee and shrugging my shoulders. "Look, I'm sorry we disappeared, but not for the time alone. To leave said ivory tower." I gesture around us. "I thought we'd be fine. I was for years on my own."

"That's because no one knew who you were." He drums his fingers over the counter. "He doesn't have that luxury. What if those men were hitmen? Hired from a rival crime boss?"

I scrunch my brows in confusion. Wait…they weren't mobsters?

Jameson catches my confusion, cocking his head a little. "He didn't tell you?"

"Had other things to talk about, and I figured he wasn't going to tell me if it was mob related."

"Well, it wasn't." He picks up his mug, glancing over his shoulder toward the bedroom. "You were followed by four men. Two were close to him, while another two almost grabbed you when you ran back to the building. Ringer and Pretty Boy were already close by, canvasing the area for you two. They were hired kidnappers. They have a record of kidnapping socialites for ransom, three accounts in the past, they made bail each time."

I stare at him as I place my coffee down.

"They probably saw Leo's appearance at the gala, because two others from that event were almost kidnapped hours prior." Jameson's face is severe, disappointment and anger lining it. "And because it was so public, police had to be involved and then press arrived, which is why Leo had you come up here."

How long was I in that lobby? It felt like minutes, but from what Jameson is saying it had to have been closer to twenty or thirty, perhaps longer. Fuck, I was really out of it. I stare at the ground as it sinks in that Leo and I escaped our own Wayne Family evening.

"We're taking care of it, press and all, because it's a nightmare. Thank fuck it's Thanksgiving, so people are more concerned watching the parade or football. But what you two did was reckless. What if something worse had happened to you?"

"My thoughts all of last night waiting for…" I almost say my husband, but clear my throat, "…Leo. I'm not sorry for wanting some normalcy with him after these past few weeks."

"Wake up, Autumn." I blink up at Jameson, who scowls deeper. "He's a famous businessman and a mafia don, there's no such thing as normalcy."

We stare at each other. Words sinking in.

Oh, trust me, I knew all too well who Leo was. Sometimes I forget the expanse of his influence, things I never had to think about before him, but I knew who he was. What's expected of him. The paperwork last night will be seared into my memory forever.

"I know."

Jameson steps closer, jaw tightening as his brows pinch together. "I can't tell you what to do, not my place. We've had our discussions and I know you want him to be happy, I can see that, but be aware of *who* he is. You have a duty now, like the rest of us, to support him. So…in the future, for all our sakes, do not suggest things that may hinder his public status."

I've got to admit, Jameson is probably the only one out of the *Forgotten Demons* to have the balls to speak to me like this. Don't fully mind it, he keeps me on my toes by being blunt, but it's what he's *not* saying that creates agitation under my skin.

Behave.

The kettle starts to whistle, and I pull it off to break away from Jameson's stare. I busy myself as I make Leo's Americano. Calmly, I say, "In the future, Jameson…if you ever even suggest how I should behave, you may end up being punched."

Our gazes meet, stone cold against hard warning.

There's noise from the bedroom, causing us both to separate as Leo walks out. His steps falter for a moment before he enters the kitchen and tells Jameson, "You're early."

"We need to discuss the press release that Carrie is sending out about last night."

"We agreed on meeting tomorrow."

"She wants part of the story out this morning. For once, I agree. The announcement needs to be out sooner than later, and Thanksgiving festivities will keep it from blowing up."

"What announcement?" I ask as Leo picks up his coffee, coming up behind me to wrap his arm around my waist. Both men are quiet, exchanging a look. "Leo?"

"Our engagement to be announced publicly. We're staying ahead of any reporters from digging into your past or mine, distract them with something shiny," Leo answers, holding my left hand up as he kisses above the ring.

Jameson watches us as he picks up his mug, clearing his throat as he begins walking toward upstairs. "We hammer this out now, then no work until tomorrow morning."

"And you say I'm a workaholic," Leo comments.

"Don't almost get mugged then." Jameson leaves the room.

"He is not a happy camper," I say. "But I don't think he knows."

"That's all that matters right now," Leo murmurs, kissing my cheek. "He'll relax when this blows over, which will be soon. He just hates that we have to meet with Carrie in person."

"PR woman, right?"

"Yes." Leo sips from his mug, following after Jameson. "I'll be down soon to start breakfast, no cereal, dear Watson you need real food."

I feign a gasp, and I can hear him chuckle as he disappears.

With a deep sigh, I lean back against the counter again. Deep down, I know Jameson is just protecting Leo, and not just for personal gain. They've been together for over a decade, almost two. I've shaken things up a bit, changed how some things are done, which can be jarring. Not to mention, he was probably scared last night, too. Yet, it still hurt with how he spoke to me.

As I'm on the verge of overthinking, there's another knock at the door. I glance at the time as I open the door and find Julio there. He smiles faintly, wearing jeans, a blue button-up that's opened to show his dark t-shirt strained over his strong gut. He trimmed his beard.

"Jameson wanted some things," he says, holding up a folder and then a box. "Also brought a gift to ask for forgiveness. Acted like a gringo who got stood up at a bar."

I wave him in, but hug him before he can pass me. "You're forgiven."

He follows me into the kitchen. "Got any coffee left?"

"Yup, I'll pour you a cup before I start yelling about what's in the box." I grab another mug and check how much coffee is left in the pot. If the Crew keeps showing up one by one, I'm gonna need more.

"It's just the computer Iron Buffalo and I got you." He places the box on the island, flipping it open to reveal a brand-new laptop.

I quickly set his coffee down, pulling it over to look at the new model. "Holy cabooses, this isn't cheap."

"Only the best for the only person to outshine me, *hermana*." Julio winks, taking his coffee to add cream and sugar.

"Leo's upstairs with Jameson," I say.

"Should've figured," Julio grumbles, shaking his head. "May wait with you to see if Sombra survives giving Spartan another ass-chewing."

We both snort as he sits at the counter, and I join him as I pull over the laptop. I quickly notice the new software, checking the firewalls and systems is like riding a bicycle.

"Still think you could provide some of your services to us," he says quietly, sipping his coffee.

"Better for me to stay out of it." I sigh, closing the laptop. "I'm out of practice anyways. Maybe I'll use it for what other people do like blogging."

"Already know it's gonna be about those movies of yours," he chuckles.

I laugh with him. "Yeah, but thanks for this. I'll tell Owen later. By the way, do y'all usually spend Thanksgiving together?"

"Have for the last decade, but first time in the penthouse. Spartan's already hired someone to bring the food, so after handing this paperwork off, all done for the day."

"Good. Y'all need a break, especially after last night," I murmur the last part.

He pats my shoulder. "Look, we're a bunch of bikers stuck in a city and monkey suits, when all we want to do is ride. We get it. Sometimes you just gotta go, but uh, tell us where you're going next time."

I smile faintly at him, and then look toward the stairs. Well, there's no yelling so that has to be a good sign, unless Leo has forbidden such actions from the penthouse. Actually…he may have.

"So, why Enigma?" I ask abruptly.

"Checking off all the road name origins?" I shrug and he laughs. "Am the last one?"

"Nope, sorry. You could wait to tell me if you want."

"Nah." He rolls his shoulders back, getting up to pour more coffee into his mug. "Pretty easy origins. It's because none of the *Demons* have figured out who I truly am; I am an *enigma* to them. Had a few other names, but Enigma stuck."

"Yet they passed up on calling you Zorro," I say deadpan.

He lets out a boisterous laugh. "I always left the mask at home and whips sting like a bitch."

We chuckle and he leans onto the island counter across from me and nods his head at the laptop. "Go to the FBI database, already put it in for you, don't worry they can't track you." Eyeing him a little, I do as he says. "Now, look up Julio Guillermo Hernandez."

I do so, finding an old profile of an agent, Julio, but there's barely anything there. I glance over it, not finding much. If anything, he looks like some computer desk jockey who never left the office. Pretty certain he was anything but that.

"Not the only one who learned how to erase their past," he murmurs. "I learned to not only bury my skeletons, but burn them to a crisp, too."

"So, the club has no idea who you truly were."

He grins playfully, giving me a wink. "Earned my spot as a *Forgotten Demon*, that's all that matters."

I shut down the computer. "Yeah."

"Or maybe it's because I never told them where the three stab wounds in my back came from," he says casually as he scratches his beard. I gape at him. He shrugs. "Ex-lover spat between Jonathan and Mark in, uh Yuma. No wait…Miguel and Anthony in Puebla."

I raise a brow.

"Or it was Ronald and Stanley in San Diego," Jameson's voice suddenly interrupts.

He and Leo return, both appearing a bit disgruntled. Julio grabs the folder he had, handing it off to Leo, who hands it Jameson.

"Have to keep living up to the name. Could always tell her about yours, Sombra," Julio smirks, going back to his coffee.

Jameson exchanges a look with Leo, before looking at me as I hold my hands up. He clears his throat, heading for the door. "Another time. I'll be back for dinner."

The door thuds behind him, leaving Julio and I to exchange a look before I glance over at Leo, who starts preparing breakfast. Alrighty, not gonna talk about it.

"You staying for breakfast?" Leo asks Julio, a bit roughly.

"Nah, pres, off to tinker on the bike and will be back tonight."

"Don't be late."

"Gracias for the coffee, *hermana*, I'll bring the mug back." I grin, waving him off as Julio leaves.

Leo goes about cooking breakfast as I watch him, and suddenly it feels like forever since the morning before. I get off my seat, walking up behind him and place my arms around his torso. He pauses at the stove, placing his hand upon my arm as I lay my head against his back.

"Would've thought you'd cook Thanksgiving dinner," I comment.

"Not for eight bikers," he mutters.

He's quiet as I hold him as his hand grips my forearm.

"Leo?"

He turns around, making me let go, but not for long as he grabs me and lifts me. He sits me on the other counter, standing between my legs. His hands drift up my body, soon cupping my face before kissing me gently. The kiss is tender. The tension in his body disappearing as he holds me. Finally, he pulls away and then brushes his fingers through my hair. "My dear wife."

I smile softly, knowing he won't tell me what Jameson and him discussed, but I could provide some peace for now. "Want to teach me how to make pancakes this time?"

Leo's small grin is enough for me.

Chapter 17

Shower Talk

I stare at the phone on the counter, cradling my face in my hands.

Well…that didn't go as well as I'd hoped.

Phone call with Nan. Another with Trix, and one more with Leanne. All of whom were not happy campers. Sure, they were excited I was engaged, but definitely were mad that they found out from word of mouth due to the public announcement.

So much for telling them in person.

A warm hand moves up my back, and I look over my shoulder at Leo. He kisses my temple. "How'd they take it?"

"Confused. Mostly happy. Mad they found out through *other* friends and the news," I huff, letting my head fall forward to hit the counter. Leo catches my forehead before I bang it into the marble with his palm. "It's almost 10 am! How could it have reached them that quickly?!"

"Some people live for that kind of information."

I grumble more under my breath, thinking of ways to make it up to them. I guess trying to give them space to be with their families yesterday was not the best…best friend move. I may have to hand that card back in for not calling them the night I got engaged or after the potential kidnapping. How was I supposed to know that's what you do?

"They'll forgive you," he tells me, rubbing my back.

I sit up with a smirk. "Oh, they'll forgive me. How do you feel about me acquiring that fancy credit card of yours?"

He comes in close to whisper, "*Ours*, my dear wife."

"One thing at a time."

Leo chuckles, spinning me in the seat to face him. "Are you implying you're trying to *buy* their forgiveness?"

"No," I say sassily. "Planning to *distract* them with their own shiny things to forget about my shiny thing…for like five minutes."

He snorts at me, sliding his hand down my arm, and taking my hand to kiss my new shiny thing and then my wrist. I smile as he places his other hand under my chin, tilting it up. Hazel eyes meet mine as he steps between my legs, caressing my neck.

It's been a chaotic 24 hours. We had a somewhat quiet morning yesterday, until the caterers showed up and then the Crew for dinner. It was good being with them all, even though it felt like the first half was them apologizing for acting like jackasses the night before. They stayed pretty late, some of them watching football, too, which felt weird. It was funny listening to them cheer for their teams.

Later in the night, Leo got a call that everything for the press release was done. Leo was officially declared off the "most eligible bachelor" list, which seemed to overshadow anything else. This Carrie person is good. Guess she must be after working as his main publicist for six years still has no idea he's the mafia don of the city. From what I could overhear on the phone, I don't think she would care. And from the constant irritated looks Jameson gave, I don't think he quite likes her.

My only hope—I'm not in the room when Carrie, Jameson, or any of the Crew find out we're secretly married. I'm hiding in my hoard of movies like the film dragon I am.

I attempt to shut my mind off from everything, closing my eyes as I inhale Leo's warm, spicey scent. I clutch his hand, feeling his breath brush over my skin. His lips press softly against my cheek, then my neck as I hum at the contact. My hand glides over his chest, moving it up to his nape and into his hair. Leo then brings his lips to mine, kissing deeply.

"Check in," he murmurs against my lips.

"Green."

Leo wraps my legs around his waist, picking me up to walk us into the bedroom. I hold on tightly as he continues to kiss me with a bruising force, having him this close lights a fire inside me.

A hand grips my ass a bit harder than usual, and I gasp into his mouth. He takes the response to squeeze again, grinding me against him in the process. My breathing picks up as the heat in my stomach flourishes, coiling deep and down into my legs.

Leo lays me across the bed, sliding his hands up and under my sweater to begin taking it off. He kisses my jaw, down along my neck after he does, leaving me only in my sweatpants. His hands move down to remove my pants next with fingers brushing lightly over my skin. My breath hitches as my hips involuntarily kick up.

"You're very responsive today," he whispers, kissing the middle of my chest and then each of my breasts. Hot breath encases my nipples, making me wiggle under him with a groan at the warm sensation that causes tingles down to the apex of my thighs. "I absolutely adore it."

Leo's voice is rough, causing another shiver to wreck my body. His breath drifts over my skin, playing along my breast. His hand skims under the hem of my underwear, teasing.

My muscles tighten. Hips bucking slightly, but Leo holds me down against the bed as he continues to lavish my breasts. An odd sensation travels up my spine. Momentarily I'm brought out of the moment as my heart rate picks up, sudden worry slinking in. Leo moves his hand over my hips, gently caressing my skin as he sucks and twirls his tongue around my nipple. I reach to grip his hair, holding onto him as my back arches more into his mouth.

Leo pulls back as I'm left panting for more. He removes his shirt quickly, nodding for me to take my underwear off. I sit up, yanking it off as he follows suit, and then goes to the bedside table to grab lube. I spin towards him, watching the tattoos on his body ripple. The edges of the demon wings reaching toward his hips, the flaming sword almost ablaze now as I stare at the ink. My gaze has moved down to one of the skulls near his tailbone when he turns around, and find him smirking at me. I almost blush staring up at him from the bed.

"Am I as interesting as your flowers?"

I bring my legs around as his climbs onto the bed. I say in a rough voice, "I think I'll take you over the flowers."

He slides his finger into me, and I grab his shoulders. I inhale sharply as he slowly thrusts, spreading the lube as he pushes another finger in. I bury my face into his shoulder as his hand moves up my leg, gripping my hip. The coiling inside me flares which makes me open my legs more. Leo kisses my neck, trailing his tongue up the curve of my throat to behind my ear. I gasp as he scissors his fingers, then circling his thumb over my clit gently. My legs start to shake as I grind against his hand, moaning against his shoulder when his fingers hook inside me. All of a sudden, he pulls out and sits between my legs. Leo lifts me to straddle him, guiding his cock into me.

My legs shake as he fills me until I'm fully seated. He lets out a long groan, clutching my ass harshly as he grinds up into me. Leo thrusts upward, causing my breath to hitch and whimper at the deepening of his cock, stroking my inner walls. He raises his hips, then brings me back down as I make another sound of need.

I lift up, bringing myself back down onto him hard. I go to move again, but Leo grasps onto me, keeping me pressed down against him as he grinds into me. The groan of pleasure is loud as he squeezes my ass unforgivingly. The odd sensation comes back, flicking up my spine that makes my muscles clench. My body shakes as the lusting heat starts to vanish.

It's like my chest is constricting, making it hard to breathe as I dig my nails into Leo's shoulders. I grip onto him, clenching my jaw as he lifts me to slam back down upon him.

Suddenly the pleasure is gone, only filled with terror. It strikes through me like lightning as I gasp. My mind spirals to dark places as I try to stay in the moment, hope it stops. Until Leo lifts me again, fear trickling up my spine at the idea of another panic attack. A part of my brain tells me to get through it, keep quiet, it'll be over soon. Go numb.

Shut your eyes.

Deal with it.

No.

"Red," I plead in a broken whisper.

Leo stops.

Quickly, he pulls out of me, placing me on the bed as he pulls the blanket over me. He clutches my face, trying to give me space from the rest of him. I tremble as tears form in my eyes as I struggle not to sob.

"Are you hurt? Autumn?" He asks. I shake my head. "You're safe, breathe," he murmurs, rubbing his thumbs over my skin.

The softness of his voice makes me whimper and I can't help the old responses as they pour out of me. "I'm sorry. I'm sorry…I don't know—"

"Shh, it's alright."

I can't stop the tears, hating that this came out of nowhere. We weren't doing anything different. No new positions, no stupid walls, it was fine! I pull my knees in close as Leo continues trying to soothe me.

"Autumn—"

"Everything was fine…I'm sorry, I don't—"

"Good girl." I hiccup through a sob, looking up at him as he cups my face. "Good girl for calling red." My chin quivers. "You did exactly what you were supposed to do. I'm so proud of you for calling red."

My mouth works as I try to figure out words.

"Autumn, no matter what, I want you to call for help if you need it. To stop." I nod a little. Leo places more of the blanket over me. "Do you need me to touch you?"

I can only nod my head. He pulls me against his body, keeping me wrapped in the blanket as he cradles my head against his chest.

"We're not going to continue, we'll try in a day or so at the earliest," he murmurs, continuing to rub my back. "Your body said no, there's nothing wrong with that. Nothing for you to overcome or prove. I'm not going anywhere."

I shiver. "I don't...don't want to be a burden. For you to keep taking care of me."

Leo lays a kiss against my hair. "I will never tire of taking care of you, sweetheart. Knowing I'm the one who cares for you, loves you, and protects you gives me purpose. You'll never be a burden or too much."

I nod, burrowing closer to him as he holds me close. The silence stretches on until the trembling stops and my chest doesn't feel like it weighs a hundred pounds. Leo kisses my head and instructs gently, "Stay here."

He lets go of me, getting off the bed and heads into the bathroom. I keep an arm around my knees, holding them tight against my chest.

"Son of a nutcracker," I mutter.

The shower turns on and Leo comes back to gently take my ring off, placing it on the bedside table.

"Come here." I move for him to pick me up, leaving the blanket behind. "Good girl."

Leo carries me into the bathroom, walking us into the shower, and setting me down to stand under the warm spray. I let out a sigh as it pours over me, leaning my head back as I inhale deeply. Leo remains behind me, running a washcloth down my back.

"Feeling better?" He asks.

"Yeah." He kisses the top of my head, continuing to wash my back in slow circles.

Leo takes his time as the hot water pours over us. Each passing moment it's easier to breathe and the bricks in my chest disappear. He turns me around, keeping my head tilted back as he starts to wash my hair. I stare up at him, noticing the furrow in his brows as he concentrates not to get soap in my eyes, rinsing the shampoo and conditioner out. While watching him, I recall the book titles Dr. Maxwell gave me and prior conversations with Leo.

Maybe they're both onto something. I also want a distraction that isn't entirely about panic attacks, societal politics, and secrets.

"Hey, Leo?"

"Yes, dear Watson?" I smile at his response, and he gives me a smirk. "What?"

"Is this...more of what you meant about being a soft Dom?" Leo goes still, and his smirk falls away. "I haven't done much research into the BDSM world, that's on me, but you said taking care of me gave you purpose. Guessing it also plays into how you always, well, handle me."

Leo clears his throat, concentrating on rinsing my hair. Once he finishes, he grabs the washcloth again and answers, "Yes, at least something reminiscent of it."

"It's *not* the same?"

He begins to wash my front, trailing the soft cloth over my skin. "We're in a relationship, and any good relationship functions best with communication and trust. Except, we're not in a specific dynamic for me to say I have been your...Dom. I've only used pieces of what that particular relationship could be. Does that make sense?"

I grab the washcloth from him, then the soap. "What does entail for that kind of relationship?"

"First, would be the consent of the wants of the parties involved, and agreement of the functions within that relationship." I purse my lips, nodding along, somewhat understanding what he's talking about. I move to start washing his chest, but he stops me and gently clutches my wrists. He guides my head to look up at him. "Meaning, you have to agree to being my Sub, which can entail giving me full control in certain scenarios. You'll still have your safe words, but it takes a different amount of trust, especially if you fall into subspace."

"Subspace?"

He nods, letting go of my wrists. I go back to washing his chest.

"Subspace is when the submissive goes into a particular mindset during a scene, not necessarily sex," he explains. "For some it's the goal to reach; for others it's not. It's different for everyone, but it's a type of euphoria."

"Okay, maybe I definitely need to research more," I mumble, trying to remember where I put that paper of book titles. I'm gonna need them. I turn Leo around to wash his back next, stepping further into the water. "Isn't that, well, orgasming? Or am I missing something?"

"You know the feeling you get while dancing? Or riding the Harley's with me?"

"Losing me."

"The moments like your favorite dance with a partner you enjoy and have a connection with. The rides where it feels like the world falls away, all that exists is you and the bike. Like this sudden feeling of floating or letting go."

I pause, remembering our first rumba or the morning rides he and I took. "Yeah."

"Similar to that. You feel everything at once, and at such a state will be willing to do anything to stay there. It can be extremely emotional in various ways. Some need help out of it, and others may even forget to use their safe words if a scene involves impact play or other harsher elements."

"So, someone who's being whipped can go into subspace too far?"

"They won't notice if they're bleeding or having pain that's beyond their threshold." My breath hitches, and I blink quickly. That sounds dangerous. "It's not always like that, most Subs are able to call a safe word to stop, if need be, but that's the trust you place in your Dom. They'll know when to stop even before a Sub may know, avoiding that from happening in the first place. The goal should never be to get someone to say their safe word. That's someone being a fucking unresponsible sadist."

"If that could happen, why want to go into subspace?"

Leo turns around, taking the washcloth back. "It's a release for many, giving up control and letting go. Subspace for some, brings them safety, knowing they'll be taken care of. There's a blissful feeling you can achieve and a freedom that comes with it, even for those who get tied up or bruised. It's a different form of control and release."

"Aren't you giving up that control?"

"Not entirely, you're just *trusting* those involved to give you what you need and want. A power exchange." He puts the washcloth away.

Alright those words make more sense. Leo goes to rinse the water off him as I contemplate what he said. "What does a soft Dom entail then?"

He pauses a moment, brushing the water down his head and over his shoulders.

"Soft Doms focus on leading scenes through praise, encouragement, and reward. We take a more comforting approach in dominance. Whereas stricter Doms are those who express dominance through more severe forms of control. A strict regime that gives a Sub security in their submission. Rules to follow is a common way. They're two sides to a coin. Some Subs need punishment, something that helps them take back control or wipe the slate clean. Others find freedom through degradation, having an environment that's safe to do so. And then there's Subs who need praise; to be given encouragement through a scene without feeling embarrassment or shame."

I run my hands over my arms, thinking. I understand that need for praise, to not feel like I'm wrong or a disappointment. Fuck, it happened almost twenty minutes ago. Before him, it's all I ever seemed to feel, not just with sex. Huh. A few more little things click in place when Leo's voice pulls me back to reality.

"Autumn." I find him tilting his head, arm poised up as he rinses his hair. "Do you want to be my Sub? Is that why you're asking?"

My eyes widen as I blink quickly. Leo turns off the water. "You don't have to answer—"

"What would change?" I blurt. He stops, furrowing his brow. "I mean...I don't, well, Okay I'm gonna start rambling soon."

I put my hand over my face, about to scrub at it like we just started the shower. We took the bigger step of marriage in secret a day ago, how could this be more nerve-wracking?

Leo guides me out of the shower, pulling my hand down as he grabs a towel to wrap around me and then one around his waist. He uses a smaller towel to carefully dry my hair.

"I'd walk you through everything," he explains. "I don't want a 24/7 dynamic, so we'd only scene when we both agree. Preference of where could be negotiated, meaning only here or at the hotel. I could reserve a suite only for that." I blink under the towel, surprised and yet not for how much thought he's already put into this. "Hard limits won't change, unless discussed to become soft limits. Behaviors and certain honorifics would also remain only in scene, as I said I don't want a 24/7 dynamic."

"Don't we kinda, sometimes do that?" I giggle suddenly when the towel tickles the back of my neck. Leo pulls it away and I suck my lips in to stop giggling. He smiles and I release my lips to smile back.

"We'd use different honorifics while in a scene, along with other aspects. It's important to have those lines drawn to not overstep those power exchanges. If lines are crossed during or outside of it, we'll talk. Lastly, there would be aftercare delegated for both of us."

All of that actually sounds, well, nice.

Hazel eyes meet mine, and I already know my answer. Never thought I'd be willing to try BDSM, I've mostly known just the harder side of it before him. Those parts of it never appealed to me. What Leo is suggesting, whilst saying what he prefers, too...we sound like a pretty good match.

"Okay," I answer.

"Okay?"

"I'd like to be your Sub." His expression softens, the lines above his brows disappearing. "Or should I say I want to? Or do I ask? You did mean being your Sub, right? Cause I'm not sharing—Leo!"

He picks me up suddenly as I screech, flinging my arms around his shoulders as he walks us out of the bathroom. A giggle comes out of me again as he kisses my neck.

"Have I told you how perfect you are?"

"Not today," I smirk.

"You are perfect."

"Cause I said yes?" Thrice in like four days, his record is solid.

He sits us down in the living room, clutching my face as he kisses me deeply like I'm oxygen for him, making my own breath hitch. Finally, he says against my lips, "Because of how much you trust me to try new things, especially after what just happened."

"That's kind of why." Leo brushes my damp air back, brows furrowing in question. I whisper, "You stopped."

I lay my head against his shoulder as he hugs me tight.

"It's easier to be brave when I know you'll catch me," I say.

"Always, my dear Watson."

Chapter 18

PR and the City

Ow are they still arguing?

I glance at the clock. Twenty minutes. I wonder if Leo and I could escape without being noticed. I whisper to Leo, "Could this be an enemies to lovers thing?"

We sit in the first-floor office of the *Italian Lily*. Leo's arm is draped over my shoulders, while the other holds a glass of scotch. It's almost one but we've been on this couch in a meeting with Carrie and Jameson since noon. More like a furious debate.

What I wouldn't give to be back in the penthouse, discussing adding a BDSM dynamic to our relationship. Unfortunately, Jameson practically threatened Leo to get here before he strangled Carrie. I couldn't keep from laughing at how desperate Jameson sounded, and was roped into joining. We arrived just as Carrie almost threw a pen at Jameson, and now I see why they don't get along.

They disagree…a lot. Such as riding being a liability, but could draw in other clientele? Or drive them away? Not sure at this point.

"Not likely," Leo whispers, brushing back my hair. "Both are too good at their jobs, but I'm not about to let her go when she's the best out there."

I purse my lips in pretend thought. Leo places a tender kiss behind my ear. I stifle a giggle at the tiny gesture. I slightly shove him, but he holds me close and does it again.

"Leonardo." Carrie interrupts.

From the corner of my eye, I notice the faint curl of his lip and furrowed brows. Whelp, he's about to add to the colorful conversation that's been happening. I tease, "Busted."

Leo's expression softens as I grin at him. He gives a soft exhale, leaning back into the couch with an almost bored expression.

"Have you finally stopped arguing enough to have an *actual* conversation?" Leo questions bluntly.

Carrie stands straighter, practically pointing her nose in the air.

Oh, crud muffins. He just had to stir the pot.

Carrie Hayes is the complete opposite of me when it comes to looks—long curly blonde hair, tall, curvy fit, and a chest I'm not entirely she was born with. She's wearing a silk purple blouse with a tight pencil skirt and heels. Her blue eyes are sharp, lined with black while her lips were redder than Aurora's. She's practically a young Dolly Parton look-alike, city version.

"It would be smart to have you do a couple of interviews," she states.

"Never done them before, why have him start now?" Jameson asks.

"He was single. Now he's not."

"What does that have to do with anything, Carrie?" Leo asks.

"The public, that's what." She walks over to the desk, grabbing a paper and holds it up. "*Leonardo Luciano, who's built a hotel empire from the ground up...*"

I give Leo a look and he narrows his gaze at me. A giggle escapes as I try to cover my mouth to stifle it.

Carrie continues, seemingly ignoring us. "*... and well-known notorious bachelor, has done the remarkable of settling down. Although some would speculate that the self-made millionaire had chosen someone within his circle, his fiancé appears to be of the* normal sort."

"I'm normal?" I ask, attempting to hold back laughter. Leo struggles to keep his composure.

"If we could have some restraint, please?" Carrie asks, glancing at me.

"Not really in her vocabulary," Jameson comments. Can *I* throw a pen at him?

"This is one of the stories editors are wanting to print," Carrie says, holding up the paper. "They want a deep dive on you, of why now and what changed. Is it due to family obligations? Not to mention reporters on my phone asking about Ms. Watson and her pedigree or involvement with your business."

She did not just say pedigree like I'm some mutt.

"Carrie," Leo warns.

"Leonardo." She puts the paper down, leaning against the desk. "We both know how nosey the press can be. It took me *months* to keep them from hounding you for statements when you moved to New York and opened this hotel. Somehow, I was able to provide publicity for the *Italian Lily* that barely included you, due to your... reclusive nature. Over five years, they've scrambled for those exclusive interviews, in which you've allowed for *six* in that time. And now, the infamous, hotel mogul under 35 from California, multimillionaire is no longer single. He's *engaged*. People want to know who's made you turn a new leaf, and the more we hide—"

"How is announcing the engagement hiding?" I ask.

Carrie glares at me suddenly, and I kinda want to shrink into the couch.

Leo's hold tightens over my shoulders as he warns, "Fight with Jameson all you want, but I suggest you watch your tone and how you even look at my fiancé."

She flicks her gaze to him, and then points at him. "*That.* That is what we can use. The stoic millionaire and the sweet fiancé who balances him."

Okay, the woman has a spine of steel.

"They're not entertainment," Jameson argues. "It's a fucking engagement. You're trying to turn it into a fucking tv special."

"I have successfully kept him out of the spotlight for years," she argues. "I've helped his hotels garner five-star success, maintaining his pristine image across the United States *and* Europe. Not to mention doing this upkeep whilst he ignores parties, skips openings, and disregards interviews."

"What does—"

"I know what I'm doing," she practically seethes at Jameson. His jaw tightens, crossing his arms over his chest as he glares at her. "The least you all could do is give me *something* to make him relatable, especially if you have plans to open hotels after Boston, such as Denver or Chicago."

"The hotels are doing well enough to sell publicity on their own," Leo argues calmly. "We've surpassed needing me on most accounts, that was the whole goal eight years ago."

"Leonardo. Engaging new potential clientele is still crucial here. This image of 'cutthroat businessman and his sweet fiancé' makes good PR." Cutthroat is one way to put it. "Not to mention she has a relatable background, which can appeal to those wanting to splurge on a luxurious night at a Michelin starred hotel. We could break through another financial bracket."

"I think I'm gonna go," I say, standing up as Leo's arm falls from my shoulders.

There's a sinking feeling in my stomach. I don't mind being out in public with Leo but being made some prop bothers me. My background, no matter how fabricated, isn't for others to get a kick at for their own pleasure. Access to Leo's fortune now or in the future wouldn't matter to them. I'd still have an orphan fucking Annie story arc.

If Leo helped me walk away from the mob, then I'm walking away from this next.

Carrie and Jameson both go to say something as I leave, but Leo growls at them as he walks me to the door. He shuts the door loudly behind us, letting out a sigh.

We ask at the same time, "Check in."

I smirk as he gives a half-smile.

"Starting to see why I haven't met her before," I mutter.

"She's good, almost too good," he speaks low, peering down the empty hall. "She's been able to keep my name out of the wrong mouths; has strong connections, unbreakable work ethic, devious, and isn't afraid of me."

"One of the few times I wish someone was," I muse.

Leo straightens his jacket, but then stops and sighs, "I'm sorry you were subjected to those ideas."

"Not your fault for what I'm gonna be seen as," I say, crossing my arms. "Knew that long before the ring, I mean, remember our first conversations?"

The line over his brows softens. We smile. It seems forever since those days.

"Do you still have that first fifty I tipped you?"

I shake my head. "I may have...*tipped* Bailey with it on my last day." He furrows his brows again. "Don't worry about it."

I give him a sassy wink, and he smirks, gesturing for me to come forward. I move closer as he cups my cheek, then kisses me affectionately. I smile against his lips, running my hand up his chest. He breaks the kiss, adding another on my cheek.

"I'll take care of it, you go," he tells me.

"You sure? Kinda don't want to leave you alone with them."

"I've been dealing with them for quite some years, dear Watson. I know how to handle them, especially Carrie and her approach to PR."

I peek past him to the closed office door, then down the hallway before I whisper, "You know, I'm starting to understand your conniving planning, because getting married in secret may have been the sanest decision for us."

He smirks before kissing me again. "I'll likely be late, so we'll stay here tonight and through the weekend."

I step back, giving him a mock salute. He gives me a mischievous look, and I yelp as he reaches for me. I jump away, laughing as I jog down the hall, and glancing over my shoulder to notice his brief smile before he opens the door.

Just like that, a frown replaces it as he disappears into the office.

I shake my head, entering the main lobby. The place is somewhat busy with early-check-ins. I go to the desk, finding Oliver, who smiles as I approach and lean on the counter.

"Good afternoon, Miss Watson, how are you today?"

"Surprised you're here, usually you're working the late shift, apart from random early mornings. Thought afternoons were your kryptonite."

"Christmas season has started."

"Does the place get decorated for it?"

"Oh, completely. Mr. Luciano has us wait until the start of December before we begin playing the music. But decorators will be coming in this weekend."

"Ahh, that's exciting."

"Do you need anything?"

I freeze. I've no freaking clue.

Could go to the apartment to watch some movies, but been doing that a lot and I'm antsy. Leo could be really late, too. I think for a moment, debating what to do and an idea pops up.

"Is Chiari working today?"

"She's in her office."

"Oh, where is that?"

"The assistant manager office down the hall." I blink at Oliver, realizing I've never heard Chiari's title before. Did I miss it on her name tag?

"So, she doesn't just work the front desk?"

"Correct," he says. "She'll oversee the front desk at times."

Yeah, hotel hierarchy was not part of my college curriculum.

"Said down the hall?" I ask, glancing back to where I came.

He nods. "Down the hall, take a right, and you'll see a door on your left with her name on it."

"Thanks, Oliver." I give him a wave, following his instructions and come upon her office door. I knock, waiting a few seconds before it opens to reveal a grinning Chiari.

"Miss Watson, wasn't expecting you."

"Can we go with the first name basis? It's just us," I practically plead with a wince. "Already been called *Ms. Watson* too many times today."

Chiari places her hands on her hip. "Carrie?"

"You know her?"

"Unfortunately," she mutters, gesturing for me to enter.

Her office is filled with dark colors of greens and browns. There's shelving labeled for ledgers and binders. Her desk has a couple chairs sitting in front and she has a small wet bar and loveseat. Pictures of orchards cover her walls, and there's a bonsai tree on her desk, which entices me to go inspect the tiny thing.

"I think we have similar impressions of her," I say, tracing a finger daintily over a branch. Chiari leans against her desk as I look up at her, stepping back quickly. "Ah, crud muffins, probably shouldn't touch, sorry."

"You're fine, just be careful with the branches." I go back to looking at the tiny tree. "I rarely interact with Ms. Hayes. I usually only need to when...*hiding* information about Mr. Luciano's businesses."

Something tells me if Carrie knew Leo was a mafia boss, she wouldn't change tactics. She'd be worse.

"If you and Jameson don't like her, yet Leo keeps her hired, she's gotta be good."

"You've no idea. She's stubborn. Her way or the highway, but with her skills and connections, finger on the pulse of society, he'd be an idiot to hire anyone else."

"How often should I expect to be around her?"

"Rarely, she travels a lot. Most of her time is spent in California, where his hotel franchise headquarters is located. The original, first hotel is the *Four Seasons* of the west."

"What's that one called?" Leaving the cute bonsai tree alone, I sit in the loveseat.

"The *California Rose*. My favorite room is the *Matilija Ballroom*. It's gorgeous."

I'm starting to think he likes flowers more than he's letting on.

"Water?" She asks, and I nod.

"You worked here before it became the *Italian Lily*, right?"

Chiari hands me the water, sitting beside me. "Right. The name changed and most of the inner workings of the hotel shifted, too, away from a traditional hotel system when he bought it."

I go to drink some of the water, but freeze. "I'm not keeping you from work, am I?"

She waves it off. "I could use the break, skipped lunch again. You're better company than paperwork."

"You're better company than the squabbling Musketeers," I mumble.

She chuckles, and then gestures to see my hand. I hold it out for her to inspect the ring, tilting her head in appreciation. Thankfully she says nothing of the faint bruising still there from the day before. "Man always had good taste. Emerald suits you."

"Thanks."

"Well, I want to avoid paperwork and you want to avoid Carrie, how about I officially show you the hotel?" I raise my brows. "If you're interested, of course. Unless you'd rather do another *run through* of it."

Well, isn't she cheeky?

I smirk with a small wince. "Oof got me there. Sure."

"I'll introduce you to those who've been given certain directives about your presence here," she says, getting up. I give her a questioning look. "He was particular that every manager knows who *you* are."

"Every manager?" She shrugs as I stand up, putting my water down. "Does that mean…um, do they know what happens at the… top of the tower?"

Chiari walks over to grab her blazer, pulling it over her burnt orange blouse. "A select few do, including hand-picked cleaning staff and security. Only those who help maintain the top floors and the apartment know who he is outside of ownership of the hotel."

"Do they know he usually lives here, too?"

"A select few, including the *last* head manager of the hotel," she answers, heading for the door.

"Last one meaning?"

She pauses at the door. "The day you…took some vacation?" I clear my throat and nod. "The head manager was fired for reasons outside of the hotel."

I should not be prying. I know that tone, and there's no way she's *not* referencing the part of Leo's life I agreed to step away from. Except I can't help asking, "Such as?"

Her faced becomes filled with concentration.

I think of attempting to take it back. Remain "oblivious" of that side.

"The manager was using the kitchen to smuggle drugs and other items, if you get my drift. I'm certain he endured most of the frustration Mr. Luciano was feeling when you were gone before he was removed of his position."

Yup, don't need that translation or imagination to know what happened.

"So, no one's replaced him yet?"

"Currently, I am, temporarily along with other duties, while Oliver oversees the front desk and other logistics. The next general manager for the hotel will have to be aware of *all* businesses involved and have a full background check."

"Why not solely you for it?"

"Then we'd have to find someone with the same criteria for my position," she answers, opening the door with a smirk.

"Well, if you want it, I'll put in a good word for you. I know the owner." I wink at her, and she laughs as we walk out. "In the meantime, off to the castle workings!"

I've never craved to be called just "Autumn" so much in my life until today.

After twelve maids, two managers, and three cooks "Ms.

Watsoned" me I gave up attempting to correct them. Their perplexed looks told me this was gonna be a long battle. Chiari kept a calm demeanor the entire time, but at times she'd give *that* commanding look. Got to admit, the woman can be scary. So, I'm just letting them call me whatever.

Chiari showed me where the storage areas are, discreetly pointing out exits and passages for future needs. I note them all, memorizing as we approach the main area for housekeeping. I glance over everything, noticing the cleanliness, yet the tiny dishevelment which reminds me of *Blue Java*. A slight tug of sadness pulls at me, missing those simpler days.

Fuck, I kinda miss working.

"Ms. Pierozzi, visitors are not allowed—"

"Grant, this is Ms. Watson," Chiari interrupts a man approaching us. "She's Mr. Luciano's fiancé, who I thought could see the hotel in its entirety."

The man, who seems to be in his early fifties with graying hair swept back, matching the stubble on his jaw, stops. Grey eyes flit to mine as he purses his lips, and then straightens his jacket and clears his throat. He's about as tall as Animal, but a bit heavier set. I recognize him from around the hotel. There've been a lot of people I've seen glimpses of but have never gotten to meet. Grant gives me a tight smile.

"Ms. Watson. Of course." He nods briefly.

"Grant is the head butler for a number of floors and suites, including being in charge of the cleaning staff for Mr. Luciano's apartment here." Chiari explains succinctly.

"Oh." I give him a warm smile, but he only looks more perturbed. He gives a small glance over my attire. I clear my throat, continuing to smile. "Well, thank you for helping keep the penthouse tidy. I'd do it, but Leo won't even show me where the broom is."

"That is because it does not have one," Grant says in a rough voice.

"There goes my idea to revive *Bed Knobs and Broomsticks* in the living room." Not only does he not laugh, but his smile disappears. Ok, it was not *that* niche of a joke! "It's a joke."

"Yes, I understand that." I steal a glance at Chiari. "The care and cleanliness of Mr. Luciano's personal space is not of your concern or yours to tarry over. If there are any changes that must be made to accommodate you, then you'll need to take it up—"

"Hold on, that's not what I'm saying," I interrupt, holding up my hand to emphasize. His eyes go wide. I could allow him to lecture me about his importance, along with others' jobs, but I'm already worn out for the day. I'm not up for this 'this is how things are done' spiel.

"That apartment is practically perfect. I'm not asking to do someone's job, I was joking. Not complaining." His face is a mask of neutrality. "Truly, Grant. I just wanted to see more of the hotel today; learn how it functions and meet some staff since I haven't really. I promise you I won't get in your way."

Suddenly, his eyes go extremely wide. Chiari peers around me and her breath catches.

"Correction, my fiancé will *never* be in the way because she will do as she pleases in *my* hotel."

Son of a biscuit. Who snitched on where I was?

I turn to see Leo approach us, Owen directly behind. I can practically feel Grant shaking in his shoes behind me, while Chiari has gone rigid. Given what Grant takes care of, he knows *exactly* who Leo is. Lately, anyone who's bad-mouthed me has gotten a warning or kick in the teeth. Thing with service industry, news travels fast. Fine, Mila had a small point.

Leo's signature furrowed brow is on display, along with tense jaw and commanding presence. Owen remains pokerfaced; Leo's doing enough for the menacing department.

"My apologies, sir," Grant speaks. "Of course, I would never insinuate that she—"

"Good. I'd hate to replace one of my head butlers after the last few managers we've lost recently," Leo interrupts, stopping next to me. His eyes darken as he scowls at the man, who may be trembling in his spats. "Shouldn't it be time for you to oversee said apartment cleaning, along with other rooms? Or shall I suggest a change in position in *my* hotel, Mr. Wadsworth?"

"No, sir. Have a wonderful afternoon, including yourself Ms. Watson." Grant bows his head briefly, then swiftly leaves the maid quarters.

I glance up at Leo, giving him a slight exasperated look. He barely changes from the stony look he wears, which tells me the meeting with Carrie didn't go well. Still, did he have to scare away the butler?

"I will not tolerate any disrespect toward you from *any* staff of mine," Leo says suddenly, in a very cold, numbing tone.

I stare at him, a warning ticking at the back of my neck. Not at Leo, but that something else may have happened aside from the meeting with Carrie. I cross my arms over my chest, tilting my head. "I don't think he was being disrespectful, Leo."

"Chiari told him who you were, yet he still took a tone with you that was condescending. Once informed who you are, should be enough without—"

"Except it's not," I argue.

He's far from the tiny playful mood he was in earlier, so arguing with him may not be the best of ideas. Except, I can't have him demanding respect for me. None of the staff will trust me. He can lay a wall down between me and the mob, but not the hotel. He can't take the same approach as he would as a mafia boss…right?

Leo starts again, "I am the owner—"

"And I'm just the *fiancé*," I interrupt again, emphasizing the word with a raised brow. There're hushed tones in the hallway, and I peek over to Owen, who gives me a reassuring look as he keeps people away. "Leo, they don't know me apart from that title, and I don't want to automatically have their respect because of it. Or because they *have* to. I'll earn it. This isn't like what Carrie was suggesting. They're your employees, who have no reason to just accept me cause of a ring on my finger, and I won't expect them to."

Leo scowls with muscles ticking along his jaw. He snaps a glare to Chiari and Owen when there's a cough, nodding once at the other hallway. Without another sound, they leave us completely.

Something in me shudders at the demand. I see the mafia boss before me again, covered in blood and terrifying expression. The rigid callous look on his face.

My mind is trying to catch up on why the change from a couple of hours ago. I'm wrangled by thoughts as he brings his attention back to me, distracted by his strict demeanor and harsh tone I forget where I am for a moment. A brief glimpse of the past—Steve yelling at me, to stop being irrational. As memories shift, Leo raises his hand.

I flinch.

My body jolts, eyes squeezing shut as I instinctively wait for the stinging pain. I let out a sharp exhale, remembering where I am and open my eyes to see his widened gaze. The scowl is long gone. Any hardness before has vanished and replaced by horror.

"Autumn—"

"Sorry, I flashbacked...remembered, fuck..." I put my hand over my face, focusing to not start hyperventilating next, "...I forgot where I was."

I'm met with silence. A few more grounding breaths, I finally pull my hand down to look at him. He's taken a step back. His hands are glued to his sides as he stares at me with...fear. There's legitimate fear in his eyes. And then I watch as his mask, that stone, cold mask cover his face.

"Leo."

"You're right. I shouldn't demand respect from others for you. I overstepped. Your relationships within the Crew are yours to develop, so should it be with the staff here." His voice is distant. My chest squeezes at the sound, hating it as he starts to withdraw into himself. He clears his throat, averting his gaze as he glances at his hands. "I'll leave you to finish and shall see you tonight."

Oh, no he fucking *doesn't*. If I can't run away, neither can he.

Leo turns away, but I quickly grab his arm and he stiffens.

"Don't you dare walk off on me," I rasp in an almost broken

whisper. His gaze is still averted, but he doesn't move. "I flashed back, that's all. You didn't hurt me. Please do not walk away because you may think…well, I don't know what you're thinking, but don't walk away. Please."

He remains silent. There's muttering in the hallway, footsteps, and a door closing. The tightening feeling in my chest worsens, and I grip him tighter.

"Please talk to me," I whisper faintly.

He squeezes his eyes shut. Finally, he says, "I triggered you."

"Not on purpose. It's okay."

"No. No, it's not. I promised I'd never hurt you, in *any* manner."

"Leo, you're human who gets to make mistakes. Do you blame yourself for this morning, too?" He doesn't say anything.

I scramble in my brain as to why this shook him. He seemed composed this morning, even during times I've safe worded before or had a panic attack. Why was this different?

I let out a long sigh, moving in front him and placing my hand on his chest. "Leo, look at me. Please."

With that gentle command, he does as I ask, and I can see the shadows that haunt his eyes. Sadness or guilt, I'm not sure, but it makes my stomach plummet. I reach up and place my hand against his jaw. He shudders, finally unclenching his jaw.

"It's okay. You didn't do it on purpose, otherwise *that* would be the issue," I say softly. "We both know triggers can come out of nowhere in the oddest places, even when things seem fine, right?" His breathing is shallow, watching me with anguished hazel eyes. I rub my thumb over his skin. "You're not them, Leo." His breath hitches. "You'd never intentionally hurt me, I know that. You were just being 'scary Leo' which threw me for a loop is all."

"*Scary* Leo?" He finally speaks.

"It's your…bossy side." I shrug.

"Bossy side?"

"You keep asking questions like this is new." I smirk, trying to get the hurt in his eyes to leave. He just continues to remain stiff, staring at me with trepidation. I sigh again, wrapping my arm around his torso and slide my other hand down his jaw to the side of his neck.

"I love you, Leo," I whisper. "You are my husband, and I trust you. You're not them."

After a few moments pass, he finally moves and strokes my cheek with a shaky hand. I lean into his touch, feeling the rigidness in his body ease. He breathes more deeply and embraces me, hugging me tight.

"Meeting not go well?" He makes a sound of disgruntlement. I hug him tighter. "Okay, don't have to talk about it."

Carrie didn't *actually* suggest a TV special, did she?

I rub my hands across his back, feeling him relax under my touch. He pulls away slightly, kissing me tenderly. I return the affectionate gesture, trying to convey I'm okay.

"I love you, my dear Watson," he whispers. "I was angry and frustrated, then almost took it out on you and Grant."

"It happens." I rub his chest a little, giving a small smile. "If you're ever angry cause of something else, just tell me. Or if you need space, a laugh, or me not arguing in front of others making it worse."

"Autumn, I was being a cold-hearted asshole."

"Hey, mister no name calling." I point at his face. Almost a smile. "Look, I appreciate you standing up for my place here but give me a chance to jab my own zingers and earn being annoying to them."

"Was that your plan?"

"I was thinking about it." I pat his chest. "But seriously, you really don't need to scare the crap out of people because of me."

"Even Carrie?" I pause, and he raises a brow.

"I'm thinking." He snorts a laugh, which I take as a win. "How about whoever may worry about losing their job?" Given what Chiari told me, not just being fired.

"Are you saying Grant…" I give him a sympathetic look, and he sighs, looking to where he disappeared, "…I'll assure him later he hasn't lost his job."

I go to step back, but Leo won't let me budge. I give him a look, before he reluctantly releases me, but keeps his hand in mine. I ask finally, "So, who told you I was snooping through the halls like McCallister lost in New York?"

"Isaac." Should've known it was my shadow. "What else did I interrupt?"

"Not much, I think Chiari was going to show me the laundry area next."

He clears his throat, then kisses my left hand quickly. "I'll leave you be then."

"Back to work?"

"Meetings this evening and later," he answers with eyes telling me what kind. Different kind of PR I guess.

"If not until later, why not join us? It is your hotel." I squeeze his hand.

"Dear Watson, if you want the staff to be themselves, it may be best if I'm not around. We both know transparency around the owner or who holds their paychecks is…rare."

"Look, you may have your scary moments, but you're still a good boss. Got others to attest it." I begin to lead him to the hall. He goes to say something, until I call over Chiari and Owen and wave at them as if our argument never happened. "Sorry, we had to discuss something. Good to finish the tour, and Leo will be your secondary guide." I glance at Owen, who smirks. "Owen's final backup."

"Well, I think all that's left down here is the laundry area and then we can venture to the shops of the hotel, including the café," Chiari answers. She starts down the hall and I follow with Leo close, my hand clamped around his.

We're about to pass through a door when there's a shout. We stop, looking back to see Jameson and Julio. Well, crud, I know *that* look.

Leo nods at them once, gesturing for Owen to go ahead. He walks away as Chiari gives us space. Leo exhales sharply, "Might be for the best. I'll see you tonight."

He kisses my cheek, but that frustrated, partially exhausted look on his face worries me. I quickly hug him tightly and whisper, "Check in."

Leo stiffens, then answers, "Yellow, but I'll be fine."

Before I can protest, Leo steps away and stalks toward the others. His entire body shifts into that stern persona as he disappears with the Crew. I'm beginning to think this week may be cursed. Or maybe a mirror I broke seven years ago is coming back to haunt me. Probably, several mirrors at this point.

"Autumn?" Chiari asks. I shake my head, giving her a weak smile. "We all have off days, even him."

"Yeah," I mutter as I follow her through the door. "Are people *actually* scared of him?"

"I think only those who know him...personally, are wary. I believe for the others it's just jitters from being around the boss, you know? Did you ever meet the owner of *Blue Java*?"

"No, they don't live in the state. But I see what you're getting at...even him." I decide to let it go, allowing her to show me the laundry area. It's fucking huge as she shows the setups, beginning to turn us around to head back upstairs. I stop abruptly when I see an area filled with bins of sheets, blankets, and pillows that seem clean but aren't with those folded on the way to be redistributed to the rooms.

"What's that? Extra?"

"Oh, those are linens that have been recently replaced. We have a policy of replacing linens every year, and anything that's been torn or doesn't meet standards."

"You do this every year?" Here I was using the same blanket for over five.

"Luxury Hotel, Autumn," she says smoothly. "When linens are used by multiple people through the year, washed, and bleached they become very worn. We can't have such linens, so we regularly replace them."

"What do you do with the old linen?" I gesture toward the bins and bins of them.

"Mr. Luciano has a policy to recycle everything as much as possible in the hotel. All his hotels do, which includes those."

I stare at everything piled, waiting to be taken away. Well, I guess that's good and less waste. Yet, something tugs at me. That's a lot of usable blankets.

"How many rooms does the *Italian Lily* have?"

"285, not including the apartment."

I hum as gears turn in my head. "Does it matter what happens to them? Like do they *have* to go to the recycling center?"

"Not under contract to do so. Why?" She glances at the laundry.

"I may have an idea for a new policy."

Chapter 19

Hot Linens Off the Press

I went to bed alone.

Around dinner, I received a message from Owen that Leo left the hotel late, so I went to the *Giglio Giardino* for dinner. Christopher was delighted to see me, constantly checking on me as I chatted with my waiters, Lincoln and Tyler. They kept me entertained until I was back in the apartment, in bed alone, hating it.

For years I was used to it, but now it sucked.

I drifted to sleep, hugging one of the pillows close. In the middle of the night, I feel the blankets get pulled back and the pillow taken from my arms.

"Leo?" I ask muffled.

"Go back to sleep, sweetheart." He quietly maneuvers me, adjusting me to lay across his chest as he pulls blankets back over us. His hands caress my back, traveling over my limbs as if he's checking that I'm real. A kiss is placed on my head as I begin to drift again.

The steady beat of his heart is the last thing I hear before I fall asleep.

Elm Jed

I wake up alone.

I sit up stiffly, glancing at the empty space where Leo was last night. I rub my eyes, and then find a note on the bedside table, recognizing his handwriting.

I apologize for missing dinner and breakfast. I'll see you soon, dear Watson. Love, Leo.

A sharp exhale leaves me as I put the note back, then place my ring on. I smile at the shimmering emerald, until I hear a clatter from the kitchen. Gotta be Pretty Boy Bond.

I get out of bed, pulling on some fuzzy socks before I head out to the living room. Yup, there's Isaac at the stove, flipping pancakes and listening to what I think is police chatter or a very, *very* boring podcast. After a few seconds, I realize it's a boring podcast.

"We should talk about your choices of background noise," I say, circling my finger at the scene.

He turns, smirking as he grabs a mug, fills it with coffee, and places it on the counter for me next to the sugar. I purse my lips, sitting down as I watch him plate a couple of pancakes.

"Y'all know I can fend for myself for food, right?" I ask as Isaac turns off his podcast, and then places a cup of juice with the plate of pancakes in front of me.

"Yes." His short reply makes me snort. "But I volunteered as tribute, because..." his voice trails off as he places maple syrup in front of me, "...we both have a sweet tooth."

I grin widely, pouring the syrup onto the pancakes and start eating.

After a few bites, I ask, "So, do I wait until after a cup of coffee to ask where Leo is? Or is this a morning where I don't ask?"

Isaac leans against the stove, holding his own mug while giving me a not so innocent expression.

"You've given me maple syrup, just give me the spark notes."

He gives me a sympathetic look before explaining. "There were issues last night, he'll be dealing with it all day, on top of other meetings held off because of Thanksgiving."

"It's Saturday." Another sympathetic look. Right, doesn't matter.

"He won't be at the hotel, right now he's..." he checks his watch, "...at the shipping docks."

"The docks?" My throat suddenly tightens before I stave off the old feelings. "That means it's..."

"Yes."

I nod my head, sighing as I distract myself with a bite of pancake. Pretty good, but I'm biased in liking Leo's more. "Can I ask how dangerous it is? Or would that be going against the whole...staying away from it thing?"

"I think you're allowed to ask about his well-being, no matter what the circumstance," he says softly. "He's not in danger."

"Except it's the mob."

"Yes, but this situation is low profile. The work at the moment is tedious, requiring his presence to maintain a tight leash on a handful of underbosses and territories."

That's enough inquiring about the mafia, I've hit my quota.

"Apart from that, how busy is he going to be?"

"I won't lie to you Miss Autumn."

"Great start," I say deadpan.

He smirks. "He'll likely be busy until Christmas, and into the New Year. Most of the Crew will be, too. I'm rarely at the hotel during this time of year. Between the holidays, end of year business transactions, change over from the fiscal year, and the winter season coming it causes feathers to be ruffled. A bit more than usual due to him disappearing upstate for those few weeks."

My gaze meets his blue gaze for a moment.

"It's not your fault," he quickly says. "I just mean to explain why he may be gone."

"I know." I take a deep breath, scratching my head. "Just sucks. I've not been one for Christmas or whatever, but was kind of hoping to get into the spirit this year."

It felt like I finally had a reason.

I sigh, looking down at my coffee. It's a month away, but my odds are not looking good. With friends traveling and Nan basically being gone all of December while the bookstore is renovated, I'm looking at another lonely winter holiday. Well, damn.

"I'm sorry," Isaac says.

"Not your fault."

"Sentiment remains. Apart from the upcoming Christmas season, being separated after recently getting engaged cannot be a good feeling."

I stare at the ring on my finger. My chest tightens, wanting Leo here for ten minutes of breakfast together. Five minutes. Anything. Hopefully tomorrow we'll get that bit of time.

"So," I clear my throat. "What are the rounds today? You this morning and then Chesty or Animal later? Or shaking it up with Ringer?"

"As I said the rest of the Crew will be unavailable."

"Meaning?"

"Throughout the day I'll be with you, unless you want privacy. Hotel security will be on call for the evenings. Or me if you want. If you wish to leave the hotel, I'll arrange for one of the Crew or a security team member to come along." I raise my brows. "I was told you met some of the men in the garage the day Steve attacked you, a few have passed security checks."

Alrighty then.

"This is cause we disappeared, isn't?"

"Can't say it was all Leo's idea for your personal protection detail."

Jameson's not fooling around, huh? Well, after the past week guess I can't fully blame him or Leo. Or Jameson's proving a point.

Holy shit the past week. Been to a charity gala, got engaged, secretly married, almost kidnapped, had thanksgiving, PR fiasco, and sprinkle in anxiety and panic attacks. I've got a full-on villain origin story fit for Arkham. Here's hoping the week of Christmas doesn't involve the Grinch stealing presents.

"I can talk to him or Jameson if none of that sits well with you," Isaac says.

"No, none of this is surprising. I knew what I was getting into, including him being busy. I just had a job and all to keep *me* busy. But I'll keep you updated on the emotional scale of things. Guess it's back to you and me again, Pretty Boy Bond."

Isaac grins, sipping his drink as I eat a bit more of the breakfast he made.

"It's still early, and it won't be hard to grab more security if you'd like to leave the hotel, although it's advised to stay. But is there anything you'd like to do?"

"Well, I have an idea and we get to stay in the hotel, so less work for you," I say, pointing at him with a pancake filled fork. "This idea may even keep me busy for a bit." Isaac pauses, staring at me in confusion. "I'm not gonna ask you take over the world Pinkie, calm down."

He waves his hand for me to continue.

"I want to slightly change policy on old linens and towels at the hotel." Isaac tilts his head in question. "Leo recycles mostly everything here, but I think there's a way to be more helpful. Not to mention..." I quickly get up, grabbing my new laptop and open it, "...I did some research."

"On?"

"Donating it all to homeless centers, including women's and men's specifically. There're over 285 rooms worth of linen, ready to go. I started going through the inventory with Chiari and one of the head managers for laundry, there's more than enough to be donated to several shelters, depending on their need, which will run out after everyone's 'good Samaritan' boost for Thanksgiving fades."

Isaac clears his throat. "How soon do you want it donated?"

"Next week? Give time to call the shelters, see what they'll need, inventory everything, and then get it ready to be delivered. *Without* interrupting work schedules unless they really want overtime. If the shelters can't take stuff just yet, then there are areas I know where people gather, and we can just take stuff to them directly. Give them a way to survive the cold easier."

Isaac watches me a moment. "Miss Autumn, when were you homeless?"

It's then I decide that I'm done with breakfast, sliding the plate away as I grab my coffee. I look down at the dark liquid, a faint smile comes over my face as I remember a cup with crappy coffee. Bobby. Walter. The last night I spent in that shelter with them. Both were good to me those couple of weeks, but Bobby always seemed to find me. Until I decided not to be found again.

"During winter," I say finally. "Everyone, meaning Leanne and Nan, thought it was only a few weeks, but it was a couple of months. I dropped off the map, even from them after month one. Spent most of my time in shelters when they had beds open."

I meet Isaac's gaze. His body stiffens a moment. "Does Leo know it was for that long?"

"No," I answer quickly. "It's a touchy subject for him." I sigh, taking a long sip of the coffee. "I can't help everyone, but I can give what I can. Right now, that's bins filled with blankets, towels, and pillows that can be used."

He smiles faintly, taking my plate. "Then we have some work to do."

⁂

Ramona flips a paper over her clipboard as she walks with me towards the laundry. She's a bit taller with ochre skin, brown curly hair pulled back with a defined heart-shaped face. Her eyes flick over the paperwork, adjusting her suit jacket. Isaac's close behind, wearing his usual dapper suit, while I'm the odd one out in jeans and my old Metallica sweatshirt.

"I'll be contacting the shelters this afternoon, Miss Watson," Ramona says as she opens the room with the bins of linen. "I'll go through the list you provided, and see what they'll take, from there we'll divide everything available into their respective areas for transport."

"Who's going to do that?"

"Mr. Olstin will schedule cleaning staff and laundry personnel."

I glance at Isaac. He murmurs into my ear, "Frank, house-keeping manager."

"Ah, Frank." Problem with mainly learning only first names—not many seem to use them. "It won't cause work conflicts, will it?"

"No, of course not, Miss Watson."

I force a smile at her as she gives me her pleasant one. "When the schedule is arranged, let me know? I want to help."

"That's not your—"

"It's my idea," I interrupt, and she shuts her mouth quickly. "And if my idea is going to suddenly cause more work for people, who already have other duties, then I'm going to help. I've done similar work, it'll be fine."

Ramona flicks her gaze to Isaac, who I catch giving his stern, warning look. "Yes, of course, Miss Watson, whatever you decide."

"Thank you, now who's going to be delivering it? Does the hotel have its own or does it hire out?"

"We have delivery drivers who belong to the hotel," she answers a bit more chipper. "We have strict management for over-seeing anything that leaves or enters the hotel, everything is handled by our own personnel."

I glimpse at Isaac with a raised brow. Oh, gee wonder why.

"I'd like everything to be delivered before end of next week, that doable?"

"Our staff is always prepared for overtime, don't worry."

Yeah, heard that before. I don't think Ramona, Frank, Chiari or any of them are bad managers. In fact, they're great, but it means the job comes first. Hotel comes first. I want to help people, but not at the cost of overworking others to appease the "boss' fiancé."

Ramona continues, "Now, the organizations you spoke of—"

"I'm sorry to interrupt again," I interject. "Are the delivery people here? I want to speak with them."

Her eyes widen before she nods, gesturing to follow her toward the loading dock, but then turns away. I follow closely with Isaac right behind as we enter a break room. Immediately, everyone from maids, line cooks, or whoever pause.

Ramona strides towards a back table where a couple of men sit. Both slowly stand, adjusting their stance as they notice Isaac. They wear dark cargo pants and long-sleeved shirts. One, who's much older, has a gut, worn skin, and some scruff on his face. The other is a bit younger, squarish jaw, and has a burly build with a dark beard.

"Gentlemen. This is Miss Watson, she's the hotel owner's fiancé and has some questions for you," Ramona says abruptly.

I raise a brow at her, noticing the steely demeanor as the men sweep their gazes to me.

"Okay Hoss, it's not that serious," I mutter under my breath. All eyes flick to me, to Isaac, and then back to me. I shake my head, smiling at the men and hold my hand out. "Hi. I'm Autumn, but everyone has this fascination to never call me that."

The older guy scrutinizes me briefly before taking my hand. "Carl, Ma'am."

"Ouch, that's worse!" I joke, shaking his hand. "Pretty sure I'm at least a decade younger than you."

"Alright, Miss Watson."

I turn to his partner, who takes my hand next. "Wayne, Miss Watson."

I give up.

"Gotta give ya consistency," I mutter, then fold my arms over my chest. "You two do the deliveries for the hotel?"

"Main ones, yeah," Carl answers.

"Well, I'm about to add more to your plate," I begin as others leave the room, murmuring as they go. I spend the next ten minutes explaining, including where the shelters are located throughout the city. Basically, it's a shit ton of driving. "So, that's the plan, but I wanted to know your opinion on how long you think it'll actually take."

Carl and Wayne exchange a look, and Wayne slightly grimaces. Carl clears his throat, glimpses at Isaac and answers, "Sure it can be done."

"Be honest. As much as I'd like it all to go out in one day, given your faces something tells me it's likely impossible."

"It's just that..." Wayne begins, flicking a look to Isaac and I step in the way of his sight, "...there's a snowstorm coming this week. Like Friday."

"Big one," Carl adds.

"So, either we gotta get it done before that or wait until after."

I look over at Ramona and Isaac to confirm, and she nods. "A winter weather advisory was sent out this morning, but I'm sure it'll be fine."

"Uh-huh," I mutter. "May not be a driver, but even I know roads can be dangerous with ice."

Isaac snorts and I scowl at him.

"Could it be done before the storm?" I ask.

Ramona starts, "Of course—"

"I wasn't asking you Ramona," I interrupt gently.

The men exchange a look as I feel Ramona shift on her feet. She's not the one driving, they are. I can almost feel Isaac go rigid behind me.

Carl answers, "Possible, even on short notice. Long as everything is ready to go without much hassle for us."

"It'll be faster delivering to shelters closer to each other in one swoop," Wayne adds.

"So, like divide deliveries over two days? First day, closer to the Bronx, second to where we're located. That way if the storm hits sooner, it'll be a shorter distance."

"Doable, yeah," Carl says, rubbing his chin. "Will have to work late."

"Or just start really early," Wayne says.

"How about this? I'll wake up as early as you want, help get everything into the trucks and make sure if you do work overtime, you get paid double." Both their brows go up. "I'm already helping organize the linens, so I can help you pack up trucks that'll work best. That way you won't be late with other deliveries before this storm hits. Does that help?"

"Well—" Wayne starts, but Carl jabs him in the side.

"Get paid enough, don't worry," Carl says, chewing on his cheek. "Don't have to bend over to get us—"

"Careful," Isaac stops him. "She's being generous."

Carl glances over him, while Wayne shifts on his feet and glimpses at Ramona.

"Easy, bodyguard," I mutter, patting Isaac's shoulder. "Maybe I should talk to them alone."

"Miss Watson, myself and Frank can take care of their overtime pay and schedule for the two days. It's not really within the men's discretion to decide," Ramona comments.

I take a deep breath, not liking the tone she's taken. I'm one step away of completely overstepping bounds, but those linens need to get distributed before that storm hits. The shelters will need it *before* it comes, not after. It also means things need to be done quickly, but I'm not going to risk safety for it without compensation. Or let people be talked about like their opinions don't matter in front of them.

"I'm sure they know the streets better than you and I, so they should be more involved," I say in a calm tone. "If you could Ramona, please go start calling to confirm, that way *I* can begin dividing linens today." I give a look to Isaac. "A moment alone with them, please."

Isaac's blue gaze sear into me, but he turns and nods for Ramona to do as she's told. She straightens and strides out of the breakroom. Isaac follows, but I can hear him position himself by the doorway.

"Never knew a *fiancé* could tell them what to do," Wayne mumbles, followed by Carl's grumbles.

Oh, I knew I was pulling the strings attached to the emerald on my finger. Of course, none of them know I technically own this hotel with every right to change any policy I wanted, but I can't do that outright. Instead, they're gonna do what I ask in order to not get the similar threat Grant received yesterday.

New slippery slope. I really just *had* to dive right in with both feet.

"I'm scary with coffee," I finally say, sitting at their table. "Also, I hope I'm not interrupting your break."

"No," Carl replies shortly, sitting down and then Wayne.

I fold my hands and smile softly. "What I'm asking is a big ask. I will make sure you're paid more for helping, especially with a winter storm coming. And will be sure you're included on how deliveries will go."

"Where'd you work before you became engaged to the...big wig?" Carl asks suddenly.

"Barista."

"One day he just walked in, decided you were it?"

"More like confused due to me laughing after having coffee spilled all over me," I explain, and Wayne's eyes widen. "As I said, scary with coffee."

"But don't work there anymore, huh?" Carl continues, tilting his head. Almost judging.

I inhale deeply, knowing what this looks like. I lean back, ignoring the prick at the back of my neck as I glance at the doorway.

"No," I reply. "Doesn't mean I won't forget what good hospitality looks like, though."

Carl's gaze meets mine. He frowns a bit longer, but then hums. "Well, can't turn down such hospitality then."

"Plus, sounds like it's for a good cause," Wayne adds, nudging Carl. The bearded man grins at me. "So...about that bonus."

<hr>

I spend the rest of the afternoon helping make calls to the shelters, organizing the linens, and discussing best route options with Carl and Wayne. I missed doing simple tasks for hours. I fall back on the sofa in the apartment. Tomorrow I'll be up early to load the delivery truck. It was a challenge to finagle everything, but hopefully it'll go smooth.

Staring up at the ceiling, I wonder if Leo is in his office. I haven't heard from him all day. Isaac suggested not to try contacting him directly, but to go through him first.

With a sigh, I get up and take a shower, grab something to eat and a mug of hot chocolate to set up shop in front of the television. I watch *The Adventures of Buckaroo Bonzai Across the 8th Dimension* and then *Lethal Weapon*. The evening ticks by as sleep tugs at me, listening to Danny Glover talk about being too old for shit. I'm briefly awoken by someone picking me up. Instantly, I know it's Leo as he presses a kiss to my temple. I hum against his chest as he takes me into the bedroom, laying me down and pulls the blankets over me. I grumble when he leaves, starting to groggily look for him, but he's quickly back to tug me into his arms.

"Go to sleep, dear Watson." I settle into his arms. He kisses my head as I take comfort in his warmth. The beat of his heart lulls me to sleep.

I jolt awake with a gasp. Sitting up, I breathe heavily as the alarm goes off. I rub my chest, glancing over and turn it off. The bed is empty. As I start getting out of bed, I realize how early it is. There's another note on the bedside table.

Have a relaxing day, dear Watson. I love you.

Guess we're both having early mornings.

I put it back and get dressed quickly, ignoring the tug at my chest. I head to make coffee, but notice it's already been done. Huh. I pour myself a mug to go, grabbing my phone, and head for the door. Isaac agreed to meet me downstairs, but I text him I'm on my way.

I walk out to the elevator, waiting as I sip my coffee to wake up. When the doors open, I'm surprised by a security guard for the hotel standing there. His brown hair is shaved close to his head and has eyes match in color. He smiles, showing dimples as he nods and gestures for me to enter.

I glance at his nametag, and grin, "Morning, Logan…not even allowed to take the elevator by myself?"

"Just doing my rounds and caught you, ma'am," he responds.

"Want any coffee before heading down? There's at least another cup," I jab my thumb behind me to the apartment.

His brows raise. "I'm good."

I shrug, getting on. "I didn't make it, but you could've had street cred having coffee the boss made."

He snorts, pushing the button to the basement floor.

We're quiet on the way down. I lean back, drinking my coffee and try to wake up more. Once we reach our destination, I wave Logan goodbye and stroll down the hall to find Isaac. Within the next hour, we have everything loaded and ready to go for Carl and Wayne. I check with Ramona about the next delivery in a couple of days. Everything is already set.

Cue boredom kicking in.

Isaac practically drags me back up to the apartment for a "proper" breakfast, an impromptu nap, and to finish watching *Lethal Weapon*. In the middle of the afternoon, I finally cave and ask Isaac to help me get the books that Dr. Maxwell suggested. He'll have them delivered in a couple days.

I just had to last until that long.

Nan calls telling me about her grand-nephew and being in Georgia, not missing the cold. I listen to her, nodding along as I pace the apartment, attempting to ignore the grey color. Next is a call to Leanne and then Trix, who I have to leave a voicemail for.

I go to bed early. When I wake up, the only indication that Leo ever came to bed is another note.

Elm Jed

That day drags on, trying to fight the unease as I distract myself with movies, checking out new laptop, and Isaac teaching me how to make London Fogs and biscuits.

The next morning, I wake up early, ignoring the note this time and get changed to go down to the loading dock. In the kitchen, I find the coffee already made again. Humming in contemplation, I pour my cup and then grab another mug on a whim. The sun isn't even up yet as I make me way to the elevator, it opening to reveal Logan once more.

"Still sticking with the original story?" I ask.

"Yes, ma'am."

"Oh, please just Autumn, and here's an offering to make it so." I get on the elevator, handing him the coffee. I lean back against the wall with a huff.

He chuckles, "Alright…Autumn."

This time on our ride down, I learn a few things about him. Such as he's worked here for six years and prefers nights. The door dings open, and he follows me down the hall, stepping away when we reach the security room.

"The, uh, mug?" He asks.

"I'll come back for it, otherwise leave it on the foyer table." I salute him, walking away to meet Isaac at the loading dock along with Carl and Wayne.

Carl looks more surprised that I'm back a second time, while Wayne appears delighted. Once they drive off after we finish, I gaze up to the sky as snowflakes begin to fall. Just in time.

"Breakfast, Miss Autumn?" Isaac asks.

"Yeah," I numbly say, rubbing my head.

These past few days went by too quickly and yet, not quick enough.

"Got any plans for today?" I ask, following Isaac to the elevator. "Or back to movies and learning more British culture?"

"Whatever you want to do."

"Please help with ideas, I'm about to go nutty here on boredom, Bond," I say with a sigh.

"You just accomplished donating over 300 sets of linen to multiple shelters in less than a week. Where's the boredom in that?" I shrug in response. He hums, opening the door for me. "We could check on the bookstore renovations for Nan."

"How long is it gonna take to get someone to ride with us?" He gives me a side glance. "That's what I thought." We approach the elevator. "I've never missed having a job more than right now."

I walk into the elevator, lightly tapping my head against the wall.

"If you could not injure yourself while I'm watching you, that would be delightful," Isaac says, walking in behind me with an extra flair to his accent. I glare at him. "I have an idea."

"Oh?"

"Can't go riding, but have you changed a motorcycle tire yet?" I shake my head. "Would you like to?"

Harleys to save the day.

Chapter 20

Mechanic at Heart

I've successfully changed the oil on the Knucklehead Chopper that Ringer custom-made himself.

Didn't have that on my bingo card.

Isaac finishes showing me the entire process on one of the Harley's for changing a tire. It's one of the bikes from Leo's estate, brought down here with a few others. The Classic Heritage is the one I'm apparently changing the rear tire on.

No pressure.

I help Isaac situate the tire, and then get air into it with the air compressor they have down in the garage. There's some tools spread out near the other bikes, leftover from whoever was here last. Probably Chesty.

"Do you miss riding Ducati's?" I ask, going back to our previous conversation when the compressor turns off.

He shrugs. "They have their pros, but I like my soft tail more. Ringer and Enigma are the ones to blame for that switch."

"Think you would've been kicked out of the club if you stuck with a non-Harley?"

"Those aren't explicit rules, just an overall..." he glances over at me, and I raise my brow, "...Ringer would've kicked my ass if I tried riding a Ducati with them."

I laugh as he finishes the job, and I hand him the last of what he needs to get the tire situated. He stands, straightening himself as he grabs a rag to clean his hands. He changed into some cargo pants and tank top, while I changed to jeans and an old band t-shirt.

"Any questions?"

I peek over to the Classic Heritage. "You sure Leo's okay if I work on his bike?"

"He has over two dozen bikes, Miss Autumn," he reassures me. "But it's just like any of the others you've worked on. It's not one of his prized bikes *and* Ringer assured me it's fine."

I'm not sure why I'm nervous. I've done more invasive work on Chesty's choppers or the exhaust system with Animal's sportster project. Maybe it's the idea of it being Leo's.

"Alright, let's do this." I get on my feet, help Isaac get the bike off its blocks and then set up the Classic Heritage to remove its rear tire.

Isaac stays off to the side as I get to work removing it from the bike, him only helping when it looks like I'm gonna fall over. After decompressing the tire itself, I'm almost ready to remove it when the sound of vehicles disrupt us.

"Stay here, Miss Autumn," Isaac instructs, walking over to the couple of SUVs that have arrived.

How I'm situated, I'm mostly hidden by the bike from whoever just came into the garage. I peek over the bike seat as doors slam and there's rough voices. Quickly, I look away and focus on the tire in front of me. Learned my lesson last time. Don't snoop.

A tickling prick moves up my spine, but I push it away even as my chest tightens.

It's fine. It's just the Crew's moonlighting gig that you are completely ignoring, and pretending doesn't exist as you change your secret husband's motorcycle tire.

My life could actually be a Nick Cage movie.

I continue to ignore the noise, grunting under my breath as I try to pry the tire off the rim and realize I'm gonna need more WD-40 or something. I double check the air is all out, sighing heavily. I'm concentrating so hard, that when someone approaches with their heavy boots I almost tumble back against the concrete wall.

"Doing good here, *barchën*?" Rudy asks, looking down at me over the bike.

"Hey, Rudy, just changing my first tire."

"Pretty Boy said you were."

"It'd be great to get the *actual* tire off."

"Remember to use the bead breaker, then the tire levers." He nods at the tools on the ground next to me.

"Thanks, knew I was forgetting something," I mutter.

"You'll be a mechanic before you know it." We grin at the other. Someone calls for him from the other side, and he peers over his shoulder with a scowl.

"Go, and thanks for the tip, Rudy." He gives me a wink, walking away.

With another exasperated sigh, I grab the bead breaker and remember what Isaac said and attempt round two. I change my sitting position, kneeling over it and stick the tool against the tire rim. Full into concentration mode.

"The lubricant spray may be better."

I yelp, dropping what's in my hand as it clangs against the concrete. I look up at Leo who stands there with a faint smirk. He's wearing a full black suit with a dark button-up. Classic Leo.

After catching my breath, I smile a little. "Hi."

"I'm sorry for being gone the past few days."

I blink up at him. "Isaac explained. It's fine. Always knew you were a busy man, right?"

He gives me an affectionate look, nodding as he scans me and my work area.

"It's alright if I'm working on your bike, right?" I ask.

"Of course, I trust you."

For some reason hearing him say that about his motorcycle, one of them, but the one I first rode on makes me giddy. A bit more pride flutters inside.

"Would you like help?"

"Supposed to do it on my own." I glimpse over the motorcycle, finding the garage empty of other humans. "Although my teacher slash bodyguard is now gone."

"Told him to leave. Give us time alone." Leo begins to take his suit jacket off, draping it over the bike's seat.

"And how long…" my voice trails off when he takes his shirt off, revealing the black tank he's wearing. I'm full-on staring as he easily shucks off the clothing, muscles moving and tattoos on display.

"Autumn."

"Give me a minute, it's been a couple of days," I mutter, still staring as he pulls his belt off next with a snap.

Why was that hot?

Leo chuckles as he crouches in front of me, placing his finger under my chin, lifting it to meet his gaze. Hazel eyes sparkle, but for a flash I see exhaustion. Something hidden like he just finished a long run. I'm quickly distracted from it when he kisses me, moaning against my mouth. I'm tingling all over. The kiss feels over too soon when he breaks away, moving to grab the tire levers.

"Allow me to help?"

"Don't tell the teach," I say with a wink.

"As you wish, dear Watson."

Leo works with me to change the tire, being the muscle that I apparently needed to get the damn thing off. The groans I've given from frustration have not been pretty, yet every time I look over at Leo he appears infatuated. Before I know it, I'm getting the new tire on, and Leo is showing me how to add ceramic dust or beads to help balance the tire.

There's something calming with him talking about the motorcycle's functions, much like the rest of the Crew. This is the first time he and I have worked on a bike together. After we get the tire fully attached and locked, he continues showing me parts of the motorcycle. I'm able to understand the verbiage he uses, which surprises him with glints of pride that flash over his face. I crouch next to him as he points to some of the modifications he had Ringer do for the engine.

Maybe it's because I've missed him these past few days, but I can't help staring. My gaze moves down his arm, following the patterns of his tattoos, glancing over the Roman shield and Latin. I catch sight of a tattoo I haven't fully noticed before, along his bicep. It's practically melded with the wire braided with thorny vines, but there's a number and skull with an eye patch below.

"Which tattoo is it this time?" Leo breaks me out of my thoughts, and I blink rapidly as I catch his gaze. "Or should I continue talking about valves?"

"Maybe if it's the ones Chesty's replacing throughout that Larry Knucklehead over there," I point to one of the choppers. "But it was this one." I trace a finger over the skull and number.

"Wonder when you'd ask about that one." He moves his own hand over it, catching my hand and guiding us both to stand fully. His arm rotates to show off the brilliantly colored tattoo. "A memoriam tattoo for the man who helped me get my first motorcycle. Road name was Eye Patch Willy. He died from cancer in 2005."

"The bikers up in Connecticut, right?"

"Yeah."

"It's a brighter tattoo than the others, like bolder."

"American Traditional. His favorite style."

My gaze meets Leo's. There's no sadness, just calm.

Leo caresses his thumb over my wrist, holding it against his chest. His posture relaxes as he positions his arm back to normal. I bring up my other hand, lightly gliding my fingers down his arm over the other tattoos that I'll ask questions about in the future.

"Thanks for the help, though I think I prefer working on the engines than tires at this point."

He smiles softly, stepping closer as his hand moves against my neck and slides up. Fingers massage into my hair, probably getting grease in it, but I don't care. Leo leans in close, his breath falling over my skin.

"Do you know how sexy it is to watch you work on my motorcycle?"

My breath hitches. Well, *now* I do.

"Probably on the same level of watching *you* work on it."

Eyes flick down to my mouth, a small moment before he crushes his lips against mine. I gasp at the abruptness, gripping at his arms as I press my body against his. The hand in my hair clutches me as heat rises inside, coiling down toward the apex of my thighs.

"Leo," I rasp against his lips.

"Check in."

"Green, but Leo—"

He practically growls, "I don't want to fuck you on my bike. I want to pleasure you until you're screaming my name."

Leo suddenly picks me up as I yelp. My arms fling around his neck, holding on tightly in shock as I stare at the man carrying me to the private elevator. He somehow maneuvers to have the elevator open quickly, shutting behind us.

"Evading work again?" I whisper, still in a daze from the shift and the words he just said.

"Focusing on you," he answers, pressing his face against my neck and breathing deeply. "I've missed you."

There's longing in his voice. Almost strained. He kisses my neck repeatedly, tightening his grip. A shudder wrecks through my body. The loving touches continue until the elevator reaches its destination. He steps out and into the short hall to the apartment but pauses. I look to see what's stopped him and laugh.

Logan left his mug.

The confusion on his face makes me giggle more. Leo smiles, going back to his task at hand, whilst whispering, "There she is."

We finally make it into the apartment with him slamming the door behind us and stopping in the kitchen, sitting me on the counter. "There's something we haven't done in here yet."

"Oh?"

He unbuttons my jeans, swiftly lifting my hips for him to tug them and my underwear off. Leo then steps beside me, washing his hands and I almost chuckle at him as he smirks. It's almost hot as he cleans himself, knowing what he's going to do. After he dries them, he licks his lips, eyes meeting mine as he slowly sucks on his fingers. I swallow hard as he steps between my legs, pulling his fingers out of his mouth, glistening with his saliva.

Leo kisses my neck once more, traveling up to behind my ear to whisper, "I've not fingered your *muffin* while in this kitchen."

I immediately break out laughing, but its cut short when he inserts his finger inside me. I gasp as his other hand goes back into my hair and holds me still. He stands between my legs, keeping them from closing as he hooks his fingers and scissors them inside me. Leo thrusts his fingers, causing me to pant and fight for breath as his mouth trails down my throat. The hold he has on my hair loosens, massaging his fingers into my scalp as I clutch his shoulders.

In one fluid motion, his hand is removed from my sex for him to swiftly pull my shirt off. The sports bra I wear doesn't deter him as both his hands slide up my torso taking my bra with them. My clothing is tossed somewhere, but I couldn't care less as he yanks his tank off next.

"Check in," he murmurs against my head, slowly pushing his fingers back inside me.

"Green."

"Good girl." His head moves down, kissing as he goes and then begins to suck on my breast. My head tilts back as my hand snaps to his head, grasping at his hair as he nips and swirls his tongue around my nipple. His fingers press inside me, hooking up and stroking my inner walls with a caress that makes my legs shake. I moan louder, needing him as I try to keep my torso up with my other arm.

Leo moves from one breast to the other, while his free arm snakes around my back. He helps me stay up, holding me firmly.

My one arm shakes as warm, tingling sensations spread up my spine and between my legs.

His mouth pops off my nipple, moving to the center of my chest and kissing gently.

"My dear wife…my beautiful, gorgeous wife."

A third finger joins the other two and his thumb circles, moving up against my clit.

I gasp loudly, body jolting at the sudden tremors he's causing. The arm holding myself up moves to clutch at his shoulder. Leo easily keeps me up with his own arm, continuing the movement below and trailing his tongue over my skin.

"Leo…" I gasp, digging my fingers into his hair as he kisses my chest again and then does something with his fingers that makes me scream, "…Leo!"

"Good girl," he worships, moving his thumb and does the movement again with his fingers. It's finally enough to cause the impending orgasm to crash into me. My entire body shudders, legs shaking and then everything going rigid. I clutch onto him as I come hard upon his hand.

He slows, helping me ride out the wave of pleasure as I unclench my hands from his hair. He kisses up my throat, taking his time as he sighs against my skin. I let go of his hair completely, leaning back on my hands as he stands to his full height and pulls his fingers out of me. He sucks on them, cleaning what's left of me on his fingers.

"Next round in the bedroom?" I ask a little breathless.

He glances at the kitchen clock, shaking his head. I scrunch my brows at him, flicking my gaze down to the tenting of his pants. I start to say something, but Leo touches my jaw. "I said I'd pleasure you and make you scream my name, dear Watson."

Surprise flits over my face. A faint smile is what I get in return as he gently kisses my lips, and then my cheek. "And if I don't go soon, we'll have company that neither of us want."

"Ah, so hit and run." Leo goes rigid. "I'm kidding," I quickly say, touching his shoulder and kissing him again. "It's mid-afternoon, course you still have work. Surprised they haven't come knocking yet."

"Careful, if we say their names three times, they'll appear."

"That gives me an idea on what to watch tonight," I joke as I touch his cheek, running my fingers over the stubble. "Will you be late again?"

Those hazel eyes, which were filled with awe before are exhausted again, hardened. I try to give him a reassuring smile. "Okay, don't worry about me."

"I always worry about you, dear Watson." Leo picks me up, wrapping my legs around his torso as he walks us to the bathroom, and then sets me down on my feet. "For now, all I'll do is tell you to take a shower and get the grease out of your hair."

"The grease you put there?" I raise a brow at him.

He smiles, and he leans down to kiss my cheek. "Yes. Have a good night…my dear wife."

Leo walks out of the bathroom, closing the door behind him. I can only stand there. The touch of him lingering on my skin as it chills.

Chapter 21

Like Falling Snow

I sit in the closet.

For I don't know how long, I sit with my knees pulled to my chest. The good emotions, working on the bikes, and Leo pleasuring me just… poof…gone. A deep loneliness settles over me. I dragged myself through the shower, purely to complete his tiny command, but could only get myself to sit in the closet after. Bed felt too lonely. Kitchen meant cleaning up my clothes. Or feeling like calling Isaac, that's if he wasn't suddenly busy, too.

I stare at the clothes around me, frowning at the stuff I don't wear hanging on the rods. Even with everything Leo has gotten me, I still wear what I owned from before. Such as the Guns N' Roses t-shirt I'm currently wearing with leggings and an old knitted sweater. I fall back onto the carpet. My eyes scan the clothes again. I did just donate all that linen to the shelters. What if I finally did the same with the clothes?

I sit up, maybe finding my next project.

Quickly, I start grabbing sweaters I know I'd never wear and carry them out to the bedroom. They're tossed onto the bed just before I scream when I see someone at the doorway. I stumble back and fall, tripping over my feet as the other woman shrieks along with me. The young woman with bright red hair, braided down her back and freckles stares at me. Another heavier set woman quickly appears beside her, saying something in Spanish to the one who scared me as she approaches. Closer, I see the wrinkles near her downturned eyes, dark curly hair with wisps pulled into a bun. They're both wearing the maid uniforms for the hotel.

"Miss Watson, are you alright?" She has a heavy Spanish accent, similar to Julio's. The woman kneels next to me.

"Uh, yeah, just scared the Dickens out of me." I blink up at her dark brown eyes. "You're the housekeepers I've always seemed to miss, huh?" She holds her hand out to me, helping me up as she nods with a pleasant smile. "So, uh, hi I'm the woman you've been cleaning up after, Autumn, but you already knew that."

"I'm Alba, and that is Charlotte," the woman introduces them.

"I'm sorry, Miss Watson. If we'd known you were here today, we wouldn't have—"

"It's fine, been wanting to meet y'all anyway. No harm done." I brush myself off and let out a huff but freeze when I notice the clothes in Charlotte's gloved hands.

Oh, *now* I'm embarrassed.

I point at the clothes in her hand. "I can take that if you want."

Charlotte glances down and then tries to hide her smile. "It's fine. We've cleaned up worse after Mr. Luciano. You're quite cleaner than his other, um…"

Her voice fades as Alba gives her a look.

I slightly roll my eyes, walking over and take the clothes from her hands and toss them into the hamper. They'll probably collect said hamper, but I'd rather not see them pick up the actual clothes.

"I know about my fiancé's…conquests before me." I sit on the bed. "Do I need to leave for you to finish?"

"No, we should be the ones to leave," Alba answers.

"You can continue. I've seen a vacuum and broom before."

Charlotte giggles, and I smile at her.

"Very well, but I shall make you your dinner if Mr. Luciano is not here tonight," Alba says, gesturing for me to follow her. "Come. Charlotte, take care of the bathroom."

I'm about to protest and then remember it's their jobs. Right, new way of living. I follow Alba out to the kitchen, which has already been thoroughly cleaned.

"How long have you worked for Leo?"

"Since he first arrived," she answers. "I've worked for him the longest, apart from Ms. Pierozzi." Her eyes flick to mine. "Charlotte and I know *exactly* who Señor Luciano is before you ask."

I let out a long breath, finding relief in not having to hide that bit. "Does that mean you're the maids who…uh, clean upstairs?"

She gives me a knowing look, and I don't inquire more.

She begins to cook dinner, which consists of some chicken and rice. "Are you from New York?" I ask.

"Puerto Rico, then Miami, and then here."

"I'm not originally from New York either," I say, trying to have some kind of small talk. Alba glances over at me. "I don't do well with the whole not talking thing or acting like you're not here."

She hums, almost assessing me as she continues making dinner. Her and Grant must get along well.

"Would you like me to hang up the clothes from the bed for you, Miss Watson?" Charlotte asks, leaving the bedroom with, yup, bag of laundry from the hamper.

"Just Autumn, and I uh, no…I'm planning to give'em away."

Both women pause, exchanging a glance. Charlotte asks, putting the laundry in the hallway, "Why?"

"I don't wear most of it. Leo's given me a lot. There's more at his penthouse I'd like to donate, too, but not in this storm." I look outside at the wintery white.

Alba plates my food, placing it in front of me. "We need to finish other duties for the day, but we can help you go through your clothes or do it for you tomorrow."

"You'd do that?" I raise my brows.

"Somewhat part of the job," Charlotte says with a small grin. "And I'm not going to say no to going through that closet." Alba gives her a look, and Charlotte quickly schools her expression. "I mean, sorry, we'd be delighted to help."

"Okay, I don't know what the usual protocol is," I say, waving my hand between them. "But just be yourselves. Please. If Leo hired you, that means he trusts you, which means I do, too. I've been poor most my life, and this much stuff is something I'm still getting used to, including having maids or the fact that after almost six months I finally met you…which kinda feels weirder."

Charlotte raises her shoulders, slightly sighing. "Part of the job, be invisible."

I should've been a maid instead of a barista.

"Well, you don't need to be with me. And thank you for dinner, Alba, it smells delicious."

The older woman smiles warmly at me, and then reaches over to pat my hand. "He chose good." She then nods at Charlotte. "We'll be back at 2:30 tomorrow to clean, señorita. After, we will help you go through your closets."

"Thanks, and it was nice meeting you two finally."

They bid me farewell, taking my dirty laundry and all. Not sure what else to do, I eat what Alba cooked and blink at how good it is. Leo may have competition.

Once done, I clean the kitchen and find myself standing in the living room, back to not knowing what to do. On the verge of going through my closet now, there's a knock at the door. I go answer and find Chiari on the other side.

"Special delivery," she greets, holding out a bag.

I take it and peek inside, finding the books I asked Isaac to get me. Well, now I have books to combat the boredom. "Thanks."

"My pleasure, and it sounds like everything went well with the linens. Ramona received confirmation on every delivery. The shelters were very grateful by the sounds of it."

"Good."

"Planning on donating anything else from the hotel?"

"Just my closet," I mutter, and Chiari raises a brow. "Alba and Charlotte are going to help me tomorrow."

She chuckles, leaning against the doorway with her arms crossed. I'm pretty sure it's the most relaxed I've ever seen the woman, which makes me grin.

"So, if you have those cart things to help take stuff down, that'd be great."

"Sure…" she clears her throat, "…you're struggling with his lifestyle, aren't you? This side of it anyways."

"Adjusting. Not the same when you're dating and just go home to a small apartment. Plus, the not having anything to do part or job, even spending 4-5 hours working on motorcycles isn't enough to fill my time. Does the hotel need another maid?"

She snorts, shaking her head. "I may just hire you to see Grant's face or watch Carrie have a heart attack," she chuckles. "But I can see why you worked so much as a barista."

"Could also say holiday spirit has hit early?" I wince teasingly.

"I'll have some trolleys set aside for you, let me know if there's anything else you want to donate due to your *holiday* spirit." She walks away with a wink before she disappears onto the elevator.

I close the door and lay the books across the coffee table.

Not sure what else to do, I begin reading about BDSM dynamics and what exactly it means to be a dominant or submissive.

"**C**harlotte just take it."

"But—"

"No, buts. I said I'm donating, so I'm donating to *you*," I say, handing the dress back to her. It's a Calvin Klein, which made her squeal way too excitedly to not give it to her. I've also given her two Chanel jackets and a Prada dress.

I've spent the last hour or so with Alba and Charlotte, going through my closet. We've collected sweaters, pants, dresses, blouses, and even undergarments that I didn't even know I had. The shoes were another story. The bedroom is somewhat of a mess. Isaac has been helping take items out to one of the trolleys Chiari sent up. My side of the closet was practically a store. That makes Leo's side the *Men's Department*.

"Yet this place is still cleaner than my apartment," I mutter to myself as I hold up a sweater, shaking my head and hand it to Alba. Charlotte leaves with hangers filled with dresses.

"You are the one who brought in the flowers, yes?" Alba asks suddenly as I grab another dress. I stop, looking over at her and nod. She hums. "He's always insisted on it being empty, not wanting…things. Always nice, but never open. You've opened him."

For a moment we just stand there.

"He's a good man," I whisper.

Her hand lands on my shoulder, squeezing gently. "Sí, he is."

Quickly, she changes her expression and takes the dress from me, frowning. Before I can ask, she says, "You still need good dresses to wear. For parties, keep this, it goes well with your complexion. This one can go."

Alba walks away with a different dress, frowning at it.

Nan and her would get along.

With a deep breath, I continue going through the clothes, brushing my hands over the soft materials. It feels all too soon when we finish, hanging everything up on the trolley. Isaac is out in the foyer on the phone, speaking gruffly as I peek over at him while Charlotte finishes cleaning the bedroom and Alba takes care of the kitchen.

I lean against the counter, crossing my arms as she puts away some packs of noodles.

"If I wanted specific stuff in the kitchen, would you be who I go through to get it? Or should I just take my butt to a grocery store?"

She chuckles, murmuring something in Spanish before answering, "Depends on what you need."

"Hold on a minute." Quickly, I grab some paper and write out what I'd like, and then hand it over.

She grins, then tsks lightly as she reads over the paper. "Not proper food, Autumn."

I give her a mischievous grin. "Indulge me if you could."

She nods, putting the paper away. "Anything else?"

"No, just get home safe. Seems like most of the storm has passed, but still looks pretty snowy out there." I glance out the windows to the darkening sky.

Charlotte comes back with a grin. "All set."

Alba says something to her in Spanish, and they converse briefly before Alba leaves giving me a small nod and smile. "Eat proper food tonight."

I mock salute her. When she's gone, Charlotte and I giggle. "She's like a mama you've always wanted," she comments. "She does the same with me."

"Beginning to see why Leo's had her around for so long."

She sighs then shrugs. "Anything else you need, Autumn?"

"Wanna help teach me some Spanish? I think I need to start learning."

"Sí," she answers with a wide grin. "I'll help with some basics next time."

"Gracias," I say, and she scrunches her nose. Damn she is adorable. "Get home safe."

"I will, stay cozy the next couple days." She waves, leaving the apartment.

It's another fifteen minutes before Isaac comes in, still on the phone and says he has to leave. I nod, gesturing for him to go, too.

Once again, I'm back to where I was the night before—alone.

I'm getting tired of this schtick.

Grey walls and emptiness greet me. I rub my hands over my arms, slowly pacing the living room until I stop at the windows and stare at the falling snow. It's peaceful. Too bad my mind can't get on the same page. My shoulders feel heavy as I wrangle my thoughts, trying not to think about where Leo is. What he's doing. What's keeping him busy.

This morning I woke up to an empty bed and a note like the others. Will tomorrow be the same?

I focus on regulating my breathing as the pressure around my chest worsens. I rub at my sternum, trying to find anything to think about other than speculating what Leo is doing or about the things I said I'd walk away from. The thoughts don't relent, not as the grey walls press in. Mocking me.

Letting out a long groan and on the verge of pulling out my hair, I turn on my heel and head to the bedroom. Time to go back to the basics—exploring.

Chapter 22

Friends in All Places

The hotel sparkles with glistening lights that resemble snowflakes. Poinsettias are scattered throughout the decorations of evergreens, and the tree near the front is huge. I blink at the extravagant decorations of the hotel for the winter season. Overnight it seems they turned the place into a luxurious winter wonderland.

People stroll through the lobby as I wind through the crowds coming in for late check-ins. I notice Oliver at the front desk, and even Chiari as I make my way to the shops. It's still early enough that they're open, and I've not explored this part of the hotel as much. I step through some sliding doors that separate this section of the hotel from the lobby. There's a jewelry counter, another for handbags, accessories, a shop for clothes, and a café. I venture down the lane, glancing at the jewelry, stepping away before a woman approaches me. My steps halt as I pause outside a shop with clothing, noticing the coats and scarves. Tilting my head, I stroll in to stroke the soft scarves and find them so plush they're almost squishy.

I'm half tempted to rub it against my cheek.

"May I help you?" I turn to see a man with a shaved head, wearing a pristine blue suit and green tie. He gives me a tight smile.

"Just looking."

His gaze flicks over me before he walks away. I glance at myself, and then at the woman he helps next, who wears a skirt and heels. What did jeans ever do to them? Or is it the baggy sweater I'm wearing?

Maybe this wasn't the best idea.

Sighing, and turning for the door, a shout stops me from behind. I peer over my shoulder to see George, who'd done my nails weeks ago. I look at my bare ones and wince.

"Autumn, how are you?" He greets with a wide smile.

"Hey George, I'm good."

He goes in for a short hug, and I accept it tentatively. Suddenly, he has my hands in his, looking them over. "I had a friend who grew up in foster care, too. They still have hard days."

I stare up at him, forgetting a moment *Autumn's* backstory and then a twinge of horrified shock to what George is implying. He smiles warmly, and whispers, "Sorry, darling we all talk, but myself, and others got your back."

I clear my throat, trying not to listen to the embarrassment and guilt in the back of my head. It was weeks ago, but I don't want to think about my destruction of the ballroom.

"Thanks," I murmur.

"You should let me do them again, just to match this ring!" He exclaims, gasping at the emerald on my finger. "Your engagement has been all the buzz, but this is a beauty! Congratulations! *Perfect* for the holidays."

"Thanks," I say again.

"Love a non-traditional ring." He pops his shoulder for emphasis, getting me to smile.

"Yeah, he knows I don't do well with the traditional stuff," I say, and then change the subject. "What are you doing down here? Escaping work?"

"Visiting my work wife." He nods toward a petite woman with short blonde hair, who helps a customer into a dressing room. "Not that busy given the storm, and the short lull between holidays."

I give him a pressed smile, nodding along. The pressure around my chest is coming back. George means well, but the sudden talk about stuff I'm not used to is making it hard to breathe. Or maybe the reminder that I've barely seen my fiancé/secret husband the past week.

"Yeah, I'll let you get back to visiting your work wife," I say.

"You okay, Autumn?" He puts his hand on my arm, rubbing it a little. His cheerful demeanor dims, dipping his head closer.

I blink up at him, clearing my throat. People don't usually notice when I'm struggling. Usually, I'm better at hiding it. Needing an excuse, I answer, "Long couple days."

"I've heard." I pinch my brows. "Again, we all talk like southern Baptist ladies, terrible with gossip here. You're all the talk with donating hotel blankets and now your clothes, got a golden heart there, huh?"

He lightly taps my chest above where my heart is.

"Y'all talk as much as baristas," I tease half-heartedly. My mask is breaking down, reminded too much of Leo's softer demeanor. I try shrugging it off. "It's not a big deal. People donate stuff all the time."

George hums, and then grabs my left hand. "Tell you what, let's take care of these nails now. Then I can share the hotel gossip with you, while you tell me which of Mr. Luciano's security team bats for my side."

I sputter out a laugh at his abrupt subject change. "What makes you think one of them does?"

"Oh, girl, no way are all those scrumptious men not a leather daddy needing someone cute like me in their life," he says, waving back at his work wife. "Tina! I've got a new appointment, see you later, darling!"

"Leather daddy?" I ask as he leads us out of the store.

He pauses, giving me a look of astonishment. "Oh, we have a lot to talk about," he says patting my hand.

I relent quickly as he continues to talk, keeping my arm in his as he takes us up the stairs to the salon. Didn't even know the hotel had *actual* stairs to the next two floors. I may have been more focused on other aspects. Everything is decorated for the holidays, adding grandeur to the already beautiful *Italian Lily*. After we reach the spa, he continues to give me the gossip of the hotel. I'm surprised how much he's telling me, but fully realize he's not intimidated like the others. He doesn't care who I'm engaged to. It's nice. As if I'm back to chatting with Mabel again.

I even hint that Julio may be who he could set his sights on.

George ends up giving me acrylic nails, explaining they'll last longer and harder to damage. They're a dark green with silver embellishments. He kept them short and told me to come back in two weeks for upkeep. These I can do. Once done, I'm leaning against the front desk of the salon as Wanda types in my next appointment with him.

"We'll have someone call to remind you," Wanda says, smiling more genuinely than the first time I met her. Pretty sure I have George to thank for that.

"What about payment?"

"Taken care of. Mr. Luciano has made it clear that any service you want is provided for."

"Really? Any service?"

George cradles his chin in his hands, trying to be cute. "Does that mean you'll listen to Lisa and get that pixie cut and some new color?" I scowl playfully at him, and he huffs. "I'll tell her I tried."

Wanda scoots him away. "Ignore him, but yes even that. Mr. Luciano's information is all in the system."

I flick my gaze to George, and grin at the guy who's been doing his best to uplift my spirits all evening. "I can leave tips?"

"Yes."

"You don't need to," George protests. "Having the boss' fiancé as my client is good enough cred. Don't worry."

"Part of being engaged to the big wig, right?" I nod for Wanda to hand over a pen and paper. She hands it over, giggling as she keeps George away for me to write down the amount and hand it back to her. Wanda nabs it before he does.

"Don't worry. I don't play favorites. Yet," I tell him.

He snorts out a laugh.

There's a flash of memory to *Blue Java*. Suddenly, I'm on the other side of the counter as it were. And maybe, I understand where Leo was coming from back then. Not trying to impress, but helping a little more because he could.

Never been in this position before. Maybe the holiday spirit has hit me.

"George, your work wife is Tina, right?"

"That's her," Wanda answers.

"She asked me not you, I'm the favorite right now." She rolls her eyes at him. "Yes, it is."

"Okay, thanks for tonight and the nails. I appreciate it." I walk away, waving at them as I head for the elevators.

"Have a good night," Wanda calls.

"See ya, darling!"

I stare down at my nails as I ride back up to the apartment. They really do compliment the ring now, and the sparkles are fun to look at. The delighted emotions are dampened when I return to the empty, very clean, grey apartment. I glance at the time. I know Isaac said to only contact Leo through him, but I don't want to wait.

"Five minutes, that's all I ask." I pull out my phone, pressing the speed dial for Leo.

It rings.

And rings.

Suddenly, it just disconnects and my heart sinks.

"Well, crud muffins, he's *that* kind of busy," I mutter. Tossing the phone onto the bed, I go change into pajamas, but quickly come back when it rings. I pick it up with a less sunken heart. "Leo, hey, I just—"

"It's Sombra." I stop, glancing down at the caller ID. Still Leo's. My stomach twists. "Autumn, did you need something?"

"Yeah, I just, um wanted to talk to Leo. Can you put him on the phone?" I murmur, suddenly feeling very small as I sit on the bed.

"He can't talk at the moment," Jameson answers shortly. "Is there a message I should relay to him?"

Well, for one, being spoken to like a business associate feels wrong.

I swallow hard, pressing my hand against my forehead. My throat tightens with the need to cry. Again, I swallow and hope it goes away.

"Uh, can you tell him I need that card he was talking about. I need it for tomorrow."

"What card?"

"His credit card."

"I'm sure if there's anything you need, Isaac or Chiari can—"

"Look, Jameson, I don't want to get into it, but I need his card, bank info, or whatever. I can't keep going through others. Leo said I could use it whenever I wanted, and I doubt I need *your* permission to ask for it. Otherwise, find five minutes for him and I to talk or I'll come directly up to the office."

"We're not at the hotel." My sinks, tears pricking at my eyes.

He's busy. Don't ask further. You're not supposed to know.

"Fine. But the only one who's going to tell me no is him." I try to keep the sting out of my voice.

There're muffled sounds in the background. Something sounds like steel slamming together. After a moment, he responds, "I'll tell him."

"Thank you," I say roughly.

"Autumn—"

I hang up, tossing the phone across the bedside table. Tears stream down my cheeks, hating this feeling of sudden abandonment. I hold myself close, rocking gently. I should call one of the Crew, Leanne, Nan…but I can't bring myself to do it. It's not Leo.

Unsure how long I've sat like that, I finally get up and go to the kitchen. I make some tea, but the walls seem to crush me, and I smell the faint scent of urine. Shit, I'm flashbacking.

I sip my tea before I cradle the mug close.

I don't want to be alone. I'm *afraid* of being alone.

The salon will be closed by now. Chiari should be going home. It's getting later and later as the snow falls outside. I should watch a movie. Read.

Instead, I pour another mug of tea and leave the apartment. It's quiet as I ride the elevator down, doors opening to the basement hallway. I continue towards the security room, pausing in front about to knock with my foot, when I realize I didn't even put shoes on. Just socks.

Suddenly the door opens, revealing Logan.

"Tea? It's peppermint." He glimpses down at it, brows pinch together as I peer past to the monitors, one showing the private elevator. "Unless you dislike tea."

"No, peppermint is good." He takes the mug.

"Working late tonight?" He nods. "Okay if I sit down here with you for a bit? Apartment is kind of…lonely."

He blinks, frowning briefly before he looks over his shoulder and asks, "Autumn, I mean, Miss Watson wants to chill with us, that cool?"

"You've heard the boss, whatever she wants," a deeper voice responds.

Logan gestures for me to enter. The office is filled with monitors for all the major spaces in and around the hotel. Screens flicking from one angle to another. Near one of the desks and computer, sits a large black man with a beard and short tight curls on his head. He stands, and I swear he's the only one who could take on Rudy with size here at the hotel.

"Hi, I'm Autumn," I greet him as Logan pulls a chair over. "If I'd known there was someone else here, I'd have made another cup of tea."

"Know who you are, and no worries. More of a hot cocoa guy

myself." He shakes my hand, sitting back down. "Name is Michael, but most call me Mikey."

"Nice to meet you, Mikey. Should've known you knew who *I* am." Not surprising at this point for any of the hotel staff. I sit in the chair Logan provides as he sits. I glance at the camera feeds.

"Maybe not why you think," Mikey says, grinning. I look at him in confusion. He turns to the computer, types up something, and a monitor screen changes. It's one of the ballrooms, empty until I see me. I watch what I did the first night at the hotel, sliding around the dance floor.

"Pretty entertaining that night. Didn't have the heart to stop you."

I cover my face, groaning a little.

"Should work on your distance," Logan comments.

"You try sliding on worn-down socks," I argue, pointing to the screen.

"Can't say either of us have," Mikey says, grinning large as Logan chuckles. We all start laughing as I race across the floor and then fall on my butt. "Ouch, that makes *me* pained."

For the next few hours, I hang out with Mikey and Logan. They're pretty open about their lives, especially Mikey who just got divorced and has two kids. He was ready with photos of them to share. While Logan on the other hand is single, living with a couple others in an apartment, thus why he likes working nights. As I continue to talk with them, the sensations of crying and darkness disappear. It's just past midnight when I start yawning.

"Should head back up," Logan suggests. "Before we have to carry you up."

"Yeah, and don't know if we have permission for that," Mikey jokes.

"Very funny, but yeah I'll go and try to get some sleep."

"I'll take you up," Logan offers, walking me to the door.

"Hey, Autumn," Mikey calls. "Come and chill with us anytime. But remember that hot cocoa, huh? Put some of your barista spin on it if ya want."

I smile. "Sure, and thanks."

He winks as we leave. When we make it up to the foyer, I give Logan a small salute after he tells me to go to bed. When I enter the very quiet and empty apartment, I know I ain't sleeping. Both mugs are placed in the sink as I head to the television room and put in *Moonstruck.*

Nick Cage to the rescue.

I stayed awake until Cher slapped Cage.

No nightmares, but I awake squeezing the covers over me, sitting up when I realize I'm in bed and not on the couch. I glance at the clock, seeing it's just before eight and fall back into the bed. For a moment, I lay there, turning my head to see a note on the bedside table. I stare at it, not wanting to read it.

Ignoring the note, I get out of bed and head to the kitchen for coffee. I stop when I see a piece of paper and a black credit card sitting on the island counter. Quickly, I run back to the bedroom and grab the first note.

> *My dear Watson, I'm sorry for not answering your call. Know that I hate being away, knowing you're within reach. I won't be gone much longer, I promise.*
>
> *I love you.*

I go back to the kitchen, picking up that note.

> *Use this however you wish. I trust you. Remember whose money it is. I will not be angry with how you use it; not matter how much you spend. My only request is to not buy a building without discussing it*

first. I love you. Go enjoy and pamper yourself. - Leo

Beneath the message are details for the bank and then a checkbook. I pick up the heavy card. It's not flimsy plastic, which is weird. Needing a moment to realize he gave me one of *those* cards, I move to go make coffee. I definitely need it.

Halfway through coffee being made, I dial for room service.

"Miss Watson, you're up early, how may I help you?" Oliver answers.

"You're one to talk." He chuckles in response. "I've never used room service before, but does *this* place include it? I suck at cooking." I open one of the cabinets and find a bucket of dry oatmeal. "Oh wait, I found the food of champions. Oatmeal."

"Doesn't sound appetizing. What would you like instead?"

"Anything but plain oatmeal," I mumble. "Got any recs?"

"Our French toast is delicious, not to mention fruit would be good for you, or perhaps eggs benedict."

"Oh, fancy, how about French toast with eggs and fruit. I've got coffee covered."

"Very well."

"Real quick, when do the stores open?"

"Ten."

"Thanks. Have a good day, Oliver."

"Have a good morning."

I hang up, then take the credit card and head into the bedroom to change. I throw on some jeans, old shirt, and a sweater, and then use the bathroom. I head back for my coffee when the door opens and Isaac walks in, stopping in his tracks when he sees me.

"Wasn't expecting you'd be awake," he says, staring a little.

"Keeping you on your toes."

"What would you like for breakfast?"

"Already covered."

"Meaning?"

"That I ordered room service," I answer, pulling down a mug for Isaac.

"Why?"

"Because I wanted to." My voice comes out a bit more harshly than usual.

Isaac goes to speak, but there's a knock at the door. I open it, finding Grant and other waitstaff with a trolley of the breakfast I ordered. Grant gives me a quick nod, gesturing for the man to bring in the food.

"Hwan, please set everything in the dining room," Grant says, following behind him.

Oh, right, keep forgetting we have that room.

They set up the table in there, and the young man leaves with a smile. Grant pauses to give me a short bow.

"Thank you, Grant, although you're here earlier than I thought."

"Always a pleasure to serve you, Miss Watson," he says, ignoring part of my comment. "Alba and Charlotte will clear the table when you're done."

"They don't..." I clear my throat when Grant's posture straightens more, "...yeah. Sure. Thanks."

He nods again, leaving as I sit down with my coffee. I didn't just get an order of French toast, I got a platter. As I begin eating, Isaac sits next to me, staring as he was before.

"Want some?" I point at the copious amount of French toast and eggs.

He's quiet, nodding as I place some food onto a plate for him. It's good, and I'm glad I took Oliver's recommendation.

"I apologize for being gone most of the night, and the night before. There were some issues I had to attend to."

"It's fine," I respond a bit too numbly, waving my fork in the air. "Occupied myself."

"Your nails look good." The softness of his voice makes me pause. I glance down at the glittering nails. "Very sparkly."

"George's idea. He's learned I like it. Pretty sure I've got a standing appointment with him every two weeks now." I take another bite of the toast.

We're quiet as we drink our coffee.

"Leo has been—"

"I know," I snap. As soon as I do, I close my eyes and breathe deep.

I didn't want the same conversation again. Another explanation. More excuses. I know what he's doing, an inkling anyways, but didn't want to keep being spoken to like some distraught... housewife.

I put my fork down, hating the lingering feeling of loneliness. The uncertainty. "Sorry. I don't want explanations, Isaac. I know, trust me, I can't *forget* what Leo may be doing. Just not having him around or even being able to reach him sucks. It just sucks."

Isaac reaches over to place his hand over mine, trying to be encouraging. "Miss Autumn, let me tell him that—"

"No." I shake my head, pulling my hand away before I lose my appetite. "I'll be fine. I told him from the beginning I wouldn't get in the way of his work. Besides, I have another project to keep me busy."

"Another? Wouldn't happen to be Leo's closet, would it?" The small tease is enough for me to look at him, both sharing a faint smile. He sighs, leaning back in his chair. "What is this project?"

"Can you get me some guys and couple of SUVs to borrow?"

"Today?" I nod. "I'm sure it's doable."

"Good. I'm doing another donation, cause fuck it."

The last of the boxes are stacked inside the fourth SUV. Each vehicle filled with what I bought from the hotel's shop. I sought out Tina, making sure she got the commission, and didn't look at the final price. The clearing of Isaac's throat and Tina's gasp though...I think I may have hit 10k.

I basically bought out the store of coats, scarves, gloves, and hats. With Oliver's suggestion, I ordered more from another two stores down the block, buying another couple thousand dollars' worth of clothing. Isaac had to argue with someone about getting the cars, but it's now mid-afternoon and we're off to one of the homeless shelters I used to frequent. Two more SUVs are going to a different center for kids. Isaac drives us to our destination, while Animal follows us in the final SUV.

I look at the checkbook Leo left me, writing out an amount and signing it.

"You're quite noble, Miss Autumn," Isaac comments.

"No, I'm not," I murmur, then become distracted briefly by the sparkle of the silver on my nails. I glance outside at the snowy landscape.

"Miss Autumn—"

"Being compassionate doesn't have to be noble, especially if I'm somewhat doing this to feel less guilty for...not being there anymore."

"Whatever your reasons are, selfless or not, it's still helping others." He meets my gaze fleetingly. "I think the only way this would *not* be is if you expected praise or another means to an end. You're not."

I lean further back in my seat, feeling the heavy coat over my arms. "I don't want them to feel forgotten," I whisper.

Isaac white knuckles the steering wheel. "You're not."

"I know...I know." His grip loosens. "Doesn't make the thoughts any easier."

The air feels heavy as he continues driving. We come to the final block, pulling up at the delivery area. I'm about to get out when Isaac stops me.

"This won't be the first time," he says in a solemn voice. "I wish I could make this easier for you, but you should know how common this is for him. Whether it's one business or the other."

"You know I'm pretty sure he tried to warn me over the summer."

Our eyes meet, his filled with guilt. "When you showed up, it had slowed. And…Matteo wasn't acting out as he is now. He's making things more difficult."

The last part is barely murmured, and I keep myself from asking questions.

"I knew from the beginning how busy he was. I knew who he was and what he did even before…" I shake my head, sighing, "…but I think I get why the apartment and penthouse are bleak and empty. He really is never there. They're shells for a reason."

Isaac frowns more, breaking away from my gaze to stare outside at the snowflakes falling. I lean my head back, exhaling longingly.

"I was really used to being alone, Isaac, but after so much work of being around people, it's foreign now. I'm not that person anymore who'll hole up in a corner. He was such a large part of it, that I can't seem to help myself from occupying my time to do something, *anything* to fill that void. Especially knowing what he's up against, but I can't seem to help. My hands feel tied. But I need…to fill that emptiness somehow."

His hand touches my shoulder. "What can I do to help? I can call Dr. Maxwell."

"Have an appointment next week, nothing's gonna change between here and there."

"Then I can speak with the *Forgotten Demons*, with Leo."

"What's that gonna change? I gotta learn how to live in *this* lifestyle."

"Except it isn't good for you or him."

"But it's all we have right now, isn't it?" He inhales sharply, letting out a sigh of frustration. "I understand my reality, Isaac. I'm also grateful that there's privilege that comes with it, cause I could be back in there." I point at the shelter. "I appreciate you listening. Maybe right now it's just harder because I don't have a purpose yet. No job. No Nan or bookstore to busy myself. No undercover work. But I'm gonna keep looking. Right now, it's donating to every fucking shelter and soup kitchen I can think of."

He nods when Animal comes up next to the window, smiling

through the glass. I get out, but his smile falters as he rubs my shoulder. "You alright, sister? Or his driving need improvement?"

"I'm fine, Animal. Let's get everything in."

The next hour is spent getting all the clothes inside, working with the main coordinator, Susan, as some mobsters deliver the goods. It's almost enough to giggle at. When we're done, I hand over the check to the coordinator, who looks at me in surprise.

"You've already given enough," she gasps.

"Well, hopefully this helps with any other supplies and repairs to the place."

"It will, thank you." She shakes my hand, going to her office and calling a volunteer over.

Through the exit, I see the other car leaving. Animal and Isaac stay behind, strolling back to the building. I glance at the inside of the shelter, watching as they hand out the clothing. A smile rises on my face, tears pricking my eyes as a young man says something about taking gloves to his daughter.

My breath falters when I notice something familiar. A hat.

I weave through the crowd as people get in line. My stomach tightens with a small prick at the back of my neck, nerves running through me as I approach a man bundled up in an old Carhart jacket and thin beanie.

"Autumn," Animal's harsh whisper from behind doesn't stop me from tapping on their shoulder.

He turns and I'm met with familiar eyes.

"Bobby," I whisper with a faint smile.

His skin is burnt along his jaw, beard now short and speckled with gray. His gaze narrows, scowling and I abruptly remember that I don't look the same. The slight changes may be enough to not recognize me, and it's been almost four years. Shit.

"Sorry, didn't mean to bother—"

"Sarah?" His broken whisper almost shreds me to the bone. Tears form in my eyes as I nod. Unexpectedly, Bobby stands and pulls me into a hug. I can hear my bodyguards get closer but I wave them off as I embrace Bobby. "I thought…thought they got you kiddo."

"They did," I answer against his ear. "But it's Autumn now. The name."

He steps back, brushing his hands down my shoulders as tears form in his eyes. I peer around him. "I wouldn't be lucky enough to see Walter, would I?"

He averts his gaze, frowning and it feels like my heart is about to break. "Bobby? Where's Walter?"

"He, uh…" he clears his throat, taking my hands, "…that cough of his was pneumonia. Real bad. He died a few weeks after you disappeared."

My throat tightens as I squeeze his hands, and then can't help myself from hugging him tight as the tears come. He holds me close as I cry into his shoulder. "His family got him. So, he's resting somewhere up north."

I nod against him, hating I left. Hating I vanished in the night. That I never said goodbye.

"He'd be happy to see you okay, though," Bobby says, rubbing my back and I suddenly feel calmer. "And walking in here with new clothes and shit."

"How'd you know it was me?"

"Your eyes, kiddo." He pulls away, holding me by my shoulders again smiling sadly. "Can't forget those eyes of yours. Lost those glasses again?"

"No, I can see without them. Not as blind as I used to be."

"Not as blonde either." He touches strands of my hair. "Really glad you're alive, thought after Walter died you were gone next… shit you changed your name?"

I nod. "What about you?"

"Name still Bobby." I smack him lightly, both of us smiling. "Jobs here and there, same old. Tried a kitchen, not for me."

"You and me both with cooking. Doing good otherwise? Staying warm?"

"Yeah, you know I can take care of myself." He glances over me again, and then at the group of people behind us. "You the one who brought all that?"

"Yeah. Long story."

"Have to tell me sometime." His voice lowers, and I peer back at Animal and Isaac, who both watch us diligently. He mutters, "Maybe not now."

I stare down at his hands in mine. The scars over them and burns. "Do you know the *Italian Lily*, further into Manhattan?"

His brows scrunch. "Fancy hotel, right?"

"Yup, if whenever you need anything, I mean *anything*, just go to the front desk and say you're there to see Autumn Watson. If they question you, um…" I think quickly, and then jog over to Isaac. He seems to know what I need, because he pulls out a card for the hotel and his own. I take them all and head back to give them to Bobby.

He inspects it briefly. "Really took care of yourself, huh, kiddo?"

I swallow hard, "Yeah, I did. You should come by so I can tell you about it."

Bobby puts the cards in his coat. "Sure, and then I'll take you out for coffee. The good kind that doesn't taste like leftover grounds."

He's gonna bust a gut laughing when I tell him about my years as a barista.

We hug again, lingering. Finally, I step away and point at the clothes. "Get yourself a new hat, cause I know that ain't the same one from years ago."

"Don't knock my style." He grins with a wink. I chuckle at him, waving as I walk away with a bittersweetness in my heart. Animal flicks his gaze past me.

"Old friend?" I nod, walking out of the shelter. "Does he need help?"

"It's Bobby," I answer quietly. "He'll come when he's ready. I hope."

They're both silent as we head to the vehicle, and I climb into the back for Animal to sit in the front with Isaac. Except, Animal gets into the driver's seat while Isaac sits in the back with me. We're barely a hundred feet from the shelter when I start to cry. Isaac holds me silently as I sob against his coat.

I've gained friends this week to aid against the darkness, but the one I didn't know I lost cuts deep.

Chapter 23

Hearing Sleigh Bells

Holiday spirit or not, I've been on a "giving" rampage for the past week.

I've visited Mabel twice at *Blue Java*, the second time I gave her and her mom a week's worth of spa treatments at the *Italian Lily*. I did the same for Leanne and Trix. I was able to have lunch with Leanne once, but Trix will be traveling until the New Year. Perhaps out of guilt from what I learned about Walter, wishing I'd been able to be there for him, I donated money to three organizations who focus on medical treatment for those who can't afford it. I finally slowed my roll after Chiari and Mikey said to go easy. And then Dr. Maxwell reminding me I can't save everyone. Nor was it my responsibility to.

Night after night without Leo. Each morning with a new note.

No whys or where he was or what he was doing.

And like every night this week, I sit in the security room with Mikey and Logan watching one of the ballrooms become undecorated after a company party. I hug my cocoa close.

"Ballrooms aren't used as much as I thought they were," I say.

"Everyone wants the *Coliseum* or *Pantheon* cause of size and design," Mikey says, sipping his cocoa. "The *Narcissus* and *Orchid* ballroom aren't used as much as the others."

"Yeah, more likely they'll be empty right up until Christmas," Logan adds.

"Seriously?" I ask.

Logan scoots his chair, types into his computer. "Yup, *Narcissus* isn't reserved until three days before Christmas, so we'll use it to hold extra chairs and such. *Orchid* reserved this weekend, but then it's open until the day after Christmas. People have their parties in offices, not ballrooms."

I tap my mug, staring at the ballroom video feed. There's a couple of weeks until Christmas. Yup, new idea.

"Could I reserve it?" I ask.

"Well, yeah," Mikey answers. "Why? Wanna throw a party?" I give Mikey a guilty look, and he chuckles. "For who?"

"Hotel staff. Could do it like a week before Christmas, in case y'all traveling."

"Not many of us do," Logan comments with a shrug.

"But do you think you and others would come?" They exchange a glance.

"Would it be mandatory?" Logan asks.

"No."

"Bring our families?" Mikey asks.

"Duh."

"Would staff have to work it?"

"No, I'd do it," I say, leaning over Mikey to bring back the feed for the *Narcissus*. "I'll even organize the tables and chairs. I'll provide food, set up decorations, and provide gifts."

Cause it's not like I have all the time and money in the world right now, which may be slowly driving me batty. See, it was dangerous letting me out from behind the counter.

"Honestly, Autumn?" Mikey asks.

"I prefer that over lies."

"Well, after the last couple weeks, and since *you're* the one throwing it, people would show."

I sit up straighter. "Is Chiari working late?" They flip through camera feeds, bringing up the lobby to show her. "Looks like I've got a party to plan."

I stare at the ballroom ceiling like it's gonna give me answers.

Isaac, Frank, and Chiari stand next to me. I'm determined to get this place party ready. It's just the small details now.

"Our event staff can set up how you want," Chiari says, holding up a finger for me to wait before speaking. "They're already scheduled to take care of the *Pantheon* and *Dahlia* Ballrooms. It won't be extra work for them."

"Evenings are when we have decorations go up," Frank explains. "Housekeeping will clean before the final decorations and lights are set."

"I don't want them cleaning a space they're supposed to be using. Have them drop off their cleaning equipment and I'll do it, not sleeping much anyways. Can do it tomorrow. No one will be in here."

"Miss Watson—"

"I'll help," Isaac informs. I side-eye him. "Never said the party was for me."

I relent, mainly because Frank looks one step away from a heart attack.

Chiari grins, continuing, "I contacted a catering company we've used before to handle the event. They're a nonprofit, small, but they don't seem to have many clients until the New Year."

"Great, whatever estimate they have in cost, double-it." I kind of like doing that. Chiari goes through a few more things on her list, and that she's sent out the invite to the staff.

She and Frank leave with Isaac and I trailing behind.

"Should've known you'd have found a loophole in your 'holiday spirit,'" he smirks.

I grin, hopeful that at least a handful will come. Help give the staff and workers time to just relax and enjoy the hotel like I have in some ways. Charlotte seemed excited when I saw her this afternoon. That's one.

We step onto the private elevator as I count the days down until the party. "Okay, so I'll help put up lights tonight, clean for the main crew tomorrow. Day after that, I'll do any last needed things to decorate. I gotta figure out presents for everyone."

"There'll be a lot of people," Isaac comments. "Are you sure?"

"What's the point of having a holiday party and not have presents? Even at *Blue Java*, Yuki made sure we got something. I'm not half-assing this after the shenanigans I pulled with the linens." I cross my arms, and Isaac starts laughing at me as I scowl at him. "Or breaking the ballroom."

He holds his hands up. "Apologies, your dedication is astounding and amusing."

I roll my eyes at him, thinking of something small I could do. Apart from bonuses, but that *definitely* seems like a subject to discuss with Leo first.

As "willy-nilly" I may have seemed in spending, I have been paying attention to what I've spent on that card. I haven't reached building buying level yet.

We arrive to our floor, and I'm about to ask Isaac about an early dinner, when his phone rings. I enter the apartment, hearing him mutter on the phone and then arguing through the door when it closes. A sinking feeling hits me as I get to the kitchen, waiting for Isaac when he comes inside. He stops. "He's not…" Isaac's voice trails off, not finishing the sentence.

How many days has it been now? When can I stop counting? How the fuck have we spent less time being "engaged" than dating?

"A shipment went wrong," Isaac murmurs. "I know you're not supposed to know, but a warehouse was infiltrated. There were casualties, but not him or the Crew. So…you can't leave the hotel either."

I nod my head stiffly, steering my gaze toward the apartment

I've come to hate. Each time I despise it more with its grey-ass fucking walls, bare and empty. I'm surprised I haven't painted it with fluorescent pink yet. I sigh, leaning back against the counter as Isaac comes over.

"It's been longer than when I…" my voice feels unsteady, and I swallow past the lump, "…I left. It's starting to seem like that. Five minutes. Five damn minutes, or a fucking phone call. Shit, I checked in with Roger more often than this."

I rub my hand over my face.

Isaac touches my shoulder gently. "He's in places he can't call from. It could compromise you. Nor does he want you near that… he's protecting you."

I can only nod, not having the energy to tell him *I know* for the hundredth time.

"Even this is abnormal for him," Isaac continues. "Shit happened in Italy; he's trying to fix things here. There's been miscommunications and blackouts."

My gut clenches as I rub my stomach. Tears slide down as I start to wring my hands. Carefully, Isaac pulls me against his side to hold me. It's not Leo, but he's warm against the swirling emotions.

I just miss Leo. And I feel lost. Every day I'm not sure where I'm going.

"I'm sorry, Miss Autumn. I'm so sorry. You don't deserve this," he murmurs.

Tears run down my face, trembling a little as Isaac attempts to console me. Once they're gone and my cheeks mostly dry, I ease back and wipe away what's left.

"I'm fine," I mutter, taking a deep breath and glance at the clock. "Should eat before helping with the lights."

"Are you sure you're up for it?"

"I need the distraction. It's worked in the past. Anything to not overthink."

He purses his lips. "Would it help if I made you a proper cup of British tea? I'll call the desk for dinner as well."

I give him a thumbs up. He starts the kettle as I head to the bedroom for a moment. I fall back onto the bed, staring at the ceiling. Didn't I already do all this? Repeating damned patterns to feel like I'm living? After a few deep breaths, I realize music plays from the kitchen. I sit up hearing the lyrics about a hippo.

A chuckle escapes me as I go back to the kitchen and Isaac winks at me. "Thought you'd like this song."

Sneaky Brit.

Isaac does an excellent job to distract me from my tumultuous thoughts. We have dinner and tea, then meet the event staff in the ballroom. He's with us for a few hours, before having to leave. I assure him I'll be fine. I do feel better, a bit less anxious, especially with twinkling lights around me.

It's late. The stage where the tree will be is brought in, and there's a wall of lights against the dark fabric as the backdrop. More lights are strung up over the ceiling, crisscrossing on hooks that have long been installed for such events. Some connect to the couple of chandeliers. Almost done, we now stand in the middle of the ballroom, wondering what to do with the last of the string lights.

"We could just not use them," Zack says, who's tall and lanky with blonde floofy hair.

"There should be somewhere we can add them," Sandy, an older woman with brown hair pulled back into ponytail, argues. "We've used them all before."

"Not like this," he gestures.

"Sandy's right, we can add them...just where?" I murmur, walking in circles.

A couple tables were brought out to get an idea for arrangement, and the dancefloor is still down from the last event. I told them to just leave it. I stop on the wooden flooring and ponder.

"Near the tree?" Zack asks.

"Too busy," Sandy counters.

"Over the doorways then," he suggests.

"Getting tacky there, Zack," I rebuke. "Even for me and that's saying a lot."

"Well, I'm running out of ideas, other than don't use them."

I turn around, catching sight of Sandy as her eyes light up. She peers above where I stand, and then nudges Zack. "How long are those lights when they dangle?"

"5-6 feet."

She points to above my head. "We hang them around the chandelier to border the dancefloor. It'll be like a curtain, like a willow tree in winter. They won't be long enough to cause issues."

I gape at her. "You're a genius."

"Damn it, why didn't I think of that," Zack mumbles.

"Cause I've been doing it longer." She pats his back and nudges him to grab the lights. I let out a long yawn as she collects the ladder. "Go to bed, Autumn. We got this."

"Yeah, you've done more than enough to help. Two-person job anyways," Zack comments.

"Thanks for helping. Made it easier to get everything where you wanted it," Sandy tells me.

"Think it's good?" I ask, looking around at the warm white lights intermingled with blueish ones. Winter wonderland with less chill.

"Better than the tacky 90s Christmas lights for the other parties," she grumbles. "We'll see you tomorrow when we check the lights for the tree."

"Fine, good night!" I wave to them both, leaving the ballroom.

Once the doors are shut, I slump against them and feel the weight of running around hit me. At least I feel less depressed.

I try to remember the melody of the hippo Christmas song, humming it as I close my eyes. For a few moments I let myself slip and forget everything around me. I take off my shoes, going bare foot. With shoes and socks in hand, I start spinning and following the designs on the carpet as I hum the Christmas song in my head.

Halfway to the elevator, I start singing a classic. The chords are imagined in my head as I recall the melody, play the invisible instruments as I hop to the elevators. Just as get to the doors, I spin and sing under my breath, "*...new old fashioned...wa—*"

The elevator dings, scaring the crap out of me as I screech, drop my shoes and socks, then promptly trip backwards. My arms whirl to not fall on my ass, but it's useless. I brace for the hard ground, but get swiftly grabbed and fall against someone instead. Air is knocked out of my lungs, and I groan slumping to the side and onto the carpet.

I open my eyes to find hazel ones as I slightly sit up.

Leo's face is filled with concern, searching me for any injury. Relief floods me as I look over him, tears threatening to come. Slowly, his gaze meets mine and his expression softens.

"Hi," I whisper. "Seems like I'm still falling for you."

"That you are, dear Watson." His voice is rough like he's been yelling or hasn't had water for hours.

I stroke my hand over his cheek, moving into his hair as his eyes flutter close. I pull him closer, bringing his lips against mine. He shifts his body, holding me closer as we kiss tenderly on the carpet. He cradles my head, while his tongue skims my bottom lip and I taste him for the first time in days. Tears fall, streaming past my ears. I clutch him, needing him.

Leo breaks the kiss, and I nearly whimper at the loss. Another kiss is placed on my cheek, and then forehead. He sweeps away the fallen tears.

"I've missed you," I whisper brokenly.

"So did I." Leo begins to stand, helping me, too. He then quickly picks me up before I can grab my shoes and socks. "They'll get picked up."

His grip tightens around me, refusing to let go and I just nuzzle against his neck. I tremble a little, relief mixed with fear that this is just a dream. Or worried of how long I'll have with him this time. I focus on him. Leo gets on the elevator, and without touching a button or code we ascend.

"I'm sorry, sweetheart. I'm sorry for being gone," he murmurs.

I keep my head against his shoulder, open my eyes, and I see it. Hidden under the seam of the dark sweater he wears is dried blood. My throat tightens as the doors open and he carries me into the apartment. I close my eyes, not wanting to look at it again just yet. Leo continues to the bedroom, sitting us down on the bed. He holds me close, clutching the back of my head as if I'm the one who'll vanish.

"I love you." His voice is gruff, almost shaky. He repeats those words. Soon, I realize he's trembling throughout the rest of his body.

I lean back to grab his face. Those eyes of his searing into me. There it is. The exhaustion. The weariness.

It wasn't just me who was lonely. Both of us lost without the other.

I kiss him more fervently as he inhales quickly, breath hitching. My fingers thread through his hair, weaving into the strands as I straddle his lap. His arms wrap around my waist, pressing my chest against his and a tingling sensation jolts down my spine.

I murmur against his lips, "Check in."

His eyes look to me in wanting, but with a different need. He swallows hard as if he doesn't want to answer. I stroke down the side of his face, rubbing my thumb over his jaw. Finally, he softly whispers in a voice that makes my heart crack. "Red."

"What do you need, baby?" I ask. His eyes glisten as tears form. I kiss his forehead, remaining there for a moment as I try to keep myself calm. "What do you need, Leo?"

"You. I just need you."

"I'm here. I'm right here." I hug him close, cradling his head against my chest.

After what seems like forever, I'm able to pry myself from him to lead him into the bathroom. I get him to change, but stop him before he pulls another shirt over his head. With a small washcloth, I wipe away the blood he missed. Blood that I know isn't his because there's not a scratch on him. The only markings are his busted knuckles I finally see in the bathroom light. Leo keeps still as I clean him, then toss the washcloth aside. He doesn't put the shirt on.

Once we get into bed, our arms and legs become wrapped

around the other. I keep his head against my chest, stroking his hair.

"I love you, Leo. I'm right here," I whisper, kissing his head.

"I'm sorry…I love you, I'm sorry—"

"Shh, Leo. You're safe right here."

My cheek presses against his head as he clutches me. We cling to each other, regaining the lifeline we'd lost and needed desperately.

Chapter 24

My Sweet

I jolt awake, attempting to sit up, but am held tight in a pair of arms. Eyes blinking open, I stare at the dim light of morning. A sigh releases from me as I realize it's Leo holding me, snuggling closer. He hums against the crook of my neck.

"Nightmare?" He asks in a muffled voice.

"Don't think so." I hold his arms against me. "No early morning?"

"Not today. Threatened job and limb to be left alone."

I snort a laugh under my breath, turning in his arms to kiss him. He smiles against my lips, squeezing me gently. Already he seems better than last night, calmer and not so tense.

"Want to know what I thought when I saw you last night?" He asks, kissing my nose, causing me to giggle. "There's my wonderful, lovely, sweet wife. I missed your smile."

"I missed you, too, mister."

We finally slowly separate to look at the other. Leo strokes my hair. "How about some breakfast? Been worried about you eating."

"I can function without you," I laugh lightly as he begins to leave the bed. "Don't always like it, but I can. The hotel makes it easier not to starve either."

"I've heard you've been using certain services; a few people have given their elation at the news," he says walking toward the closet.

"Really?" I sit up, ruffling my hair. Didn't think it'd be that big of deal they'd tell Leo.

"Some people live to serve. They take pride in what they do."

"Guess I gotta learn how to give orders," I mutter, putting my ring on as Leo pauses. I head into the bathroom, take care of business, and toss the bloodied washcloth into the hamper along the rest of his clothes.

"Autumn?"

I walk out and find a puzzled Leo. "What?"

"What happened to your clothes?"

He's just now noticing? He really was occupied.

"I donated them to a women's shelter. Alba and Charlotte helped."

Leo blinks slowly, turning his gaze back to my side of the closet. Suddenly, my stomach sinks wondering if I should've talked to him first. Yeah, it was mine, but he had been the one who gifted them to me.

My hands come up to start tugging at the other, but I quickly force them down and then wrap my arms around my middle. "It happened over a week ago," I whisper.

Leo comes over, grabbing my arms gently to take my hands and kiss my palms. "I should've noticed earlier, and I did tell you I would donate what you didn't want. They were yours to choose what to do with, I'm just surprised by how much you donated."

"I kept what I usually wear." Mostly my stuff. "And some dresses for fancier occasions, per Alba's advice."

"She has a good eye."

I ask in a small voice, hating that it is, but the anxiety crawling up my spine needs to be squashed, "You're not mad?"

"No." He kisses my hand again. "I can just buy you more."

"Leo," I groan as he smirks. "That kind of defeats the purpose of what I just did."

"Then donate those clothes," he says, walking out of the bedroom. "Then I'll buy you more, and you can keep donating."

"A very vicious cycle," I playfully argue. Charlotte is gonna love me.

I follow him into the kitchen. He starts pulling skillets out as I start on the coffee. Leo passes behind me several times, each time stroking a hand over my skin. He reaches up beside me, pausing as he opens a cabinet. I follow his gaze and start snickering as he pulls down a box of my favorite cereal, the sugary marshmallow kind.

Thank you, Alba.

"You've made allies," he comments.

"I made friends." I grab the box from his hands, putting it back. "Hey, you left me alone, I'm gonna create an entire army ready to devour sugar for breakfast, donate clothes, and catching coffee is next."

Leo nabs my waist, tugging me back against his front to hug me tight. I peek over my shoulder to grin at him, but falter when I see the glint of guilt and disquiet in his gaze.

I know he didn't want to leave me. I've watched him rearrange his entire schedule before, skip meetings, and even disappeared upstate to take care of me. The times he can't, I know it's serious, that's why I try not to complain. We can't change it. It's just awful when he's gone and lonely.

I swallow hard, and whisper, "I knew you'd be back. Just had to be patient."

He inhales sharply before burying his face against my shoulder, like he's trying to hide there. I'm beginning to think it's his new favorite place or he's truly trying to hide. I understand the feeling.

"So," I say stepping away and grab mugs for coffee, "I don't know when you need to go back to work, but I do have some things I have to finish today. Otherwise, I may be up past midnight decorating."

"Decorating?" He glances at the penthouse.

"Not here. I'm throwing a Christmas party for the hotel staff in a couple days. Since I don't want anyone to work it, I'm going to get the ballroom cleaned and set up for the party. By the way, any ideas for gifts? I've never had to, and please don't say ornaments."

I ramble as I make him his Americano, not noticing he hasn't moved to start breakfast until I'm almost done. His brows are fully furrowed when I face him finally, holding out his drink. His head tilts. I blink at him and ask, "What?"

"You've been busy."

I shrug. "No job, no bookstore, friends are busy or out of state, and the Crew were also busy. May have gotten a little stir crazy."

Leo takes the mug, smiling faintly. The haze of guilt and unease is still there, but his expression does soften as he sips his coffee. Last of those dark emotions swirling in his gaze vanish as he leans down to kiss my cheek. "Thank you for the coffee. Why don't you tell me more about this party you're planning and almost giving my head butler an aneurysm?"

I gape at him in mock shock, picking up my coffee. "That how you keeping tabs on me?"

"Not just him," he muses as I sit down.

I lean my head back dramatically, clutching my heart. "The betrayal! Giving away my secrets!"

"Were you even trying this time, dear Watson?" He turns on the stove and begins cracking eggs.

I grin. "Touché."

He starts asking more questions about what I've been doing and the party. We never discuss for him. Either because it's mob-related or it's not worth him talking about. Leo keeps the conversation on me, even commenting on my nails and that they fit me better than the last. He suggests gift ideas for the staff, but none stick.

Once we finish breakfast, I do expect Leo to disappear, but he doesn't. Instead, he gets dressed into more comfortable clothes with me and heads down to the ballroom. We walk in, finding all the cleaning supplies I'd asked for and the last of the lights strung up.

"Good job so far," he comments, peering around the place with his hands in his pockets.

"Thanks, but Sandy and Zack mainly did the lights. It was her idea to put them around the dancefloor." I point to what was finished after I left.

I grab a vacuum, rolling it across the carpet and find a place to plug it in.

"You're *actually* going to clean? Autumn, it is their job—"

"And this is something I'm doing for them for *doing* their jobs." I look over my shoulder, smiling. "You know I've used these things before, right? Had to clean a coffee shop for three years, you've literally seen me mop."

"Not what I mean."

"I know, but still...not that big of a deal, besides Isaac will be down later to help."

"I told him to take the day off," he says as I pause. Leo continues flicking his gaze around the ballroom. "Now his argument makes sense, but the moment I said I wouldn't work today he caved. My apologies, I didn't know."

"It's fine." I wave him off. "Honestly not that big of a job. Carpet isn't stained with coffee, no grounds that I need to hand-pick off the floor, or whipped cream to scrub. Just simple vacuuming, setting up tables and such. Easy-peasy."

Leo chuckles as I plug in the vacuum, assessing where to start as I unwind the cord. I'm debating starting in a corner and moving along from there when Leo comes over to plug in another vacuum.

"What are you doing?"

"Helping."

"You? Clean?"

"Are you now saying *I'm* incapable of doing so?" He raises a brow.

"Not what I said, mister." I point at him. "You don't have to help, it's alright, it's essentially your day off."

"We're partners," he counters. "In cleanliness and grime."

I start laughing, unplugging my vacuum and point to the other side. "Alright, *partner*, I'll start over there you take care of this area. I'll even be nice and play music like a proper cleaning party."

I roll my vacuum, pausing at the stereo system and plug my

phone in, starting a playlist of 80s and 90s rock. I'm about to start vacuuming when Leo calls over, "Autumn?"

"You can't hate this music, it's Aerosmith!"

"Not that…how do you turn it on?"

Do not laugh at your husband. Do no laugh at your husband who's probably not touched a vacuum in over a decade.

"Coming, honey," I tease, while he playfully scowls.

The loud music and humming of the vacuums fills the ballroom space. For his first time in probably over a decade vacuuming, he does a good job. Once we finish that, he helps me arrange the tables and chairs, then cover them with their dark green cloths. Into the afternoon, he practically carries me away for lunch when the event staff show up to bring in the decorations.

He takes us to the *Giglio Giardino* for lunch. We're seated instantly in the back away from other patrons, not long after Leo orders for us, Christopher appears with a wide smile.

"Good afternoon, Mr. Luciano," he greets, then turns to me. "Hello, Autumn, how's the party planning?"

"Finished cleaning, final touches are next," I answer as Lincoln appears, delivering coffee.

"Are you planning on attending?" Leo asks.

"Yes, sir," Christopher answers with a warm smile. "How could I not? She's invited every staff member of the hotel, restaurants and all. Very kind of her."

I shrug, grabbing my coffee. "Just trying to do something nice for y'all."

"And we appreciate it," Christopher says. "Although I wondered if you would donate food from the kitchens next."

"That's when spring cleaning hits," I joke.

"Very well," he laughs. "I'll inform Raoul and Giulia."

"Oh, that reminds me, can you tell Raoul that the pasta he made the other night was delicious? It's a newer recipe he's trying out, Hwan mentioned him wanting my opinion."

"Of course," he responds, nodding to me then Leo. "Anything you need, sir?"

"No, thank you, Christopher."

"Always a pleasure," he says then disappears.

Leo stares at me a moment, and I look around. "What?"

He reaches across the table to take my hand, stroking my fingers. "You are a delight."

"Wanted to do something nice, I mean, I've skidded into your lobby. Broken into ballrooms, escaped hotel security, technically twice, broke furniture, and given your head butlers and managers mini-heart attacks. Least I can do is offer a party for surviving my antics."

"And mine," he murmurs.

"We both know you're the behaved one in this relationship."

"You have your moments, too."

His thumb strokes over my skin as he peers down at our joined hands. That haze of guilt and disquiet comes back. Worry gnaws at me every time I see it, unsure what's happening to even cause it to frequent his expression. Deep in my gut, I know that blood I wiped off was hardly the tip of the iceberg.

"Leo, should we talk?" I ask tentatively.

He clears his throat, not making eye contact with me. "We agreed to not have you involved."

"I'm just worried about you."

A soft smile crosses his face. "Don't. I'm alright. I'll make an appointment with my therapist after New Year's if that will help you feel better."

"The one I want to feel better is you," I whisper.

A different kind of softness comes over his face, tender, as he gestures for me to sit beside him on his side of the booth. I do so, and he puts his arm around my shoulders and murmurs against my ear, "All I needed was time with you."

The anxiety doesn't leave, tickling down my spine. "If something was truly wrong, you'd tell me, right?"

He tenses a moment, inhaling sharply. "Please trust me. I'm figuring...things out at the moment."

"I do trust you, Leo, I just want you to be okay."

"As long as I have you, you're all I need." He tilts my head back to finally look me in the eye. The glints of guilt are gone, replaced by that of affectionate longing.

I swallow hard, knowing I shouldn't make him talk if he's not ready. I can't force him. Not after all the patience he's given me. And if he'll talk to his therapist, then that should be fine.

"Does that mean you don't want anything for Christmas?" I ask, attempting to change the subject.

"I already got what I want," he answers, nipping at my ear, which makes me giggle as it tickles. "But what about you?"

Leo places my coffee mug in front of me, maneuvering things around the table for us to sit next to each other, instead of across.

"Unless you want more clothes that you can donate later?" He adds.

I scoff and roll my eyes at him.

The food arrives with Lincoln delivering it, easily setting things on the newly organized table and leaving promptly. Leo adjusts in his seat as I get ready to dig into my pasta but pause with an idea.

"Maybe there's one thing I want for Christmas," I say, and he raises a brow. "Come to the party and have fun?"

"As you wish, dear Watson."

I smile, satisfied and take a bite of pasta with a hum.

"Will you let me take care of the gifts for the staff? You've already done so much."

Half a noodle hanging from my mouth, I glance over at him. An easy smile rises on his face as I slurp it in and nod. Leo reaches over, passing his thumb under my lip to wipe away the white sauce. The loving tenderness on his face makes my heart squeeze, pushing away those worried thoughts. He discreetly licks the sauce off his thumb, then nods for me to continue eating.

Time stills as I hold onto the small moment. The only true thing I wanted for Christmas, albeit common, was peace.

Chapter 25

This Christmas

The caterers finish setting up as I walk through the ballroom, dressed in a comfy green sweater, jeans, and socks. Didn't see a reason to wear shoes.

"The place is gorgeous! Can you take over the Christmas parties for my department?" Leanne asks as she comes up behind me.

She's wearing a bright green sweater with jeans, and unsurprisingly shoes. Last minute, I invited her when I realized she was still in town. Figured that's one person for sure coming. I glance over to the three Crew members who could make it: Isaac, Julio, and Animal.

"Thanks," I say. "Just hope everyone has a good time."

"Course they will," Animal says, walking up alongside Isaac. "Place is a Christmas Hallmark movie."

"And you're already engaged to complete the plot," Leanne chuckles, holding out my left hand.

"You've done an excellent job, Miss Autumn," Isaac adds, smiling.

"First guests arriving," Julio calls, pointing towards the back doors.

I turn to see Charlotte, Alba, a younger couple, and then children being guided through. I rush over to Charlotte, who squeals in delight.

"Autumn! This is so *fancy!*" Charlotte exclaims, hugging me.

"Feliz Navidad," Alba tells me, coming in for a hug as I reciprocate the greeting. "Come. Meet my daughter and grandchildren."

"Then you can meet my best friend," I say, waving Leanne over.

The next fifteen minutes I'm being introduced to Alba's family, and then introduce Leanne to the hotel staff as they arrive. More and more show up, even those I haven't personally met yet. Logan appears with his girlfriend, and then Mikey with his kids, who I meet briefly before they run off to play with the other children. Ramona, Grant, and Frank even show up. It's about an hour into the party when George, Lisa, and Tina arrive with a couple of others from the spa. Then right before I call out the food is ready, Chiari arrives with her mom.

The entire place is filled with music playing, laughter, children running about, and people eating. At some point, I sneak over to George and point out Julio who stays near one of the entrances with Animal. He smiles at me, winking at my little nudge as I run off to go eat with Leanne. I'm finishing up checking on the caterers when I notice Isaac and Animal slip out into the hallway. The warm feelings I've had sink suddenly as I quietly step around everyone and sneak out. Both men turn around with solemn expressions and I already know.

Leo isn't coming.

A tightness wraps around my throat and the plummeting in my stomach makes me feel sick. I try to concentrate past the disappointment and hurt, waging war inside me.

Animal starts, "He tried—"

"Is he okay?"

"Yeah."

"The rest of the Crew?"

"They'll be fine," Animal answers again as Isaac watches me closely. I nod, although the want to sob claws at me, making it hard to swallow.

"Miss Autumn, he wanted to be here, truly," Isaac murmurs.

"I know, but shit happens…right?"

Both men nod stiffly.

He's not doing it on purpose. I know that. I do. Yet, a part of me doesn't believe that. Another part wants to disappear, not go back into the ballroom. I'm half-debating to actually go and hide, when Leanne opens the door.

"Hey, Chiari said she…what's going on? Hun, what's wrong?" Her arm slips around my shoulders.

"I, uh…just need a minute," I answer softly.

I stare at the carpet, trying to convince myself to move. Do something. Fuck sake, I have an entire crowd of people in there I'm supposed to entertain.

Leanne shifts beside me, and says, "Can you two tell Chiari that Autumn will be there in like a minute?"

"Of course," Isaac answers. Both men leave silently.

"He's not coming," Leanne states. I can only nod my head, trying to concentrate. "Is he alright, at least?" I nod again. "Hey, look at me."

Leanne takes my shoulders, turning me to face her and I see that bright, hopeful expression of hers.

"I know you wanted him to be here. Why wouldn't you? He's your fiancé. And okay, it sucks, he's not going to make it. But others have shown up. The ones *you* are throwing this party for and they're amazing people who've been sweet and wonderful to you. So, let's go have fun with them. Him and you can go throw another party. Don't let his absence take away the joy that could be now."

She takes a few deep breaths with me and slowly I start to smile.

Leanne's right.

It sucks he's not here, but I can't change it. This party was for those in there. A thank you to them. I smile faintly, the anxiety somewhat calming.

"Okay," I whisper.

"I could just hand you over to Alba, who I'm sure won't let you cry," she teases, leading me back into the ballroom.

"No, that's Charlotte's job."

"That girl is the bubbliest person I've ever met. I'm not sure she's real. Can we arrange a date for her and Trix?"

"Why not you?" I giggle.

Leanne shakes her head. "Nope, Trix could do bubbly, I need…" her voice trails off as we enter the space, both our attention moving toward Chiari and Isaac, "…more stoic."

I lightly smack her shoulder and she starts laughing, pulling me towards Chiari who beams when she sees us. I'm handed off, not knowing what's happening until Chiari grabs a mic and announces, "May I have everyone's attention?"

The music fades as Chiari and I stand by the large, decorated tree. I raise my brow at her as she smiles toward the quieted crowd.

"What are you doing?" I whisper, hoping to not have a panic attack from everyone staring at me next.

She gives me a knowing look, almost sad, but quickly brightens.

"Let's all give our thanks to Miss Watson for putting this beautiful party together for us," Chiari says, rubbing my arm comfortingly. Oh, goodie, she knows he's not coming either.

People applaud and I sheepishly raise my hand in recognition.

"She's been busy the past couple of weeks, keeping us on our toes as she found ways to give to those less fortunate than many of us here. She's done a bit to make this holiday season easier for a handful of us as well, and I guess she's not finished yet. There's still a few things left on the agenda tonight, an idea from her and Mr. Luciano."

I scowl, briefly looking over at the Crew, who all shrug. Leanne, who's beside them, also gives me a confused look as Chiari pulls out a letter.

"From the owner himself," Chiari starts, and then reads, "*Thank you all for a wonderful year. Perhaps, going forward these parties will become tradition for the* Italian Lily. *My dear fiancé was adamant about gifts for hotel staff but struggled with what was meaningful and best for you. So, I decided to emulate her giving nature. First, all staff of the hotel shall be given two extra weeks of paid vacation."* Chiari pauses as some people gasp, while others laugh in shock. *"All those required to wear uniforms will be given a new set. You and your families will be given three complimentary meals to dine at the restaurants of the hotel, free of charge. Lastly, staff will receive an extra $2000 bonus at the end of the year. May your holidays be filled with joy and peace. Signed, Leonardo Luciano and Autumn Watson."*

Holy fucking shit.

The entire room is quiet, people gaping in shock as they stare at me. I stare at Chiari as she quietly folds the letter, a soft genuine smile on her face. I attempt to do the math in my head of what he's just gifted, but give up when I realize that many zeros make me dizzy.

"I didn't ask him to do that," I whisper as the room erupts in cheers.

"He's always had a good heart," she murmurs, grabbing my hand. "But I think you're the

one who reminds him that he does."

She hugs me as I stand there stunned. Music starts playing, unsure how to respond. I blink as some tears fall. "I'm sorry he's not here, Autumn, but we all got your back."

I clear my throat, pulling away. "Thank you."

Chiari grins, stepping away as people begin approaching to thank me. A few times I think I may hyperventilate from the attention, but Leanne or Alba shoos them away. I'm swept away by it all, forgetting the hurt in my heart. The evening wears on as I sit next to Mikey, watching Leanne pull Isaac onto the dancefloor.

"If he gets that guy to open up, I'll be surprised," Mikey comments as I follow his gaze to George and Julio. One looks happy as a clam, the other seems interested but distant. Julio is the latter.

"Maybe it'll be a slow burn," I say.

Mikey snorts. There's a screech of laughter as the kids start sliding around on the dancefloor as the music changes. He gestures toward the dancefloor with a wink. "You should show them how it's done, or maybe *they* should."

I gape at him. "I am a pro!"

"Andrea!" Mikey calls, and one of his little girls come running with her beaded hair bouncing. He tugs her in close and whispers in her ear, she then beams and comes over to take my hand and starts leading me toward the twinkling dancefloor.

"Skate!" She shouts.

I frown at Mikey playfully, shaking my head as I go over with Andrea. Once we reach the wood, I begin pulling her around and she squeals as she slides. Older kids join us, skating around the floor in our socks. My stomach hurts from laughing as we race each other, going in circles with the sparkling lights surrounding us.

All the kids soon wear me out, landing me on my butt upon the wooden floor. It takes Leanne and Animal dragging me off to allow the young ones to continue running around. The party continues into the evening, slowing down as people leave for home. It seems in a flash it's filled with people, and then almost empty. The last to leave are Chiari and her mom, who wave goodbye. I'd long sent the Crew home. Leanne left a bit ago, still having work tomorrow and was escorted out by Isaac and Julio.

Pieces of the heaviness comes back as I look around. It's not that messy, but I decide to keep myself busy. I flick through the playlist, and then start playing some holiday classics as I clean-up a little. Andy Williams sings of chestnuts as I check that all the leftover food was cleared, which will be taken to a soup kitchen the catering company works with. I pick up some tinsel that's landed near some tables, beginning to dance as I toss it into the trashcan and roll it around.

I partially sing, dancing around the tree and through the lights. I twirl again, shaking to the music as I grab some cups to throw way. The song fades out as I smile to myself, spinning one last time, but stop in my tracks.

A version of *O Holy Night* gently plays as I stare at Leo.

He stands off to the side of the still glittering dancefloor. A ghost in the shadows. The jeans and long-sleeved shirt he wears aren't clean, rumpled with dark stains. No red.

Silently, I walk over and give him a faint, half smile.

His brows are furrowed close, expression on the edge of shattering as he frowns. Heavy breaths leave him as he swallows hard, almost making a choking sound when he tries to speak but stops.

He looks like shit.

"Check in," I ask quietly.

"No," he whispers. "No, don't I fucked up...I..."

"Leo, I'm not mad." I stop almost a foot away from him. He averts his gaze, refusing to look at me. I reach for his hand, and he almost flinches away. "I knew what I was getting into at the beginning of this, that means missing things, work you can't avoid, or whatever. I'm hurt you couldn't make it, but you're here now."

The quietness of my voice doesn't get him to look at me.

I gesture to the dancefloor. "Found out I gotta up my sock sliding, but I guess I have an entire year to practice. You can help me prep. And everyone was really grateful what you did for them."

"It wasn't much," he murmurs.

"No," I counter, stepping closer to place my other hand against his chest. He closes his eyes completely. "Giving them a day off or an extra two hundred in their banks isn't much. You just made their lives a bit easier. To not worry about bills for the next month at least. You did that because it's you. Leo with the golden heart."

He shakes his head. "No, Autumn, that's you not me."

"Yes, it is you."

"I promised to be here."

"Mistakes happen, it's okay, you're here now..."

He holds my hand tighter, finally bringing his gaze to mine. Tears fill them as hurt contorts his face. "I wanted to be here," he rasps. "I wanted to be *here*. With you."

My heart breaks.

Of course, I was upset he couldn't make it. I hate it whenever we're apart, but I know he's trying. He doesn't have much choice at times, he warned me of that before I agreed to date him. Leo couldn't be like many of us to just step away and enjoy life. He couldn't easily take breaks without costing him time. And every small break he takes doesn't feel like enough as he keeps coming back bloodied and in grime.

All he's ever known is work.

"Come here." I pull him after me, ducking under the lights to stop us in the middle of the dancefloor. I gesture for him to stay. "What's your favorite Christmas song?"

He stares at me a moment, then answers quietly, "Silver bells."

I jog to the stereo, looking up the song along with a few others to place into the que. As the song begins, I head back to Leo and put us into waltz frame. Dean Martin begins singing and for a moment, I think I may need to be the one to lead, but Leo sways to the music before leading us into a waltz.

We dance slowly within the sparkling lights. There's no over-the-top spins or moves, no extravagant gliding across the floor. Just a simple box step as we dance softly to the melody and crooning of Dean Martin.

"Autumn," Leo whispers, moving a hand down my back. "I'm—"

"No." I shake my head. "Don't apologize. It sucked to not have you here, but I'm okay. There'll be other parties, dinners, or events. We'll find time. We'll figure this out, Leo."

Wham! starts to play next, causing us to stop as Leo strokes my cheek with his knuckles.

"You're allowed to be angry with me," he whispers. "Don't push aside your emotions for my sake. Be angry with me. Be disappointed. You can be mad and tell me off, I broke my word to you."

I stare up at the man who pleads with me.

Memory flashes to a late night in his office; begging him to be angry with me. Hate me. Condemn me for what I'd done. To be punished. I'd hated what I may have done to him, and wanted him to hate me, too. Shoulder the blame. Make it easier to be the bad guy.

I place my hand against his cheek as his hand falls. "I hate not having you around, but it's not always possible. We *will* figure this out. Find that balance. I will not be angry with you for things you can't control or when you're placed into predicaments where you have to make the hard decisions. Not happening. I love you, and no matter how long you leave, I'll be right here waiting for you to come back. I promise. Secret marriage or not, I'm staying."

I pull him down into a crushing kiss. He inhales sharply, wrapping his arm around my waist. He clings to me as he cradles my head, kissing me with a bruising force as I grip him just as needily. The kiss shoots a warmth down my spine and through my legs, making them feel like jello.

So much of me loves him, I can't hate him. I can't fully be angry when he's trying, tearing himself apart to do "the right thing" by me. Even if that may not exist. My biggest fear is losing him, and right now, I'm worried that may not mean physically, but other parts of him. We've both been alone for so long, I don't think either of us know what to do.

"I love you, my dear precious wife," he murmurs against my lips.

"And I love you, my dear husband. I'll be there in the dark when you need me, just as you have for me."

He holds me tenderly, before placing another searing kiss upon my lips. I taste him, trailing my tongue over his. We kiss like there's a bush of mistletoe above us, breathing heavily until the music changes and I pull away with a grin.

"Right on time," I say as the high notes ding in the air before Mariah Carey's voice fills the space.

"For?"

I start to sing along with Mariah, stepping away and dodging him through the lights. I act all dramatic as I sing to Leo. Not my complete best, but the snort Leo gives when I clutch my heart pushes me on. I pretend to play the piano as well, sliding onto the dance floor through the lights. Affection grows on his face as I sing and dance around him, turning to keep his eyes on me as I slide and swing my hips, and then twirl in place and point at him, "*You!*"

Hands grab me, causing me to squeal as he tugs me into a hug. Leo pulls back, keeping my hand in his and spins me. For the rest of the song, he dances with me. As the song fades, he swiftly picks me up and starts walking us off the dancefloor.

"Wait! I have to turn the music off!"

He stops, giving me a disgruntled look, but relents and walks us over to the stereo. Music now off, I smile and gesture for him to continue for the exit. He strolls out with my arms wrapped around his neck into the quiet, dim hall.

"Gonna let me down?"

He grunts in protest.

We ride the elevator up to the apartment, and only when we reach the foyer does he finally relent in putting me down as I raise a brow at him.

"Thank you. Now, how about some hot chocolate and roaring fireplace to keep that Christmas spirit? Maybe I should've brought up some tinsel," I murmur the last part.

"You won't need it," Leo says, opening the door for me.

"Leo, even you have to admit…"

I stop.

It's decorated. Garland hangs near the ceiling with lights and tinsel around the fireplace. In the corner by the terrace is a small pine tree, shimmering of gold and silver. There are random decorations of nutcrackers, gingerbread houses, fake snow, and more spread throughout. The apartment that was once the cold space he never changed and empty is now the perfect quiet holiday picture. You can barely tell it has those grey walls, creating an ease that falls over my body. It's stunning.

Leo decorated the apartment. For me.

I turn to him, his expression tender and almost bashful. "Merry Christmas, dear Watson."

My heart feels like it swells in appreciation and love. "Always the suave, smooth talker, even when you don't need to talk."

I take his hand, leading him to the bedroom. We get changed into pajamas and fuzzy socks; new ones that he got. I make hot chocolate and he opens a bottle of scotch, getting ready to settle in front of the TV.

"Do you have any Christmas movies in that hoard of yours?" Leo asks, sitting down.

"I'm not sure if I should be offended that you called it a hoard."

"Compliment in your collecting skills."

"Or maybe because you think I don't have holiday films. I am no amateur, mister."

"Thus, why you have a hoard."

I roll my eyes at him, crouching to grab the only movie we need tonight. I grin when I find it, popping it in and go sit with him on the couch. A few minutes in, Leo chuckles low.

"*Die Hard*?"

"Not officially Christmas until Hans falls from the Nakatomi tower," I muse.

"I agree."

I raise a fist into the air. "Yes! Married the right guy!"

Leo smiles warmly, pulling me close to snuggle under the blankets together. I breathe easier, pressed against him as I listen to his steady heartbeat. Even with the heartache earlier today or even the past few weeks, I wouldn't change as long as we had these moments.

The moments where I have him. I have my Leo.

Chapter 26

Times Be Changing

"So, I'm going to ask the inevitable, question," Leanne says, leaning back in her seat after she sips her drink. "When are you thinking for the wedding?"

Whelp, she wasn't kidding about 'inevitable.'

It's mid-January and I'm having an early lunch with Leanne and Trix. The rest of the New Year went smoothly, as one can be while secretly married to a mafia boss.

The last few weeks have been slow, Leo disappearing only a couple of days at time, but when I do see him it's brief. Leo doesn't seem as tense as before, but the unease around him still lingers. Most times when I see him, it takes a while before he can meet my gaze. I don't ask questions, trying to adhere to our agreement of me not getting involved. Worry still gnaws deep, even when Isaac tries to reassure me. Dr. Maxwell said to trust my own gut; if I truly needed to confront Leo about what may be causing his stress it wouldn't be unwise. Unfortunately, Leo being who he is, that list could be extensive, not including the mafia.

"Maybe a summer or fall wedding?" Trix asks, grabbing a fry off her plate.

My stomach drops, remembering the conversation that I'm in

the middle of. I press on a smile, shrugging nonchalantly. "Haven't really thought about it."

My days lately have been filled reading about BDSM, working on motorcycles, and hanging out with hotel staff. I'm on my way of converting Mikey and Logan into Nick Cage fans.

"Just don't say it's in two months, that'll *really* make our heads spin," Trix chuckles.

"Course not." *Cause I already have you beat.* "Enough about me and shiny rock, what about you two?"

The subject change works in my favor. Leanne bashfully says something about an old classmate who showed up at her Christmas family event. She keeps saying she's not dating, taking a break, but I notice her flicking her gaze past me. I'm split between ignoring it, they're adults, to the other side of meddling. I decide to focus on Trix discussing her project with the schools.

"After those schools outside the state agreed, how could they still be dragging their feet?" Leanne asks.

"Funding, as always," Trix answers, shrugging. "Paperwork's been greenlit, especially after Boston agreed, competition basically, but now I have to wait for a board to approve money."

"Who's supposed to provide it?" I ask.

"The university itself, putting it on the list of other building projects. Another way is through donations, fundraisers, or a bene-factor basically."

"Or you could wave in their faces with flyers that say 'hey, A place for DV victims to have security is a good idea' could work," Leanne comments. Trix snorts.

"Wait, can anyone give money to go to this center?" I ask.

"Technically, I mean large donations from alumni and supporters of a university happen all the time. It's how sports complexes happen," Leanne explains. "Most alumni are sports related though, so they *say* they want their money to front a project and then get a shiny plaque for their good deed."

"Long as the school allows it, which they hardly *ever* say no," Trix says, finishing her drink. "I mean, private schools depend on donations, but in my opinion almost every college practically is on how projects are done."

"Don't get me started on *that* area," Leanne huffs.

"So, a board approving a building project, even to renovate an already built space, is slim," Trix finishes. "Saying yes, they look good, but actually doing it? Well, that's the hard part."

"Even if it could help students from all backgrounds?" I ask.

"It's a public university that I'm trying to get this done at," Trix explains. "This center won't just be for the students who are effected by domestic violence, they'll have priority, but others can have access to it as well. Like a hub. A place to grow and finish one's education in a safe manner, but I don't think a board will move forward unless it's *only* for the university or students living on campus. Even though it can be a solution to not push more kids to a homeless shelter."

I hum, tapping my fingers on the table. A thought starts forming in my head.

"Uh-oh," Leanne murmurs, grabbing her drink and hiding her smirk behind her glass.

"What?' Trix asks.

"How much do you need?" I ask Trix.

"For what? To convince the college its worth doing or just paying for a building?"

"Either."

She goes still, narrowing her eyes and then gapes.

I've supported Trix since I've known her on this project. It started as just programs to help protect survivors of DV, and now it's growing into actual spaces at colleges. It was more than just a passion project for her. It was turning into her life's work, and I don't want some "board" deciding that future for her. Not if I could help after all she's done.

"Autumn, hun, what are you suggesting?"

"I can talk to Leo," I quickly say, grabbing her hand. "He already funds the women's center, and you know his other philanthropy endeavors. He could help you do this."

"It could be a conflict of interest, with him still funding *Luna Stella*..."

"Then have a meeting with him or have a couple of conversations," I continue. "Have a full business meeting to discuss details and your plans. If it doesn't work, then we can say we tried. I'll ask him to talk with you, and *Luna Stella* doesn't need to be a part of it. He could front the money himself without another company affiliation."

Not like the man doesn't have options.

Trix stares at me. She flashes her gaze to Leanne, and exhales sharply, "Remember when we were the ones offering her help?"

"It's a nice change," Leanne smirks.

"I'll think about it," Trix says, squeezing my hand. "But thank you for offering."

"In the meantime, she's paying for lunch, cause *that* she doesn't need permission for," Leanne jokes, waving the waiter over.

I roll my eyes at her. "No matter how hard you try, I ain't gonna be your sugar momma."

"All these years wasted!" Leanne dramatically exclaims as the waiter approaches. I hand him the card, catching the quick look of surprise before he disappears.

Why couldn't Leo have given me a card the doesn't scream millionaire?

It's what I get for having Chiari make the reservation, but the food is really good, along with pristine tablecloths, shiny silverware, and an upscale bar for my shadow to sit. I miss simple pizza parlors.

"How about next time we go somewhere simpler?" I ask.

"Hun, you don't have to pay every time, it's okay," Trix tries to reassure me. "One of us can next time. I'll be back, going to the bathroom before we leave."

Trix steps away as the waiter returns, putting the card and receipt on the table. I thank him, writing down a tip and close the booklet after I sign. Leanne stares at me as I do.

"What?"

"Was that *his* card? How can you sign for it?"

I glimpse at the card, quickly putting it away as my heart starts to pound. I've been careful the past month, acting like I'm using a card he gave me or just using cash. Except, I just clearly signed my name on a bank card that clearly had *his* name on it.

"Some joint account he made," I answer, keeping my voice calm. "Trying to give me freedom, whilst paying for everything. Weekly allowance is better pay than being a barista."

The joke comes off a little flat. Leanne narrows her gaze as I try not to break under her stare. I've mostly told the truth. He *did* make a joint account so as not to raise any flags with Jameson or the others either. They just didn't know I was on them as his spouse.

It hurt to lie like this again, but I can't let the cat out of the bag.

To keep myself from accidently giving away the truth, I stand up and gesture for her to leave. "Let's meet Trix at the entrance. Give Isaac time to pay whatever tab he started."

It distracts her enough to move her gaze to him. I breathe easier, exhaling hard as we stroll to the entrance and meet both Isaac and Trix there.

"Have a martini, shaken not stirred?" I ask him as he holds the door open for us.

"We both know I don't drink on the job, Miss Autumn."

"What do you drink when you aren't?" Leanne asks as we all step outside.

"An Old Fashioned," he answers, straightening as he flicks his gaze over Leanne. "Yours?"

"Depends on the date."

A blush begins to form on Isaac's neck, and he pulls his scarf up, clearing his throat as he nods for us to continue.

"Alright, you should head back to work," I say. Trix starts giggling, walking towards the subway station as I quickly hug Leanne. "Quit making him blush."

"But it's so easy!" She exclaims under her breath, grinning madly. She then winks, waving as she goes the opposite direction.

Trix and I walk together to the subway station, Isaac not far behind. She whispers in my ear, "You don't think those two would…you know?"

I give her an exasperated look. I'm not sure if I'm ready for *that* rom-com.

"Well, Leanne's probably just having fun flirting, I think that last guy messed with her head a little," Trix says as we head down the steps to the subway platform. "They seemed serious, and he just left."

"Some jobs are really important to people."

"Yeah." The train pulls up and we quickly get on, finding a corner to stand in. Once we start leaving the station she abruptly asks, "Are you serious about donating?"

"Yeah, but it'd be Leo's company or personal funds," I answer, smiling softly. "Maybe, I'll be your sugar momma before Leanne though."

Trix laughs, putting her arm around my shoulders to hug me.

"Thanks for even considering talking to him. Don't feel any pressure. I know you probably feel a kinship to those I'm trying to help, but it's…it's not your fault if you can't help."

I lean against the window, watching tunnel lights flash past.

"I'm trying to figure out what I'm supposed to do still," I say, and her face softens. "Nan's still gone, even though they finished renovating the bookstore, but…not sure working there will be enough. Could go back to being a barista, but when I was fired Nan mentioned it was time to move on. Before everything went topsy turvy. You know, randomly, sometimes I think if I *could* get pregnant, well, least I'd be occupied."

"Oh, hun."

"When I say randomly, I mean rarely, and I blame holidays just passing," I quickly try to reassure, not certain where that came from. "I'm just figuring things out, but I'm in this position where I can do more."

"Doesn't mean you have to."

"But I *want* to. This time, not give up my own freedom or autonomy again."

Trix smiles, rubbing my shoulder as she leans her head against mine. "I'm proud of how far you've come, Autumn. If you think my idea is the place for you to start finding your footing again, then I won't say no. I appreciate you as a friend and as survivor. You'll figure it out, without having to play into expected social norms."

"Thanks, and I really do believe in you. This center *will* happen."

"I hope so." The train comes to Trix's stop. She gives me a quick, hard embrace. "See you later, love ya."

She steps off, disappearing through the crowd on the platform. A seat opens up, and I sit down as Isaac shuffles closer, hovering. I sit and quietly recite part of *The Raven*. Not sure why. I'm not anxious or feel the prick at my neck, but I find myself staring at the ground as I murmur the words.

We get to our stop, stepping off the train and a bit of nostalgia hits me. It's the stop I used to get off for *Blue Java*. I sigh deeply, heading up the stairs toward the greyish skies and brisk wind. I pull my scarf up as Isaac comes to my side, pausing at the cross-walk. I glance across the street at the shop and see Bailey working.

"Want to go for round two?" Isaac asks.

"Nah, I'll be petty another day."

"Not even to show off the ring?" He muses as the light changes, and we begin crossing.

"Tempting, but I don't wanna go through fifteen minutes of her complaining it's not a diamond, probably fake, or whatever she concocts."

"Good to know you're determining which arguments are worth having."

"So, don't ask about how you've seemed to become a little flirta-tious around Leanne?"

He quickly clears his throat, but not before almost tripping over his own feet. I start giggling, almost in shock, but mostly amuse-ment. I'm half tempted to tease him more when we approach the hotel and one of the valets, Charlie, greets us, "Good afternoon, Miss Watson."

"Hi, Charlie, slow day?"

"Normal weekday in January, so yeah."

"Stay warm out here." I step into the lobby, hearing Isaac murmur something to the young man. Charlie is far younger than me, but finally stopped calling me ma'am. Most of the staff have. Now to just have them call me by my first name.

Isaac is catching up to me when commotion near the front desk catches my eye. Two daytime security guards are there with a man between them, dressed in a ragged coat.

Isaac stiffens next to me, adjusting his stance to easily grab for his weapon. "Miss Autumn—"

"Wait." I stop him from dragging me upstairs.

There's no shouting, but voices are raised as security grab the man and Oliver appears worried behind the counter. The man they're handling roughly, drops a blue hat that's exactly like the ones I donated last month.

"Miss Autumn, I think that's—"

I jog over as my heart rate quickens, stomach dropping. Oliver catches sight of me, nervously looking at the man who's being held by security.

"Miss Autumn, we have it handled, please—"

"Autumn?" That familiar voice makes me hurry, bending down to scoop up the hat and recognize the man as Bobby. Relief covers his face.

I look at the guards holding him; one is Rhonda, who is tall with blonde hair, pulled back in a bun, and the other I don't know. He's a big dude with steely blue eyes.

Oliver begins to walk around the counter. "Miss Autumn, this man said he knew you and had a card from the hotel. Mr. Morton's name was on one, too, but he wouldn't leave—"

"He's a friend of mine," I state, then give Rhonda a look. She gives Isaac one before releasing Bobby. The other guard doesn't. "Please let go of him before I give Mr. Morton permission to do it *for* you."

My voice is colder than I anticipate, but seeing Bobby roughhoused causes irritation under my skin. Isaac barely moves an inch to make good of my threat before the guard listens, stepping back.

"I'm sure you two have other duties to attend?" I ask. Rhonda nods, then nudges the other guy to walk away. I give Bobby his hat back, then give him a hug.

"Think you came just in time," he whispers. "They didn't believe me. But, uh, good security. Pretty safe here."

He has no idea.

I step back. "It's good to see you, what are you doing here?"

"Oh, doesn't matter, you just walked in from somewhere, I can come back…"

"No, I'm free. Why don't we get some coffee? I swear it won't rot your teeth with sugar." I grab his arm and swing my gaze to Isaac. He gives me a nod, walking away to where those guards disappeared to. Maybe I should be worried about them, but they were being a bit too gruff for my liking.

They're hotel security, not the mob.

I stroll away with Bobby, waving at Oliver as I lead us to the hotel's café. We pass through the lobby, already I feel people staring. Bobby tenses, stopping us before we reach the café.

"Maybe we should go somewhere else. Don't think they want people like me here." Bobby's voice is nervous and quiet. The short time I've spent with him, he's never sounded like that—ashamed.

I lean close, whispering, "I own part of this hotel. *Anyone* is welcome. Practically every staff member knows me, too. It'll be fine. Trust me."

He narrows his eyes, then glimpses up at the ceiling. Shaking his head he exhales deeply, laughing under his breath. "Really changed some things around, huh, kiddo?"

"Yeah, and why don't I start telling you my long story over good coffee? That you don't have to steal." I get us walking again.

"Never stole, *acquired*."

I giggle at him as we enter the café, where the barista greets us warmly. Bobby gets a plain coffee as I order a latte, then head to a corner table. For a couple of hours, we talk about the last four years. I tell him what I can, mainly that I got out of the mob, Steve being imprisoned, the assault, and then about Leo. He tells me about the jobs he's had, moved out of the city a short time and then came back. He even told me about Walter's final days. Since the end of summer, Bobby's been floating between jobs.

"Next step then?" I ask, tossing my empty cup.

"Who knows? Between jobs but was doing some maintenance stuff. HVAC. Better at it than cooking and less wear on my fingers than trucks." He holds up his fingerless gloved hands, scarred and stained. "Oil's a pain to get off."

"Where'd the burns come from?"

He waves it off, scratching under his chin where some more burns are. "Dumpster fire. Didn't wake up fast enough."

"See, that's why you're supposed to have a guard cat."

He chuckles. "Yeah."

"Want another coffee?" I nod toward his own empty cup.

"No, no I'm fine."

The tapping of fingers and the soft ambiance around us is all the noise there is. He adjusts in his seat. The unease he had before is coming back. My heart sinks for him, knowing that feeling of not belonging. I reach over to grab his hat, holding it up with a smile.

"Finally listened?"

He smirks. "Fine, I admit it. My old thing wasn't doing much anymore."

Deciding to take the plunge, cause he sure as fuck ain't going to ask. "Do you need a job, Bobby?"

His eyes meet mine, lips pursing a brief second before he takes the hat from me. I give him time, waiting for his answer as he looks out at the small mid-afternoon crowd.

"Come a long way, kiddo. Even with all the shit, you found your way out."

"Bobby," I say softly.

His gaze stays on the crowd, frowning as he scratches his chin again. "Yeah, I could use the cash. I know it's a lot to ask, but yeah," he finally says in a quiet voice.

"It's okay to ask for help. You told me that, remember?" He looks over to me. "Think I got here on my own?"

"Nah, but...well, at the time, I had to help you. How could I not?"

"Well, my turn now, and I'm not letting my friends get turned out." I get up, holding my hand out to him. He scowls at it. "Come on, you old coot."

That gets him to snort and smile.

He takes my hand, following me to the front desk. "If you're too uncomfortable with it, that's fine, I'll find another way to help, but I want you to stay here. Temps are gonna be colder than a frozen margarita tonight."

"Stay here. *Here*?" His voice raises an octave.

"Look, I know it's not a shelter, but I think it'll do," I tease.

"Well, hard to live up to stiff cots."

"The *Italian Lily* has a lot to live up to. We're trying here." We share a smile as I walk him around the counter, away from where others are checking in. I wave Oliver over, who flicks his gaze between us.

"Miss Watson, how can I help you?"

"I need a room for Bobby here. Put it under my account. Whatever he wants, he can have. Except for diamonds."

"They're terrible with my complexion," Bobby jokes. Oliver's eyes go wide, turning around to type on the computer. Bobby comes in close. "Don't have much humor, huh?"

"Different kind," I whisper back. "How long do you want to stay?"

"Oh, you're serious, kiddo. Giving me a room and all?"

"However long you want. I'll speak to the hotel manager for a job position here. You'll stay here until you can talk with her or another manager. Do you have a phone?"

"Just a burner," he says.

"Alright. Stay however long you want. Order room service, clean your clothes, and anything else. Oliver, can you make sure he has access to my information, including contact up to the apartment, and Isaac?"

"Of course. Would you like me to call Ms. Pierozzi?"

"Just let her know I want to chat tomorrow, and that I have someone to hire." I look back at Bobby who watches in disbelief. "He has me as reference. And have all his info sent my way, too."

Oliver nods, unstiffening as he pulls out a keycard and slides it over to Bobby. I double-check the room number, and then order clothes to his room.

"Okay, hopefully tomorrow evening you'll have someone calling up about a job here. In the meantime, relax. I'll be here in the hotel if you need me."

Tears form in Bobby's eyes, shaking his head as he tries to hide them.

"Not sure why you're doing this," he says in a rasp. "It's been years since we've seen each other, even then only knew the other for a short time." I sense Oliver going still nearby, listening. "For all you know, kiddo, I could be scamming you for money. Maybe run off with a vase or fancy pillow."

"If that's all you're gonna run off with, we need to discuss your acquiring skills." I smile, and then take his hand and say in a gentle tone, "Bobby, someone taught me a bit ago about compassion. And then another, in a New Jersey diner, made me realize we sometimes need kindness from strangers. To listen. To feel human. I'd rather give you a chance."

"Why? Just some old, forgotten man with nothing to his name."

"Because I was once a younger, forgotten woman with nothing to my name, but someone believed in me and gave me a chance."

He smiles softly, hugging me as I let out a choked laugh as I wrap my arms around him. I find Oliver watching, but his attention is taken by a ringing phone.

"Now," I say, pulling away. "Time for the longest bath you've ever had, get some good sleep, and food. Maybe watch some cartoons. Hey, Charlie!" I wave over the valet, who comes and

pauses right before approaching us. "Can you help Bobby find his room? First time in a hotel this big."

"Oh, sure, Miss Watson! What room, Mr. Bobby?" He beams, energetic and ready. Bobby gives me a look, and I wink at him. They leave with Charlie telling him about the hotel.

I exhale a long breath, hands suddenly shaking as I press them against my thighs. He's fine. He'll be okay here and safe. I swallow hard, taking another long breath as Oliver hangs up the phone.

"I'll inform Chiari to meet you tomorrow. She has meetings with other managers in the morning."

"Thank you, Oliver."

"I'm sorry how I acted towards him." I blink at Oliver, his apology throwing me. "I should've believed him and not called security."

"You were just doing your job," I murmur, smiling faintly. "I'll never yell at any of you for doing your job. But, maybe, next time be weary of *how*? Not everyone is who they seem."

He gently smiles back. "I'll make sure he's comfortable."

I reach over, touching his hand. "You *are* wonderful at your job, Oliver."

"Thank you…Autumn."

I nod, heading towards the elevators, but suddenly veer towards Leo's office instead. It's open as I walk in, sitting down on the couch where Leo first handed me that drink. The night I fell into this hotel, and he'd given me refuge.

I can't help everyone, but today I could help one.

One day at a time.

My finger circles around my ring, wondering with unease if one of those people may be Leo.

Chapter 27

Tiptoe

"**Y**ou really think I'd deny your request?" Chiari muses.

I roll my eyes, leaning back in the loveseat. It's just after one, and we've discussed Bobby getting a job here. She found a few places that could work given what I told her of his background.

"I'm sure he'll do great," she continues.

"He doesn't have a suit that I know of. He's only really done blue-collar work. Don't want what he's wearing in an interview to effect his chances."

"It won't."

"You're gonna make sure he gets a job because I'm asking, aren't you?"

"Yup." She smiles, sitting back in her office chair. "Not just because you're engaged to the owner, though. But because I trust your judgement."

Well, some perks are nice.

"How's *your* supposed replacement coming?" I change subjects as she files a few folders.

"Not great. We're looking at in-house candidates, someone who knows our operations within. Except, those who do know about it will need management training. Not just for the hotel."

"All around manager. Why not have two positions then? One for assistant manager and the other for, you know…mob stuff?"

"An entire new position would need to be created, and then there's upfront payment, legal payment, not to mention…" she sighs, rubbing her temple, "…trying to pass off an extra management role would be difficult. Not just for staff here."

My mind flicks to Roger. It's like a game of chess, small pieces and movements at play. One wrong move? It's over. It's one thing to hire a butler, kitchen line cook, or mechanic like Bobby, but the prestige of a management role in a famous hotel? Not as easy.

"Other options?" I ask.

"Hire someone who has no idea, just let them be an assistant manager." Chiari shrugs, typing into her computer. "It'd be difficult some days getting through red tape, hiding things from them, or not including in certain instances, but may be my only option."

"Wouldn't that mean you'd have responsibilities as the new head manager *and*…"

My voice trails off as she gives me a knowing look.

"It's not that bad, and I like my work," she says. "Would it be nice to have an assistant manager to handle all of it? Yes. But Mr. Luciano pays me handsomely, so it's worth it most days. I've paid off my debts and then some, I'll take the win."

"Except for working all the time."

"Used to it." She waves it off, leafing through a folder. "May not have much of a social life, but I've always been an introvert at heart. I knew what I was getting into. I'm good at what I do, and I enjoy it."

I stare down at my hands. That's the kicker, isn't? Enjoying what you do, long hours or not. Wasn't I the same way at the coffee shop? Even at times undercover? Made it worthwhile. It was fulfilling at times. Those jobs kept me from falling apart.

"Honestly, Autumn? I don't want someone to fully replace me."

I look at her as she glances through a file.

"Perhaps it's from working for him for five years, but I'd rather be in charge of Mr. Luciano's assets and security here." Chiari's voice is quiet. "Then again, I may just feel I can't trust just anyone to handle such delicacies given recent situations."

Her voice is strained. Her posture going rigid.

I shouldn't ask. Not peer behind the curtain. I walked away. Yet…

"What situations?"

Gingerly, she puts the folder down and leans back in her chair. "Autumn, Mr. Luciano has made it quite clear about your position regarding that. Not my place to tell."

There's a flash of anger inside me. Anxiety crawling up my spine that I hate.

"Can you at least tell me if I should be worried or maybe something I *could* do?"

"No, they're handling things."

Not only has Leo and the Crew shut me out, but even Chiari is doing it. Suddenly, the twist in my stomach is too familiar to ignore. I stand up, holding myself close as I lean against her desk.

"Leo's been distant," I whisper. "We agreed about me being separate from the mafia stuff, but I'm worried. It'd be one thing if he enjoyed what he did, but he doesn't. Every time he comes back, there's this look in his eye. Like he's slowly dying inside." Her brown eyes meet mine. "Leo takes pride in his hotels, other businesses, but not this. There's no pride in his eyes or even certainty. So, if you know *anything*, I am asking you to tell me. I won't tell a soul if you do."

Her solemn expression makes my hands shake. I keep them close, concentrating to not let the trembling overcome me. She's silent as she touches my hand, helping it stop. Chiari gets up, locks the office door and grabs two glasses and a crystal of scotch.

Great. Wonderful. We love that. Not.

"Doesn't leave my office, and I'm only going to tell you what I think you should know. The rest, he needs to tell you." She pours a drink for us both. "But you're his fiancé and you not knowing what he's fully doing, I think is bullshit. You're stronger than what he and the rest of the Crew think. Otherwise, you'd have never walked back here on your own two feet."

She hands me the glass. "Thanks for the vote of confidence," I say dryly.

Chiari gives me a sympathetic grin. It disappears quickly as she glances at the door as if someone is going to crash in. I've never seen her this nervous. A warning sensation develops at the back of my neck.

"I know about Leonardo having plans to leave the mafia," she begins. "Those escape plans were mainly for him and the Crew, but myself and a handful of others were included. If we wanted to follow, otherwise we'd be absorbed into the next reign, as it were. Honestly, it looked good for the past year. Maybe three more years, we could have safely stepped away. In December something... happened. He may have no choice but to stay as mafia don, until... well..."

"Arrest or death," I mutter, throwing my drink back. "Or find a successor who won't stab him in the back."

"Given who the other crime bosses are...never gonna happen," Chiari murmurs. "Unless you have kids, then they could take over, if he allowed it."

"I can't get pregnant."

I hold my glass out to her. Those sharp eyes flash to mine, and she lets out long sigh, pouring me another finger.

"The assault?" She whispers. I nod. "Bastards, least they're dead."

"What happened in December?"

Chiari knocks back her glass, and then pours herself another.

"I can't tell you," she says solemnly. "I gave my word. But if anything happens to him, Autumn, who knows what becomes of everything from the hotels, companies, or even the mafia." We both stare down at the ring on my finger, and it feels like my heart is in my throat. "If it's something they truly think they couldn't handle, they'd tell you, I think. They're trying to fix the damage. They'll make a new plan. Always do."

"Yeah," I murmur.

I can't tear my gaze away from the ring. Did he know something like this was going to happen? He said it wasn't the reason, but how much of this factored into our marriage? Safeguarding what he built from the wrong hands? My memory flashes to the paperwork, what I agreed to. No, it was to protect *me* if something happened to him. In my heart and gut, I knew he was doing everything to make sure that happens. But at what cost? When I thought I lost him, I spiraled.

Damn it, Leo. He's trying to protect me *again*, but this time he may be sacrificing a part of himself that's destroying him.

"His exit plan was Matteo," I state. She nods her head. "Did something happen to him?"

She shrugs. "They won't give details. I'm just holding off hiring other staff until they do figure it out. Stalling."

"They don't trust people."

"When has that MC *ever* trusted anyone outside their group?" She muses. "Besides you."

I snort, putting my glass down as my stomach churns. We sit back against her desk. "Thanks for saying something."

She gulps down her drink, rotating it in her hand. "Usually I'm not this bothered, but you're not the only one who's noticed something hasn't been quite right. Almost worse than when you disappeared for a week."

"Meaning?"

Chiari leans back, letting out a long exhale. "He's the head mafia don for a reason."

Thoughts swirl in my head. I stand up, rubbing my hands over my arms as I glance over at her shelves of paperwork. My chest constricts, knowing deep down what she means. Leo does have a dangerous streak, but as dangerous as he could be, it's in no comparison if someone like Gabriel took over again. I've seen what those men can do; been part of their scheming and malice. Lead sinks in my stomach, thinking of what could happen if his exit plans fall to pieces completely. Choices taken away. Arrest or death isn't a choice. Neither is agreeing to a botched deal with the feds or witness protection. You're always watching your back. I should know.

Unless you have leverage. Another escape plan. Or blackmail.

I stare hard at the folders. New thoughts cloud my head, battling against what I agreed to and what my gut is telling me. Anxiety ticks up my spine. Except, if don't do anything, I may have no future whatsoever with Leo.

"I have an idea," I tell her. "It'll give me a hobby, get my feet wet again, and help you."

"I'm listening."

"I need a job before I go insane, and it sounds like you have the *perfect* opening."

I't's early evening when I get back to the apartment.

The Christmas decorations were taken down a couple weeks ago, beginning of January. I glance at the clock, realizing it's been a while since I've eaten. It's dinnertime and I decide instead of calling down to one of the restaurants, to make an easy meal instead.

Nothing like cereal for dinner.

I head to the television room with my bowl, wondering what to watch. Finishing up the last of the marshmallows and drinking the milk, I put the bowl down and crouch to skim through the movies. After a few minutes, I plop down behind the couch to browse the titles as indecisiveness sets in.

Hmm, maybe *Elvira?* No, not tonight. *Tremors?* Oh, Kevin Bacon sounds good.

Searching for *Footloose,* I hear the door open. My entire body freezes when I hear the agitated voices of Jameson, Chesty, Owen, and Leo.

"Look, we tried everything to contact him," Owen says.

"Apparently not, because I *know* he's not fucking dumb enough to blackball me," Leo responds gruffly. Something slams shut and I jump, pushing myself against the couch as I hold my breath.

"It's only been three weeks," Chesty intervenes. "He's been gone longer without contacting, maybe he's—"

"What about that stunt he pulled in December? November? He almost cost us multiple shipments," Jameson argues. "Not to mention millions of dollars."

"He said he had to shut down the ports cause of the feds," Chesty counters. "Renato confirmed it."

"Maybe he did, but where's the evidence?" Owen adds. "Renato doesn't trust Matteo; doesn't even fucking like him."

"Matteo put a spotlight on *our* ships from being that complacent," Jameson says. "He's bringing attention to us we don't need."

"Already doing that, without Matteo's help," Chesty says gruffly. I shuffle to the side, keeping against the wall as I peek to see the men stand around the counter. Leo's not there. "He's going through mobsters like they're used tires."

"It's keeping them in line," Jameson argues.

"By fucking torturing them?" Chesty snaps. "Leaving bodies everywhere?"

It feels like knives have struck my chest, making it hard to breathe. My body trembles as I clutch the movie against my chest. Torture? Bodies? I concentrate on breathing, not making a sound.

"Saying they don't deserve it?" Jameson questions. "Rapists, murderers, pedophiles..." he switches to Spanish suddenly, and then back to English, "...should've purged them years ago."

"There's a better way," Chesty argues.

"One. Sure about that?" Owen asks. "And two, you gonna be the one to tell *him* that?"

All three go quiet. Owen leans against the counter with his arms crossed.

Chesty questions, "How much longer we gonna be able to keep the police at bay?"

"However long it takes," Jameson practically growls.

"He'll calm down, always does," Owen adds. "Let him get his

anger out on those who deserve it. Fuckers had it coming. And so he doesn't do anything stupid like pissing off Renato next. We're all fucked if he cuts ties."

I want to be sick. What the hell is Leo doing?

"We need to get into contact with Matteo *before* Gabriel does," Jameson says harshly, slapping papers onto the counter. I flinch, white-knuckling the movie case.

They're not after you. They're not—

"First, you all need to not tell me what to do, this ain't club business." Leo's voice enters the room. "They all deserve what's coming to them."

"Boss—"

"Question me again, Waylon," Leo warns. The cold tone makes my stomach churn. It doesn't sound like him. Like any of them.

Stop it. This isn't you. Stop.

There's silence and I carefully peek around the corner again to see Leo's back. He's in a fresh suit, adjusting his cuffs.

"I know what I'm doing," he says, almost too calmly with a lethal undertone. "I'm getting rid of trash, and only a few bodies are left. Cleaning up like I should have done *years* ago. And gathering information."

"Liar," Chesty murmurs.

Leo's voice is cold and irate. "Careful, *Waylon*."

All of the Crew go quiet, stiffening. My heart pounds in my chest.

Chesty clears his throat before speaking, "Don't want things to go belly-up. Don't need traces getting back to you, especially after all the work we've done to keep businesses legit."

Leo responds, "That's why we have protocols, speaking of, someone…*anyone* get a hold of Matteo. Use a fucking carrier pigeon for all I care. And don't involve Renato."

"Enigma and I will try other contacts," Owen speaks. "Unfortunately, most of interpol is in Renato's pocket."

"Don't remind me," Leo growls. There's heavy steps and the clink of crystal. "And someone tell Captain Wolfe to fuck off. Not my fault his *prized* detective went missing, which for some reason we have no leads on. If we can't find Gabriel, then fucking find that bastard Caltz before someone else does."

My eyes widen. What?

"It's only been 12 days," Jameson says. "Sweeped his house, it's clear. Either he's dead or left town. Good riddance either way."

"Then if he's dead, I want his fucking body to toss into the morgue," Leo snarls. It sounds like glass cracking. "If alive, drag him here, and *then* I'll toss him into the morgue. He's a liability. He knows who Autumn is."

"We'll find him, dead or alive," Jameson answers. "Investor meeting is in fifteen. Then we need to be at the warehouse by ten."

"I know," Leo snaps.

It becomes quiet and someone releases a sharp exhale.

"Where's Autumn?" Leo asks.

My hand moves over my mouth to keep me from screaming. I should get up; tell him I'm right here, but I'm frozen.

"Isaac said she's with Chiari," Owen answers.

"Make sure Alba cleans before she returns," Leo instructs. "Have Isaac inform her I'll be late tonight."

I peek around the corner with most to all their backs to me, except for Chesty who leans against the wall. Leo continues talking to Jameson and Owen about meetings. Suddenly, Chesty makes eye contact with me.

His eyes widen with horror, face becoming pale as his entire body stiffens. My chin quivers, tears threatening to come as the rest of me feels like stone. His gaze is yanked from me as Owen and Jameson leave the apartment, Leo following.

"Leo," Chesty says, and I hold my breath. Quickly, I move behind the wall again, silently begging him not to tell. Chesty clears his throat as Leo's steps halt. "I'll tell Isaac. Autumn will probably spend most of the night with Logan and Mikey anyway."

"Their backgrounds were double-checked, correct?"

"Yeah, they're safe men, boss."

There's a deep sigh. "I shouldn't have snapped like that."

"Been a rough couple months, it'll pass."

"Yeah." Footsteps leave the apartment.

I look around the corner again, finding Chesty peering over at me. He mouths, "Don't run." He follows, door slamming behind them.

I can't move. It's like cold steel has wrapped around my spine as I sit frozen. My heart thunders in my chest with a hard twist in my stomach.

Long hours, fine. Overworking, I knew about it. Me stepping away from the mob dealings, okay, but he lied to me. He promised to tell me anything pertaining to me. Roger fucking missing counts. Matteo going dark and I guess even Gabriel disappearing, too. And who was he torturing? What was Chesty talking about? What bodies?

I try standing, holding onto the wall for support as I drop the DVD and stumble through the living room, feeling the weight of betrayal. Emotions I once felt years ago of being deceived or treated like some child who shouldn't know.

The counter is cold against my gripped hands. My gaze slides to the bedroom, remembering Leo mentioning Alba. In a daze, I walk into the bedroom and look around to find nothing amiss. The twisting in my gut worsens, throat constricting as I swallow hard against the vice around it. Slowly, I push open the bathroom door and see the bloody washcloths. A blood-soaked shirt once light blue, now a deep purple, draped over the hamper. Blood spattered pants. So much of it. Everywhere. More than what I'd seen after he killed those men. After he finished with Steve. Was it one person or several?

Bile rises as I race to the toilet. I puke out the cereal with a groan, heaving out the alcohol I had earlier with Chiari. Tears run down my face as my stomach clenches as I puke into the toilet bowl. I'm beginning to dry heave when doors open, and there's footsteps.

"*Senorita*!" Alba exclaims, suddenly behind me as she kneels as I try to stop the convulsions. She rubs my back as she places her hand against my forehead.

She murmurs in Spanish for me to breathe. Her voice a mantra as I feel empty, gnawing through my stomach. Finally, the convulsions stop as I clutch the porcelain and sit heavily on the floor.

"Aye, Dios mio."

"Alba…what happened?" Charlotte practically shrieks next.

"Get rid of the clothing," Alba instructs. "Clean up all the blood, ahora."

Charlotte moves, cloth rumpling as she works behind me. I try to get up, but Alba keeps me in place. "I've seen blood before, I'm fine…"

"No, stay. Breathe through your nose," she orders gently, rubbing my back still. She holds me carefully as the tears run silently down my face. Minutes tick by before she allows me to stand, cleaning me up, and moving us to the living room.

I sit as Charlotte brings me water, and asks, "Are you alright?"

"Just didn't feel good. I'm fine." I glance at Alba who sits beside me, her face filled with concern.

"I know this may sound cliché," Charlotte starts, wringing her hands in front of herself. "But are you pregnant?"

An empty laugh escapes. How the fuck has that subject come up so often the last two days? "No."

"Are you su—"

"I don't really have a uterus anymore. It'd be short of a miracle for it to happen." Her eyes go wide. Alba scolds her in Spanish, some words I catch as Charlotte responds in an apologetic tone. "Please don't, you didn't know. It's fine."

Alba tells her to clean the bathroom, and Charlotte sighs, leaving to clean up *my* mess now. Great.

I sip more water, hoping to clean out my mouth. The bitterness mixed with sugary sweets is disgusting. I begin to stand, but Alba protests.

"I need to wash my mouth out." I stand fully, heading to the kitchen sink and swish around some water to spit out. Alba appears with my bowl from earlier and I wince.

"Not a proper dinner."

"Well, if it makes you feel better, I doubt I'll have cereal again anytime soon," I mutter, putting my water aside and she grabs my glass to clean.

Can't even have one dirty dish.

An oncoming headache begins to form as I clutch the counter. Alba goes still next to me, drying the glass. "I'll make you a better dinner."

"You're already working late, go home."

"I'll make some rice and vegetables to help with your stomach." She starts to make dinner, and I shake my head. Charlotte comes back, passing the kitchen to the hall and comes back with a cleaning bucket and sponge. I glance over to the cart they've brought up, Leo's bloodied clothes on top.

"Is there anything else you need?" Charlotte asks me, and I pull myself back to the present.

"Uh, no, thank you. And sorry you've got to clean that up."

"It's fine, but are you sure you're okay?"

"Just not feeling the greatest. Maybe flu season."

"Oh, that would be the worst."

"Yeah, thankfully, Alba's cooking should help."

"She makes fantastic tostadas, so you should try them when you're feeling better." I nod as she leaves for the bathroom.

Slumping against the counter, Alba works around me as she slices vegetables. The sick feeling remains, churning with the raw emotions. My gaze flicks to the kitchen knives across the way. Anger mixes with betrayal and hurt.

"He won't harm you," Alba's voice breaks my concentration from the knives. "Señor Luciano never harms those who are loyal. Never raised a hand with me. Charlotte. Staff. Blood is just blood."

"I know he won't." I rub my hand against my face. "He just wants me safe, but I'm...I'm afraid of the path he'll take to achieve it."

Alba hums, moving around the kitchen, and then stops near the sink as she washes the rice. Her gaze remains averted, concentrating on her task.

"People do incredible things when they are in love," she murmurs. "Dangerous things when they fear they'll lose it. He has always been passionate, bearing responsibilities, and protecting what he cares about. Fear can drive a man to the ends of the earth."

"I get that, really I do." I pull at my hair, pacing a little as she continues washing the rice. "Part of me knows him so well, that I *know* he'd destroy the devil to get what he wants. Fuck, he'll destroy hell itself. It's how he's doing it, thinking I need it, when it hurts me. We're supposed to be partners; to talk and be honest like he fucking promised. Instead, each day it feels less and less. Hiding from me, isn't helping me…it's hurting me. Fuck, I feel so alone, Alba."

I groan, leaning my head back as some tears slip down my cheeks. I choke out, exasperated, "People change, but this isn't change…it's not healthy and it's not working. I'm not going to survive any more of these secrets. He knows that, he *should* know that, why doesn't he *know that*?"

"Because he doesn't know." The faucet is turned off and I look at her. "How can he know you're hurting if you don't tell him? Cannot always assume, even with those who know us best."

"I can't tell him," I rasp. "He hates the idea of hurting me. Alba, if I tell him then—"

"He'll know the truth," she interrupts, turning to me. "It may hurt, but it's the truth. You say he's protecting you, and it's hurting you. Well, you're protecting him, and it may be hurting him. You cannot expect change if you don't do anything."

Suddenly, I feel like I'm sitting in a session with Dr. Maxwell.

I wipe away some tears, whispering, "He has to know what he's doing isn't right, hiding stuff from me? It's Leo. He always seems to know me better than me at times, why is it with this, he doesn't?"

I'm not sure why I ask Alba, grasping for answers. Anything to make the hurt less or to make sense without falling into an abyss of other questions. Her answers hurt but feel true with each word. I've pushed down so much, not wanting to rock the boat. There were difficult things happening, but did that mean I had to push away my own needs? Did he?

"It is because he is trying to do the right thing," she says, going back to cooking. "Just like you are trying to do the right thing. But…you're making hard decisions without the other." She comes over, holds up my left hand. "Work does not stop after the ring. More must be done."

She points at the counter, swiftly grabbing a plate and pouring a cup of juice next. I take the hint and go sit. I'm quiet, letting her words sink in.

I told Leo at the end of the party we'd figure it out together. Yet, what have I done to do that? Sure, I haven't been sitting around complaining, but I sure haven't done much to change anything either. I've been keeping busy…avoiding.

"Thank you," I whisper.

She looks over her shoulder. "Being in love isn't easy. Maybe harder with who he is, but you're strong."

"Yeah, tell that to my puking."

"That's from terrible dinner choices," she chastises me.

"Alright, fine, cereal only as dessert."

Alba chuckles. I change the subject to hotel gossip, needing the distraction to not overthink. When I'm in the middle of eating, Alba and Charlotte finish their duties and pack up. It's almost an hour later when they leave.

The door shuts behind them as I stare at my mug of tea. Maybe I should listen to the women who've worked for Leo for years. They're the only ones who don't seem scared of him. I snort at the thought.

I messaged Isaac that I'd taken care of dinner and was in for the night. No messages from Chesty, which made me hopeful he didn't tell Leo.

Fuck. I'm gonna have to face him at some point. Or act like I wasn't here, that I didn't overhear their conversation or that he tried to hide what was in the bathroom. My stomach twists again.

My thoughts are like mashed potatoes as I get up to grab some ice cream. I climb and sit up on the counter, eating it out of the container as I grapple with what to do. How the fuck do I even start talking? I'm pondering for so long the ice cream starts to become soup. I put it away, uncertainty tugging at me as pieces of my brain scream to get out. Run. I'm fidgety as I pace, pulling at my hands as I look around at the grey walls that encage me. Anger crawls over my skin, making me want to scream, throw, or break something.

"Men like him —"

"He's a good man —"

"Fuck!" I yell, stopping in the middle of the room. I smack the side of my head, wanting thoughts to disappear. Those memories to recede.

I'm tired of being understanding all the damn time. I'm tired of pushing for communication. I'm tired of these cycles, feeling insecure, feeling broken, or waiting to get fucking hit again. Control slips from my fingers as I crave it. *Anything* at this point.

And I wanted to be angry. So, *fucking* angry.

I look around at the empty shell of the cold apartment. The grey taunting me. I'm pulled in different directions. One to tell me to grab the knives, end it already or take it to the damn walls. Another part of me wants to storm up into Leo's office. Or third to run away.

Don't run.

My hands shake as I look down at them. The ring that once meant freedom, weighs heavy. I could be cruel. Absolutely cruel to him as I have with others. Punish him—

"No, don't do that," I say out loud, pacing again. "Don't become like Roger or his brothers. Don't do that."

Fuck, I can't stay here.

I go to the bedroom, pack a small bag and sling it over my shoulder. I head out the door, and take the elevator down as my headache worsens. Some of the anxiety dissipates as I look at the colorful interior. No grey. Once the doors open I head to the front desk, where Mikey appears, and then Oliver.

"Still working?" I ask Oliver, seemingly ignoring Mikey as he stands off to the side, watching with a frown as he adjusts his belt.

"Took an extra shift. Not that late, but what…" he glimpses at the bag in my hands, "…Miss Watson?"

"I need a favor." He nods, giving me his full attention. "I need a room."

His brows pinch together. "Did something happen with Bobby—?"

"It's for me." Oliver's eyes shoot up as Mikey steps closer.

"Uh, Autumn, you can come down to the security room if you need," Mikey says.

"Not up for people right now," I whisper. "Just need… I need something different. It's too empty." I turn to Oliver. "Anything available? I'll pay myself."

"No, whatever you need is yours," he says, typing into the computer. He pulls out a keycard sliding it over. I glance down at the room number and let out a breathy laugh.

Same room as the first time.

"You can check out anytime," he assures me.

"Thank you, Oliver." I glimpse over at Mikey who watches me with trepidation. "And can you not let anyone know I'm there? You can use a bogus name like…Sarah."

The name is heavy on my tongue. He nods, not at all objecting. I start walking away with Mikey close behind.

"Autumn, Mr. Luciano didn't hurt—?"

"No," I say quickly, turning toward him as we reach the elevators. "Nothing like that. I just need…somewhere to think. Space to think."

He nods slowly, inhaling a deep breath.

"Do you want me to tell him if he asks where you're at?"

"No…I mean, only if it's emergency."

He presses the button for the elevator. "Let me escort you up?"

I nod, quietly stepping in with him. He doesn't say another

word as he walks me to the suite, sending me off as I slip in and double latch the door. It smells of lilac and fresh linen, a little bit of vanilla. I put my bag in the kitchen. Everything seems smaller than the first time, but it's nice. Relief fills me as I look at the soft lighting, yellow cream walls, and painted visions of green. No fucking grey walls.

I breathe deeply, and head to the bedroom in hopes of sleep and clarity.

Chapter 28

Broken

Leo

Mila follows Leo through his office and into the bar as he goes behind the counter to pour a glass of bourbon. It's thrown back before the bile in this throat can escape.

Shouldn't have gone that far, he thinks. *Shouldn't have taken that long.*

Yet, he can't get the mile-long rap sheets of the men out of his head. The pictures. Teenagers, they were practically *children*. Some of them fucking were. His own damn brother hired those bastards.

Guilt gnaws at him. He should've done this years ago, gotten rid of trash like them when he first took over. Except, he'd been so caught up shipping Matteo to Italy, getting Renato off his back, and dealing with Gabriel that he didn't think about those beyond this office.

Leo's mind flicks to the photo of Sarah Marie. One of many who took the brunt of the cruelty he should've managed years ago. Mob or not, those men went too far.

"Boss," Mila interrupts his thoughts of self-hatred. He scowls as she stands firm. "Bodies have been disposed of."

"Good. See you in the morning," he says in a rough voice. She doesn't move at first, arms remaining crossed over her chest. "Is there something else?" Her jaw works a moment. "If not...then you're *dismissed.*"

Her gaze flicks to his next glass of bourbon, clears her throat and leaves.

Leo turns his gaze to the amber liquor before knocking it back.

Pieces of him felt like they were cracking, splintering through his insides. He flexes his left hand a few times, staring at it as footsteps approach. There should be a ring on that finger. It shouldn't be bare.

How many times has he seen her since the New Year? Spent longer than five minutes with her before leaving to deal with those monsters? Lonely agony tugs at him as he glances at the clock to see it's almost two in the morning. He goes to pour another drink, but someone grabs the bottle to place it back on the shelf.

Leo glares at Jameson practically growling at him.

"I fucking defended you earlier that what you're doing is *sane,*" Jameson whispers harshly, even though there's no one else in the office. "Quit drinking, go home. We have more business to finish tomorrow, the kind that *doesn't* include a knife."

"Who's boss, you or me?" Leo retorts. Jameson glares back, both men standing to their full height.

"You are," Jameson answers. "Even though we're a weird little outlaw club, don't make me or the others pull a democratic election on your ass."

"None of you would dare."

"Don't give us reason to." Jameson grabs the glass, putting it in the sink. "Never been overly prideful before, don't start now."

"Who says I am?"

"Me. The one cleaning up your messes as you slice and dice—"

"I'm protecting her."

"Men who don't know her name?" Jameson questions.

"Remember her face? For fuck sakes' she's engaged to you, mafia don of the city, how much safer do you need her to be?"

A flash of the k-bar in Autumn's hands strikes Leo. The band aids on her legs. The screaming. The rain pouring down over her as she responded to her old name.

His face darkens. "Until the message is clear."

"To the mob? A missing or possibly dead detective? Gabriel?" Jameson steps closer, but Leo doesn't stand down as they come face to face. "Or you giving a warning to your family?"

Leo's expression becomes cold, all emotion becoming void.

"The past two months have been shit," Jameson continues. "That doesn't mean you lose your head. We need you level-headed or everything goes down the shitter. That includes us covering our asses, not pissing off crime bosses by killing their men, or using resources on finding people who clearly are gone or dead. Because if Matteo tries to—"

"I know," Leo mutters. "He'll see reason."

"Will he?"

"Yes."

"Leo—"

"I'm not giving up on him," Leo states, walking out of the bar and heading towards the doors. "He's just having a pissing match with me."

"I know he's your younger brother, but he's becoming a flight risk."

"Which is why someone better get into contact with him." They walk out into the hall, and Leo punches the elevator button.

They're silent as the elevator doors ding open, both getting on. Silence consumes the small space until they open again. Leo steps out, but Jameson causes his steps to falter. "We have two meetings in the morning, don't forget."

"How can I forget, when you never let me?"

"I'm trying to keep your businesses in the clear, I suggest you focus on the same."

Leo goes to retort, but the doors have already closed. He stands there for a moment, staring at his warped reflection in the doors. He turns and stalks into the apartment, closing the door quietly before he leans against it to take a few breaths, running his hand through his hair. Sighing, he goes into the bathroom silently, noticing it's been cleaned and begins to pull his shirt off until he realizes *how* quiet it is.

He steps out of the bathroom, peering into the darkness. The bed is empty.

There's an ache in his chest, knowing she may be sleeping on the couch again, but it turns into fear when he sees how empty the living room is. Alarm rushes over him as he checks the television room. Empty.

She should be here.

"Autumn?" He quickly checks the other rooms, heart pounding in his chest. "Autumn?"

Glimpses of the night she left pierce him, making him almost stumble as he looks around the apartment. *Where is she?* Panic makes the liquor he drank hard as a rock as he grabs his phone, calling Isaac.

It rings twice. "Boss—"

"Where is she? Where's my—" His voice chokes out before he can say the word, breathing heavily. "Where's Autumn?"

"Home."

"Hotel or penthouse?"

"Hotel. Been here all day. Why?"

"She's not here, Isaac."

There's noise on the other end. "Shit."

"Get hold of security. *Now.*"

<hr>

Autumn

My phone won't stop ringing.

I grumble, pulling the pillow over my head and debate

turning it off all together. Finally, I grab it and answer without looking at the ID. "What? Hello?"

"Autumn?" Mikey's voice comes over the line. The nervousness in his tone makes me sit up.

"Mikey, what's—"

"Look I'm sorry, I know you wanted privacy, but if I didn't give him your room number, I think he may have shot Logan or I."

That wakes me *right* up.

"Wait, what? Who—" Oh, no.

Suddenly, there's pounding at the door of the suite. It's loud, and someone else tries to call me. I glance down, noticing Leo's caller ID. I don't answer. Same when Isaac tries to call.

"Autumn, we didn't give him a master key, but Logan is taking one up. He's trying to take his time, do you want—"

"No, no it's…it's fine. I'll handle him."

Mikey clears his throat. "Are you sure?"

"Yeah, trust me, thanks for the heads up." I hang up, walking out to the living room area as the door is pounded on again.

Through the hard wood, I hear him, "Open the door. Please. Open the door, Autumn."

My chin quivers, chest tightening as I listen to the plea. I rub at my chest, unsure what to do and feeling trapped. Here I am acting like a child once more, hiding and locking the door. The logical side tells me to talk to him; while the other says run.

He knocks harshly again. I swear under my breath, knowing if he keeps doing that, he'll upset the other guests. It's practically 2:30 in the morning. Staring at the door, knowing Logan will arrive with the key soon, I call him. It barely rings once. "Check in."

I almost want to laugh at the absurdity. Instead, I answer quietly, "Red."

"Autumn, open the door, let me in. Let me help you."

"I don't think you can," I whisper.

He inhales sharply. "Autumn, sweetheart, open the door… just—"

"I was in the penthouse." The words stumble out before I can

think. "I heard everything. I saw what you left behind. All of it."
Leo swears under his breath. Tears fall down my cheeks, stepping
back from the door. "You lied, Leo."

"Let me explain."

"No, no I am tired. I am angry. I am hurt. I am…lonely. No more
excuses. I can't hear anymore, I can't."

"Dear Watson, please," he practically begs over the line and
through the door.

"I hid from you," I say in a small voice, vision blurring as I
stumble back against the couch. "I… I thought…"

"I'll never hurt you. I promise you. I *promised* you."

"Except you have this habit of breaking them." A sob catches in
my throat, clutching my head. "Said we were partners, but how
can we be when I never see you? I agreed to step away, but not to
be lied to. Not to be hidden from. You said you'd tell me if it
involved me. You promised to talk to me if it got bad. You
promised…I trusted you. I trusted *you*, to tell me the truth! No
more secrets! Unless you stopped trusting me, maybe I did something wrong—"

"You did nothing wrong," he says abruptly. "I trust you with
fucking everything I have. You know what I've given you—"

"The money doesn't fucking matter!" I start pacing, anger
rising. I hate feeling like this, emotions swirling inside me as panic
ticks at my neck. "None of that matters; it doesn't prove anything!
Not when doors are closed in my face. Not telling me where you
are. Not picking up the damn phone. Disappearing for days!
Leaving me! You left me! *Alone*. You left me alone, all of you!
Expecting me to just be fine! I wasn't *fine*! Everything and anything
became more important than me, no matter what I did. You
promised me…you promised me."

My knees hit the carpet, sobbing as I hold myself. There's a slam
against the door, but I can't even look as I continue to cry through
every heavy emotion of the last few weeks. Months. The turmoil.
Isolation. Old forgotten feelings.

"I've been trying…" I plead as muffled sounds come from the

other end, "…I kept trying without you. I don't want to get in the way, but I don't want to be forgotten. I just…I just wanted…"

There's ding from the key card going through.

It jolts me as I scramble to get up, dropping the phone on the glass coffee table. It clangs, causing me to shout and then the door slams open. The extra lock pings off, flying across the room as flight kicks into my defense system. I fall back, struggling to fight anyone off of me. Hands reach for me as the darkness encompasses my vision, trying to drown me in panic.

"Let go! Don't—" I shout as Leo grabs my wrists.

It's only a momentary glimpse that I see him checking my right wrist, and then my left. I freeze. Sharp reality hits me like cold water as I realize what he's doing. Leo only takes a moment to check if I self-harmed before he pulls me into his embrace. I blink through tear-filled vision and see three others at the doorway.

"I'm sorry, I'm sorry…" Leo's broken, whispers ring through my ears. He kneels before me, arms shaking around me. They're still trembling as he pulls away to inspect my arms again, as if he doesn't believe it. "I'm sorry, I'm sorry…"

"Stop," I plead. "Stop."

Tears cover his face, eyes red, and horror encasing them. The terror in them reaches into my fucking soul. He thought I cut again.

"I never meant to hurt you," he rasps, grasping at my face. His entire body trembles. "I was trying to protect you. I fucked up. I'm sorry. I fucked up, Autumn. I love you, don't leave me, I fucked up."

I can't take it anymore, body screaming to be held.

My arms wrap around his shoulders as my legs go around his waist, gripping him for dear life. We're shaking violently as he holds onto me as if I'll vanish.

"I swear I trust you," he murmurs, burying his face against my neck. "I swear. I love you, please don't leave me. Please. Anything you ask, anything." Leo begs against my skin. The clutch he has on my body reminding me of…me.

We remain there for what seems like forever. Whoever had

come with him is gone, the only noise being the click of the door shutting. After a few minutes, I look to see a piece of the lock on the floor.

"You broke the door."

He grunts.

I could have scoffed if I wasn't so worn out. His grip tightens as I bury my face against the crook of his shoulder. He begins to stand, grunting as he struggles a moment, but gets up. As he starts heading for the door, I begin shaking again.

"Stop," I choke out. "Don't take me upstairs. Please. Don't."

"Autumn."

"No. I can't be alone again, not with those…walls. Please. I can't."

My words are muffled as I dig my nails into him. His hand caresses my back in attempt to soothe me. He starts to hush me gently, taking us into the bedroom instead.

He yanks the blankets back, getting into the bed with me still clinging to him. His arm remains around me as he pulls the covers over us, resting my head under his chin. I listen to his thundering heartbeat. It doesn't soften as he strokes my head. I begin to untangle my legs from his waist, and then realize his pants don't feel right.

"Are you wearing slacks?" He nods. Not showing signs of letting go. "You can change."

He grumbles, tightening his hold. "Take them off, Leo."

Barely a few moments pass before he moves a hand down, unbuckling his belt and shimmies out of the slacks. Using only one arm doesn't quite work, so I help him and toss them across the floor. He holds me close again as exhaustion takes hold.

"I love you," he murmurs. "I love you more than life, my dear Watson."

I stroke his jaw unable to fight anymore. The last of it leaves me as the weight of today, the past months yank me into oblivion. "I love you. I'm not leaving…I'm not leaving."

Chapter 29

The Ecstasy of Autumn

I gasp awake, grabbing for the covers. Eyes pop open to not find grey walls, but warm ivory. I attempt to catch better air as my brain processes that I'm in the hotel suite. Hands pull me toward a warm chest.

"You're safe." Leo's voice drifts over my ear. "You're safe."

It isn't until the second time he says it I realize how tense my body is. I relax, going limp. We lay in silence. Dim morning light peeks in. I hold his arms that are around me, curling against him. My mind flits over the events of yesterday; remembering what I overheard. A slight headache begins to form as I begin to feel sick, almost woozy.

I fidget, attempting to get up, but Leo keeps a firm hold. I grunt against him, but the only response I get is him pressing his face against my neck, placing a soft kiss. The tender touch makes my heart ache. Craving it. He does it again, and I get the sneaking suspicion I'm not the only one who wants to forget what happened last night.

"Leo." He moves one of his hands down my side. "Leo, what are you doing?"

Hot breath trickles over my skin. I shiver at the sensation, battling against the craving.

"Leo," I say his name again as he glides a hand over my leg, stroking up my thigh. "We need to talk."

"We will." His groin presses against my backside. Oh, look, someone *else* is awake.

"What happened to 'responsible' Leo?"

"Gone after he broke the door," he mutters. I shiver again as hands skim my side. I want to fall into his spell, forget what happened, but *someone* needs to get us to talk and it's not gonna be him.

Quickly, I turn and grab his hands, forcing him onto his back as I pin his wrists above his head and straddle his waist. I move up his torso, trying to ignore his erection. His eyes widen.

"The *one* time I want responsible Leo, really?" I grumble, somewhat glaring at him. He goes to open his mouth. "Don't make me use the stoplight method, mister." He shuts his mouth. "We're talking first, cause I'm tired of crying, puking, hiding, and..." I glimpse at where the broken lock is, "...us breaking the hotel."

His face turns serious, but his eyes are filled with regret, and the lingering guilt comes back. Yeah, *that's* what I've been trying to avoid altogether. But we can't keep dancing around each other. Isaac, Chiari, and Alba were right. We need to talk.

"Months ago, near a playground," I begin, slowly. "I told you I'd give you a chance, but you *had* to talk to me. Not assume what I'd say. We agreed I'd step back, yes, but what's happened is that I've been completely shut out. Treated like I should just...shut my mouth and don't ask questions. That's not what we agreed on. This is a team effort. You broke promises by not telling me about Roger going missing, Matteo causing you stress, or the truth about leaving the mob crumbling. *All* that pertains to me, too."

Leo's brow furrows deeply. I almost want to smile at the frown lines that I've missed seeing. The right ones, not the kind that creates worry.

"Don't ask how I know," I continue. "Was undercover without

you noticing, so don't try me. Next, I told you I don't care what happens behind closed doors, if you don't want to tell me, fine. But don't try hiding it like some damning secret. The more you push me away in an attempt to protect me or whatever, the more heartbreaking it is to find what's left behind. I puked my brains out when I saw those clothes yesterday. Not at the blood, but at the *why*. For weeks I asked you, and you said nothing. I *knew* something was wrong, but you wouldn't talk to me. Kept saying you were handling it. It felt like you didn't trust me. Like I couldn't handle it. I know those first few weeks of me losing my shit didn't help, but, fuck, Leo I don't—"

Suddenly, Leo breaks from my hold to pull me down for a kiss. We crash together, swallowing up my words as I sink into him. It's tender and loving. He breaks away far quicker than I anticipate, and I blink down at him

"I'm listening, but you were about to panic ramble," he says, putting his hands above his head again. I groan, putting my hands over his to "pin him" as I thud my head into his chest.

"Why can't I be mad at you for more than five minutes?" I grumble.

He clears his throat, not answering.

I sigh sitting back up. His gaze moves over me, a bit worried still. Taking another deep breath, I say in a quieter tone, "I was lonely. Didn't want to fully admit it. To feel like a burden. I wanted to be supportive of you, give you space, thinking that's what you needed. Everyone kept telling me how much you worked, that this was normal, and I gave in to those excuses. I didn't want you to feel more guilty being away when I knew you were trying. I hated you being gone, not even being able to fucking call you. When you didn't come to the party I was upset, but when you showed up... you looked so defeated, I couldn't be mad. I couldn't. You kept coming back so exhausted and barely here, I didn't want to add on."

I pull my hands away from his, placing them on his chest as I look down at my ring. Tears form even though I'm unsure how there's any left. Leo brings his arms down, one to hold my hands and the other to wipe away the first tear.

"It's been so fucking hard keeping our marriage a secret. *Our* secret, but you weren't here. Days and nights I felt truly alone, more than I had been before." Leo squeezes my hands, wiping away another tear. I swallow hard. "I love you Leo, but it's been so hard. The one person who's been my rock, for figuring out my head stuff, anxiety, and gave me peace wasn't there. Then, I find out you've been hiding what you were doing, and it made me feel like...I wasn't enough."

He cups my cheek, softly stroking his thumb. "You will *always* be more than enough. Don't ever doubt that."

"It's hard to believe that when you're stuck alone with your thoughts," I whisper against the lump forming in my throat.

"I know I've said it a hundred times, but it won't be enough. I am sorry for what I ended up doing to you, causing you to feel this way. It was never what I intended. If I'd known—"

"It's my fault for not saying anything."

"Autumn." Leo sits up, cupping my face, which elicits me to look at him. He strokes his thumbs over my skin again as my chin quivers. "Perhaps, we'd have talked earlier if you'd said something, but it's not your fault. I wasn't around. That is my error. It was me who left you alone, and I knew better. I *do* know better. At some point, any human being would start feeling lonely. Because I was...I was lonely, too." Leo lowers his hands. "May I speak?"

My sarcastic side is screaming, *about damn time.*

Instead, I ask, "Do you wanna switch? Pin me down. Seems equal."

He smirks before twisting us, making me fall onto the bed as he hovers over me. He doesn't pin me, instead leaning on one arm while stroking my hair with the other.

"Better?" He asks.

"I'll take it."

"You were right. I was being dishonest with you," he starts. "I said I had a handle on things but didn't. Not really. I was frustrated, angry, and overwhelmed. And then tried to handle it the only way I knew—working. Thinking it would help, but it hasn't. It made things worse. What I'd done before you isn't going to help anymore because…" he looks away, face twisted in a scowl as his fist clenches beside me. I brush my fingertips over his stubbled chin. "…I hated being away from you. Damned if I worked, damned if I didn't."

Leo still won't look at me but takes my hand against his cheek and kisses my wrist.

"I fucking hated it," he continues. "The very thought of you unsafe or in danger again blurred any lines of right and wrong. And then the exit plan I had for us, disintegrated. Continues to. The idea of failing you bore a hole in me, so I concentrated on what I *could* do, no matter how heinous. How bloody." He closes his eyes, clearing his throat. "Put simply, I was a coward to not tell you what was happening. I didn't want to burden *you*. You are strong and capable, Autumn, but there are some images I cannot forget. The thought of failing you over and over grew that guilt to the point that I didn't know how to tell you what was wrong. Not without worrying you'd try to take the blame."

My heart feels torn and heavy. I nudge him to look at me, but he refuses.

"I did the exact opposite of keeping you safe," he whispers. "I hurt you; pushing you away when I shouldn't have. I trusted you, but it was myself who I didn't trust. Not after…after we were attacked on the street or…when you flinched."

My stomach drops. "Leo."

"I fucked up. I'm why you felt the need to hide. Nothing I did was excusable. I made you run—"

"No, no you didn't…I just needed space." I clutch at his face, trying to get him to look at me. "I…I had to think, to breathe. I didn't know what to do, but I wasn't leaving."

"You told Oliver to use a fake name."

"I needed space, Leo…a different space." A tear falls down his cheek, and I quickly brush it away. I gulp, knowing I need to be honest about another reason I had to leave. When had we lost that open communication and vulnerability? How did our innermost confessions just…stop?

"Look at me, Leo," I urge him. "Please." Finally, he does with my soft ask. Those hazel eyes glisten with tears.

"You didn't fail," I whisper. "I'm angry with you for not talking, not being fully honest, hiding things, but I love you. I'm sorry I disappeared, but I wasn't leaving. Those…the apartment…it reminds me of the interrogation." His brows furrow closer together. "The grey. It's the same color. Sometimes I forget, and I couldn't think last night."

His face crumbles. "Fuck, Autumn, I would've changed the damn paint in a day if I'd known. I'm sorry—"

"Not your fault, I didn't—"

"I don't want to be a source of your pain, yet that fucking cold apartment has been." He sits up, holding his head with his back turned to me. "And I fucking left you there."

"Leo, you didn't know. This is why I didn't want to tell you. You take on every burden of mine you can, and that's not fair to you." I sit alongside him as he stares down at his hands. "I'm sorry, I should've talked, too. But…Leo, I know you don't want to hurt me, but please talk to me. I shoved shit down, because you were pushing away and every time you do, I feel worthless again with no room to complain."

"You're worth more than the damn stars, dear Watson."

"And you're worth more than all the planets, mister." I press my forehead against his shoulder. "You've always understood me better than anyone. Always given me time and never faltered. What changed for you to pause? It couldn't have just been the flinch, I have before. Was it cause I called red that morning?"

"No. Never feel guilty for calling red."

"Then what? Why put walls up or not trust yourself around me to talk? What are you afraid of?" He continues to stare at his hands, flexing them. His gaze becomes distant. "I don't want to make you talk, but…I don't know what to do."

Silence stretches. Inside, I beg for him to speak to me. For both our sakes at this point.

"I've done terrible things," he finally says as I watch him stare at his hands with a blank expression. "I regret none. Although, it might make me no better than Gabriel or my father, I just have a better leash on myself. The justification. Pain replaced the anger, frustration, guilt, blame..." Leo turns his hands over, and I notice the scabs over his knuckles and the rawness, "...their pain. I've come to terms with what I am. These past weeks I've hurt, killed... tortured those that Gabriel hired under my nose. Every single person he hired to assault, rape, and kill those who didn't deserve it. When it wasn't enough..." he swallows hard, dropping his hands to his lap, "...I went after every single person you came into contact with undercover."

I go still.

I'm not sure how long I hold my breath. Mind going blank as his words sink in. My eyes flit to my wrists. Those seconds last night of him checking for cuts. The fear in his eyes.

"I wanted them to pay," he murmurs. "What they did to you. What they did to others like you. While...trying to absolve my own sins. I became judge and executioner, even if it meant becoming the monster. I didn't care. I wanted every single one to suffer."

Holy fuck.

I close my eyes as I take a deep breath. Okay, I understand him not wanting to tell me. Past couple months he's been pulling the most morally-grey villain arc in the shadows. Alrighty, Mila's caution was more warranted than I thought.

My heart clenches at how he's been handling all this. Keeping the pain of seeing my aftermath to himself. I reach for his hands, bringing them up to kiss every bloodied knuckle of his. Finally, his solemn gaze meets mine.

"Speak to me before you decide to destroy more of my demons, allow me to decide their fate, not you," I say softly. "What's done is done, but don't take more of my past on your own. You should know; I won't approve you taking such measures always. I understand you know the difference of someone looking at me wrong or suggesting bodily harm, but just putting it out there."

He scoffs lightly.

"I love you. Even when you don't trust yourself or when you take matters into your own hands. Maybe you fucked up, made me angry, or accidentally hurt me along the way…but I know you'll never, *ever* break the one promise I care most about." I turn his hand against my cheek, leaning into its warmth. He sharply inhales. "Whatever you do in the shadows, fine, but don't hide from me. Talk to me when it feels too much. Let me be there for you, too."

"You're not…horrified?"

I shrug. "Surprised, but uh…" I swallow hard, easing down the anxiety trying to build up my spine, "…I know who you went after. And this world is better off without them. Maybe that makes us both monsters."

His expression softens, shaking his head faintly. He leans his head against mine.

"I'll talk to you, but promise me something," Leo says. "You'll be selfish. Tell me to come home. Stop working. Anything. You won't be in the way. Never let my position or power keep you from wanting. Be selfish."

"Are you giving me permission to tell you what to do?"

He leans away, stroking my hair back with a tender gesture and smile that makes my heart lighten. "Only you."

I move to wrap my legs around him, straddling his waist. Leo's breath hitches before putting his arms around me, then burying his face against my neck. I'm certain it's where he prefers to hide.

"Thank you for telling me finally," I say. "I do forgive you."

"I love you, my dear Watson."

"I love you, mister Americano."

We remain there silently. Except my mind continues to reel, wondering what to do as I clutch him to me. A thought rises at the back of my head, snippets of what I've read these last few weeks. What Dr. Maxwell suggested in understanding Leo in a different light. Why this compulsion to not "save me" but to "protect me" from the world so vehemently. There will always be blood spilled in the mafia, no matter the reason, it's not what I worry over. It's the why.

Chapters float through my head. What he's told me about what he needs as a Dom, then suddenly it clicks. He's a soft Dom yes, but also a caregiver. He takes full responsibility because he craves it, needs it as a purpose. Much like me, he needs reassurance. Reminders that he's good enough. It's himself he lost trust in, not me. So, he isolated himself.

Like I'd done.

I immersed myself in "work" again to not feel. To not think. I secluded myself without admitting out loud what I needed.

We needed to find that rhythm again. First steps needed to be taken, which meant finding that vulnerability we had before.

"Let's go shower," I whisper to him.

He pulls back slightly, glancing over me and then nods his head. I remain wrapped around him as he gets off the bed, heading to the bathroom. It's smaller than the apartment, by a long shot, but the shower will fit us both. He sets me down quietly, turning on the warm water as he tugs his shirt off.

Leo freezes when I place my hand at the center of his back. I trace down the blazing blade, back up to the hilt. My eyes search over the demon wings upon his back, the hellscape that covers his skin.

"It's the Archangel Michael's sword, isn't?" I ask softly.

His breath comes out in a soft exhale. "Yes."

An angel for warriors. The angel of righteousness. Was that sword representing the path of Michael or being slayed *by* him? I look over the leathery wings, remembering depictions of the angel having feathered wings instead.

I spread my hands over his back, leaning in to kiss the hilt of the sword. His breath hitches as I turn him to face me. My hands trail up to his jaw, making him look down into my gaze.

"Be not afraid," I whisper, and his eyes widen.

I've not been religious for most of my life, but it's clear that pieces of his own beliefs have clung to him.

"I want you," I say, beginning to take my shirt off. "I need you, Leo. Just as much as you need and want me."

I get completely undressed as he does. He's stiff, taking his time as if he's waiting for me to bolt. To run. Suddenly, I see that child left, forgotten for days. Left behind by the death of his mother. By the cruelty of his father. I see myself tossed aside by my parents. My sister. Beaten and battered into nothing. Treated like nothing. Seclusion was always safest. No one can hurt you.

I take his hand, leading him into the shower. It pours over us as he closes the gap. Water streams down his tattooed skin. Leo gently pushes back my hair, allowing the water to fall down my back. My hands glide over his skin. We continue to feel the other, taking our time. I turn, pressing my back against his chest as he runs his hand down my torso and across my stomach. His fingers trace over the faint scars. I sigh against him, leaning into his warmth as the hot water cascades down our bodies.

"I *was* afraid," he whispers. "I am always afraid of losing you."

"I'm right here. I don't plan on leaving you, Leo, in any sense."

He turns me around, cupping my face in his hands. Gold flecked green eyes sear into mine. "I never want to be why you hurt."

I move one of his hands down, placing it against my neck, not taking my eyes off his. "You're why I'm *alive.*"

His breathing picks up. The hand against my cheek trembling.

"The only one I trust with my life, my body, my mind completely is you," I say, going the route of declaration as he's done for me. "I love you despite your mistakes, misdeeds, or attempts to be perfect for me. All I need is Leo. *My* Leo, and husband. He is the only one I will *ever* trust to replace every touch that's harmed me with his pleasure. Body and soul."

Leo's gaze scorches into my soul. Hand flexing on my neck ever so slightly, he gently pulls me forward to kiss me deeply. I reach up, gripping onto him as I kiss him back, needing him to understand that no matter what he does, I love him and will stay.

Our bodies become flush, warm wet skin sliding against the other. My body practically writhes in need as I cling to him. Leo continues to ravage me in a passionate kiss, picking me up and carrying me out of the shower. He sits me on the counter, clutching my head to continue kissing until what feels like eternity.

"Autumn," he rasps.

"I need you, baby," I plead, stroking down his stubbled jaw and neck. His eyes snap to mine as I continue to run my hands over him.

He kisses me again, opening my legs a bit more as a hand slides down between them. His fingers brush against my sex and my breath hitches against his mouth.

"Check in," he whispers.

"Emerald. Check in."

"Peridot."

His fingers thrust in gently, making me gasp. He continues the slow movements as he clutches my hair, keeping me still as he kisses me. Our tongues tangle, almost frantically trying not to let the heat inside either of us diminish. His hand moves slow below, almost teasingly as his thumb circles around my clit. I gasp into his mouth when he presses forward. He eases the kiss, moving his lips over my jaw, down my neck and above my breasts as I lean back.

Suddenly, Leo pulls his fingers away and steps back. I'm left panting on the counter for him, feeling flushed and needing more. He brings his fingers up to his mouth, cleaning them almost reverently.

"Step down," he instructs faintly, then swallows hard. I do so. "Turn around, put one leg up on the counter." His voice is hoarse as he instructs me what to do.

I turn and carefully set my leg up on the counter. It slides a little from the water, but Leo comes up behind me, bending my leg so my knee rests on the counter. Gently, he leans my torso forward closer to the counter. I look up at the mirror, finding the reflection of Leo's tattooed torso directly behind me as he takes a hand to stroke my sex again.

"You don't have to make eye contact, and if you feel like you're cramping, tell me," he says tenderly as his other hand caresses my hip.

"Okay."

Slowly, Leo bends a little and helps guide his cock to my entrance. I stare down at the marbled counter as he enters. I clutch at the hard surface as he slowly pushes forward, moves back, and thrusts again gently. One of his hands holds my hip while the other cups my ass cheek.

The angle and being bent over like this, his cock hits different spots of nerves. I gasp as he thrusts forward, causing tremors along my limbs. Leo leans over, going at a steady pace as he fucks me against the bathroom counter. Tingling runs up my spine, which coils in elation that forms in my core. I look up.

My eyes catch Leo's form over mine. Water and sweat drip down inked skin, falling onto mine. His dark hair, longer than usual, almost covers his forehead drips upon me. His hand on my ass slides up, cupping my breast from the side. I moan at the contact, unable to tear my gaze away from our reflection. Butterflies fill my stomach almost shy at the intimacy it provides, until his eyes find mine in the mirror. He pauses only a moment before slamming his hips against mine. I cry out as he continues the sensuous torture. Pleasure and bliss beginning to blind me as I lose my breath. Leo's eyes never leave mine as he deepens his thrusts, pulling me back against him.

Euphoria, pure and craving uncoils deep within me. Before I know it, I'm coming hard. My entire body tenses as Leo thrusts into me one more time, holding me there as my body shakes and convulses from the intensity.

We breathe heavy, gazes locked in our reflection of ecstasy.

Chapter 30

The Other Cheek

Breakfast is placed on the dining table. Hwan refuses to make eye contact with Leo, who sits back in his chair on the phone. He's canceled multiple meetings, which means Jameson will be down to wreak havoc before we're done eating. My bet is before the coffee is cold.

"Thank you, Hwan," I say, then gesture for Leo's wallet. He hands it me without looking up as I follow Hwan to the doorway. I give him a hefty tip, mainly to overcompensate for the shock in realizing he was serving breakfast to the hotel owner. "Thanks for the quick service."

"Anything for Mr. Luciano." He takes the tip, glimpsing past me. "Does he…sorry, I shouldn't intrude."

I lean in. "He's not that scary. He's ma—engaged to me, right? And I'm told I'm a delight." Hwan pinches his brows. "And remember that bonus."

He suddenly smiles, nodding. "Right. Have a good day."

"You, too."

I shut the door as Leo pours the coffee, talking sternly on the phone. Once we cleaned up in the shower (again) he called room service and then started canceling meetings for the morning. I hadn't realized it was barely eight until I came out to assess the door's damage.

He hangs up as I sit down. "Pretty sure you almost gave Hwan a heart attack."

He raises a brow. "How'd you know his name?"

I unroll the napkin from around my utensils, cutting into my eggs benedict as Leo starts on his omelet. "I know him and a few other servers. He's working while in college, studying science, can't remember which 'ology' though," I answer. I glance over at Leo staring at me. "What?"

"I understand a good amount of the staff came to the party, but how many have you gotten to know?"

I shrug. "Not sure. Servers, restaurant workers, housekeeping, front desk, most managers at this point, handful from the spa. Not to mention a few valets, oh, and security guards. Mainly only Mikey and Logan."

"You know many," he says in a quiet tone.

"Well, you own half a dozen hotels, Leo, with thousands of workers. Bet you know all the board members. I don't. You're not gonna know everyone. Besides, I had time on my hands and they helped keep me busy."

Leo's quiet as I sip my coffee. He stares at his plate then abruptly breaks out of whatever spell he was in and continues eating. He's stiff and almost robotic.

I put my mug down, then place my hand on his thigh. "They kept me company. You don't need to know every single one. But do know you have good people here."

"*We* do."

I smirk, grabbing his hand to kiss his knuckles. "Yeah, but they don't know that, yet."

He smirks back, bringing our joined hands up to kiss mine. "Perhaps I should just give the hotel to you."

"Calm down there, Hoss, one thing at a time," I nervously laugh, letting his hand go as my breath becomes shaky.

Leo places his hand behind my head, guiding me to look at him.

"I didn't mean to scare you. Just a thought. Since you refuse to sleep with a potential boss, but what happens now that you own *him* and his hotel?"

I snort rolling my eyes. "Obvious. Plan world domination, Pinky."

He chuckles, kissing me before going back to breakfast. I breathe easier, relief in having this semblance of normality back.

After our second shower, we talked a bit more before breakfast arrived. Discussed emotions, wants, and needs, including spending time together daily. Something to ground us to face the world. We'd move forward. Eggs is a good start.

"Speaking world domination," I say after taking another bite. "I told Chiari I'd help with her manager duties, since she seems overworked. Just part-time."

Leo nods. "I worry about her at times. I put a lot on her shoulders, yet she always remains steady."

"She's good."

"That she is." He sips his coffee, raising a curious brow. "Is this the part where we discuss salary?"

I snort. "No. Unless cuddling will be part of payment."

"Could be arranged." He winks, making me giggle.

"And one other thing, okay, two," I say quickly. He raises both brows, pausing before taking another bite of his omelet. "I've been a busy gal." He gestures for me to continue. "A friend was looking for a job, so I offered him one here, but he *will* go through an interview process. I also gave him a room here indefinitely because he's homeless."

He leans back in his chair, nodding slowly. "Is that both things? The room and the job?"

I clear my throat, knowing I'm asking a lot. "No. You said to discuss with you before buying a building."

Shock covers his face, brows somehow higher than before.

"I told Trix I'd talk to you about funding or donating some money for a center she's been working on establishing for victims of domestic violence. It's for a university or two, but lack of funding is keeping her back. Donations can do the trick. She can explain it better, but I told her you could meet."

"Then we will."

I drop my fork. The stoic expression isn't helping the surprise. "Really?"

"Yes, *Luna Stella* isn't the only place I help fund, Autumn," he answers. "Apart from my own, slight unconventional ways of handling deals, I'm open to other options." I snort loudly, and his impassive expression almost falters. "Who's this other friend?"

"Bobby," I answer immediately. A surreal feeling rushes over my chest as I poke at my expensive eggs, remembering not eating for days. "He and..." I clear my throat, blinking past potential tears, "...and Walter kept an eye on me when I was homeless. Checked on me."

"Where's Walter?"

"He died. Pneumonia."

Leo inhales sharply, touching my hand. "I'm sorry."

I shake off the old memories, grabbing for my coffee instead.

"He won't be able to stay at the hotel long," Leo states suddenly. "Due to policies of loitering and such, whether we're paying for the room or not. Not to mention nosey guests will likely complain." Leo places his mug down, going back to breakfast as my heart sinks. Until he makes it flutter. "I'll arrange an apartment for him. Give him his own space."

My throat feels tight, swallowing hard as I stare at him. "He may not accept it. Got a prideful streak."

"Then I'll have a discussion with him." Leo cuts away at his omelet like we're talking about the weather, not changing a man's life. "We'll discuss the best role for him to work here. You've told me in the past, sometimes we must put our pride aside and accept help. No shame in it. For anyone."

There's a clack as I put my mug down. Leo pauses as I go sit on his lap, putting my arms around him. I say softly, "Thank you."

Leo strokes my hair back. "I think I'd rather help those who were good to you, than punish those who were horrific nightmares. Perhaps *that* will ease my guilt instead."

"Less bloody," I tease, and he faintly smiles. "And the whole spread kindness to the world spiel, too. Yada-yada."

We smile at the other and then I abruptly smack his shoulder. He looks at me wide-eyed. "See? This is why we need breakfast talk; we figure shit out during this important time."

Leo chuckles, kissing me hard until there's a hard knock at the door. It pounds again, and then his phone buzzes. Well…coffee is nowhere near cold. The disruption continues as Leo grumbles under his breath.

"I'll get the door," I say. Leo goes back to breakfast like no one is vying for his attention. Oh, so we're going the route of ignoring, huh? Cause *that's* worked so well.

I go to open the door right as the pounding starts again, behind it is a disgruntled Jameson, surprised Owen, tentative Isaac, tired Julio, and…Mila.

"About damn—" Jameson cuts himself off when I don't budge from the doorway.

"Can you not knock so loudly? Guests are probably already complaining about last night, let's not add grievances," I state. I look to the others. "Good morning, and Mila, hey, this is a surprise. Beginning to think you ghosted me." Not even a flicker of a look in response.

Good to know she hasn't changed.

"I need to talk to him," Jameson says.

"Later. You've had plenty."

"He has businesses to attend to," Jameson argues, raising his voice enough for Leo to hear. "He skipped two meetings already this morning. *One* in Florida. He's been canceling *all morning.*"

"If I remember right, he *owns* those businesses and has a say of when and where for meetings, too. Not you, not board members, or anyone else pulling him in every direction." Jameson's eyes widen, almost gaping at me as Isaac clears his throat and Julio snorts. Owen attempts to hide his smirk.

"That's not how it works," Jameson rebukes. "He doesn't—"

"We're reevaluating some things, including a lesser workload for him, especially since he has people who *can* do it as well."

Jameson narrows his gaze, brows pinching. "We need to talk. *Alone.*"

"Don't try ordering me around next." I stand my ground, even as anxiety creeps up my spine. I hold onto my arms to help my fingers not tremble. "Maybe try asking."

His eyes flare next before taking a step toward me. Owen quickly grabs his arm, warning under his breath, "Watch it. He'll fucking disembowel you after last night."

I glance over my shoulder, noticing Leo standing beside the table with a hardened, terrifying look.

"That's *why* he needs to work," Jameson bites back.

"No, that's *why* he has me," I counter. We stare down the other, until I cave before my stomach attempts to upchuck breakfast. "Fine, let's talk." I spin on my heel, heading for the bedroom.

I take a few grounding breaths, repeating the first few lines of *The Raven*. Anxiety spikes, warning me to be careful. I take another breath, reminding myself Leo is nearby. Jameson wouldn't hurt me. He's just frustrated.

He walks in, closes the door, and frowns at me. "What the hell are you doing?"

"Protecting my fiancé." The word 'husband' wants to rip out of me.

Jameson scoffs. "Disappearing last night, practically getting him to shoot hotel security, threatening staff, almost throttling Isaac, is you doing that?"

"That's not my fault."

"If you were protecting him, you'd have stayed in that fucking apartment where you *should* have been."

I gape at him, anger boiling in my gut. "Excuse me?"

He steps closer, pointing at my face. "*I* know him, known him for fifteen damn years. He needs to work before he does something stupid like burning down his own hotel for his *fiancé* who disappeared. *Again.* For fuck sake's Autumn, he went on a rampage the first time you left, what do you think he'll do next time? Who he may hurt? Think before you decide—"

"Shut up," I suddenly say, hands now shaking. My stomach feels like lead as I try to keep my ground. "I'm not dumb or someone you get to order around."

"I'm telling you to think—about him, the pressure he's under. That's why he has to focus on work, get shit taken care of before it's too late."

"Except it's shit he can't control!" I throw my hands up. "You *can't* control Matteo or Gabriel. Not to mention Roger! Believing you can will only drive him and every one of the *Forgotten Demons* insane! Maybe that's what Gabriel wants, mayhem and you at each other's throats and—"

"You don't know Gabriel."

"But I know Roger," I argue, stepping into Jameson's space. "*I* know him. He will find loopholes and work them against you—"

"You don't know—"

"Yes, I *fucking* do!" I yell, nails digging into my palms. "I know more about how your damn mob works than any of you. I was in the worst of it, not you! I knew what Gabriel was doing before any of you. I am telling you *right now*, if Roger disappeared, either he did it on purpose or was kidnapped. He did *not* leave the city. He is vindictive and manipulative. He will do *anything* to bring the Marchetti family down."

"Autumn—"

"No!" I scream as anger heats over my skin, my entire body shaking. "I agreed with Leo to step away from the mob, for both our sakes, but don't tell me what I know or don't. From the very beginning I said you had no fucking say in our relationship, that includes him stepping back, too. He needs a *break*."

Jameson stares at me as muffled voices come from the other side of the door.

"Fine," Jameson answers, scowling harsh. "I won't interfere with your relationship; you've made that *very* clear. But…when it comes to business, to everything we built...*I* have first say. You're his fiancé, not his business partner. So, stay in your lane and I'll stay in mine."

"Jameson—"

"Just because he gave you a fucking credit card, doesn't mean you get—"

"That's *none* of your—"

"His money is my damn business!" He scolds. "Do you know how much you've spent? Generous donations or not, a shitload. Not to mention, you have no right acting like you own this hotel by changing policies, telling housekeeping what to do, or giving jobs to anyone off the street! How the fuck do you think that makes the hotel look?" My eyes widen, heart thundering in my chest. "Throwing parties is one thing, but you're acting like some bored, housewife, gold-digger with no regard to his—"

The door slams open, and I flinch from the sound. Jameson's head suddenly whips back as a fist hits his jaw. He stumbles back. I look up, expecting Leo, but it's Isaac behind the punch. He breathes heavily, snarling at Jameson who holds his jaw in shock.

"Watch. Your. Mouth," Isaac warns.

"What the fuck are—"

"You have no right—"

"I had every—"

Isaac goes to hit him again, but Julio and Owen jump in. Owen keeps Jameson back, pushing Isaac away as Julio starts scolding Jameson in Spanish. I catch a few words, none being nice. The two go at it as Owen frowns at Jameson. Mila stands in front of Leo at the doorway, her hand on her firearm, ready to intervene.

My heart pounds as the men fight, slowly stepping back. I recite *The Raven* in my head, attempting to block out the noise. The shaking in my hands hasn't stopped, vibrating up into my chest.

"Miss Autumn." I look up to find Isaac's worried blue gaze.

"*Enough*," Leo's voice cuts through like a cold wind. The room goes silent as I turn toward Leo's dark expression. "Get out."

For a moment, I think he's talking to me. Leo flashes a look to Jameson. "Leo—"

"*Get. Out.*" The statement isn't for me, yet it chills me to my bones. "Isaac. Mila. Wait in the kitchenette. Julio. Owen. Get him out of here."

Jameson tries to speak again, "Leo—"

"We can go by club rules or mafia," Leo says in a deadly calm tone. "How do you think the Crew will respond knowing you verbally went after my old lady?"

The room becomes cold. The other three men exchange a glance before Isaac steps out of the room. Mila disappearing with him.

"He's got a point, Sombra," Owen says low. "Handle this with Spartan later."

"Or Ringer is gonna pommel you, along with Chesty," Julio mutters. He says something in Spanish, and I catch something about Leo being in a merciful mood this morning.

Finally, the three men walk out. Julio and Owen nod once at Leo. Owen peers over his shoulder at me, giving me a quick reassuring smile before Leo shuts the door. His expression immediately softens, opening his arms. "Come here."

Without hesitating I go to him. His warmth instantly eases me as he cradles my head against his chest, kissing my hair. My body shudders, melting into his hold. He continues rubbing my back, helping me breathe more normally and I can think more clearly. "I wasn't trying to start a fight. I swear."

"I know. He's not someone you can easily stand up to, I should know, but I wanted to give you space to speak your mind. I'm proud of you." He kisses my hair again. "Good girl."

I laugh nervously. "I wanna puke, can't stop shaking, yelling—"

"You stood your ground," he says, cupping my cheek. His eyes search mine and lets out a long sigh. "He's frustrated. Under a lot of pressure, which he'll blame on other things. He'll do anything to not look at the actual issue, admit being wrong, or say his pride has been hit. Not excusable, but I don't want you to think he hates you. Or meant half the shit he said."

"He's worried about you."

His jaw tightens, nodding once and looking away a moment.

"Which is my fault, not yours. My actions are my own, including last night." My chin quivers a little as I nod my head, still feeling sick. Leo places a kiss on my forehead. "I'll speak with him later, but until I say, do not be in a room with him alone. Understood?" I stare up at him, trying to understand the meaning behind those words. "A consequence for disobeying me, not because I think he's dangerous." I nod finally, letting out a long breath. "Let's go finish breakfast or at least coffee."

"You're not leaving?"

"Not yet, dear wife."

He kisses my cheek, keeping a hand at the small of my back as he leads us back to the table. Mila and Isaac stand quietly as we sit.

"Isaac," Leo starts, going back to breakfast and business. "Although, I appreciate you defending Autumn, you crossed a line punching Jameson. Due to your insubordination, which includes towards me, you'll be stripped of your duties concerning my security, the Crew's, and other immediate security teams."

My head whips to Leo. He doesn't even look at me or Isaac as he speaks, just his mug as he sips his coffee. I look at Isaac in horror. His own expression blank. Leo can't be serious. He's firing him?

"Julio and Rudolph will take over those responsibilities, have a complete turnover by the end of day. Tomorrow, you'll begin working solely for my fiancé in *anything* concerning her, including her protection or updating her on my whereabouts." Leo's tone is level, but I think my brain just restarted. What? "Autumn will be helping Chiari soon, so assist her through that new role, however she sees fit. You are to answer to her, and only her, aside from myself, are we clear?"

Isaac's expression changes from blank to gratitude. "Yes, sir."

"Good. Go start turnover now." Isaac nods and gives me a hidden smile before turning away. "And Isaac?" He pauses before the door, glancing back at Leo. "Thank you."

"Of course, boss," he answers, walking out.

I stare at Leo. He continues having breakfast like the past twenty minutes didn't happen. I grab my coffee, needing something to do with my hands.

"Mila," Leo says her name in the same strict, authoritative tone. "I'll be cutting back on meetings with most of the captains and underbosses, you'll be going in my stead, determining if I *actually* need to be present. We'll discuss later your security detail."

"If there are complaints?" She asks.

"Within house, tell them they'll answer to me directly in *my* office," Leo's voice darkens as he takes another bite of food. "Outside of it, use whatever means necessary to get the point across. I trust you'll make the proper decision in maintaining control."

"Yes, sir." She flicks her gaze to me. "Would that include the meeting at *eXtasy* tonight?"

Leo pauses a moment, casually sitting back. My hands are wrapped around my mug, trying to ignore the rocks in my chest as he plays the part of mafia boss.

"What time was it for again?" He asks.

"Ten, sir."

Leo glances at me. "No. Take care of it."

Mila hesitates, before replying, "Of course, sir."

"That's all. I'll see you at one for the briefing."

"There is one thing I wanted to inquire about."

"What?"

"Six people are left on…*that* list, we have addresses. Do you want them before the end of the week?"

This time Leo fully stops with jaw tensing. His gaze shifts to me, fingers beginning to tap the table. Ah, *that* list. The room is quiet.

Before he responds I ask, "Do you have the list of the names, Mila?"

Her gaze meets mine. Leo clears his throat loudly. Mils responds, "Yes, ma'am."

"Read them off, please," I say. Leo's hand slips over my leg. I put my hand over his. Not ready to look at him as Mila pulls out a paper and reads them off.

I'm not sure why I needed to hear them. If I'd even recognize them.

But I do.

Fragments of clubs. The streets and docks. Their names unlock memories, reminding me of other victims. How insidious the underbelly could be. Any empathy I had toward those Leo had killed vanishes. These six weren't even that bad compared to the others. I'm sure he took care of the worst first. And he'd begun with the man who chased me into his hotel. This wasn't weeks of handling what haunted me, but *months*. Scourging the earth as it were as my mind flicks to the sword on his back.

Leo squeezes my leg softly, and I blink. Shit, I was dissociating. Mila watches me curiously. Without another moment, I say, "Yes, bring them in."

Flicking her gaze between us, she answers, "Yes, ma'am."

"You may go, Mila," Leo instructs. She leaves the suite and we're soon left alone. "Check in."

"Yellow," I murmur, pushing my plate back, not having much of an appetite left. I truly haven't spoken much about those worst days and nights, not even to Dr. Maxwell. For some reason, I do now.

"The third one used girls as ashtrays," I say quietly. "The fourth would bring in barely legal women to the clubs and lock them in dancing cages for hours. The sixth, well, strippers always ended up dead after a night dancing for him." Leo remains a steady force as the words almost feel torn from me. "If you, um, needed any ideas. Eye for an eye."

"Dear Watson, look at me," he instructs gently. I find hazel eyes without a hint of forgiveness. "They'll never harm another again. I promise you."

I nod stiffly as Leo kisses my temple.

Chapter 31

Lilacs

The locksmith fixes the door at the end of the hall.

Yup, lots of people complained. Most were compensated.

"Miss Watson." Grant's voice drifts from behind, and I turn toward the head butler. His neutral expression and hands placed behind his back are a bit too resigned. I glimpse past him, smiling at the housekeeping staff and wave. "I've been told you're helping Ms. Pierozzi in her duties, including interest in housekeeping."

"Uh, yeah," I reply. "Wouldn't that fall under Frank's duties?"

"Usually, unless concerning *certain* guests." I scowl, unsure what he's getting at. He clears his throat. "We have three checking in today. Two politicians and a real estate broker from Miami."

Oh. *Oh.* "Oh!" I slap my hand over my mouth. Right. *Those* guests. I rub my forehead. "Sorry, long morning should've gotten that faster. I'm not sure how I can help though."

"I suggest you shadow housekeeping first, while they prep suites to gain a better understanding of what we do," Grant answers. The neutral tone is a little unnerving. Feels like he's the older brother stuck with the younger sister. Oh, joy. "Best for you to be accustomed to what their needs may be."

Fingers crossed Leo doesn't bring drugs in for them or something. I cough to myself at the thought, remembering something Charlotte said that it wasn't allowed.

Grant turns on his heel, heading for the elevators with me jogging behind to the private elevator. He swipes his own card.

"Three floors are dedicated to our most valued guests," Grant explains. "We keep accurate accounts of each one, including whom they cannot interact with, which is why there're multiple floors."

"Politicians need to be separated, huh?" I comment. Grant side-eyes me. "So…no sarcasm today? Only chance is on Tuesdays?"

The elevator opens. "Yes, they're usually separated." I bite my lip, trying not to laugh, and follow him out. "We spend approximately 45 minutes to an hour per suite."

"An hour?"

"They're given more care and precision than others. Alba and Charlotte are part of the staff who prepares them." Said staff disappears into a suite, leaving the cart outside. "We'll be finished just before guests arrive; one of them at 3:30 and another at five."

"Okay, so I might be wrong, but I've seen in movies, uh, do you greet them when they arrive? Or is that just bellhops?"

Grant pauses before a suite door. A plaque next to it: *Lucca Suite.* I peer down to vaguely read others, *Milan Suite, Verona Suite,* and *Florence Suite.* Well, Leo's consistent.

"For these guests, myself, Ms. Pierozzi, and Mr. Olstin will greet them along with maids or bellhops to put away luggage and necessities."

"Do other guests get this?"

"Depends on status." He walks into the large suite.

The suite I stayed in was pretty, but this was *heaven.*

The floors are marbled with umber and gold, matching pillars that lighten into a golden sheen. Ivory walls with dark vines climb the corners, trimmed in deep brown like dark, fresh soil. The counters are granite, including the large kitchenette, while the plush furniture has lighter tones. Grant stops in the main space, and I walk in further to find the bedroom, where a large four-post bed with pillows sits illuminated by sunlight.

Oh, the luxury apartment is now just plain sad.

"It's freaking gorgeous in here," I gasp.

"For these suites, cleaning staff comes through daily, and while others prepare for the next guest. We divide the work to give ample time for preparation."

I nod, following him through the rest of the suite, staring at its beauty. Grant continues talking, opening velvet curtains to allow more sunlight in. I smile.

How different is each one, and are they decorated to represent each city namesake? Was it Leo? My mind sparks, realizing how much I want to ask. We've talked about some things regarding it, but not the rooms themselves. The little details. More and more I see why it's such a highly regarded hotel.

I swallow hard when I remember he said we'd have dinner today. We'd had a long breakfast before he left. A torn emotion bubbles up to believe him or he won't show again. I focus on the opulence of the room, remaining distracted.

Everything seems perfect, even when Alba and Charlotte arrive, who still redo the bedding. Charlotte manages the closet, stocking the bathroom and kitchen with specific requested items. Whoever it is, they love pickles, sardines, and lots of bathroom wipes. Not something I planned on learning today. If I ever need blackmail—I'm going to housekeeping.

Charlotte sets out little soaps shaped like flowers, not allowing me to help. I watch as she puts everything out with interest, how precise she is.

"Want to practice more Spanish?" Charlotte asks. I nod and she switches the language. *"Last night was quite loud."*

"Yes. Very."

"Mr. Luciano was worried?"

"Yes." I try to think of another word. She smiles. "Sorry, I mean…lo siento."

"Takes practice, you're doing good." I smile at her.

We continue small conversation, helping me get used to the language change and her teaching me more words. We walk out of the bathroom, and I notice Alba placing a small flower on the bedcovers.

"Qué flor?" I ask.

Alba smiles at me with a look of gratitude. "Lilac, and good pronunciation."

"Gracias. What do I gotta do to get those on my bed?"

She chuckles, gathering linen. "Fill out a complaint card."

I laugh, following her and Charlotte as they do their final sweep through. Grant begins to explain the needs for the next suite for the real estate broker, who'll be staying in the *Verona Suite*.

This suite has darker decorations with black marbling, flowers in cooler tones like the sea. The smaller foyer leads into a kitchen, living space with a fireplace with teal accents, and a bathroom twice the size of the *Lucca Suite*. This suite would be perfect for the god Neptune with the accents of blues and gold.

Grant shows me how he arranges the dining area, due to the guest having an immediate meeting when he arrives. I'm enamored by Grant's care with the silverware, prepping of wine, glasses, and placement of every utensil. There's a knock at the door near the end of his explanation.

"That will be the servers," he says. "I'll be staying to greet him. You may shadow Alba in the bedroom."

I give him a small salute, which he doesn't seem to appreciate. I walk into the bedroom area, where Alba sets a lilac on the bed. She goes into the closet. I peek back at the dining area, noticing Hwan is one of the servers.

"*Are you learning well*?" Alba asks, putting up hangers.

I take a minute to translate what she said, and answer, "*More than...I thought*." She smiles, nodding. "Guess I thought the same before working a coffee shop," I say switching back to English. "Some things seem tiny, but people will pitch a fit over non-fat lattes and oat milk."

Alba chuckles.

"And if you meant learning Spanish, well, you think Rosetta Stone will help?"

"Talking with *people* will help, not some book or CD," she says, waving her hand about.

"Guess, that means more time with you and Charlotte, hope you're ready for that." Alba laughs under her breath, patting my arm as she gestures with the other for a hanger.

I'm about to ask more questions when there's commotion in the foyer. Alba sighs, and that's my only warning that I'm about to see something I shouldn't. We step out as bellhops, and maybe assistants, enter the suite. A larger man with light ochre skin, high-fade cut dark hair, and suit speaks on a phone. Alba moves quickly, taking the luggage into the closet. I step aside, watching Grant navigate the staff and speak with the two assistants. The guest speaks in a gruff voice, interrupting Grant multiple times.

I have a gut feeling I'm not gonna like this guy.

The man then ignores Grant, getting off his phone and looks at me. He does that "up-down" thing with his eyes and my jaw clenches.

Oh yeah, we're not gonna be friends.

I glance at myself wearing jeans, a loose shirt, and a cardigan that hangs to my hips.

"Is Luciano letting in riffraff now? Or he hiring charity cases?" The man smirks. He tosses his phone at an assistant, who brings him a glass of scotch. "Perhaps he's finally relented and allowed *entertainment* to be brought in."

Ohhhh, update, we're gonna be enemies.

I scowl, biting back harsh words.

"This is Ms. Watson," Grant intervenes. "She's shadowing housekeeping, Mr. Ludwig."

Someone push me over with a feather. His name is *what*?

Mr. Ludwig grunts, scowling toward the closet. "Be careful with those suits. They're imported from Spain and Germany."

I peek over to Alba, who is already taking good care of his clothing. I'm half-tempted to go old school and dump *Italian* coffee on it. Full European trip. Five minutes with this guy and I already want to push him out the window. The feeling worsens as he speaks gruffly with Charlotte. I don't want to think about his comments toward Hwan as he leaves. I do learn his assistants' names, Emily and Kevin.

"Mr. Ludwig, dinner reservations are set for tomorrow along with the meeting with the investors," Kevin informs.

Mr. Ludwig glances at his watch before taking his jacket off, tossing it onto the bed. He pauses, snatching the lilac and holds it up to Grant. "I didn't ask for something as ridiculous as *this*. Do I look like I have a snotty *wife* with me? Or is it for potential *other* guests?"

His eyes flash to me.

"Of course not, sir," Grant replies, walking over to take the lilac and putting it in his pocket. I glance at Alba, who's expression is passive.

Just one shove out the window, that's all I ask. I want to yell or throw something at him. It's like being at *Blue Java* again as someone screamed at me or Mabel. Just like back then, all I can do is stand and watch with an aching heart. Swallowing hard, my chest squeezes as I watch the nastier side of their work. I busy myself and help Alba put away the luggage.

"I'm sorry," I whisper.

"Used to it."

"They're not all like this, are they?"

She shakes her head. "No, but most aren't divorced three times."

I stifle a laugh and she winks at me. Light humor to get through the day, some other things never change.

I straighten, wink back and follow her into the living space when we finish. Alba leaves the suite, while Charlotte picks up left-over cleaning supplies as I pause near Grant. He finishes the dining area as Mr. Ludwig sips his drink, tossing his tie off.

"Can I have the lilac?" I whisper to Grant.

He side-eyes me but reaches into his pocket and hands it to me discreetly. I hide it in my pocket next.

"I presume dry cleaning is still a service here?" Mr. Ludwig asks.

"Yes, sir," Grant replies.

"Any more *staff* who come through should be in more proper wear than just...jeans," he mocks, moving his gaze over me again. And then speaks directly to me. "Surely, there's extra maid outfits for you to wear. Maybe you'd even look cute. Perhaps a skirt, too."

I almost step forward, but Grant stops me. While the asshole sneers smugly, Grant nods for me to leave ushering us out of the suite, then closes the door.

"Give me two reasons why I can't go in there right now and stab him with a dull butter knife!" I hiss under my breath. "I've dealt with shitty customers, but the arrogance of that man is unbelievable!"

"All part of the duties, Ms. Watson." Grant nods to Alba and Charlotte. "Please check the suite below. Mr. Luciano's apartment will be dealt with tomorrow evening, per orders." They nod, giving me a smile before leaving. Once they're gone, cart and all, Grant turns back to me.

"Grant—"

"Part of this job is to keep one's emotions in check," he tells me, and I scowl. "I've been informed you were a barista, which I assume you understand when those needs arise. Sometimes with the most perfect preparation, items go amiss. When that occurs, we take care of the issue and repair what we must."

I want to yell at him. Neither him nor the others should be treated like that. Doesn't it bother him? Except, I *do* see hurt in his eyes. It's hidden in the corners. The same Mabel would have or Yuki. It's the look that you don't want to admit that someone awful got under your skin.

"You're stronger than me," I murmur, glaring at the suite.

"Pardon?"

"You spent time and effort to prepare that suite for him. Down to the smallest centimeter, and...I can't imagine staying quiet while someone dismisses your work, your staff, and time."

But I could.

The aftermath of being undercover. The hurt. The dismissal. Every strike to the heart of feeling worthless. Any pride in your work for nothing. You're just left with the pieces.

Grant remains postured before me, watching silently. I clear my throat, feeling the lilac in my pocket.

"So," I start. "Asshole *Beethoven* may not say it, but I will. I'm proud of what you did and everything was immaculate. If the apartment or penthouse was even *close* to looking like that I'd be inviting you to dinner or taking photos for magazines."

"A new insult and compliment from you, dear Watson."

I yelp, almost jumping into Grant who grabs my arm to keep me balanced. Leo stands behind where I was with a stern expression, but his eyes dance with mischief. He's alone.

I narrow my gaze at Grant. "And you didn't say anything."

A bored look is my response. I roll my eyes. Leo peers past me, prompting Grant to explain. "Ms. Watson was shadowing housekeeping to understand preparation for particular guests, sir."

"Oh?" Leo looks over to me.

"Ms. Pierozzi thought it'd be beneficial."

"And fun," I add, smiling a brief moment before glaring at the suite plaque. "Apart from other things."

"Such as?" Leo asks.

I snap my attention to him. "Uh, well…"

Perhaps I wished for the guy to be pushed out a window, but knowing what Leo's been up to the past couple months, well, I'm fearful he may actually do it. Which means another meeting with Carrie, and I kinda want to avoid that at all costs.

Grant steps forward. "Sir, might I explain?"

Leo nods. "Very well."

"Mr. Ludwig disrespected Ms. Watson and the housekeeping staff," Grant answers. I freeze. "He showed unsightly behavior, to which he commented on her clothing, going as far to call her riffraff, insinuating she was a prostitute, and suggesting she wear a skirt. Not to mention his rude comments towards Charlotte and

Alba. He does not know who Ms. Watson is, but I'm sure you can inform him if you so wish."

Holy shit, he tattled.

I want to applaud him but remain frozen as Leo's expression becomes menacing.

"Grant, go announce to Mr. Ludwig that I've arrived. Take Autumn with you."

"Of course, sir." He nods, gesturing for me to follow. I blink, not sure what else to do but follow. Grant enters the suite with a knock, Emily opens the door and steps aside for us to enter.

I whisper, "Grant—?"

"Some things I cannot achieve," he answers quietly as we stop before the dining area as Emily walks over to the petulant man. "Hands are never truly tied when you know the right ears to whisper in. Watch and learn when you use power *accordingly*."

Mr. Ludwig glares at Emily, then at us. He snorts. "I thought I said no riffraff—"

"Mr. Luciano is here for your meeting," Grant interrupts with a schooled expression.

"What?" The man's eyes go wide. "But he's, he's—"

"Early, I know," Leo finishes as he strolls into the suite. He peers around the place, stepping past us and says, "Perfection as always, Grant."

"Thank you, sir."

"You may leave. Ms. Watson and I will handle the rest." Grant bows slightly and departs. Leo turns to the man and his assistants, who've stepped back and avert their eyes. Leo's commanding presence seems to have sucked the life out of Mr. Ludwig.

"Leonardo, if I'd known you were—"

"I've been informed you've not been kind to my staff, Stefan," Leo talks over him, stepping toward the dining table. "When you insult my staff, you insult *me*."

Leo's tone darkens as he trails his hand over the back of the chairs. Stefan remains silent, frozen in place.

"I was willing to keep our meeting because you poised quite an offer, but now I have reason to rethink it." Leo pauses at the head of the table, cocking his head. "I'll need time to reflect on *any* further business with you and your companies, so I'm canceling. I'd rather spend an early dinner with my fiancé than with your belligerent, disrespectful mouth."

"I…Leonardo, we've completed similar business transactions without fail," Stefan speaks in a shaky voice. He nervously laughs while Kevin and Emily step further back with worried expressions.

"Yet, I can always make similar deals with those that don't insult my hotel, my staff, or my future wife." Leo walks toward me.

Stefan's brows furrow, pinching together in confusion until he pales. He swallows visibly, staring at me as sweat forms at the top of his head. His eyes dart between us.

Leo stops next to me, reaching for my left hand and kisses the knuckle above my ring. He lets go and turns towards the others. "I take my future wife's opinion very, *very* seriously and she doesn't have a good impression of you. I'll give us both the evening to think about our potential futures. For myself, whether I buy out and liquidate your properties, then sell to the lowest bidder before terminating any chance of business in Miami again for you. And you Stefan…can determine the best option in convincing me to continue business. In *any* sense."

"You wouldn't, what, not over…miscommunication, I mean, I didn't know—"

"Correct." Leo adjusts his cuffs casually. "Not over miscommunication. For what *you* did, I may be more inclined on giving certain receipts to the proper authorities. There's a police commissioner or two I can think of."

Stefan's mouth works as he attempts to apologize to me.

"If you even think of speaking to her, ever again," Leo warns, making the man shut up as venom practically drips from Leo's words. "I will cut out our tongue, feed it to an alley cat, then slowly carve out your eyes. That way I am *sure* you will never look at her again. Do not tempt me to take your hands and feet, too."

Emily and Kevin stare at their boss. The room chills, deadly silent. Leo places a hand on my shoulder, walking us out. He pauses to tell them, "Be sure your suite and rooms are up to your liking. I'll have my own people contact you *if* I decide to have a meeting while you're in New York."

Leo leads us out, keeping a hand at the small of my back as he shuts the door. We walk silently to the elevator as he pulls out his phone and calls someone.

"Cancel every meeting with Stefan Ludwig," he says in a less threatening manner. "If he tries calling tomorrow, tell him I've made my decision. Set up a meeting with Graydson in the next couple of days and place the *Verona Suite* under surveillance until Ludwig leaves, including the rooms for his assistants."

He hangs up as we step into the private elevator, rubbing my back in a comforting manner as the doors close. It immediately starts going up to the apartment. I've yet to figure out how he does that. He glances over at me, and I give him a small smile.

No anxiety creeps up my spine. No inkling of panic. Nothing.

"I'm okay," I say.

"Didn't overstep?"

"He's your business whatever." I shrug. "Maybe Autumn months ago would've been upset, but I've learned you usually have a clear head regarding real estate and handling asshole businessmen." He snorts. "Not sorry for him, especially after almost crushing Alba's lilac."

"Her what?" The elevator stops, and we walk out with me pulling the lilac out. "You meant actual lilac," he chuckles.

"She puts them on the beds," I say, heading into the apartment and pause. Back to grey. Yup, now the place seems drearier after being in the suites. I hold the lilac up to smell, taking a deep breath of the soothing scent. Leo steps up behind me, rubbing my shoulders.

"Painters are coming in tomorrow. We'll discuss furniture after they're done," he says softly.

I smile up at him as he walks past, taking his suit jacket and tie off, tossing them onto the couch. He rolls up his sleeves, going into the kitchen. "Are you done for today?"

"Yes. Ludwig was my last meeting," he says, pulling out pans. "So, we have an early night in, which will include shrimp linguini."

Worry still gnaws at my spine as I put the flower down on the counter. I watch him, making certain he's not actually going anywhere.

"Did you threaten him with a *Princess Bride* reference?" I ask.

Leo smirks over his shoulder. "You caught that." He starts to fill a pot with water. "Your films are rubbing off on me."

Slowly, I sit at the counter, still not convinced that he's not gonna just disappear. I clear my throat, and ask, "Did you name the suites?"

"It was my idea to name them after well-known places in Italy, but others decided the exact names."

"Same with ballrooms?"

"Yes."

"Is each suite designed to represent that city then?"

"Are you asking me what Italy is like, dear Watson or for decoration ideas?" He raises a brow, and I shrug. "Each is more of an interpretation of those cities."

"Can you tell me about them?"

Leo smiles gently. As he makes dinner, I listen to him talk about Italy, and slowly my nerves wash away.

Chapter 32

Curiosity

February may be my lucky month.

Okay, not *that* lucky.

Roger was still missing. Julio placed a surveillance team outside his house, waiting to see if he'd show, but nothing. The police are "looking" for him, but he's become a cold case given it's been over a month since his disappearance. Then there's Gabriel, who's still missing, and every person sent to find him shows up dead or never being seen again.

At least Matteo contacted Leo again, including contacting Renato, whom I still barely know anything about. Not to mention my time with Leo and the Crew, who've been better at dispersing work and not overwhelming themselves. Some days they don't have much choice, but others they do.

Like today.

I lean against the elevator and look over at Rudy. He has his usual frowny look, but this time due in part to running into Jameson in the garage. Himself, Isaac, and I were working on a chopper when Jameson and Owen drove in. I've gotten an apology from Jameson and not mad at him anymore. The rest of the

Forgotten Demons? Well, let's say it's a good thing for Jameson and Isaac that the Crew doesn't operate like most clubs.

"You know I forgave him," I say, smirking at my current shadow. Isaac had to settle some business with Chiari for my work schedule next week. And apparently taking the elevator up to the apartment is dangerous.

"I know." His gruff voice makes me sigh, and I scoot to bump my shoulder against his arm. He looks down at me.

"Rudy, you're gonna have to forgive Sombra, too. So, *I* don't have to be *his* bodyguard against you."

He snorts.

"I don't agree with what he said or did," I continue. "But he was stressed. We all were. Cut him some slack." Still nothing, and more scowling. I'm remembering he was a wrestler with the lines forming over his forehead.

The elevator opens, and I sigh, walking out towards the foyer where the mugs I told Logan and Mikey to drop off are on the table. Leo still has some late nights, and those I still spend with my favorite security guards. I pick up the mugs, about to head into the apartment, but pause when Rudy speaks.

"He needs to learn to share him." I face Rudy, who stands more casually at the foyer entrance. I raise my brows at him. "It was him and Spartan for almost two decades. Like a sibling who doesn't want to..." he waves his hand a little in front of him, and exhales sharply, "...accept the bride. Afraid of being replaced."

"I'm never gonna replace him."

"That's what he's gotta learn. Why we gotta be hard on him. To accept you."

"Pretty sure he does."

Those kind eyes of his soften, giving me a look that I may not be right. Huh, here I thought Jameson was just the hard hitter for other reasons, maybe it was for personal reasons. Fear of losing someone? Yup, get that.

He comes closer and then pats my shoulder gently. "For me,

barchën, whether you end up wearing our patch and leather one day or not, you'll always be a *Forgotten Demon.*"

My heart flutters, and I smile up at him. "Danke."

"Bitte." He pats my shoulder again, then turns for the elevator. "You should work on your German. Maybe while tinkering with the chopper's engine next time."

"Oh, yeah, let me add that to the Spanish and Italian I've been attempting. Y'all are gonna give me a broader range in learning than my actual college education."

He lets out a belly laugh, walking onto the elevator and winks at me.

"Maybe I should get Rosetta Stone," I mumble as the doors close, heading into the apartment. "How do others speak multi-lingually? Oh, right they start young and not when they're almost thirty."

I shake my head, place the mugs into the sink and look up at the apartment that doesn't make my stomach churn anymore. The space is now a burnt yellow with dark trim and some white to contrast the dark flooring. The furniture was replaced to match with Leanne and Trix's help, who were all too happy to. There's even a couple of paintings I put up with Alba and Charlotte from a local artist they know, and finally flowers that are regularly replaced. A very happily subdued version of the suites within the hotel.

No longer the cold apartment.

I head to the bedroom to change out of my "mechanic" clothes, glancing at the bedroom that's similar to the rest of the apartment. Warmer colors and softer edges, no hint of grey in sight. I pause near the bed, noticing the bundle of lilac on the pillow and grab it with a smile.

I take a shower and change into comfier clothes, and then hear the front door open. Footsteps follow as I pull my sweater on, and arms wrap around me. I smile, holding onto Leo's arms as I lean my head back.

"Hello, my dear wife," he murmurs against my ear, kissing my neck.

My smile falters, noticing the exhaustion in his tone. It's barely five. I turn in his embrace, and he presses his forehead against mine. He breathes in deep, rubbing his hand over my back, almost clinging to me.

"Check in," I say.

Leo's movement falters. "Yellow."

"Wanna talk about it?"

"More like I want to forget," he mutters, and then places a brief kiss on my lips. He goes to sit on the bed, tugging off his jacket and unbuttoning his shirt. He begins to pull it off as I sit next to him. His brows become furrowed.

"What happened?"

"Almost tore a couple heads off, heads I need," he answers, taking his shoes off next. "Someone is suing one of the hotels on false claims regarding their stay, but I still have to put up with lawyers. A few deals fell through on some properties, I'll have to resort to other buyers or flip them myself." I nod along, listening as he stands and changes clothes. "Most of it I can't do anything more about. Others will have to handle the rest, which makes it...well..."

"You feel out of control?" I finish. He faces me, and I smile softly. After a moment, he nods. "What would help you?"

He goes back to changing, pulling his undershirt off. "Having a night in with..." his voice trails away, jaw tensing as muscles across his bare chest flex.

Leo tosses the clothes into the hamper, then comes back to lift my chin to look up at him. I blink up at him, somewhat surprised by the gesture.

"Remember our talk about trying a different dynamic...in the bedroom?" My eyes widen and I nod. "Are you willing still? I know we haven't spoken about it in months."

"Yeah, uh, I've also read up on some things, too."

"How much?"

"Enough to know medical play is a hard limit."

Leo chuckles, but there's a smoldering look in his gaze.

"Then, I have a surprise." I perk up a little. "This may be the perfect time to explore your Submissive side. Everything's finished."

I scrunch my brows together. "That's mysterious."

"Thought you liked that about me."

"Most days," I smirk.

Leo leans down, brushing his lips against my ear. "Well, I think your curious mind will absolutely love what pleasure I have in store for you."

Chapter 33

Violet Dreams

Rudy drives off as Leo and I enter the building. I smile seeing Xavier inside.

"Good evening, Mr. Luciano, and *future* Mrs. Luciano," he greets us.

My heart skips a beat, hearing that title for the first time. Butterflies fill my stomach, almost blushing as Leo squeezes my hand. His own expression is warm and inviting.

"Hi, Xavier, hope the rest of the night is calm," I tell him.

"You as well, good to see you," he says, then smiles at Leo. "Hope she likes it."

"She will."

"Like what?" I ask as we get to the elevator. "Does *he* know about the surprise?"

Leo bends to whisper in my ear, "Only one of them."

The doors open and I narrow my gaze, getting on with him. "Still ominous."

The wicked smile on his face does not help.

My stomach is almost in a knot, excited and anxious. The usual anxiety ticking up my spine isn't there. I'm not sure why we're here specifically, but maybe he only wants to "play" here. I read about couples in BDSM having specific spaces or only doing it at clubs to separate from the real world. I glance over to see we are indeed heading up to the penthouse and not another floor that could secretly be his own private club.

Wouldn't put it past him.

The elevator arrives and Leo leads the way to the door, but steps back and gestures for me to enter first. I continue to eye him, opening it and barely make it five steps before I'm frozen. Everything goes silent in my head. Time slows along with my breathing as I stare ahead.

The floor has been redone in resin, warm mahogany with gold and amber trickling through, flowing into the kitchen that changes into sandy tiles. Entranced, I keep walking to stare at cabinets of rich brown with golden handles and tan marble counters flecked with gold and black. New soft glowing lights hang over the island. My gaze sweeps across the living space that now has bookcases along the wall, some shelves filled with books already. Through the window, the balcony has new railings and furniture, along with lamps and heaters that resembled firepits.

I step forward, trailing my hand over the counter as I stare at the soft ivory walls trimmed in brown. The new paint continues into the television room, where there's new green carpet. The modern furniture is gone, replaced by plush, soft dark brown sofas and stonework coffee tables. Deep earthen colored stones surround the fireplace.

Shock makes my hands shake as I walk down the short hallway that now has an intricately designed runner, clouds painted on the ceiling and cracks painted on the walls to replicate old buildings as ivory blends into a dark tawny color. I stop before the doorway to the dining room, where a brass chandelier hangs with antique looking furniture beneath. The stairs were even redone with new wood. My hand grips the railing for the staircase, staring at the paintings placed deliberately to brighten the place. Hillsides. Mountains. The estate up north.

Everything is comforting.

I can't even make it any further, swallowing hard against my dry throat. Slowly, I turn back towards the living room, finding Leo waiting patiently with his coat off and hands in his jean pockets. He's relaxed and appears…warmer.

I clear my throat, but no words come out.

He holds his hand out in invitation. I walk back to him, taking it and follow him down the short hall to the bedroom. I gasp at the light blue walls, trimmed in black with a creamy, white carpet. The furniture is black, less modern, but the bed is the same. Portraits of Harleys are on the walls, along with a painting of a sunrise over a hill. The bathroom was retiled and now looks similar to the one at the estate in color scheme. I get to the closet, and I instantly notice the fewer amount of clothes hanging up. On both sides.

"Finally donated most," Leo says quietly. "All the clothes you owned before are in the drawers. The rest of your stuff from the apartment is upstairs. Ready to be placed wherever you want."

Tears form as I choke back a sob. I hide my face in my hands, shaking violently as it hits me this is real. Little details I told him about that day we walked in the park were here. The pictures of the bikes. Bookcases. Earthen tones.

Leo moves my hands away, lifting my chin. Hazel eyes flecked with gold meet mine. He whispers, "You deserve a home, Autumn. This is *our* home, which means you may do whatever else you want. Including macaroni art or movie posters."

My arms wrap around him as I sob against his chest.

Home. *Home.*

Leo caresses my back as I cry. He picks me up and carries me to the living room to sit down with me in his lap. I grip his neck tight, sobbing harder at the reality of how safe I feel. No grey walls. No coldness. A safe haven.

When the tears finally dry, I start to feel hot in my coat. Wiping at my face and struggling to get out of it, Leo helps me. I don't know what else to do, but grab his face and kiss him hard. My whole-body presses against him, trying to show how grateful I am for what he's done. His breath hitches, but quickly matches my energy and sweeps his hand up my neck. The hard kiss turns passionate, and then into a very, loving tender kiss.

He pulls away to look at me with shimmering eyes. "I guess you like it?"

"A little," I tease. I move my hands down his neck to his shoulders, looking around at the living room. "It's amazing. Fully surprised."

"Not done yet."

"Upstairs?" He shakes his head. My eyes widen, glancing around the space expecting a damn puppy to show up now. "What else is there?"

"First, check in."

"Green, emerald, peridot, jade—" I'm stopped by a quick kiss to my nose.

Leo smiles and gestures for us to stand. He takes my hand, leading me back to the hallway to the bedroom, but goes past it to the doorway on the left instead. We stop outside the chestnut door as Leo pulls out a key.

"This will be our playroom or whatever you want to call it."

Oh. *Oh.* Okay, so not an entire floor.

I'm not sure what I'm expecting as he gestures for me to open it after he unlocks it. But it's not *this*.

The space is bigger than the bedroom with a different kind of comforting ambiance. Deep violet is painted on the walls with shiny onyx trim. The floor is resin with black, blue, and silver as if galaxies are beneath your feet with a plush soft rug in the middle. On the right is a wide bed with a tall headboard with rings spaced out across it. Other brass rings hang at the corners of it. The bedspread is lavender and white, complementing the deeper, cooler colors. Along the back wall are two short dressers with hangers above holding items I've read about in all those BDSM books I got.

I move my gaze past that to the small archway that leads into a bathroom. There's a walk-in shower and bathtub, and then a counter to the left, all in ebony and white tile with gold that matches the dresser handles.

To the left side of the room, there's a massage table, well, looks like one, with black padding and dark wood. Along the wall behind it is a marbled counter space with more drawers beneath and a fire extinguisher. Further to the front left of the room I think I see a chair, but realize it's one of those tiered spanking benches with rings on the side. Above it are more hard points. Lastly, I look at the St. Andrews cross that's near the back wall. It's ebony with dark purple padding. Beside it are different ropes that hang in perfectly wrapped bundles. The room is illuminated by gentle lamplight placed strategically around the room.

I don't realize I've ventured to the middle of the squishy carpet, until Leo steps up behind me and runs his hands down my arms. "What do you think?"

All I can seem to do is stare at the opulent space, which feels more regal than anywhere else in the penthouse. The thought makes me giggle. Quickly, I try to stop myself because my first reaction cannot be *giggling*.

Leo turns me around, smiling, already pulling my hands down. "That's a good sign."

"I doubt you want my first response—"

"I want any response you give me, which includes *any* sounds you make." Yup, too smooth, I giggle again. He brushes a thumb under my lip. "Besides…the design *was* your idea."

My brows pinch together, looking around the space quickly. Design? Me? No, I only talked about the penthouse and apartment that night, not about…wait.

My ramblings from the interrogation room.

I stare at him in shock.

His expression becomes soft as his hand slides down to rest against my neck, caressing his thumb over my skin. "Violet walls. Galaxies you could stare into," he whispers. "Carpet you could sink you toes into. Soft ass bed. And velvet, which we'll use in other ways."

My heart thunders in my chest. "You remembered all that?"

Leo leans in close, placing a lingering kiss on my forehead and says, "I remember *every* brilliant idea that forms in your head."

"I was *losing* my head."

"No, you were being so fucking honest that it cut through my soul." He tilts my head back to look up at him. "I swore on the other side of that glass I'd get you out of that room and build you this one."

I swallow hard, trying not to cry again. "Suave, smooth declarations as always, mister."

Leo kisses me affectionately. I lean into him, running my hands up his chest and sighing. He pulls away, letting go and nods at the space. "Have a look around."

Instantly, I get my shoes and socks off and feel the carpet with my own bare feet. He chuckles as I flex my toes. I run my hand over the bedcovers, already wanting to nap in it and trail my fingers over the dressers, glancing at the various toys displayed.

"It's far prettier than even, well, I imagined," I say finally. "Although if I'd known you were this good at decorating, I'd have teased you earlier about your other living spaces. I don't know if playroom fits as its title."

"Suggestions?"

I glance over at the rigging system on the left side of the entrance. "Sex dungeon," I blurt.

Leo laughs loudly, throwing his head back. I grin widely.

"Not what I expected you to say," he laughs.

"See? I have surprises, too, but I'm kidding."

He walks up and places a hand on the dresser. "Before we do anything, I want to show you it all and what it's meant for. No surprises there."

"Or could see how much I *already* know. Could quiz me."

He raises a bow. "Oh, really?"

"Look, I've kept busy in multiple ways, including reading some fascinating topics." I shrug, glancing around the place. "Also wanted to be better prepared and educated."

Leo kisses my hand, and says in a voice that makes me shiver, "Good girl."

Turns out I can still surprise Leo. Most of what he showed me I knew what it was and how it was used. The room's completely stocked along with aftercare supplies in the dresser next to the bed. He's reassured me several times that not everything had to be used, but we'll see if we're keeping those items permanently or not. Everything was easily accessible from water, towels, medical supplies, and more.

He thought of everything.

Every few moments I wait for anxiety to crawl up my neck, but nothing. No shaking. No worried thoughts, just questions. I feel safe in the space, which I've noticed smells faintly of lavender and citrus.

I'm back to pushing my toes into the carpet as Leo stands before me. "Check in."

I take a deep breath as different set of nerves start to trickle over my skin. I'm about to enter a different world, one I was excited and wanted to try fully.

"Green," I answer.

"Good girl." He traces a hand across my jaw, lifting my face to him. His other hand takes mine, stroking his thumb over my wrist. "We'll go over the scene and rules for this particular time, understand?"

"Okay."

"First, I want you to do everything I say," he begins. "At any point you feel too uncomfortable, anxious, need to pause, or stop use the stoplight method. No repercussions, Autumn. If at any point you *don't* do what I say, and we find you *do* have a brat side…" he smirks, and I grin, "…your punishments won't be physical like spankings. It'll be something like orgasm denial. No punishment will go beyond this room, understood?" I nod, letting out a long exhale and not realizing I needed to hear that. "We've already discussed hard limits, but are there any you want to add?"

I bite my bottom lip going over the list of things I've researched in my head. Most of my hard limits involve impact play, being tied up, anything involving intense pain, and I can't forget walls. Shit, I seem to have a grocery list of them.

"Uh, no degradation," I murmur.

Leo strokes his thumb under my chin in rhythm with the one against my wrist. He tilts his head. "What's wrong?"

I inhale deeply as my heart thunders in my chest. *He won't yell at you for not wanting to do something. It's fine.*

I repeat those words in my head and finally say, "Lot of my hard limits take out the…well, basics of BDSM and I'm worried if I add more, there won't be much left at all."

"Not as much as you think," he says, continuing to stroke my skin, and I find the small movement comforting. "BDSM has many facets and approaches, which includes a plethora of kinks. It's okay to not be into those that seem common like degradation or impact play. There are plenty of ways to play and experience pleasure that don't include being whipped, spanked, tied up, or used." I swallow, nodding my head. "Would you ever push me to do any of my hard limits? Or judge me?"

"No, never."

He smiles gently. "I'll never do that with you." I take a deep breath, letting it out slowly and feel calmer. "Anything else?"

"No spitting." His thumbs caress my skin and I concentrate on the tender touches.

"Not a favorite of mine either. Neither is degradation. Are you still open to anal play?"

A sudden giggle escapes me, and I clamp my mouth shut. Leo only smiles, giving me time to wrangle my emotions and flurry of butterflies that begin in my stomach. "Um, yeah, just small plugs or toys, been a while, and I liked it in the past, but nothing large."

"I know. We've discussed before, remember?"

"Oh, yeah, right."

"Anything else you want to discuss?" My mind goes blank, which I hope is a good sign. I shake my head. "Very well. We haven't set up specific honorifics, but I'd like to see what you use in the moment. Only one I won't accept is Daddy."

"Fine with me." I shrug. Not my cup of tea. Leo continues with the light caressing motion, and I swear he's gonna put me to sleep.

"So…are you ready, dear Watson?"

His voice is tender, but commanding in a way that helps the last of my muscles relax and the fluttering in my stomach disappear. I breathe in deep, staring into those hazel eyes. I find myself wanting to submit, let him take full control and let go. With that thought, I reply with the first thing that comes to mind.

"Yes, Sir."

Chapter 34

Burning Desire

"Strip off your clothes," Leo instructs stepping back as he pulls his shirt off.

Breath catching, I listen, but don't reply not sure if I should. I wait to see if he tells me to, but he doesn't. Instead, he walks over to one of the dressers. I strip completely, realizing it's pretty warm in here. I glance over at Leo as he goes commando, then pulls on a pair of loose slacks and black tank top.

Too nervous to stare, I concentrate on the carpet fibers between my toes doing my best to keep my arms at my sides. Leo instructs next, "Go sit on the table."

I take one step, but pause and say meekly, "Yes, Sir."

Right, that's what I'm supposed to do?

"You don't have to respond to every command," he says, I peek over my shoulder to see his encouraging smile. "I do appreciate you trying out the ropes."

I grin back and go sit on the soft cushioning of the table. It's slightly chilly, but I wiggle to make it warmer. My fingers dig into the edge as I watch him collect items. My legs kick slightly from how high I am. Okay, not *that* high, but enough not to touch the floor. I stare down at the swirls of sparkling silver and blues upon curated clouds of darkness. A smile stretches over my face, wanting to follow the warped shapes.

"Having fun?" Leo's voice pierces through my daydreaming, and I whip my head up. He smirks, walking over with a basket of washcloths.

"Sorry L—Sir."

Leo moves around the table. "I'm not a strict or high protocol Dom, Autumn. I want this dynamic to move fluidly, so I appreciate you trying out the title, but until you're fully ready to use it, you can call me by my name, too. Unless I insist on a check-in, that's the only time I need an instant response." He places things onto the counter, grabbing more items from below as I look over my shoulder. A small metal bucket and rods that look like tiny drumsticks are added. "I also will not punish or admonish you if you get lost in your own little world. I'll pay attention if it becomes dangerous for you to do so, and I'll pull you back, but otherwise just relax. We won't be in a session that will require harder concentration from you or needing instant responses."

I nod along. "Can I ask a question…Sir?"

Warm light dances over his gaze as he turns around to face me, gesturing with a finger for me to spin around. I swing my legs over the table, letting them dangle on the other side. "I'll always welcome questions from you."

"You explained subspace is like dancing or riding, right?" He nods. "Are my 'fuzzy sock' moments like it, too?"

"Personally," he begins, setting up his, I guess, workstation. "I think, it could be a route to it. Your brain produces chemicals during those moments that make you feel pleasure or happiness which helps you feel safe. Subspace requires trust and safety to let go, completely being consumed by emotions."

"Is that the goal today?"

"To go into subspace?"

"Yeah."

"Do you want it to be?"

"Kind of."

"Then today we'll see if you do." He turns around, placing his hands on my thighs. He runs them up my skin, gently pushing my legs apart to stand between them. His hands continue to glide up my sides, and I hum, shivering at the light roughness. "I'm going to detail everything I intend to do, no time limit. I may not tell you what comes next or not. Understood?"

"Yes."

"Good girl." He brings his hand under my chin, stroking his thumb as he did before. "I'm going to put a plug in you, not too big and I'll work you up to it. A vibrator will come into play, you may feel uncomfortable, but that's okay. If it becomes too much, you call your safe word, which is?"

"Yellow and red…Sir," I answer. Thrill dances through my veins when he smiles.

"Good girl." Every time he says that I want to melt. Slivers of me are willing to do anything he says to hear it or continue feeling the gentle touch of his hands. "Lastly, fire play will be included." My eyes widen. "I've done it many times before. You won't get burned. At some point, I may lay you on your back, but if you think it may trigger you, you'll stay on your stomach."

Fuck, I'm not sure if it's the anticipation of being played with, trying something I've only read about, or from the way he speaks in that calm, soothing tone as he strokes my skin that causes tingles down my spine. Excitement rushes over me and I begin to get fidgety. Leo has helped me feel comfortable and enjoy sex, but this was…another galaxy.

"Getting excited?" He asks.

"Uh-huh." A small giggle comes out. Get a grip, Autumn! Seductive I am not.

Delight comes over Leo's gaze. "Oh, you're going to be a fun Sub," he whispers, kissing me briefly. "If you're very good, which means letting go, allowing yourself to slip into Subspace, listening to me…you get to have me as your reward. Me and you on that big, comfy bed with me deep inside you."

A pulse goes down through my sex, almost zapping me. His hand travels down my thigh and I swallow hard.

"Yes, Sir," I whisper with a shuddered breath.

"Such a good girl," he tells me, and I almost whimper. He rubs his thumb across my chin, his other down my thigh and back up as his lips press against my neck, trailing down.

There's a tightness in my chest that fights back, wanting me to be fully aware. I'm at the cusp of falling into a feeling of bliss held back by my worrying, anxious side.

"Stay still," he instructs. I almost try to follow him when he pulls away. He's soon facing me again with one of the rods, but the soft cotton top is on *fire*. "Hold your arm out." I do so, and he grabs my upper arm as his eyes meet mine right before he rolls the fire down my forearm. I gasp as the quickness of heat that follows, but it's only a moment. It leaves a tingling sensation and gentle heat. I look up at him and he does it again, this time his hand following behind the fire.

"How does it feel?" He asks.

"Nice."

"Nice?"

"Yes, Sir."

"Not scared?" He does it again and I giggle.

"Not with you handling it."

Leo hums, and then steps back. "Lay down on your stomach, *Tesoro*."

I do as he says, wondering what that last word means and listening to him move things on the counter. My arms remain at my sides. Suddenly, Leo's hand brushes over my back, stilling me as he strokes over my skin. He's quiet, using both hands to massage my muscles and move down toward my hips, ass, and inner thighs. I sigh, relinquishing to his touch and relax into the table.

"There you go," he comments. I sigh as he brings his hands back up, one leaving my body, but comes back to dip his hand between my legs. My body tenses quickly, but eases again as he caresses my skin with the other hand. He strokes a finger through my folds, gently encouraging me to lift my hips and spread my legs enough for him to cup his hand against me. I press my cheek against the padding as he strokes, circles, and enters me with a finger. My breath hitches, beginning to breathe heavier as I close my eyes as the overwhelming emotions of anticipation and excitement flutter in my stomach. He continues to work me, pushing two fingers inside and then squeezes my ass with his other hand. A whimper escapes me; unsure how long he's been working me up.

I honestly couldn't care.

"Make any sound you want," he reassures. "Let me hear you."

He pushes his fingers back inside, hooking and then separating them. A gasp comes out of me next, followed by a moan as his hand presses against the small of my back. He goes at a slow pace, almost agonizingly, but I can feel an orgasm build inside me as my sex tingles, pulsing down my legs. I moan louder against the padding as I'm kept on the edge and my fingers grip the side of the table.

"Come for me, *Tesoro*." His voice is a command dripping in honey. "Let yourself go.

You can do it."

My brain fizzles, flickering from bliss as I see stars and my muscles shake. I grind against his hand. The heat coils, tingling up my spine, and suddenly it explodes when he presses his thumb upward and I moan and whimper as the onslaught hits me. Leo continues to massage my skin, helping me ride the wave of pleasure as my mind blanks out and I slump against the table.

He pulls his fingers out and I hear a small click, but I'm currently on an orgasm high so I'm barely paying attention. This is usually when we'd have sex or be done...except we're only getting started. I'm fully reminded of that when Leo's lubed finger circles my asshole.

"Bring your knees up a little," he orders gently, and I instantly do as he says, putting my ass into the air. "Good girl. You like having instructions, don't you?"

He circles the hole again as I answer quietly, "Yes, Sir."

"Why do you think that is?"

He's seriously asking questions right now? Course he is, it's Leo —the man who loves to make me multi-task.

"I…I don't know, Sir," I answer, breathing sharper when he finally presses the finger intomy ass. At the odd sensation, I whimper. It's been a bit since I've done anything back there, but it's not that uncomfortable and my hips involuntarily push back at the intrusion.

"Don't rock. Stay still," he orders softly. I halt. "That's my good girl. Perhaps I can tell you why you love instructions."

I hum as he pushes his finger a bit more and my muscles tighten around him. There's an automatic response to push him out, but I concentrate on relaxing and breathing through my nostrils. "Okay…Sir."

Leo begins to move his finger a bit more. My body jolts as he works me slowly and carefully as I cling to the edge of the table. Suddenly, he pulls his finger out completely and I soon feel the lubed plug pressed against my entrance.

"You want to be praised," he talks, twisting and pushing the plug into my ass. It doesn't feel much bigger than his finger at first, but I can tell the size difference as it gets bigger the more he pushes it inside me. I let out a long breath, concentrating on his voice. "Instructions are easy to follow. Something you can do and accomplish. The reward at the end. The want for praise. Although, the only times you truly seem to follow orders are from me."

I gulp as he pushes the plug further, stretching me and I answer with a panting voice, "I trust you, Sir."

"Oh, I know, *Tesoro*, and I adore you for how much you place in me. Want to know why?"

"Yes, Sir." He's playing with my ass now, carefully thrusting the plug halfway in and then pulling out. My face presses harder against the padding, clutching the table.

"Because I also love praise. Your responses, listening to me, or your pleasure are my version of it. It reminds me I take care of you." He starts to push the entire plug into my ass. "I protect you." More. "I cherish you." *More.* "And only *I* bring you pleasure."

The plug becomes fully seated and I swear I come again. My legs shake as I try to keep my hips up as my bottom half practically explodes in ecstasy. Oh, fuck me, how did he do that?

"Good girl." The approval in his tone could unravel me again. "Lay down fully. Time for some other play."

I lay down completely, putting my arms at my sides again and wiggle at the intrusion. The plug isn't uncomfy, but I'm quite aware it's there.

"We'll be playing with fire now, remember to use the stoplight method if you need, including with the plug," he instructs.

"Yes, Sir," I murmur. I'm on the edge of being sleepy and wide awake.

His hands stroke over my hair, and then he kisses my neck. He places another on my temple. "My very, good *Tesoro.*"

"What…what does that mean?" I ask as I feel him shift next to me. It's only a moment before I gasp as heat trails over my skin. The sensation runs down my backside and over my ass, causing a fluttering in my stomach. I tighten my muscles as he does it again, feeling the plug more and moan at the rippling sensations across my body. His hand travels over my skin, following the fire.

"*Tesoro?*" He asks in seductive voice.

"Yes."

Another pass goes down my shoulder blades, coming back up just before the nape of my neck. His other hand lingers there as he says, "Treasure. Darling. My sweetheart."

My breathing becomes shallow as I close my eyes, listening to him. The heat hits my skin again, making me warm and relaxed as if I'm finally taking the hottest shower I've always wanted. Leo continues down my sides, my ass, my legs, and leaves no spot unscathed from the rolling fire. It pushes me further into this abyss, away from the thoughts of worry or uncertainty. Nothing else exists except Leo's hands, the fire, and his voice that continues to lull me.

"Look at you being so good for me," he praises, moving the fire over my ass cheeks again. I hum and listen to the voice that tethers me to earth. "My good girl…my dear, lovely Watson."

At that endearment, I feel myself fall.

As if strings snap within, I tumble into the chasm that is absolutely nothing but Leo and the fire. What anxieties were left are gone as my mind goes blank. All other thoughts shut off. I'm floating and lost in a galaxy of safety and bliss.

"There you go," Leo murmurs, moving the fire down my spine. My body shudders at the tickling heat and I smile to myself, eyes remaining closed as I stay where I am. Everything is perfect.

"Check in," Leo says.

"Emerald."

"Good girl. Fall as far you need, but stay with me, *Tesoro*."

"Yes, Sir." My answer comes without needing to think. It's becoming automatic. If he asked me to do *anything* right now, I'd do it without question. Without thought.

He stops rolling the fire, and it's replaced by a soft washcloth, stroking over my entire body. It tingles against my already sensitive skin, making me shiver and breath hitch.

"I'm going to turn you over to your back."

"Yes, Sir."

Leo gently turns me over, and I whimper at the movement of the plug when it presses inside me as I lay down. My breath catches before I fully put my weight down onto the table. Leo's fingers trail up my center, placing his hand gently against my neck.

"Open your eyes, *Tesoro*."

Without thought I do. I gasp when I see small lights in the ceiling, flickering as they create a starry sky in the deep onyx painted ceiling. A smile spreads across my face as Leo's face hovers over mine and I sigh when I see those hazel eyes I adore. "There she is. How are you feeling?"

I swallow against the dryness of my throat. My eyes can't seem to pull away from his. A part of me wants to look at the twinkling lights, but something keeps my attention on him.

Don't look away.

My body becomes fully aware of his hand on my throat, resting there as his other skims my side.

"Good, Sir."

He smiles, which ignites a joyful thrill. "Don't know how to describe it?"

"Lots of things, Sir."

Leo releases me, coming back with a newly lit rod. "Why don't you tell me," he suggests, rolling the fire over my thighs.

I sigh as the heat hits me, laying my head back as I stare up at the stars. I answer, trying to touch upon the emotions wrapped around me. "Safe. Good. Relaxed. Blissful. Free. Safe."

"You already said that." He starts to roll the fire over my stomach. Warmth builds over my skin as the flames roll over it. I glance down, watching Leo roll the fire over my ribs. It's surreal watching him as his other hand follows behind, striking out any left-over fire that could, on the small chance, stick.

"It's how I feel with you, Sir."

"Now or other times?"

"All the time," I whisper. Tingling travels up my spine and through my limbs. "All the time. Only you."

My voice becomes a whispered plea as my sex throbs unexpectedly, heat coiling again down in my core. I'm not sure why, but the need to cry rises alongside the ecstasy, more powerful than the pleasurable feelings. It doesn't seem like any of the other emotions, a combination of those I don't quite understand. It's as if the admittance released something within as I close my eyes and whimper when he passes the fire over my breasts. Every cell inside me feels alive, sparking with desire and tugging at me. My breath becomes heavier. I don't struggle, but each long breath becomes more deliberate than the next. Every inch of my body aware of its surroundings, yet not truly here.

The fire disappears and the washcloth is back on my skin again. My mind focuses on the constant care that's Leo, who seems to be the only thing to exist aside from myself. Care. Safety. Treasure. Adoration. All of it bundles together. A tear slides down my cheek.

My skin is hypersensitive as it's touched again and again as if I'm a cherished piece of art. Oh, fuck it spills together and more tears gather.

Leo cleans his hands and comes back to place both hands against my cheeks. He wipes away the tears.

"I don't...I don't know..." I try to speak, words not leaving me.

"You're okay," he murmurs. "You're safe. They're just emotions and you're letting them out. You can let them out, sweetheart."

"Leo," I plead for him, breathing harsher as in the very, very far reaches of my mind is panic.

"Look at me, *Tesoro*." I bring my gaze to his. "Good girl. Deep breaths. These emotions are normal. This can happen. You did nothing wrong." I breathe in deeper, doing as he says. "You reached a place you didn't know you could reach; it can be scary. You've done so well, and I'm proud of you. My very good girl."

Each breath is easier as my body relaxes back onto the table. His thumbs stroke over my skin, and I want to close my eyes to be pulled back into that safe abyss again. I fight to keep my eyes open, clinging to that previous command.

It's not long before he notices.

"Look at you trying to be a good girl," he whispers, kissing my nose. "Are you trying to keep your eyes open for me?"

"Yes, Sir," I whimper.

"You can close them, *Tesoro*."

His tender voice makes me yield instantly as my eyelids drop and my body arches. All the emotions fall together and I feel myself cresting the edge of euphoria once more as Leo continues to hold my face, softly kissing my skin. I moan, not sure what it is that's making me rush to the edge as heat coils and tremors. My muscles tighten and I gasp when I feel the plug, remembering it's there. My ass presses down, pushing it inside me and I moan again.

"There you are, ride it out, sweetheart." His deep voice vibrates through every fiber of my being, making me shiver as he continues to talk and kiss my skin. "Such a lovely, good girl. I could watch you for hours and hours. Absolutely gorgeous...

Tesoro…my enchanting treasure. Remember the heat on your skin…my hands caressing your body…my lips pressed against your skin. All yours and all mine to love…cherish…worship…and protect."

A strangled noise mixed with whimpers releases from me as the pleasure builds. Leo breathes against my neck, nipping at my ear. The little touch is enough to send me over the edge of coming. My legs shake, muscles clenching as my back arches into the air. The plug pushes deeper, causing the orgasm to wash over me. My breathing halts as everything goes tense down to my sex, until it releases and what follows is paradise. My body slumps and Leo kisses my forehead.

"Good girl." I hum, my eyes still closed as I turn my face in the direction of his voice. "Are you ready for your reward or are you too worn out?"

My eyes snap open as my brain clicks to one thing. Reward.

The need for praise engulfs me and Leo grins at my reaction.

"Not that worn out?"

"No, Sir," I breathe out.

"Are you sure?"

"Yes, Sir." I will remain awake damn it.

He leans in, moving his hands down my neck and arms. "It's alright if we don't. There's nothing wrong in not having penetrative sex during a session."

"I want you, Sir. Please," I plead. I'm on the brink of begging him, needing…*wanting* him inside me. I've never fully begged for sex, but I was about to.

Leo picks me up and walks us to the bed. He stands me in front of it and gestures for me to turn around to face it. I do so, and he presses his hand on my back. "Lay down and lift your hips."

I'm reminded of the plug I seem to keep forgetting is there as I follow instructions. My breath hitches, wondering what he's planning to do. We never said anything about him keeping it inside me while he fucks me or not. I clamp down on the worry, dragging myself back to Subspace or least close to it. My face and chest press into the bedding. His hand trails down my spine, over my ass and then taps the plug.

"How'd the plug feel?"

"Good, Sir."

"Should we go bigger next time?"

"Y-yes, Sir."

"Be honest with me." His hand trails over my hips.

"Maybe not yet, Sir."

"Good girl. It doesn't always have to be yes or no. Just like we have 'yellow' to call for slowing down, correct?"

"Yes, Sir." I relax further into the soft bedding, rubbing my face against the blanket. Oh, it feels like pure fluff and clouds. Perfect to cuddle in for hours.

"Approve of the blankets?" He asks, massaging my hips and taps the plug again.

"Yes, Sir, but…"

"What is it, *Tesoro*?"

I swallow hard and admit. "I prefer you the most."

Tears prick at my eyes again. It could be from him touching me in such an open way with my plugged ass in the air. Or maybe just admitting how needy I feel for him, sounding almost clingy.

"I'm delighted to hear that, sweetheart. Relax for me." I take a deep breath, relaxing as Leo pulls the plug out. Instantly, a feeling of emptiness is left behind. "Don't move."

I stay put, hearing him walk away and come back. I'm not waiting long before he gently drags a wipe down my crack. I tense.

"Just precautions." He walks away again to throw the wipe away, wash his hands, and comes back opening more lube. He strokes his fingers down below and I sigh at the contact. "You're still wet from those other orgasms. Do you think you can do one more?"

"Uh, maybe, Sir."

"Will you try for me? Give me one last orgasm while I'm buried deep inside you."

My body shudders at the idea, and I moan as his fingers dip

inside me. Oh, shit, maybe I can. Didn't think it was possible, but then again, I practically just came from his voice alone. "Yes. I can, yes, Sir."

"That's my good girl," he praises, pulling his fingers away.

Leo presses his cock to my entrance, and I have no clue when his pants came off. Or his shirt. He ever, so slowly pushes inside me, inch by inch. The agonizing slow pace causes me to clutch the bedding beneath me, wanting to rock into him, but I keep still. Leo continues the sensuous torture, pulling back and then thrusting forward slowly again until he finally pushes all the way in and his hips are flush against mine.

He groans under his breath. "Fuck, you feel wonderful, darling."

My whimper is muffled by the blanket as my mind goes blank. I'm practically back in Subspace again, left in only feeling filled and bliss. He pulls back a little, but then grinds back into me steadily before he grips my hips, starting to fuck me from behind. A part of me already feels spent, languid and loose, but I keep my body up on all fours as he drives forward. He hits my already sensitive walls, making me moan louder and louder. The softness of the blanket, his hands on my skin, and his rough breathing surround me. I'm reminded of the fire, igniting a thrill through my veins. I gasp as he goes harder.

Leo bends over me, pressing his chest against my back. "Lay down completely."

My body crashes to the bed with Leo on top of me. He moves my hands above my head, placing one of his hands over them. I stare up at the hand that pins mine against the bed. No panic arrives as Leo entraps me with his full body. His other hand skims down my side as his thrusts become longer and deeper. The orgasm I didn't think I'd be able to achieve again starts to crest once more as he changes the quick rhythm to something slower. He fucks me slowly and deeply, his cock hitting the right spot each time.

Finally, I scream into the blanket as I fist my hands. He pulls back, thrusting back in, causing me to scream again as my entire body shakes, right on the precipice of release. The crest is right there, almost…

"Come for me, *Tesoro*…come for me."

He grinds his hips once more and my entire body locks up. I let out a longer scream, orgasming harder than before as every single muscle tightens. I stop breathing. My heart pounds as my legs shake against the onslaught, Leo groaning behind me as his grip tightens. Finally, it passes and my body slumps into the bed as the air whooshes into my lungs.

Leo breathes heavily, kissing my neck before pulling himself up and lays kisses down my back. He gently eases himself out and I whimper at the lack of contact. He returns, cleaning me below and turns me over with my body going wherever he puts me.

He picks me up, carrying me to the bathroom. My head hangs, barely able to hold myself up. Eyes closed, I hear him start running the sink water.

"Stand up for me, sweetheart." His soft instructions get me to stand on the warm tiles. I'm wobbly, but I remain standing. I'm floating as Leo uses a new washcloth to clean off anything on me from the fire play. He turns me around, taking care of all sides, and turns off the sink. After tossing the cloth, he picks me up and takes me to the bed but sets me on my feet again.

Leo takes my hands, ordering gently, "Open your eyes." I do, even against the pull to go to the land of sleep and bliss. "Good girl." I smile as he strokes the side of my face. "Do you want to snuggle in here or in our bedroom?"

I look over at the bed and then back to him. I want to answer, but all forms of speech appear to have left me. I look at the bed again, hoping he takes the cue.

"We'll snuggle and sleep in here for a bit then," he says, letting my hands go. An involuntary whimper leaves, and Leo reassures me as he strips off the top blanket. "I'm right here, Autumn. Not going anywhere. You still had some oil on you and got it on the blanket. I want to be extra careful, otherwise, what kind of Dom would I be?"

I giggle, finding how he speaks funny in my brain. I watch almost blurry-eyed as he spreads another blanket across the bed. He then picks me up, placing me down and turns off the main lights as he gets under the blanket with me. I sleepily gasp when I touch the velvety feel of the blanket, sighing contently as I cuddle against his chest.

"*Tesoro…*" he murmurs, stroking my hair, "…my beautiful dear Watson."

I hum, slumber pulling at me where no monsters, panic, or anxiety reside. It's gone. I'm completely free of myself and the shadows that haunt me.

Chapter 35

Shadows that Hover

Coffee is brewing.

I open my eyes, finding myself in the bedroom filled with soft blues. I sit up, not remembering how I got into *this* bed. I'm also dressed, and my engagement ring sits on the bedside table in its own tiny bowl.

I get out of bed, putting on my ring and venture out to the hall. Before heading toward the smell of breakfast and caffeine, I pause before the playroom's door. There's sizzling from the kitchen. Quietly, I turn the playroom's doorknob, finding it open. I peek inside, seeing the bed is made and it's been cleaned as if last night never happened. When did he do that?

Humming to myself, I close the door and pad softly down the short hall to the living room. My feet are quiet as they land against the chilled resin floor and I suddenly stop, looking down at it that feels surprisingly not as hard as hardwood floors. There's more sizzling and pans being moved in the kitchen when I gasp. Quickly, I run to the bedroom and go to the dresser, digging for them.

"Autumn?" Leo's voice calls from the living room.

Finally, I snatch a pair and race out of the bedroom and past Leo to the other hall.

"Autumn, what are you…" his voice trails away when I start pulling on the fuzzy socks, "…never mind."

I look up grinning as Leo folds his arms and steps out of my directory. With a running start on the rug, I slide across the floor easily to the other side of the penthouse. Giggles erupt. Best distance yet!

Before I can go back and do it again, Leo catches my waist, hugging me to him.

"Hold on spider monkey."

I gape at him. "Who taught you that movie? It wasn't me."

"Don't ask. And good morning, my dear Watson."

"Morning, mister." I kiss him briefly. "Fine, more coffee first."

He chuckles, kissing my head and let's go as he strolls back into the kitchen. "I was going to ask how you're feeling, but I'm presuming well-rested."

I slip and slide a little behind him, having fun but stop when he turns and raises a brow at me. I sheepishly grin as I take my mug of coffee from him.

"Best sleep ever and like I had the best massage of my life," I say, and he smiles gesturing for me to sit. He goes back to cooking breakfast, preparing more pancakes and eggs. He appears to have a lightness about him. Much like those early days of dating actually.

"You feeling better?" I ask.

"Much."

"When did you sneakily get us back to bed and me into clothes?"

"About an hour after you fell asleep, didn't have the heart to wake you," he smirks. "I didn't mean to wear you out that much."

"Not complaining."

I sip my coffee, noticing he's just drinking his regular. I'm half-tempted to make him an Americano. A few minutes pass as I watch him cook, flipping pancakes and stacking them onto plates.

"I could've helped clean the playroom…dungeon…violet galaxy room," I say softly. A twinge of guilt is there.

"Part of the duties of being a Dom, Autumn. Aftercare and cleanup."

"Some Subs help."

"Usually if they're Servants or those under stricter protocol," he replies promptly. "I'd prefer to do it as the Dom to know every item's condition after, keep better care of it."

"Still seems unfair for you to do everything."

"It's not, I assure you. When I said I enjoy and want to care for you, I meant it in multiple ways, including clean-up." He turns away, putting some pans into the sink. "And if the power exchange ever shifts, then you can."

His last sentence is a bit faint. I remember chapters about different Dom and Caretaker approaches. I watch him as he whisks some eggs and prepares to cook them next.

Some people strive to serve, just his own way, I guess.

I hum and Leo smirks. "Ask away."

"Not even giving me a chance to pretend I don't have questions?" He shakes his head. I chuckle, leaning back as I drink more coffee. Yeah, I do have questions, especially seeing Leo like he's had a complete system restart.

"It is breakfast," he adds, putting the pancakes on our plates. "And it'll make up for the aftercare conversation that didn't happen last night."

"Cause you wore me out."

"Yes."

"Okay, first, when do we lock the room?"

"I suggest when we're gone or when we don't want others to venture in there. I'd like the space to be entirely ours."

"How often do we? Like set up appointments or just… whenever?"

Leo chuckles, putting the eggs onto the plates next. "However often we want and when. Whether one or both of us need to play or want to experiment or just to have sex. It doesn't need to be concrete on how we use it, it's our own private space not a club."

"Right," I breathe out, recalling that snippet of information I've read. "After weeks of reading about BDSM, dynamics, and all, I still feel pretty naïve. Or just...really green."

"You learned the foundation of BDSM, after that it changes from relationship to relationship, every single new one can feel overwhelming," Leo says, turning the stove off and pushing our plates towards me. "That's why discussions before any play are important and continuing to do so is smart. Such as, whatever dynamic we have in there, we leave in there. I don't have expectations of you calling me 'Sir' out here or being ordered about."

Leo grabs his coffee, coming around the island to sit next to me as I set his plate in his spot. I nod along, but then a thought makes my heartbeat quicken. "Are you...uh, still gonna use 'good girl' out here?"

Anxiety ticks up my spine, worried he'll stop. What if I have a panic attack and he won't use it? Will I get confused? Or maybe—

Leo's hand lands on my thigh, squeezing gently. "I was using that long before last night, Autumn. I'll continue to use it in scenes and outside of them. Don't worry."

"What if—"

"One of the reasons I used it last night is because it *can* ground you, like it does when I'm helping you through flashbacks, anxiety attacks, or other times you struggle. It's okay to use something like that outside of that dynamic."

I release my breath, realizing I'd been holding it. "Okay. Thank you."

He gently squeezes my leg again before we start eating breakfast. We eat a bit, him grabbing maple syrup for me as I randomly stare at things in the penthouse and hum. My feet swing a bit as I eat his delicious pancakes. Leo smiles softly, watching me as he drinks his coffee.

"What?" I ask.

"Just you, dear Watson."

"Glad I entertain you."

"Was there anything last night you'd want to change?" He asks suddenly. "Verbiage, length of the scene, items used?"

I chew on some pancakes to think. "Wasn't a vibrator mentioned?"

"Yes, but I decided not to use it, given how quickly you fell into Subspace. Didn't want to overwhelm you."

"Oh, thanks, you don't need to tell me if you're not gonna use something, I'd rather know what's all on the table as options. Maybe keep me guessing a little." I smirk. "But everything was perfect. I understand why people want to get into Subspace, but also the danger you mentioned."

He pauses. "How so?"

"Well, I felt incredible, as if I was *actually* floating in a galaxy," I explain. "Wonderful as it was to feel everything, there was a point of where I felt...lost? Like I wouldn't make it back. It got, well...scary. Kind of like being in the middle of a panic attack, and while in Subspace, I almost *did* panic from being just so over-whelmed. I wanted to stay there, but was worried." I look over to find his curious gaze. "You knew what to do, though. Brought me back without me having to tell you I felt lost. I think I could've safe-worded, but even my brain seemed to forget to use it. Never occurred to me just take a break, say yellow, but you did. Even if for only a moment."

I sigh, going back to my eggs. "There's nothing I'd change. I completely trust you to be my Dom and submit to you. Maybe you used magic, sounds about right."

I mutter the last bit, glaring at my breakfast. It only frustrates me a little that he knew my tells before I did, but then again, we've talked a lot and he's guided me through panic attacks. Guess it only made sense he'd be that good. A part of me wanted to do the same for him. Know those little tells, pull him back, and keep him safe. Give him something similar. Maybe I'd learn one day.

"Thank you," he says gently.

Leo's expression is filled with relief mixed with appreciation. I smile at him.

"Thank you for introducing me to this part of you." I grab his hand, kissing his knuckles tenderly. "And everything else you've given me, including a place to truly call home."

Leo leans in close, and I meet him halfway, kissing him deeply. Bitter coffee mixes with his own taste, and I can't help the smile as his hand slides along the nape of my neck.

"I love you, my dear wife," he murmurs against my lips.

"I love you, dear husband."

He kisses me again gently and whispers reverently, *"Tesoro."*

A sigh against his lips is my only response.

***

"You're lively," Nan comments as I reshelve books.

Nan's Bookstore has been fully renovated with new paint, shelves, carpeting, and counter space for check out. Apart from the books she already stocked, there's a handful more indie authors and genres she didn't have much of before. It seems like she was gone forever, but the bookstore has had quite a bit of foot traffic since reopening.

Leanne says it's cause of the new sign and upgraded storefront; Trix says its cause there was a snippet in the business section of the newspaper about Leo acquiring the buildings over here. Either way, Nan came back to customers.

"The penthouse is just that beautiful," I answer. "Leo did a fantastic job, can't wait for you to see it."

"Surprising you with a redecorated penthouse, what will he think of next?" I smirk at her as she turns away to go ring out a group of college students.

Nan returned beginning of February. She seems a bit more chipper having taken such a long family vacation down in Georgia. I've helped work some hours with Nan. Isaac helps, too, but mostly just checks with the security placed around the block.

Leo left late morning, and I came straight here after Chiari said she didn't need me at the hotel. It was mid-afternoon when I got a call from Leo that he'd be late or not show up for dinner. At least I get warnings now.

A woman comes by looking for some history books, and I help her find them, taking her back to the front where Nan cashes her out. Isaac hovers behind Nan, giving me a half smile as I grab some books to take to their shelves.

"Oh, take these," Nan says, holding out a couple murder mystery books. "Someone returned them."

I nod, glancing over the books as I weave around a few customers, and step aside as some women pass me giggling about romance books. I find the mystery section, looking for the author, when I notice a paper sticking out the back of one of the books. I pull it out, figuring it was left behind.

My heart thunders in my chest as I unfold the wrinkled paper, recognizing the writing instantly. The books in my hands tumble to the ground as I'm frozen in place.

It's the last piece of paper I'd given Roger. My final warning to him.

Sarah Marie Mitchell died for your ego and pride. Never again.

Fuck. FUCK.

Quickly, I fold it back up and stuff it into my pocket. My hands shake as I pick up the books, shoving them onto the shelf. My vision blurs as my mind races. Someone brought these here. Nan would've recognized Roger. Was he working with someone? If so, who?

I move to the back of the store as I try to keep my breathing level. I come around the corner, keeping my gaze down and say, "Hey, Isaac, I need to talk to you. Nan, we'll be right back."

Thankfully she's distracted by more customers as I step away and disappear through the back door. I begin pacing, running my hand through my hair. I tug at it a little, trying to recite *The Raven* in low murmurs. The door opens again.

"Miss Autumn, what happened? Are you—"

I stop and pull out the paper then shove it at him. "Are there cameras directed at the front of the store?"

"Yes," he says tentatively. "Every corner is covered."

"Then we need to know who dropped off those books," I rasp.

Isaac opens the paper and his breath hitches as I begin to pace again, rubbing at my chest next. I was right, Roger is still in the city. Where is he?

"What is this?" He asks in a calm tone.

"It's the last…thing I wrote to Roger," I answer. "When I left his house."

"The red herring you gave him?" He asks and I nod. "And you know for sure this was only in his possession? Could an Agent have—"

"That's what I shoved at him when he arrested me," I say, stopping. Isaac's eyes darken, scowling as I can tell he's remembering that moment. "It's probably why he forgot to read me my Miranda Rights."

He places his free hand on my shoulder, rubbing it slightly. "Deep breaths, Miss Autumn."

"He could've been in the store," I rasp. "Someone else was in the fucking store, Isaac. Nan's store…*again*. How? It's been crawling with security."

"We'll take care of it," he tries to reassure me. "Nothing will happen to Nancy or you here. Believe me." I nod stiffly. "You said yourself he plays mind games, he's doing so now or someone else is doing it for him. Don't let them."

I nod again, gulping harshly. Isaac starts the first few lines of *The Raven*, and I go through a couple of stanzas with him. The anxiety creeps along my skin, hands still shaking, but my breathing is less erratic.

"Nan would've recognized him," I whisper finally. "He has to be working with someone else. Replaced Steve."

"He could've told someone, in case he disappeared or died," Isaac murmurs, and my stomach twists. "Maybe a police buddy. I'm going to make calls and start checking the tapes. Stay here as long as you need."

I pace once more, reciting the poem as Isaac leaves. It'll be fine. Like he said Roger is screwing with me. Trying to mess with my head again. Someone is. After a few minutes, I stop, leaning my head back and stare at the light.

How long has it really been since I've worried of my past self being found? The truth coming to light to the wrong people? That old fear yanks at me, bringing a wave of nausea. I step back, leaning against the wall carefully. I wasn't this worried with the engagement announcement, the idea of being in public, but this… how far is Roger willing to go? Perhaps further than I ever thought.

I know he's out there. Waiting.

It seems like forever before I go back out to the bookstore, but Nan is closing up the store after a couple of customers. Isaac is on the phone and there's two guards just outside the storefront.

"I'm sorry, Nan," I say, knowing they all decided to shut down the store.

"Not your fault, dear." She leads me back through the door and to her apartment. Her arm is shaking slightly as she holds onto mine and my heart cracks.

Someone got in. *Again.* Perhaps, that's what I'm more shaken up about.

"I'm sure Isaac and the others will take care of it, as they have before." Her voice becomes soft as she closes the door.

We're both quiet as she makes some tea, places a plate of cookies at the dining table where we sit. I clutch the warm mug in my hands, peering over at her. Nan's face becomes soft, almost remorseful.

"Don't start, dear. Not your fault they've found the cracks, even in new walls."

"Supposed to have stepped away, but I guess don't always have a say, huh?" I mutter, staring down at the tea. "Past few months

I've been trying. Not as easy as it was before, to ignore they exist. Thought it would be after Steve was…was…"

"Sent swimming with the fishes?" Nan partially muses.

I shake my head. "I was hoping to forget, move on, but my past won't just…die. It's not over and may never be over."

"It's not your past following you," Nan says softly, reaching over to stroke my hair back. "I was trying to leave it all behind, too." I look up at her. Those warm brown eyes tender and sad. "But like memories, our pasts remain, we just have to learn that it won't have the same hold on us as it has before. We're just not there yet. And maybe a little scared until we do."

"I sometimes wonder if it was easier, pretending. I mean, I was happy."

"Except life is more than just being happy. It's messy and complex. You know that." She sighs, leaning away from me and tilting her head. "Were you happy pretending *this* time though?"

I can't even try to fake a smile or answer, shaking my head.

"Somehow it's been harder. Instead of looking over my shoulder, waiting to see if they're coming for me…I'm trying not to look, but have this compulsion to."

Nan hums, circling her spoon in her mug, before tapping it and placing it on its napkin.

"I never truly wanted to look or even peek, even when Finn was in the mob, rarely did I know what he was doing," she starts to say. "He'd come home some days, fear on his face, but never told me. I didn't want to know details, having faith he'd take care of it. No one ever came to our door. Ah, but some nights he'd pace and pace before he'd fall asleep on the couch. I'd never ask."

"You were okay not knowing?"

"Apart from helping him here or there, I was content with *those* rose-colored glasses." She pats my hand. "But you, Autumn…I don't think you ever will be."

I shake my head, grabbing my mug. "No, I need to step away for my—"

"And who decided that?"

"Leo *and* me, Nan. It wasn't just him."

She hums low, sipping her tea. I almost give an exasperated sigh, hoping she's not going to try to pick at him again.

"Perhaps, but did you agree out of your own fears or his?"

I stare at her. I try to get words out of my mouth, but she speaks before I can.

"You and I are not the same. I was never truly cut out to know the mob or what they did. You though, were calm."

"Calm?"

"Yes, when you worked for Caltz. The times I saw you, always level-headed and vigilant, much like Finn."

I put my mug down as I try to make sense of what she's trying to say. "Because I had to, all the time. I couldn't put my guard down, and I...I..."

"Taught yourself how to survive, think during danger, and none of that is wrong to know how to do. Pretending to be blind will never work for you, because *that* part of you never truly left." Her expression saddens a little. "Sarah Marie who refused to stay down, infiltrated the mafia, and did it well."

I scoff, muttering, "Yeah, sure, look where it got her."

"I am."

My body goes still. Her words sinking into me.

Nan cups my chin, making me look at her as she whispers, "She survived. *You* survived through it all. You didn't fail or die...Sarah, you succeeded, and those monsters want you to believe you had. Moving on is fine, but don't forget the box we buried was empty."

I clench my jaw. It's as if she's punched me through the chest. Swallowing hard, I stiffly nod.

She stands and says, "How about Shepard's pie for dinner? Good and hearty."

"Sure," I murmur.

Her words continue to sink, each digging deep into my soul. I stare down at the tea where my reflection is faint in the liquid. Glimpses of that past speed past like a projector flickering upon a screen.

Elm Jed

I've spent so many years removing myself from the pain and horrors that at most times it was hard to place myself back into those shoes. But, if I did step back into that world, how much of myself would I lose again?

My eyes move to the ring on my hand. A question echoes in the distant reaches of my mind—how much of Autumn would I lose, and would she fully disappear?

Like Sarah Marie?

Chapter 36

Honeymoon Dreams

The paper was wiped clean, even of my own prints. The man who'd dropped off the books, hid his face from the cameras. The description Nan gave of what she could remember didn't help much. Three weeks later, still nothing. My anxiety has spiked, and I soon found it hard to be at the bookstore. I stopped working there altogether after Nan expressed it was best for me not to. Some of my night terrors returned; images of the interrogation room, Roger yelling at me, and the hospital. Nan believed that whoever left it was just trying to scare me, trying to reassure me that it wasn't Roger. Whoever it was, their tactics were working

Leo and I began to spend more time at the penthouse, although I knew he felt the *Italian Lily* was safer. I was getting restless again and he could sense it. Even with the change of scenery, feeling safe here wasn't stopping the nightmares and I'd wake up screaming.

It was the waiting. I hated it. After months of feeling isolated again, and now this, it was like I was cracking again. I wanted to do something, *anything*, and I couldn't get Nan's words out of my head.

"Where do you want these Scottish romances?" Trix asks.

I blink, coming back to reality as I look up at her. She stands over me with some books in her hands.

"Sorry, brain went wandering, uh, second shelf." I point to the unit behind her. "There's more romances there."

"I thought you hated mystery books?" Leanne asks, walking in from the hallway with a box. She sets it beside me, and I notice how long her hair has grown. I absent-mindedly touch mine, where my shaggy pixie cut has gotten a little long.

I peek into the box, grinning at the colorful bindings. "I do, but those are classics I found in a small store. They looked cool, and lonely, and were only 50 cents."

"Classics?" She holds one up, checking the inside. "They were published in the 30s."

"Exactly." She rolls her eyes at me, smiling. "Shelf above the romances."

Trix and Leanne came over to one: help distract me, two: get me to finally decorate more of the penthouse, and three: unpack all my books and movies. Didn't help much the new stacks I've gotten after almost diving into a couple bins while out with Isaac last week. He found it hilarious that I dove for the Marx Brothers.

Leanne's ready for spring break to start, while Trix has been busy getting two centers approved. Leo and she had their conversation, barely ten minutes, before he handed her a check. The donation helped immensely, and quickly caught the eye of the board members of the two other universities Trix has been vying for. She's just waiting for space and final approval. Their waiting games were less daunting. Leanne knew the minimum, such as the paper I found, and that Roger was missing. I couldn't stomach telling her of the messes Gabriel or Matteo seem to keep creating. Gabriel had dead bodies and Matteo had shit ton of paperwork and nosy police.

"Feel normal calling this place home yet?" Leanne asks.

"Yeah." I smile at the warm penthouse, my gaze moving out to the terrace where the first small signs of spring are showing.

"From your description I'm kind of glad I didn't see it before," Trix says, finishing her task and sitting on the couch. I walk around to join her, slumping back into the softness. "I know most of the color scheme was your idea, but even the Italian aesthetic?"

Trix sweeps her braids over her shoulder, which she got sewn in about two weeks ago. They hang down to her midsection with a golden ombre.

I shrug as Leanne comes over, sitting beside me as she puts her arm over my shoulders. "Him and I."

"Get it for him, why you?" Trix asks.

"I blame the hotel suites. Besides, never really looked into my own ancestry, maybe I have a connection and don't know it, but he's passionate about it, and I like it."

"Long as you love it," Leanne says, winking.

"Does that mean higher probability place for a honeymoon?" Trix asks suddenly, and my heart goes into my throat. Oh, right… the *other* thing that gives me anxiety—secret marriage.

"Oh, that would be *perfect*!" Leanne adds. "He'll lose you at every historic site and cute coffee shops though, so make sure he has running shoes."

"Haven't really discussed it." I get up, walking over to pick up the empty boxes and put them in the entrance hall. I come back, trying to remain nonchalant like this is any other discussion. "We're still getting used to the idea of being engaged, living together, plus his work schedule has been chaotic. And then there's the hotel in Boston going up—"

"Hold on, hun," Leanne interrupts, coming over to place her hands on my shoulders. "It's okay if you haven't thought of it. We're just suggesting, maybe help give you ideas when you start planning the wedding."

I force a smile, rubbing my hands a little. Quickly, I drop them and clear my throat. "Just…not ready for that pressure and all, yet."

"Hey, if you want a year or years long engagement, good for you, waiting is fine," Trix comments. "There's no pressure in getting married, Autumn. Whenever you two are ready." She scoffs lightly. "I doubt Leo needs the excuse of a honeymoon to whisk you away to a foreign country anyways. Surprised he hasn't yet."

"Can't leave exactly due to…work," I say quietly, and Leanne drops her hands, glancing over me briefly. "He's busy. Doubt he'd want work to follow him across seas."

Since it seems to already be following him here.

"Right," Leanne murmurs, but quickly schools her expression and steps back. "Well, most of what you wanted is done, want to sit out at that fancy balcony of yours?"

"Oh, I'm for this idea," Trix agrees, standing up.

"Grab a blanket, still chilly even with the firepit," I say as they head for the sliding doors.

Trix grabs a blanket, following Leanne out to the balcony as I walk out last and turn on the firepit.

"Let's say hypothetically," Trix starts, sitting in one of the chairs. "To get you *used* to the idea and thinking forward, where would you want to go? Honeymoon wise? Leanne and I can give some ideas."

Trix's tone changes, reminding me of her social worker side. She smiles easily as she adjusts the blanket over her as Leanne sits in the other chair. The firepit does give a bit of warmth, but I rub my arms not just because of the chill.

"I'd choose Japan," Leanne sighs, lounging back with a grin. "Always wanted to see the cherry blossoms and Mt. Fuji, the markets, and temples. Plus, the festivals."

"Not England?" Trix muses, poking her arm.

I look between them, and Leanne rolls her eyes, then swats at Trix. "Everyone wants to go there. For…whatever reasons."

Trix glances at me, biting her lower lip as she tries not to smile. I sit next to Trix, and ask her, "What about you?"

I peek at Leanne who mouths "thank you."

"Well, there's the Northern Lights," Trix answers. "Don't like the cold, thus heavy blanket, but I'd brave the snow of Norway to see them. Can only imagine how romantic it could be." She tilts her head at me. "There, now about you? Wherever you think."

My hands become very interesting as I stare down at them. I know what Trix is doing, whether she knows the truth or not, she's trying to help me see a positive future. Plan ahead and bet on there being one. I rip my gaze away from my hands, looking out at the city and feeling the warmth of the sun on my skin. Only one answer seems to keep popping up in my head.

A few more breaths, I finally say, "Rome."

"See, I would've bet on England for you," Leanne says. "To see the Globe, palace, or go to the countryside to have your own Mr. Darcy moment."

"I'm not that big a fan of Austen," I laugh.

"Pretty sure Leanne is," Trix comments. "Englishmen can be so hot, you know?"

"Why Rome?" Leanne asks, ignoring Trix.

Trix bumps her shoulder with me, giggling under her breath. She's having too much fun teasing Leanne. Thank goodness Isaac wasn't here today.

My best friend waves me on to explain. Fine, I won't let my own curiosity interfere. They've barely talked the past few weeks anyways.

"I've wanted to go there before Leo," I say. "Maybe the *Italian Lily* has progressed those thoughts, but I'd love to walk those ancient streets or explore the gardens. I'd love to see what Leo is like there, too. See firsthand why so much of it inspired the hotel. His eyes light up every time he talks about little details or the summers he's spent in Italy."

It gets quiet while I daydream about Leo showing me churches, Piazzas, or sitting at a café.

Trix nudges me, bringing me out of my daze as I blink and am brought back to reality. I clear my throat, and smile at them. "Enough about me and potential honeymoons and stuff." Especially since I don't want to accidentally let the cat out of the bag. "What about you, Trix?"

"What? Dating?"

"You haven't been outspoken about it lately," Leanne adds.

"Cause Autumn is in the wonderful, lovey-dovey stage, while I'm out here wanting to strangle people," Trix answers. She touches my arm. "By the way, I'm happy for you, it gives me hope."

"What happened to that girl you were talking to?" I ask.

"She broke it off," Trix sighs. "No explanation, one text. I should just take a break on the whole dating scene anyways. Oof, let's go back to talking about potential honeymoons, let me live through you."

"Oh, come on, don't put all the relationship talk on my shoulders," I groan dramatically, falling over Trix's lap.

"Hey, we kept that ship afloat for years, and Leanne here is struggling to flirt with a London man."

"Hey!" Leanne exclaims.

"Your turn," Trix teases me. "Give us all the fun stuff, dates, or everything in between."

"Cause let's just all admit your fiancé is the whole package, this view included." Leanne gestures out to the city, lounging in her seat again. "And we, as your friends, are grateful for it."

We all laugh, while Trix gets further under the blanket when a breeze blows through. Leanne shrugs it off, sighing as she puts her hands behind her head. For a moment, I think and realize there's a subject I haven't really talked about with them. It wasn't about weddings or anything, and I *did* kinda want to tell them. And could.

"Well..." I start, clearing my throat, "...I could share some... bedroom stuff, or whatever."

They both go still, exchanging a glance with the other.

"Hun, you don't have to," Trix reassures me. "I didn't mean everything, especially if you haven't...wait, that's not, I mean—"

"Wait, wait, Trix it's fine." She stares at me as I give her a faint smile. "We've done it. Like...yeah we've done it." And more so, but we'll wait on discussing kink. "I thought I told y'all we have."

"Well, you may have mentioned it," Leanne replies slowly.

"But we weren't sure if you *enjoyed* it," Trix says. "Leo may be a whole package, but that doesn't always translate to, well, sex. We never wanted to press it until we were sure you wanted to talk about it." Trix takes a long breath, taking my hand and rubs it in hers a moment. "You were scared for so long."

I give her a sympathetic look, and then peer over at Leanne. Her own expression softens. "So, you enjoy it?" Leanne asks.

I nod my head.

"Do you still have panic attacks?" Trix brings up next. "Or have…sorry, I'm being intrusive now, it's just…been a while since we've talked about it. After that guy from like two years ago, well, you didn't seem to want to talk about sex at all."

I shrug. "I've had few panic attacks here and there, but Leo's handled each really, *really* well. Trust me."

Trix's eyes glisten, a tentative smile appearing. "You honestly enjoy it? You're not just saying…"

"Oh, yeah…oh yeahhh. No lies here."

"Well, that's a great response," Leanne chuckles.

My gaze is fixed on Trix, who has more tears in her eyes. I keep her hand in mine as her throat works. I nod again, hoping she'll believe me a bit more. Suddenly, Trix pulls me into a hug, and I feel her tears.

She'd been there during the worst it; been in the room when I thought I was dying. I had no guardians, no one to advocate for me, or fight for me. Leanne and Nan weren't signed on anything, my attempt to keep them safe, but it screwed me over and they couldn't see me. It was all Trix in those vital hours. This woman, my friend, tethered me to earth as I bled, screamed, and cried. And then she watched me recover, one appointment after the next, trying to move forward. I wasn't the only one she's sat next to, and many didn't make it.

Leanne gets up. "Why don't I call up some delivery for dinner?"

"Sure," I say, and she disappears inside.

Once we're alone, Trix finally pulls back and lets out a long breath. A few moments pass in silence, and she finally smiles faintly. "I never gave up on you, I swear…and I hoped you were trying with him, but didn't know you…well, would look happy talking about sex."

"I hate myself less, including the guilt," I murmur as she wipes away some tears. "Leo has really helped me, Trix. He's beyond patient, doesn't blink twice when I do freak out, and helps me enjoy it. What you saw months ago, at the restaurant and the club, really is how he is. I'm not…I'm not scared anymore because of him."

She lets out a watery laugh, sniffling as she wipes her eyes again. Trix cups my face, smiling. "I'm so proud of you. All I've wanted was for you to be happy and find your strength again. I've seen so many who haven't, and there were times I worried for you. You've heard it so many times, but you really didn't deserve what happened. No one does. And I am happy he was the one to help you stop being scared."

Her words spread a calmness over me.

"Just know, Trix, I'd never be here if it wasn't for you. I'd never have made it out of that hospital without you."

We hug again, both our arms gripping hard against the other. "That was all you," she whispers. "Always has been."

I nod against her head, unsure what else to say. We remain there a few minutes, before pulling away and we both wipe away tears. She laughs through hers as I wipe mine away. She asks, "Do I get to tell him how grateful I am? No matter how strict or grumpy he is?"

I chuckle. "Maybe, but don't phrase it 'thanks for giving my friend orgasms' or whatever."

We both laugh and she shakes her head. She starts getting up. "Best to get inside before Leanne orders for us."

"Yeah, we'll have thirty California rolls to devour." We laugh again as she heads into the penthouse, taking the blanket with her as I turn off the firepit.

I shake off some of the heightened emotions, pushing away the creeping anxiety. Her words were comforting, but elicited old feelings, too. Not to mention knowing I'm still lying to my very loyal, loving friends. A sigh releases from me as I smile stepping inside.

"How do you not have takeout menus?" Leanne asks.

Trix tosses the blanket onto the sofa. "Oh, good we got here in time."

I chuckle, "Uh, well, about the menus—"

The front door opens, and Leo walks in, beginning to take his coat off. He pauses near the entryway to the kitchen, noticing all of us. "Apologies for interrupting."

"We were just about to order sushi," Leanne says. "Where's your menus?"

"My what?"

"We rarely do takeout, which is why there's none." I smirk and he scowls at me. "Xavier may have suggestions."

"Doorman?" Trix asks. I nod.

"Oh, let's ask him," Leanne says as I walk to the counter, picking up my phone to pull up his number. Leo appears out of place, starting to pull his coat back on.

"I'll leave you three be for dinner then," he says.

"Just stay, Leo," Leanne tells him. "Pillow fight portion of the evening is already done, so you're safe." Leo looks at me confused, and I can't help smiling.

He starts to protest, straightening himself when Trix chimes in. "Besides, we owe you a dinner anyways." She grins as he shifts his gaze to her. "No interrogation this time."

I hand Leanne my phone, who smirks as Leo finally relents with a long sigh, taking his coat off again. Leanne calls up Xavier and Trix joins her to discuss options as I go to Leo.

He pulls me into an embrace and whispers, "Pillow fight?"

"We'll have one later." I smirk, kissing him quickly. My body relaxes as his hand caresses my back, and then his hand goes into mine as I pull him toward the others to order food for a much calmer dinner than the first.

Chapter 37

All Tied Up

The door shuts behind me after saying goodbye to Leanne and Trix. I pad back through the kitchen, where Leo has already cleaned. Xavier gave an excellent choice for sushi. I may pretend in the future this was the first dinner I had with Leo and my friends. It went well, yet there was this unease in my stomach.

I amble towards the shelves in the living room, trailing my fingers over the books and then proceed to the shelving that holds most of my movies. Kneeling down, I look over the cases on the bottom shelf. Unease travels over my skin, while thoughts I'd hoped would disappear come back. I breathe deeply as I come upon the cases of *The Thing*, *Mommie Dearest*, and *Donnie Darko*. A debate runs through my head as I pull out *The Thing*, holding it in my hand as my mind becomes clogged with worry.

Footsteps sound behind me. I put the movie back and stand to look at the movies I usually try to watch. All my Nick Cage films are lined together, most organized they've ever been.

"Which Cage film tonight?" He asks.

I stare at the titles.

"May not be in the mood," I murmur, turning towards him and rubbing my arms.

Leo's brows pull together as he comes closer, placing his hands over mine. "What is it, Autumn?"

"For once, I don't think a movie is gonna help. Was hoping Leanne and Trix coming over would help with the anxiety, but... maybe not." He watches me, head tilting with a frown.

"Was it something you talked about?"

I shrug. "Maybe? Or just...things are getting under my skin again. Maybe that's it."

Being reminded that I'm lying to my best friends, Nan calling me out weeks ago, and keeping a marriage secret also doesn't help.

"Something tells me my usual distractions, aren't going to work." My voice is soft as I peer down at the movies again, suddenly wishing for the rest that's at the hotel. Should have them all here. One place.

Leo moves a hand up to my jaw, tugging it lightly to look back at him. The frown still faintly there, his eyes scan over my features before he asks, "What about a different kind of distraction?"

I stare at him. Without a word, my gaze flicks towards where the playroom is. I meet his hazel gaze again, inhaling deep in an attempt to calm the creeping worry in my chest. After another breath and wanting to do anything, but shove those movies where they shouldn't go, I answer, "Please."

<hr>

Bundles of rope lay across the end of the bed. I stare at the different colors, heart pounding a bit harder than usual. There's more light in the playroom than the first time. Soft, sensual beats echo through the room, coming from speakers hidden in the corners. I'm nude, standing on the rug, pushing my toes into the plush carpet. It's comforting as I keep my arms at my sides. It's not cold, but my nipples don't seem to know that. Between the ropes, standing naked in the middle of the room, and the music playing the distraction is off to a great start from my uneasy thoughts.

Leo walks out of the bathroom, wearing those slacks and dark tank top again. Shears are clipped to his waist, and he places some kind of balm next to the rope. He turns away from me again, going through the dressers a moment before coming back with some black fabric in his hand.

"Put this on, *Tesoro*," he instructs gently.

I go to grab it, and then swallow hard and answer, "Yes, Sir."

My hand wraps around the sheer black fabric, but Leo's other hand entraps mine against his. It makes me look up at him with wide eyes.

"Breathe." He inhales deeply, and I do it with him, and then let all the air out. "I know I told you this session I'll be requiring more responses from you, but not just yet. When I *do* need a reply, I'll tell you." I nod my head. "I'm pushing your soft limits tonight, and if you truly don't feel ready, we won't do it, it's alright."

"No, I want...want to try."

His expression softens before he places a kiss on my forehead. "Put this on."

Leo lets go of me, and I unfold the sheer fabric. It takes me a second to realize how to put it on, shimmying into the lingerie like it's a one-piece bathing suit. It's an extremely sheer mesh fabric with a deep V neck and drastic hiked bottom part. It's snug against my body.

I bring my attention back to Leo, finding him ever so slowly trailing his eyes over my body with a smoldering look. Whatever nerves I had before are now replaced with a different kind as hazel eyes continue to look me over. He comes close, tilting my head up with a single finger, caressing his thumb just under my lip.

"You're absolutely ravishing, sweetheart, and if I didn't have plans in maintaining your focus tonight, I'd be worshipping your body on that bed instead."

"I mean...that could work, too," I say behind a gulp.

"Where would the fun in that be?"

"Oh, I could think of many ways."

Leo chuckles, continuing to rub his thumb over my skin. "Let's go over said plans again, shall we?"

"Yes, Sir."

"The rope isn't going to truly bind you in any capacity," he explains in a soothing, low voice. "You'll be able to move your arms and legs, no attachments to hardpoints or even to your own body. I'll be using techniques and designs that are more decorative, making you feel hugged or slightly constricted. Every few minutes, I'll be checking in with you on how you're feeling. Although I don't plan to have anything tight, there's still risk involved, so you need to be aware of your body. No going off into the galaxy, you'll need to remain present."

I breathe in a long breath again, and answer, "Yes, Sir."

"Good girl." My body relaxes more. "What are your safe words?"

"Yellow and red."

"What do you need to make sure I'm aware of that I can't see or feel?"

"Partial loss of feeling in the hands or fingers, burning or tingling, and no mobility."

"Good girl." The deepness of his voice calms me, bringing that sense of safety. "At any point of time, we need to stop, use your safe word, and I'll cut you out if need be."

"Yes, Sir."

"We won't be having sex this time." My eyes widen at the statement, and I'm half-tempted to ask why. We've discussed that not every time we'll have it, but I thought it wouldn't be off the table this soon. "What I do have is a vibrator I didn't use the first session," he smirks. "And I have other plans for you that don't include my dick."

A quick retort bubbles up in my throat, but I bite down on my bottom lip to keep from saying it.

Leo's smile is knowing as he brings his face down close to mine. "I'm still going to worship you, *Tesoro;* to replace every touch upon your body with mine, leaving behind only ecstasy, satisfaction, and you realizing the resplendent holiness your existence has on me."

My breath comes up short, entire body going still.

Well, *holy* shit.

Tenderly and fervently, Leo kisses me. There's a hitch to my breath as his lips caress mine, hand still upon my chin. My mind goes completely blank as he kisses me, pulling away what feels too soon.

I remain in my spot as Leo goes to pick up one of the bundles. He grabs the deep cobalt blue rope, and then stands directly in front of me.

"Hold your hand out." I do as he says. He places some of the rope in my hand, gesturing for me to grab it. It's kind of soft with a slight scratchiness to it. "It's called jute." I nod as he takes it out of my hands. "Check in."

"Green, Sir," I answer, looking up into his gaze.

Butterflies float in my stomach as Leo begins to tie and loop the rope around my chest. He maneuvers my arms, either telling me where to place them or doing it himself. I try not to stare down at my front where he makes some knots, crisscrossing some of the rope as it's looped around my neck like a halter top. Each breath I take is deliberate as I feel the rope gently move across my skin. Each time I think Leo is done, he begins something else, wrapping another piece over my chest or tugging a portion of the rope around another.

I pay attention to my fingers or if there's tingling. What I mostly feel is the light compression of the rope as it's tightened over my breasts and under them, becoming like a wire bra without the actual wire.

Leo constantly checks in with me, his voice low and soothing as the torso of my body is practically covered in rope. He steps away grabbing another bundle. He pauses to bring his finger under my chin, tilting it back once again.

"Check in."

"Green, Sir."

"Feel all your fingers and limbs?"

"Yes, Sir," I murmur.

"Good girl, now move and wiggle your legs a little. You've been standing for a bit, don't want your knees locking on us."

He moves his hand away and I shake my legs out, bending them. I hadn't realized how stiff they'd become and now I'm really unsure how long it's already been. It could have been ten minutes to thirty, I'm not sure. Those thoughts are quickly swept away when Leo slides his hand over my hip just under where the rope harness ends.

I go still as his hand follows the length of rope up the middle of my chest to my breasts. He brushes his palm over my nipple and then over the other. A shiver travels down my spine, becoming more aware of the rope tied around my body, pressing in as my breath catches.

"Place your hands behind your head," he instructs. I do so, and then he gently commands, "Legs apart." For a moment, my breath almost hiccups as my stomach does a flip as I realize what position he's putting me in.

A high protocol position—arms up and legs spread for the Dom to see.

I swallow hard as his hand glides down my side, along my thigh. The butterflies in my stomach become like lead as he undoes the next rope and begins to tie to the bottom of the harness to begin on my right leg. It squeezes against my limb lightly, and there's a prick at the back of my neck. I stare ahead as I try to concentrate on the rest of the rope around me, swinging on a pendulum of panic and not. Leo continues to wrap the rope around my thigh, creating what I think is called a ladder rung tie.

The prick comes back, traveling down my spine in warning as I feel the rope tighten. Pieces of me attempt to grasp that it's just Leo and some rope, while other parts slither toward panic and fear. He tightens the rope, moving further down and I suddenly want to puke.

Shit, safe word, Autumn...fucking safeword.

We just fucking started. My upper body was fine, why was my leg being tied making shit bubble up?

My mouth won't seem to work as I stare forward, clutching at the back of my head, frozen in place by Leo's command and the repercussions if I do.

Check in with me. Please.

I'm on the edge of hurtling towards a panic attack, concentrating on the harness around my chest, imagining it's Leo's arms.

Check in with me, I plead inside, frozen on the outside.

Leo suddenly stops, hands going still. His voice is low and commanding, "Check in, Autumn."

"Yellow," I rasp, thanking fuck he ingrained in me to reply.

"Pain?"

"No."

"Leg?"

"Yes."

Before I know it, he has his shears out and cuts through the rope he just tied. My breath hitches as the rope falls to the ground in pieces. He stands, readying his shears to cut the body harness next.

"No," I say, breathing in deeply as relief washes over me from my leg not being wrapped in rope. I concentrate on the pressure of the rope around my chest, unsure why it's giving me any comfort right now. "Harness stays, please, Sir."

Leo reaches up under my arm to hold my hands against the back of my head. The shears are gone, and his other hand rests on my upper thigh, rubbing it lightly.

"Look at me." I finally look him in the eye. "You're safe. Breathe with me."

He takes in a long breath and then lets it out, giving me time to follow suit. His thumb begins to massage my thigh where the top part of the rope was, tilting my head back slightly to keep my eyes on his. He comes in close, his body practically pressed against mine as he calms down the panic attack from going full throttle.

"Check in."

Feeling the lead gone from my stomach and the prick of warning, I reply, "Green, Sir."

"Good girl, and for using your safe word." He kisses my forehead tenderly. "We can stop entirely."

"No, I'm okay now."

Leo frowns with brows furrowing deeply, which causes a small smile to rise on my face. He glances me over, watching my chest rise for a bit longer before he lets go of me completely. I remain in the position, my submissive side clutching to the instruction from earlier like a lifeline.

"Bring your arms down." They come down, and he sweeps his hand gently over my hair. "No more rope. Your harness will stay on, but not much longer, I don't want to push you too far."

"Yes, Sir."

"Bring your legs together. Stay right here."

"Yes, Sir."

His scowl eases as he bends down to pick up the pieces of rope he cut, taking it over to the dresser and places the rest of the rope with it. The shears are clipped back onto his pants.

I can't help staring at the pieces of rope he just cut. A sliver of guilt starts to climb, along with embarrassment. An attempt to squash it is futile, until Leo says, "It's just rope. I can always get more."

"Why didn't you just untie it, Sir?"

He stands before me again, brushing his hand down my neck and then places his palm against my throat.

"Jute doesn't cause burns as easily, but I wasn't going to chance it or take too long to get it off before you fully panicked," he explains. His other hand trails over some of the rope, brushing over my skin and then my breasts. "How does the harness feel?"

"Good, kind of comforting," I answer quietly. "I think having limbs tied may be…um…"

Leo nods, hushing me gently as he swipes a stray tear from my cheek. The scowl comes back, but this time I can't seem to smile at it.

I've been fully distracted by other anxious thoughts, but now I think those of the past linger in my head. I feel fully discombobulated, but don't want to give in. The guilt starts to deepen, coupled with embarrassment and even shame.

"Autumn," Leo says softly. Hazel eyes meet mine. He asks in a steadier tone, "Do you want to continue?"

My chin quivers, hating that my anxiety followed me in here. That I know, deep down, I was excited to try rope play like I saw in the books. I trusted Leo to take full reign, but the anxiety of the outside slipped through the cracks.

"I don't know," I whisper. "I want to keep going, but I'm not sure if the rest of me can."

His hand remains against my throat stroking gently. "Does the rope harness help or hinder you?"

I inhale deeply, causing the rope to strain against my skin. It doesn't feel the same like my leg being wrapped, instead the constriction is calming. It's as if I can trick my mind that it's just Leo's arms wrapped around me. I don't want it off just yet.

"It helps."

He nods once, and steps back, letting go of me. Leo goes over to the spanking bench and sits down in the main seat. He gestures for me to come over, but then pats his leg for me to sit. I'm taken aback by the gesture, but the calmness in his gaze soothes my reaction. I walk over, and sit gently on his lap, keeping my legs between his. One hand goes onto my thigh, stroking up and over where the rope had been, while his other arm wraps around my back to secure me against him.

"We'll try another approach then," he says, trailing his fingers down my side along the knots.

"Okay, I mean, shit, yes, Sir."

He takes my chin gently, turning my head toward him. "Unless using that title is going to help you, don't worry about using it."

I stare at him, body relaxing against him as the rope presses into my skin.

"You're a very forgiving Dom," I say quietly. He tilts his head, letting go of my chin and caresses my leg again.

"Why do you think that? Because you safe worded?"

"Maybe that, but even the other Doms I read about, soft or strict, each sounded like they needed rules to always be followed."

"One, I will never punish or shame you for safe wording, just as I know you'd never do that to me," he begins. "Two, each Dom or Top is going to be different in their desires or needs. Surprisingly, in here, I'm not one who absolutely needs harsh rules to feel as if I'm in charge, for me it's the trust given. For you to listen, which you do and comply to the best of your abilities. To be the one you're most vulnerable with, open, and feel the safest. Just as I feel when I'm with you."

My brows raise, not expecting that.

He feels safe with me? My anxiety ridden, panic attack around grass butt who forgets to eat and when I don't forget its likely sugary cereal?

Leo smiles tenderly.

"You notice when something is off with me," he explains. "You show affection by paying attention, giving your time. Whether you know what's wrong or not, you attempt to ease my worries. You give me patience, forgiveness…" he smirks lightly, and I give one back, "…and respect. It could all be attributed to your want of praise, but I don't believe so. You care and at the end of the day; I'd trust you with my life."

His hands continue to stroke my skin, causing emotions to bubble up along with his words. I place a hand against his chest.

"You help me feel safer, and you deserve it, too." My words are quiet as I stare at his chest under my hand.

Leo leans closer, pressing his face against my neck before kissing my skin.

"I am not forgiving of you, *Tesoro*," he whispers against my ear. "For there is nothing you could ever do that would require my forgiveness. Only you can remind me that I can be gentle and loving, to offer you security and I'm safe to do so. You bring every barrier of mine down. Allowing me to cherish, love, and…submit my own needs to you."

His hands go still, while the rest of me does, too.

There's an admittance to his voice I can't quite place. Hidden between the precious words he says. I'm too entranced by him, the rope harness, and sitting upon his lap that I can't concentrate on what it is.

Instead, I turn my head for my gaze to meet his. Those eyes of greens and golds, shimmering with a need that matches my own.

"I love you," I whisper.

He grasps my jaw tenderly, speaking Italian words I can understand, "*I love you, my everything.*"

The softness of his lips come against mine in a gentle kiss. It's so extremely tender that I could start crying right there. It could be hours that we're there kissing, sharing that love with the other.

My mind goes into a haze, like skipping through scenes in a movie as he has us stand, unties the rope from my body and carries me to our bedroom. There we strip down to nothing, and he starts a bubble bath. In the warmth of the water, we cling to the other. In the silence, our bodies pressed against the other in such intimacy I find relief.

Although his original plans of distraction fell apart, I became fully preoccupied with only one thing on my mind—the man who holds my heart in his gentle grasp.

Chapter 38

The Domino falls

Three weeks. No Roger; No Gabriel.

Each quiet day becomes heavier and heavier. It's been like watching a ticking clock.

As a way to grasp a semblance of control, Leo and I have "played" almost every other day. Each session either pushing one of our limits or just to distract ourselves from having no control outside of the violet room. He finally used the vibrator, and rope on my limbs is now a hard limit, but Leo really knows how to think outside the box.

Apart from those sessions, I have my less kinky kind.

Dr. Maxwell sits across from me, sipping his tea. I rub my hands together, not really wanting to answer his latest question. "No answer is wrong, Autumn."

"You sure?" I rub my hands over my thighs. "It's just, I could reconcile or not care about the others…didn't really bother me they were tortured or dead, but Roger…well…feels like I should."

"We don't have to mourn every person who exits our lives." He leans back in his chair, putting his tea down. "Death, *if* that is the case for him, does not absolve what he did to you or took from you."

"If I feel sorry? That maybe he met a brutal death? I know he brought himself to where he is, but…" I sigh, leaning my head back, "…even if I know *why* he did it, put me through hell, manipulated me, and lied I still feel sorry for him. Not angry or sad anymore…just sorry."

"Any particular reason?"

"I understand his frustrations, in the beginning, wanting to do the right thing and he…fell into a trap of his own greed. *Shouldn't* I feel sorry? That he, I guess, fell from grace?"

"You're not supposed to feel anything in particular. Your feelings, reactions are yours through your own perspective. How you react is up to you. So, I'll ask again, if Mr. Morton came in here and said Roger was dead, how would you respond?"

I rock slightly, chewing my bottom lip and then exhale a long breath. "I wouldn't care. Nothing. Not even relief at this point, as if the book is closed and I already put it on the shelf."

"And that's fine," he replies with a sympathetic expression. "It means you've moved on, Autumn. That's what healing is; taking steps forward and leaving behind what doesn't serve you. It's letting go, not harboring emotions longer than we should. We don't need to cling to them to remember our lessons, pasts, or what we've accomplished. You can have that ability to look back and not have those same emotions, to not allow them to control you."

"I control them."

"Yes. They're yours to do with what you wish. How you wish." I nod, relaxing into the couch. "I'll pose another question. Don't think, just answer what comes to mind first. What would your response be if they walked in and said Gabriel was dead?"

"Happy." My eyes widen at the automatic response. Dr. Maxwell's expression remains calm, and the shiver of fear along the bottom of my spine vanishes.

"Would you say you had a similar response when those men who assaulted you died? Or your ex?"

"Yes."

"There's nothing wrong with that. Again, death does not erase one's actions or who they were alive. You never have to forgive them. There's nothing wrong with you finding relief or peace over it. Why did you seem fearful when you said happy?"

"He's Leo's brother," I murmur. "How can I feel that way over, well, he may be awful and a lot of things, but…he's still his brother."

"Much like death, it doesn't pardon him of what he's done," he replies softly. "He still harmed you and was a cause of a large part of your trauma. You can hate him. Be angry. Or be glad if he's no longer here. Very normal reactions actually to abnormal situations."

"What about being positive? Like hope he gets better? Changes his ways?"

"All hypothetical thoughts, ones that can diminish your own trauma or place blame back into your lap." Oh, goodie glad to know some things don't change. He picks up his tea again. "Aside from that, even if he or Roger does, you don't have to forgive them. They can become saints, and you can never forgive them or give them access to your space again. *You* decide. It is *your* past and experiences, so it's your choice. No matter what relation they are to you."

I nod, rubbing my hands over my thighs again. At this rate, I'm gonna put a hole in them.

"It can be hard to accept emotions that *aren't* socially accepted or presumed," he continues. "Anger, hate, and grief don't seem as fulfilling as others, because they're used regularly for things that don't aid us. Those feelings are no less valid nor make you a villain for having them. You're human, and they're very human emotions." He places his tea down, folding his hands together. "You never have to forgive your abusers, Autumn."

My hands stop. We sit quietly as I decipher the emotions of what I feel like I *should* feel and what I actually do. I swallow hard, closing my eyes and hope to just get it out in the open and out of my head.

"I do hate them. I hate Roger. Hate that he used me, *tricked* me while at my lowest. That he continued to use me after he left me with nothing. I hate that he only ever cared about getting the bad guys to the point he helped Steve out of prison. He made deals with devils to get what he wanted, not caring who he hurt. And I hate Steve for the years of abuse, that after it all I am left with the traumatic aftermath and nightmares for the rest of my life. Finally, I hate that no matter what, their deaths will never be enough to take away the pain they caused. For me or anyone else caught in their traps."

Once finished, I open my eyes and find the doctor's neutral expression. "Does it feel better saying it out loud that candidly?"

"Candidly?"

"You've tip-toed around it before."

A lightness does come over my shoulders. "Yeah, it did."

"Hate isn't always a bad thing, it can help us fight monsters, keep us moving, and remember what we do love. The important thing is to not let it consume us or allow it to morph into a harmful state. We're humans. We'll never love everything, and hate can of course divide us, but can also help take down a common enemy."

I raise my brow. "You're not gonna suggest something like tea versus coffee are you?"

He chuckles low, shaking his head. "Not quite, but sometimes simplicity is the best path to take." He starts to stand, checking his watch. "I think we'll stop here for today's session."

"Sure, and thanks Doc."

"Of course." He starts to gather his things, and then pauses. "You said your sleep has still been erratic?" I nod. "Still no on the medications?" I shake my head quickly, knowing that I *hate* that idea. "Very well, thought I'd check in."

Both of us head to the door.

"Hope you have a good vacation," I say, opening the door where Isaac and Animal stand up from their chairs. "You deserve some time off."

"I appreciate it, but if you need me, you can call—"

"I'll survive, don't worry." We share a smile as he pats my shoulder. "I'll be on my best behavior."

He chuckles, "See you in a few weeks, Autumn." He nods once at the other two, heading towards the lobby.

"How'd the session go?" Isaac asks.

"Hate more things than I thought."

Animal does a dramatic pose, putting his hand over his chest. "Our Autumn? *Hating* something? Say it ain't so!"

I gesture toward him, and tell Isaac in a deadpan voice, "See, this is why I'm in therapy."

"Along with the rest of us."

"Hey!" Animal scowls. "I'm hilarious, and some of y'all seem to have lost yer humor of late, by the way."

"You gonna keep being dramatic or we going riding?" I ask.

His scowl shifts, raising a brow. "Thought today you're helping housekeeping and deliveries?"

"Nah, Chiari called earlier not to bother. Everything's handled and I figured I'd stay out of the way rest of the weekend. Besides, Bobby and I'll just start talking and he'll get behind work."

"Again," Isaac mutters.

I frown at him playfully. "Fine, again."

"Guess we're riding," Animal smirks. "Can even let you take your favorite."

He starts heading for the elevator, and I practically race after him. "The Fat Bob?"

"How you handled it last time, I think Chesty was right to just have you stick to it. We'll wait on the chopper." I reach him right as the elevator doors open, getting on with both men.

"Probably cause I've used it the most to practice with, it's easier to handle," I reply, crossing my arms. "Although I liked Chesty's Sportster and Leo's Classic Heritage before Ringer moved them out."

"You're one of a kind being able to adapt to different bikes so easily," Animal comments.

"It's because she learned on a blank slate and the mechanics first," Isaac adds.

"Y'all know I'm right here, right?"

They chuckle as we head up to the apartment, where I switch into some jeans, boots, and a leather jacket. We head back down to the garage, where I climb onto the Fat Bob and the other two get on their sportsters.

It's near beginning of spring, given the weather lately, my little band of teachers have allowed me to practice riding outside the hotel in secret. Neither Leo or Jameson know. Riding has been the other hobby that's helped when I'm not working at the hotel. More and more I understood why Leo loves it and I can't wait until I can ride the open road.

We fuel up while we're out, riding through the city at a steady pace, and then head to a deserted parking garage, going up to the top. It's open, free of pillars as we stop and turn off the engines. I swing my leg off the bike, feeling less wobbly then usual from the rumble of the motorcycle. My helmet comes off next as Animal takes his off.

"Figured we could—" Animal gets cut off when his phone starts ringing. He motions for us to wait, stepping away to answer the call as Isaac's phone goes off next. "Enigma what—"

Animal's face becomes serious just as Isaac answers his phone. There's shouting over both phones, including noise that makes my heart race. A prick pulls at my neck, yanking at me as both mutter and swear.

"Shit," Animal exclaims, hanging up as Isaac walks away, still arguing on the phone. Animal starts checking his bike, pulling out a gun and my stomach drops.

"What's wrong?"

"Security breach."

"Meaning?" His eyes meet mine, hard, but worried. "Drew, tell me."

"Warehouse is under attack," he says, glancing over as Isaac talks on the phone. "Someone fucked us over, we need to get you back to the hotel."

"Where's Leo?" I ask, heart pounding in my chest. "Is Leo there?"

"Yes, but—"

His phone starts ringing again, and Isaac comes jogging over as Animal answers the phone. I hear Jameson yell over Isaac's phone, "They're surrounding the hotel! Get her out!"

Isaac is already pulling a .45 from his saddlebags, putting it into one of mine. "Miss Autumn—"

"They're coming for her!" Jameson's voice pierces the air. "Get her out of the hotel, *now!*"

"Sons of bitches, the warehouse breach must be a distraction." Animal hangs up.

"We have a short window, everyone thinks we're at the hotel still," Isaac says. "We need to get you out of the city."

I start to talk, "But—"

"Miss Autumn." Isaac grabs my shoulders, making me look right at him. "They don't know you ride. You're gonna take the bike, get out of the city and head for the estate. I'll meet you there. Do you remember the address?"

Swallowing hard, I nod, going through the directions in my head that he and I have gone over multiple times.

"From there we'll head to your next safe house, but first we need to get you out of the city. Away from the hitmen." Isaac grabs my helmet and continues talking to Animal. "We'll distract anyone who may have seen us leave. Head for the Washington bridge, then break off. Traffic may be in our favor if they're in vehicles."

"Isaac—"

"You'll be fine," he tells me. "Leo, too. Now get on the bike, you know what to do. Once you're on the highway it'll be a piece of cake."

Oh, sure yeah.

I shove the helmet on my head, quickly pressing the button on the side to receive the emergency calls through the headset. My leg swings over and I turn on the rumbling engine. I glance at the other two as they get onto their bikes, heart pounding as realization sinks in on what I have to do. There's a singular ring before the helmet picks up, coming from Isaac.

"Go. We'll take care of the rest. Get out, Autumn."

Upon that demand, my head and gut come together with a singular notion: Run.

I leave the other two behind, riding the bike down and rip the throttle when I reach the bottom. Every lesson the guys taught me, races through my head as I speedily weave through cars. When I hear another engine behind me, I briefly glance over my shoulder. Isaac's not far behind. We race through the city as I aim for the highway.

The headset clicks and beeps before I hear Isaac over it. "Still clear, Animal what about you?"

Animal replies something over the headset as I turn down a street, trying to remember the fastest route to the major highway. Fuck, the subway was easier to memorize, especially as I try to avoid traffic. The familiar warning along my skin returns, tickling down my spine as my gut continues to scream *Run*.

Police sirens go off suddenly, screaming through the traffic and noise of the city and I slow down. For a brief moment, I see them pass at an intersection, causing taxis to honk their horns.

"Another distraction for all we know," Isaac comments as I pick up speed again.

"They're trying to keep Leo away from me, aren't they?"

I veer off down an alley, chest squeezing tight. There's commotion behind me, cars honking and someone yelling as I go down another back alley and glance over my shoulder. Isaac isn't following me anymore. Fuck, I want to puke as my stomach clenches.

"Yes," Isaac finally answers. "Most likely to kidnap you for leverage or blackmail."

"Who would—"

"Fuck!" Animal yells, vibrating through my ears.

The bike jolts as I almost hit the brakes, easing off as I come to the end of the alley and stop. "What is it?" I ask, searching for any sign of being followed besides them.

"Bastards, take the other street, Animal," Isaac instructs, and I hear popping noises.

"Bond? Animal?"

"Get to the estate, Autumn!" Isaac suddenly yells. "They're following—"

He gets cut off suddenly and my stomach drops. The headset crackles, and I press the button again. Silence. My hands grip into the handles, trying not to accidentally make the bike jump forward.

"Bond?" No answer. "Animal?" Nothing.

I look behind myself again. Short crackling happens again over the helmet, then silence. My breathing becomes strangled like gravel pressing into my lungs.

"Breathe. Get out. Do what he said. Get to the estate." My voice faintly echoes in my helmet against the rumble of the engine.

Listening for any noise beyond the usual, I take another moment before thrusting the bike forward and turn toward the highway. I almost rip the throttle again when I see the signs for the main highway, weaving through cars at tight angles that makes my heart thunder. Horns sound as I swerve, a couple of times almost losing control as I try to straighten the bike before completely skidding down the road.

Sirens go off behind me, and crackling comes back over my headset then disappears. I'm not sure if my body is shaking from fear or from the bike as I finally make it to the on ramp for the highway, now dumping the throttle to get the fuck out of the city. My heart hammers in my chest as I get on the wide road, a new kind of fear beginning to pulse.

I've never driven on any highway before. In *any* vehicle.

My mind screams, wanting to curl up into a ball. I battle with my emotions, trying to regain control when I hear another bike engine approaching. Hope flickers in my chest as the other motorcycle comes up beside me.

Animal.

He points to his helmet and then gestures with his hand to follow him. I nod just before he pulls ahead of me. The shaking doesn't stop as I speed up to remain close. The stretch of highway we're on feels like forever before he aims for an off ramp.

The motorcycle's engine is my only comfort as I follow Animal onto a back road. It's not long before he pulls off into an abandoned parking lot of an outlet store.

The trembling worsens as I park beside him. Animal flips his visor up and I do the same.

He yells over the roar of the engines. "You good?"

I nod.

"Keep following me until we get to the estate. Good maneuvering back there. You're a natural."

I force a faint smile.

"Focus on the bike. Just you and it. Got it?" I nod again. He flips the visor down as I do before we hit the road.

The only thing keeping me from losing my shit is the constant vibrations of the Harley.

Chapter 39

Run, Autumn, Run

It was like being hit by a truck.

My body is tired from constantly tensing. It's hours before we reach the estate, Animal guiding us down country roads to throw off anyone who may be following us. Finally, I recognize the road and see the trees that line the entry of the estate.

Relief fills me as we reach the gravel driveway, engines roaring through the quiet of the countryside as we park the bikes before the garage. I shut off the engine, letting out a long breath as I take my helmet off. Animal takes a moment longer, nodding his head as he shuts off the engine. I can hear him talking low in the helmet.

Guess only my headset is fucked up.

I glance around the property. It's quiet. No sign of anyone as my gaze scans the place. The prick at the back of my neck pulls. Finally, he mutters something, pulling the helmet off.

"Who was it?" I ask.

"Iron Buffalo. We're gonna switch out bikes, and then head to the safe house."

He gestures for me to stay put as he goes to put his pin in, opening the garage as he pulls out his .45, clicking back the safety.

"They're not sure how deep the security breach is," he

murmurs, beginning to sweep through the garage. All of Leo's bikes are lined up as they had been before when we left months ago, but the Classic Heritage is missing. "Most of the assailants were taken out or apprehended, still looking for those who were after you."

"What do you mean how deep the breach was?" I step into the garage, seeing no sign of threat. Animal looks back at me, nervousness flashing over him. "I'm on the run *again*, Drew, you better tell me the fucking truth."

"Leo was in a meeting."

"Mafia?" He nods. "And?"

"No one was supposed to know he was there. Secret meeting with another boss."

My chest tightens. Shit. "Inside job or betrayed by who he was meeting."

"Basically. Or both. Grab the gun Isaac stashed for you." I jog back to the bike, pulling it out and checking the ammo. I keep it ready as I follow Animal into the house.

It's empty. Furniture covered in sheets; lights turned off. It feels cold and dreary. A shiver runs down my spine as Animal checks the security room, and then goes through the living room and kitchen. He gestures for me to stay as he checks the upstairs. My heart thunders, pulsing through my head until he returns.

"We're good. I'm gonna double up locking shit down, you can get changed."

"Who would betray Leo?" I ask suddenly before he can walk away.

He shrugs tiredly. "Anyone can get paid off. Could've been promised better protection or pay. Sounds like a handful of them were guards you met briefly when we brought Steve in."

My heart sinks and I feel sick.

"Drew..."

"They're not Crew," he states. "Not family, hurts they fucked us over, but our family is good." I nod. "Get changed, dress warm. Temps will drop."

"Not staying in the orchard, are we?" I ask, going up the stairs.

He chuckles half-heartedly. "Nah, but you've been there before. Good place to stay until they catch the last of the rats jumping off the sinking ship."

My hands tremble as I head for the main bedroom. Quickly, I find all the clothes Leo stashed here and change. I resituate the gun, knowing why we're doing this.

History repeating itself.

Closing my eyes, I take a moment to regain my composure and am about to leave when I see the leather vest Leo gave me. The one with the *Forgotten Demons* insignia and *Property of the Spartan* across the back. Quickly I snatch it off the hanger, pulling it on and grab the jacket as I head out the door.

Animal is packing a bag for extra supplies as I return to the garage. He's wearing his vest, too. Gut decision was right then. The nod I receive is another confirmation.

Melancholy tugs at me when Animal locks the doors behind us. Swiftly, we park our bikes, and he starts rolling out Leo's black Road King. I stare at the spot where the Classic Heritage should be as he situates our supplies.

"Where's the other bikes?"

"Probably in the club's garage." Animal juts his head once toward the sheds near the helo pad. "Ringer always puts them there before moving them. It's where ours are stashed. He and Chesty don't trust the mechanic Leo has to keep his bikes running."

Once we're set with the Road King, Animal closes everything up, trying to make it seem we were never here. Helmets on, I tap mine trying to get it work. Nothing. Fuck.

"Headset still isn't working," I say.

"Enigma's backup then, hit the radio connection," he suggests.

It finally crackles to life, connecting only to Animal's headset. Guess the Bluetooth gave up. He straddles the bike and I climb on behind him. The engine rumbles to life, causing birds to rush out of the trees as we leave the estate. I glance back at what was my haven. Warning pulls tight along my skin.

Not even safe here.

The bike surges down the road.

After we've traveled a bit, Animal's voice comes over the headset, sounding like the ones on the helicopter. "Made an old biker proud. Not only traveling hours on your own, but navigating the city traffic and getting on the highway like that."

"Not sure how the fuck I did it."

"Paid attention to your mentors."

"I got some good ones."

A prick tugs at my neck, making my hairs stand on end. We come upon a wide curve, heading up into the hills and I peer back to see a car in the distance. SUV.

Animal continues to talk over the headset as I peer past his shoulder, seeing another curve come up. We lean into it, and I look back again to get a better view of the car.

I don't want to spook Animal if I'm wrong, but the warning along my spine doesn't relent. I close my eyes, steady a breath, and concentrate on the engine of the bike. Trust my gut.

"Don't change your speed," I interrupt him, pulling the gun from my vest. He tenses, but the bike's speed doesn't change. "When I tell you, slow down and hit the brakes. You'll know when to hit the accelerator and open the throttle."

"Bike ain't made for tricks."

"Trust me?"

"More than you know."

I notice they've gotten closer, gaining on us we take another curve. Ahead there's a longer stretch a road before one more. Close enough. Now or never.

"Now."

The bike jolts as the brakes are hit. Tires screech as we skid to a halt, a car horn sounding behind us as they speed past, but they're brakes are screeching next. Enough of a glimpse, I know my gut was right. Their windows begin to lower, and I pull the gun out.

It echoes as I pull the trigger, ringing through my ears as I aim for the tires. Two bullets hit the back of the car and they swerve.

Animal hits the accelerator, bike flying forward as we blast past them. I aim again, hitting a front tire. It pops and the car jerks, ramming into the hillside. Animal swerves, driving the bike defensively as shots ricochet behind us. The curve isn't far ahead as we both lean into it, disappearing from their sight.

"Guess watching action films helps," I mutter.

"Were you aiming for the tires?"

"Yeah. Figured it'd stop them faster than hitting them or the damn engine. Not chancing if anything was bullet resistant."

"Not bad, sister, not bad at all." We pick up speed as he rips the throttle. "Let's get the fuck out of here."

D arkness surrounds us with only the headlight piercing through. Last couple of hours have taken their toll and exhaustion is hitting. No one else followed us, especially with Animal's evasive tactics through small towns. I try to pay attention, but only when we come to a lone road and slow down do I recognize our surroundings. He turns the bike into the parking lot of a bar, going behind the building and shutting off the engine once parked. The back kitchen door swings open as we take our helmets off and climb off the bike.

It's Ikemba aka Snake Eyes.

"Later than I was told." His deep voice cuts through the quiet night.

"Had to make sure we weren't followed. Remember Spartan's old lady?" Animal asks, grabbing our stuff.

"Hi, again." I wave.

"Hoping next time I saw you, it'd be for a party," he replies with a half-smile. "You good?"

"Tired."

"Come in. Your Pres owes me, Animal."

"I know," Animal answers as we follow Ikemba into the bar.

Ikemba talks, leading us through the space. "Ringer and Iron

Buffalo didn't say much, but I got guys posted down the road. Most jumped at the chance to help, given what they owe The Spartan."

"Took out the last stragglers a few hours ago, haven't seen anybody since," Animal says as we skim past a kitchen, go down a hallway, and then enter a back room with a poker table and chairs strewn about. Two cots are set up. "No idea how long we're staying."

Ikemba folds his arms over his chest. Animal drops our stuff on a cot. I'd take it over Roger's guest room any day.

"Sure, you good?" Ikemba asks me.

I clear my throat, trying to remain nonchalant except my mind is racing a mile a minute. Then again, I'm so numb and exhausted. I can't stop thinking about Leo and the others, just wanting to know they're okay.

"I'm fine."

"Anytime a woman says that, ain't." I snort at him. "Being chased from home ain't easy."

"Neither is running from it," I reply bluntly. He frowns a bit deeper. "Not my first time."

He hums about to say something when Animal interrupts, "Can we talk in private?"

Ikemba nods. "I'll get something cooked up for ya, too. How you feel about chicken?"

"Sounds good, thank you," I respond softly. "Snake Eyes."

"Remember my real name?" I glimpse at Animal, then look back at Ikemba with a faint smile. He returns the gesture. "Knew I liked you for a reason."

Ikemba steps out and Animal goes to follow. "Animal...I thought he didn't know about—"

"He doesn't. Bikers take care of our own. He was told someone was after you, needed a place to hide. That's all he knows. Your Leo's Old Lady, which they won't take lightly." I wrap my arms around myself, feeling the leather vest and nod, remembering what Ringer said. "Stay here. Be right back."

Those warm brown eyes flick over me a moment before he

closes the door behind him. I slump into a chair, hands trailing over the felt table. My mind flits to Isaac explaining every security precaution, from GPS tracking in the bikes to the phones. Suddenly, my heart sinks, wanting my shadow here. I'm grateful for Animal, but why didn't Isaac make it out of the city?

He's fine. Just change of plans.

I feel sick, fisting my hands. The door opens and Animal holds up his phone. "It's him."

I jump out of the chair, lunging for the phone. "Leo?"

"Check in," he rasps.

Eyes closing, I lean back against the table in relief to hear his voice. I clutch the edge as the door closes, leaving me alone. "Yellow, I mean…green, I'm fine. I'm okay."

It's silent on the other side. Suddenly, something slams shut in the background and there's muffled yelling. My breath hitches as another door slams, then finally silence. He breathes heavy on the other end.

"Leo?"

"You can ride," he whispers.

I stare at the poker chips. "How did—"

"Enigma was fixing street footage. I saw you…through traffic and getting on the highway."

I let out a broken laugh. Later this spring I was going to surprise him at the estate. Couldn't have that, could I? "I was going to surprise you."

"How long have you…when?"

"The estate. Since then, most of my free time wasn't just mechanical, but learning to ride. Most the Crew were teaching me. I wanted to surprise you." My voice catches.

"You did. You did." The brokenness in his voice is beyond exhaustion. Pained.

"Check in."

"Red."

"Leo—"

"I need you to listen, very closely, Autumn." Bricks press down upon my chest. Each word heavier than the next. It's the lack of him saying his name for me. Chills gather as his tone changes. "We're interrogating those involved. You need to stay there until I say otherwise."

"Okay." My voice is barely a whisper. He goes quiet, too fucking quiet. "Leo?" Silence. "Leo, talk to me, please."

A beat passes.

"They were coming to kill you." Everything goes still. If I wasn't clutching the phone so hard, I'd have dropped it. "One or two may have kidnapped you instead, for greedy ransom, but they were hired to kill you. Not sure by who yet. I'm likely next."

Horror wraps around my neck, choking me.

"You own everything I have," he continues, voice colder by the second. "If anything happens to me, *you* own them. *You* are the boss, not Jameson or my brothers, *you* are next in line, do you understand? For *everything*, remember? You are *my* wife, who inherits it all. No one else. Not Matteo. Not anyone else of the family line." A lump rises in my throat. Tears falling down my cheeks. "Autumn, answer me."

"Yes."

"I will do everything, absolutely *anything* to keep you safe and bring you back to me. I promise. But I will not give you false hope." My body trembles, begging for this to not be real. "Someone is manipulating the other underbosses within my organizations to overthrow me. They're hitting vulnerable spots, taking personal routes to do so, and breaking unspoken rules we follow. You have to survive, I *need* you to, Autumn."

"Don't ask me to do this. Don't you dare." My voice shakes.

"I'm not...I'm begging you."

My knees buckle and I hit the ground. I clutch the table still, struggling to breathe through the tightness around my throat. No...no...

"Autumn...dear Watson, promise me." I shake my head. "No matter what, survive."

A whimper leaves me, flashes of the night we were almost

mugged. The blood on his shirts. The crunch of snow. The grey walls. Hot tears pour down. Flickers of dreams and hopes merging are yanked into oblivion.

Don't make me a widow.

"Let me come back," I beg. "Let me help you."

"Autumn—"

"I'm not walking away or going on without you," I exclaim under my breath. "I told you I'd stay no matter what. I don't care —"

"This is different, they will drag you—"

"They already have! I've been pummeled into hell and back. I don't care."

"*All* the crime bosses are against me, Autumn." What? "There's no one to trust. It's not safe for you. And I will not risk them finding out who you are or what you did. They've already gotten too close, especially within the hotel."

Fuck. FUCK.

His voice cracks and something snaps on the other end of the receiver.

"I can't bring you back into this," he says quietly. "I can't. I won't let you take more of my sins. My mistakes and fuck ups. You've already taken enough of my burdens, shouldered more than I could ever ask. You'd carry the worst for me, but not this time. Please not this time. I want…*need* you safe."

"And I need you," I plead. "I need you, Leo, please."

"I'll find you. I'll always find you." His voice is barely a whisper. Terror grips me. "You are my dear wife. You will always be no matter what anyone says. I love you more than life itself. I'll do everything that I must to protect you, even…even if it means I have to break a promise."

Fear slithers across my skin. "Leo."

"I love you." His voice is dark and cold, distant almost. There's nothing I can do as he says the damning words, "Goodbye…my dear Watson."

The line goes dead.

Horror snaps inside me. The phone drops from my hand as I finally scream. I shriek, tugging at my hair. Animal slams into the room. He yanks me into his arms, holding me as I shake my head and sob into his chest.

"I'm sorry, sister… I'm sorry."

I can't even fight him. All I can do is sob and scream as he murmurs his apologies, while the reality of Leo being killed smothers me like an unforgiving inferno.

Chapter 40

Yank the Wool

Two days pass. Depression almost smothers me, reminding me of Roger's house. Almost ironic. Except this time, I'm not left alone, keeping busy helping tend bar. It reminds me of *Blue Java*. The Crew have only called Animal, giving me updates that my friends and Nan are safe from the maelstrom.

It's late as I wash glasses. Donna, one of the bartenders with spikey blonde hair streaked with pink and piercings along her ears, pats my shoulder.

"Thanks for cleaning'em," she says, giving a wink. Most the time she's yelling at the bikers playfully. Tonight, she wears a midriff tank top, necklaces swinging down her chest which match her bracelets.

One of the newcomers whistle at her, causing a few of the older bikers to grumble. Donna scowls at the guy, takes his beer, and scolds him. I grab some empty glasses, a few of the bearded bikers giving me a nod and a sweet smile. Snake Eyes gave a handful of clubs I'm okay to help serve, who all wear their vests to help recognize. I wear mine, which is like my own protective blanket. I doubt any of the bikers would do anything, but it's an assurance all the same that means hands off.

Elm Jed

I turn back to the sink as my chest concaves again in melancholy. I've thought of sneaking out, grabbing the Road King and hightailing it back to the city. Get back to Leo. I can't get his last words out of my head.

"How ya doin', sweetie?" Donna asks, coming up behind me with a pleasant smile. Herself and couple bikers know I'm on basically on the run.

"Moving. Still here."

"You'll be home before you know it." She rubs my shoulder a little.

"Hey, Donna! Beer over here!"

"Oh, calm down, you just had one," she calls back, walking away to grab a glass.

"Aw, be nice Donna, he hasn't gotten laid since the turn of the century," another biker comments.

"Not my problem he can't find his dick, which has been shoved so far up his ass from riding that *crop duster* of his," she replies.

"Hey!" The first guy yells. Others start laughing as she serves the complainer but leans over to give him a quick kiss on the cheek. The older gentleman grumbles, tugging at his beard as he takes the drink.

She returns, shaking her head and gives me the dirty glass.

"Men, so fragile and easy," she remarks, snatching a towel to wipe the counter. "Trust a gal who's been around enough of 'em, if you want to hold'em to their knees…" she leans in close, "…apart from your own, just don't blink when they growl at ya. They'll be more confused than anything."

"Let me guess, smile instead?"

"Hell no, that's for *purty* girls," she snorts, winking with a smile. "You growl *back*, sweetie."

"Donna!"

"I'm coming, I'm coming!" She calls, going to serve them.

I finish cleaning, disappearing into the back hallway near the kitchen. They're finishing final orders, the pans and dishes clinking from the two cooks. I lean against the wall, careful how I do until Ikemba appears.

"Slow out there?" He asks.

"Donna's handling them fine."

"Sounds right," he chuckles, beginning to move past but pauses. "You know, I figure Spartan's permission includes the now." I raise a brow. "Meaning, haven't danced with you since you arrived."

I look out to the main part of the bar. "He trusts me to make my own decisions."

He hums low under his breath.

"Haven't had as good a dance partner as you," he adds. I'm quiet, staring down at the floor. "Nothing like dancing to remind us we're alive." His words clear some of the brain fog as I look up at him. "Wallowing ain't gonna do nothing. Gotta take care of yourself."

"Like dancing with you?"

"Could help."

"Really want that dance, huh?" A faint grin spreads on my face, appreciative of him trying to cheer me up.

"Donna steps on my feet." I snort out a laugh. "Don't worry, you ain't gotta dance with anyone else."

"Only you have special permission." He smiles broad. My grin grows and I finally nod my head. "Okay."

He offers his hand and I take it, following him out to the bar. Ikemba changes the music on the jukebox with a few bikers looking over at us, including Animal who's at one of the tables. Ikemba plays a west coast swing song and takes my hand to lead me onto the dancefloor. He goes slow, using simple moves at a leisure pace. Halfway through the song, he starts to sing the lyrics as I move around him easily.

"I know you know the words," he tells me. "Come on now."

I smile softly and sing quietly to *Wade in the Water*.

We continue slow dancing as the music fades. Not long after, another begins to play with a more upbeat tune.

"Know this one?" He asks.

I step back, pushing back as I would with a slow lindy hop and start singing the lyrics of *Sixteen Tons* and his face lights up. A few moments later, patrons give a few cheers as he spins me.

"Know your stuff," he comments.

"Had a few people that made sure I did." The last of the crooning of Tennessee fills the bar before the song ends. Ikemba smiles, squeezing my shoulder gently. "Okay, I'll admit, that helped."

"Mean to tell me, she was a dancer this entire time?" One of the men ask, raising a glass.

"Only one she's dancing with is me," Ikemba says. "Next time The Spartan comes through you can see what he says, Hound-Dog."

The guy waves him off, friendly like. Another biker pushes his shoulder. "Could ask Donna."

"Hell, no, heard she'll spear your damn toes off."

"I ain't that bad!" She retorts. "I bet you can't even see your feet with that damn scraggly beard. All you gonna see is Father time when you look down."

They all start playfully bickering, throwing insults to the others. Ikemba shakes his head at them. A giggle escapes me, until I notice Animal disappearing into the back with his phone to his ear. My stomach drops.

"Hey, Snake Eyes!" Someone calls, and Ikemba walks away.

I leave the dancefloor, quietly stepping into the back room. The door shuts behind me as he paces, phone to his ear. He looks over at me and I gesture for him to put it on speaker. He shakes his head. My jaw tenses, frustration building. I glare at him and point for him to put the phone down, having enough of the 'telephone game'. He stops. Finally, he puts the phone on speaker.

Jameson's voice is strained and angry. "...she *cannot* come back."

"She needs to—" Isaac tries to speak, but Jameson's growl interrupts him. Relief washes over me to hear Isaac's voice.

"Fuck no." Jameson's is cold. Demanding.

I flick my gaze to Animal, who places the phone on the table carefully with a scowl.

"Sombra," Animal starts.

"Animal, the last thing we need is her coming back to see him like this."

"See him like what?"

The phone goes silent. A breathy chuckle sounds, alongside a disgruntled huff. Jameson starts, "Animal, I told you—"

"She asked, well, demanded," Animal replies. "Besides, she deserves to know."

"That doesn't mean—"

"I'm still right fucking here," I interrupt. "I *do* deserve to know something. Quit leaving me in the dark. I'm already going out of my fucking mind here."

"So is Leo," Isaac mutters.

"What does that mean?"

"Nothing," Jameson answers. "We're handling it. Stay where you are."

"Jameson—"

"Whether you understand how the mob works or not, doesn't mean you get a say," he spits back. "It gets messy. It's fucked, especially right now. From Leo's orders, *his*, I'm not going to let you see this side of it. He begged me to make sure you wouldn't. I personally don't want you seeing it either."

My hands shake with anger as I concentrate on not screaming.

"Is anyone coming after me?" I ask.

"There could be—"

"Is it safe for me to come back?"

"That doesn't matter right n—"

"Tell me the damn truth," I order. "And maybe, just *maybe*, let me decide what I'm capable of."

"My job as his *consigliere* is to uphold his wishes. He's the boss, *not you*." I almost stumble back at the vitriol in his voice. The silence is deafening, pulsing through the room. Animal frowns heavily.

"At the end of the damn day..." Jameson warns with a lethal tone, "...you are only his fiancé. Not in charge or having *any* authority without his say so, club or mafia wise." His words sting. "So...for once, do as you're told and stay in your place."

My heart thunders in my chest.

We've had our arguments, but I've never heard him speak with such condemnation. From the look on Animal's face, neither has he. Whatever happened or will...isn't good.

"Just like the diner, Jameson?" I speak low. "You gonna guilt me again?"

"If it works."

Silence stretches as I stare at the phone.

"Let him get this out of his fucking system," Jameson says. "Just stay out of the way."

"Get *what* out of his system?"

He ignores my question. "He's a good man, Autumn. Just let us fucking handle him as we've done."

He's a good man. How many times have I been told that? Similar phrases from multiple people. A thought slinks through my brain, *were they trying to convince me or themselves?*

No matter who they're convincing, Jameson trying his damndest to keep us separated tells me something is beyond wrong. There are few reasons why he'd be fighting me this hard.

"Who hired those people?" I ask.

"I'm not—"

"*Who?*" I slam the table, fully expecting the name that's haunted me. I prepare myself for it as it becomes quiet again. There's swearing on the other side.

It sounds like Jameson may just hang up when Isaac answers, "Matteo."

A deep chill runs over my body.

"Stay the fuck there," Jameson orders again just before the phone goes dark.

I'm frozen, unable to speak or move as I try to wrap my mind around it all. One thing to cause problems, have a tantrum, or want more from Leo, but what could've pushed Matteo to send people to kill me? Or Leo?

"Fuck," Animal mutters. "That means he's the one who…shit."

Matteo betrayed Leo. After everything he's done for him, built to protect him. He gave up his own freedom for Matteo to take over as boss. Horror shivers down my spine.

"Why?" I rasp. "Why would Matteo do this?"

"Should've seen the signs," Animal grumbles. "Right fucking there. Others knew something was wrong, Chesty said—"

"*What* was wrong?" My heart cracks for Leo. "If he wanted to take over, I'm pretty fucking sure Leo would just hand it over."

"Not as simple as that." He shakes his head, pacing next. "But we didn't think he'd go this far, figured he was just… young! Barely old enough to drink, mature or not—"

"But he's smart," I interrupt. "He's not dumb, so why would he go behind Leo's back?"

He stops pacing, placing his hands on his hips and shaking his head.

"Fuck the deal Leo and I had. Tell me everything, *now*," I order.

Those warm brown eyes meet mine, hurt and filled with uncertainty.

"They used to have weekly meetings, discussing family matters and business. In December, Matteo began to pull back, missing meetings, starting shit in Italy, and arguing constantly. We thought it was something else, it'd pass…he's twenty-one for fuck sakes. It's why Leo took over in the first place. He's young, still naïve at times. Leo figured it was a phase to get more responsibilities, maybe rebellion, smuggling in drugs or weapons."

"But?"

"No evidence of it. Chesty mentioned something about his behavior, so did Ringer, being petty. We didn't think so, *Leo* didn't think so. Kept saying he'd talk to him. I think Matteo became threatened by you; his attitude switch happened after the engagement announcement. Enigma mentioned a nasty phone call after that meeting with Carrie. Perhaps he thought you were trying to take Leo away or—"

"What? Why would he…" my breath hitches, and Animal keeps talking, gears shifting in my head.

"He must've blamed you for the changes Leo was making. Felt pushed out. Renato was already doing it. Makes sense he'd blame the new fiancé, someone he never met or Leo told him about. And what Leo's done the last couple months, it'd be easy to convince the other bosses he's unfit like we did for Gabriel. Use it to his advantage, say he'll bring them all down or go after them next."

Flickers of the conversation I overheard in the apartment come back.

"Why? So, Matteo could become the next mafia don?"

"Probably, cause he won't inherit anything else."

Gears keep shifting, clicking into place. "Inherit?"

He slumps against the table. "Matteo's only in line for the Marchetti fortune, not Luciano or Salvadori, which Renato holds."

My gaze moves to the emerald on my finger. Family blood lines.

"If Leo dies…" my voice is soft, "…would Matteo believe he gets it all? Leo's businesses, the Marchetti fortune, and all?"

"He must think so." My heart pounds in my chest. "Only reason I can think of why he'd stab Leo in the back like this. To take everything."

"And killing me?"

"You marrying Leo means a high chance of inheriting instead of him. Figure he's making sure he's getting his cut and you don't."

Fuck.

I start pacing next. Matteo could've done this *because* he knows we're married, but Animal's right. He may be trying to stop it before it happens. But Matteo *had* to have that doing something like hiring hitmen was cruel and would tear Leo apart.

Tear Leo apart.

Shit. Wrong brother.

"What if killing me wasn't the endgame? And Leo isn't being

targeted like that? But it's to isolate Leo; unbalance his trust with everyone? Men within his own organizations and hotel were hired."

His gaze catches mine.

"*Leo's* people are being turned against him. Destruction from the inside out like a disease spreading."

"Matteo don't work like that."

"Gabriel would." Animal's eyes widen. "He disappeared and shit started going sideways. *He* has used Leo's emotions against him in the past. All of this is screaming revenge, Animal, including *using* Matteo to take out Leo, which this isn't the first time, *especially* if Gabriel believes Matteo inherits everything."

"And Gabriel would get the Luciano fortune," he mumbles. I keep my mouth shut, knowing the stipulations for *that*. "Fuck...I think you're right. No one else would have the balls."

Except me.

My gut is screaming that it's Gabriel we have to worry about. He's manipulating Matteo to take back what Leo took from him, what *I* took from him. What they didn't anticipate was Leo's little backup plan—our marriage.

A sinking feeling hits me. Did Leo know?

"Shit, he's gonna have to throw Matteo under the bus," Animal mutters. "That's why Sombra was pissed, Leo's gonna have to hang Matteo out to dry if he wants to convince the other bosses he's solid. Show them how incompetent Matteo is, like we did with Gabriel. We can't go against them *and* his brothers, the Italian mafia, fucking Renato isn't going to intervene—"

"Wait, hold on, if Matteo is being manipulated—"

"Won't matter, we need a fall guy. We don't have the time. Gabriel is still missing."

"It'll *break* him if he turns Matteo over and realizes it's Gabriel's doing."

"He could cut Matteo out completely, but that won't assuage those fuckers. It's either force their hand or give them a sacrifice, we've got *nothing* to force their hands. They don't want a mafia don losing control over his own organizations and family. The bosses don't want that mess or chance in losing their money, territories, or what the fuck ever."

Leo may have made his decisions with Gabriel, but not Matteo. Not the little brother he spent years to safeguard, came back for, built an empire to help, and did *everything* for.

"He won't," I whisper.

"He will…to protect you," he murmurs.

I swear under my breath, pacing the room.

"It's not your fault. Just know that. He's got no choice. If Matteo has gone this far to get rid of you, him, or anything for money, he's too far gone. It was bound to happen being around Gabriel, his parents, the mob, and the rest of that fucking family his whole life. I doubt he'll ever forgive him for hiring people to kill you."

"But to feed Matteo to the wolves essentially?"

Animal shakes his head. "We got nothing else, Autumn. Only way to convince them he's not losing his position within his own damn organization and family. Otherwise, they'll jump at the chance to take out the top-dog mafia family."

"I can't let Leo do this. It'll break him. He will feel like his father or Gabriel for fuck sakes; forsaking his little brother will *break him*."

Those warm brown eyes meet mine, defeated.

"From how Sombra sounded…it already has."

The crack forming in my heart shatters. Words tumbling together as conversations slam into the other. *He needs control. Anger management. We'll handle him. I couldn't be a hard Dom. He's a good man…-can't lose control. These hands…that I can be gentle. Monster.*

I go very still.

"That's why Sombra doesn't want you back," Animal whispers. "We're out of tricks and negotiating power. Leo has no other choice, and we know what that will do to him."

No choice.

Fuck that and staying in the safety of secrecy if that means I lose him. I'll beg for his forgiveness after, but at least he'll be alive and not a shell of himself.

I'm sorry, Leo...I was hiding shit, too.

"We go back tomorrow morning." Animal scrunches his brows together. "And either you're gonna help me get back or I leave you here."

"Autumn, Jameson's right, there's nothing you can do. Only Leo—"

"No, I don't give a fuck if Leo begged, I'm not losing my husband."

It takes a second for him to process my words, and then his eyes widen. "Son of a bitch."

Chapter 41

Strike the Match

Drew secures the last of our stuff on the motorcycle. It's early morning and there's a chill in the air. I'd just gotten off the phone with Chiari, checking on her end of the plan. Drew's quiet, grabbing his helmet as I receive the same look as last night.

"I said I was sorry."

He took the news about the marriage pretty well. He was more shocked we kept it secret this long. Chiari on the other hand replied with "I knew it", and Isaac's was "I *fucking* knew it." I informed them both last night, needing them for other parts of my plan. My heart races, knowing what both need to collect for me. I guess thank goodness for my paranoid, anxious side.

The rest of the Crew will know when we get back to the city. In a bit more dramatic fashion. If all went to plan.

Drew sighs, "More so pissed you didn't say anything."

"It's not cause we don't trust y'all."

"I know, and well, I'm more relived cause it's probably gonna save his ass. Rest of ours, too. Just…I know you won't turn on him, but don't, no matter what you witness, don't." He meets my gaze, swallowing hard. "Leaving Matteo that last time wrecked him, especially when the blackmailing had just happened. We dragged him out of that dark place, not sure if we can again."

I touch his arm. "Except, this time, you have me."

"Yeah."

"Rains supposed to stay north, should be dry heading south," Ikemba says, walking out the bar.

Drew nods while getting on the bike and turns on the engine. I jog over to Ikemba, giving him a stiff hug. "Thank you for every-thing, Snake Eyes. Tell Donna I say bye."

"Stay safe out there. I'll see you again." He gives me a smile as I pull away, putting my helmet on.

I get on the bike behind Drew, and we head out onto the open road. The sky is grey, clouds making the world seem dim. I hold tight to my seat as he revs the engine, racing for the estate. We'll switch out bikes again, and recoup before entering the city.

Most of the night I spent calling Chiari, Logan, and Isaac. The plan I'd slowly been cultivating would have to go into action sooner than I presumed, guess it was now or never. I barely slept, anxious if what I was doing was the right thing. My gut was telling me yes, but even now, worry floods me. I have to focus on Leo, get him out. Although my plan is a bit on the insane side, I've had crazier plans work in the past. And I didn't have backup with me then.

We ride silently through the hills. Only noise is the motorcycle as we take the wide curves. Drew tenses a moment, touching his helmet and I can hear him mutter something just before speeding up. Whoever he's on the phone with, it's brief, because my headset connects with his soon after.

"We got issues," he says.

"No shit." He snorts. "What else?"

"Caught the men who followed us to the estate." I lean back, holding onto the bike's sides.

"You don't sound relieved."

"Cause who they were. Their jobs for Leo. Our plan to go back to the *Italian Lily* may need a detour."

"Why?"

"One of them was the mechanic who checks on the bikes at the estate, keeps them running. He was in that damn SUV, knew it was us. Recognized the bike." Well, fuck. "Everyone's getting extra background checks, who knows who else Matteo got his claws into."

"Who else?"

"A server at the hotel and delivery truck driver."

My stomach drops. Trees zip past as I try concentrating on them, focusing on the vibrations of the bike underneath. "Do I know them?"

He exhales sharply. "Isaac said you did."

"Did?"

"They ain't gonna be alive when we get back." A chill runs over my skin. "They're already at the warehouse, not the hotel. They grabbed the other two this morning, taking them where, well...Leo sends messages."

"Top floor only for parties then?"

"Personal shit for him or us. This warehouse they're going to is where...damn it."

"Animal. Just blurt it out."

"Where he was those few months. It's what none of us wanted you to see, cause there won't be anything left of those men when he's finished." His voice becomes quiet, almost too quiet against the roaring engine. "The driver was hired to kill you at the hotel after therapy."

There goes my stomach again. Whether I knew them or not, those men made their bed. They'd live or die by the consequences, and I have to remind myself there's no saving everyone, especially if they fucking planned to kill me.

"Don't be mad at me," he adds.

"Why?"

"May have called backup."

"Who?" I ask, peering over his shoulder as the estate appears.

"I wasn't gonna have us go back without someone on our six, and you can pull rank on me later…boss."

I smack his shoulder. He laughs lightly, patting my knee.

We pull onto the gravel driveway. It's quiet, not a single soul aside from us, but I already see the damage. Windows shattered. Bushes uprooted and there's dents in the garage door, which isn't shut all the way. Drew stops the bike further away than last time, turning it off. Slowly, we take our helmets off, dismounting the bike. It's eerily quiet. He pulls his gun out, and I do the same.

"Shit," I mutter.

"Stay here, I'll—"

The loud roar of a motorcycle pierces through the quiet. We both spin in place, ready to fire, until we recognize the rider—Chesty.

He pulls up, parking next to us and turns off the engine. Our weapons come down as he dismounts the Harley. Helmet barely off his head, I run and hug him hard as he wraps his arms around me. His shoulder feels wrapped.

"Thank fuck you're okay," he mutters.

"Are you okay?" I pull back, yanking at his jacket.

"Whoa, sister, just a flesh wound. Worse injuries on deployment." He nods once at Animal. "Thought I was gonna beat y'all."

Animal answer, "Rode fast. Pretty Boy Bond update you?"

He nods. "Let's check out the place."

They gesture for me to stay back, opening the garage the rest of the way. No one's there, but my heart sinks. Every bike has been trashed. Tossed to the ground, windshields busted, rims bent, and pieces strewn about. There's oil everywhere. Already, I can tell some may never run again.

"Hell sucking fuckers," Chesty mutters, looking over Leo's choppers. They're demolished.

"Fuel lines are cut," Animal says, checking others.

"That fucker was a biker," Chesty growls. "Leo better rip his head off. No fucking respect, should draw and quarter him for this."

"Good thing Leo kept his prized choppers in California," Animal mutters. "Let's check the rest of the house, make sure they didn't get into the security rooms."

Chesty grunts, and both men disappear into the house. I step back outside, a bitter sadness overcoming me as I peer back at the carnage. Leo's beloved Classic Soft tail is practically in pieces.

Every single motorcycle is destroyed.

I run my hand over the vest I still wear, angry and devastated at the ruin.

The hotel. The bikes. The estate. People I knew. Everything feels tainted.

My breath hiccups, realizing one isn't here. I step out further, looking across the way to the garage Animal mentioned. Keeping the gun at my side, I jog down the smaller driveway, gravel crunching under my boots as I get to the pin pad. I try my personal pin, but nothing. Thinking quickly, I put in Leo's, and it starts to open. Inside sits Ringer's other bikes, couple of the Crew's, and… the Classic Heritage.

Thank fuck, one survived.

Quickly, I start rolling her out and close the door behind me. The other two are leaving the estate as I'm bringing the bike down. Their brows go up, staring past to where I came.

"Fuckers didn't get all of them."

"Thank the gods, otherwise Ringer would've burnt down half of New York," Chesty murmurs. "Bond's already creating a diversion, don't need another."

"They know you're here?" I ask.

He shakes his head. "Only Bond. Too busy concentrating on the five guys they're hauling to the warehouse."

"Wait, five?"

He nods slowly, then tells it to me straight. "They worked for the hotel, ordered to watch you. We only got the last two cause your friend Bobby caught them talking. He's okay but banged up trying to nab them when he overheard'em devising a plan to grab you when you returned."

I may end up puking before getting back to the city.

"I'm gonna check around, make sure they didn't leave other surprises," Animal says, disappearing.

I stare out to the countryside's grey ambiance as Chesty touches my shoulder. "How did they get that close? To us…to me?"

"Don't know, and trust me, all us are kicking ourselves. None of them were mob, just employees, but they've been planning this." He clears his throat. "By the way, congrats Mrs. Luciano."

I smile faintly at him. "Sorry we kept it a secret."

"Thrown for a loop when Bond told me, don't get mad he did, figured it'd help with the plan you're concocting. He wouldn't say much though."

"Trust me, Chesty?"

Those light green eyes peer into mine. I breathe a bit easier as he squeezes my shoulder. "Like a sergeant leading me into a firefight."

"I'm gonna protect him. All of you. I promise."

"I believe ya, and mainly cause we're out of options. Sombra's starting to worry us. If Leo goes over the edge, he'll go next." He looks away, exhaling sharply. "All hell will break loose."

Gravel crunches behind us as Animal approaches. "So, how we gonna do this? Go to the hotel and wait?"

"No, we go to the warehouse," I answer.

They exchange a look. Chesty asks, "You sure?"

"It'll give Leo more time." Warning in my gut tells me I *need* to get to him first. "Besides, this warehouse is where he sends messages, right?" They nod, neither saying a word. "Then I'm sending a message," I mutter.

"We'll have to coordinate with Bond," Chesty mentions. "Make sure the others don't try stopping you before knowing the full plan."

"Or *after* knowing it," Animal mumbles.

"Animal you talk to Chiari, Chesty you with Bond. Both your helmets can still take calls without disconnecting."

"Alright," Animal says, patting the Classic Heritage's seat. "Then you ride on her. I'll take the Road King."

My eyes meet his. "I thought we'd switch bikes."

"Nah, Animal's right," Chesty adds. "If things go sideways, you'll be able to get out easier." He smiles faintly. "Besides, you know that bike inside and out by now."

I glance over my shoulder where the dismantled garage is, knowing what I rode up here is in shambles, too. Nerves coil in my stomach, and I swallow hard as I bring my gaze to the motorcycle. It wasn't that I was nervous riding on my own again, it's because it's the only one of Leo's Harleys that's unscathed. And the first bike we rode together. I've tried it before in the garage, but this felt different.

I brush my hand over the vest again. Chesty touches my shoulder. "You'll be fine. Saw the footage of you getting out the city, this'll be a piece of cake."

"It's his last surviving Harley," I whisper.

His smile is encouraging as he flicks his gaze over my vest. "And he's gonna be proud that you rode it."

I inhale deeply, finally nodding and then debate wearing the vest the rest of the way. Both men notice my inner dilemma. Animal hands me my helmet, patting his own vest he wears and says, "Let's keep it on. You know…safety."

His smile is slightly wicked as he checks the Road King one more time. I glance at Chesty, who goes to his bike's saddlebags and pulls out his club vest next. Shaking it out first, he dons it, grinning maniacally. Both settle on their bikes as I swing my leg over the motorcycle.

All three engines turn on. Butterflies are in my stomach as I balance the bike. The engine vibrates through me as I close my eyes, inhale a deep breath as I focus on our plan. Suddenly, anger grows, knowing they infiltrated our safe spaces and were deliberate getting that close. These weren't just people Leo trusted, but me as well. They came into areas I loved and cared for. They destroyed something which brought me back to the living.

Lastly, they fucked over my husband.

Devastated my safe havens. My people. My home. My hotel.

Elm Jed

Those sudden possessive thoughts jar me as I follow Animal and Chesty onto the open road. While focusing on steering the motorcycle, it's not long before I come to terms with my reality.

It *is* my home, *my* hotel, and *my* husband that they'll regret ever fucking over.

Chapter 42

Burn the Match

Rain falls when I see skyscrapers. We took a longer route back, airing on precaution. Chesty stays mostly beside me as Animal leads the way, weaving down the highway. Every so often, Animal checks in over the headset. I'm worried we're gonna have to stop for the rain, but it begins to lighten finally.

My headset crackles as Animal speaks, "Coming up on our exit. How you feeling about the rain?"

"If I start squeaking when we arrive, I'm never making fun of y'all again." We follow him off the highway, Chesty's motorcycle roaring behind me as we go into a singular line.

We zip down streets, heading closer to the harbor. My stomach clenches as I grip onto the bike, legs tightening. I focus on the motorcycle beneath me, keeping my mind present.

I'm in control. I can do this. I *have* to do this.

"You know," I speak, hoping Animal can hear me. "Raining or not, still better than the last time coming back."

"Thought you enjoyed the helicopter?"

"The other time."

A pause occurs before he answers, "Got your back...boss."

"Am I actually that?" We reach the docks, moving between large buildings.

"Usually, no, marriage ain't enough, but if Leo put your name on everything and made you his successor, then yeah, you are."

"Advice on being one?" My heart thunders when I see Isaac far ahead, standing outside with Julio next to some cars.

"You're the one who took down the mob in a hospital bed, you tell me. So, be *you*."

Except was that Autumn or Sarah?

The rain has stopped completely when we pull over to park. I yank my helmet off, dismounting and inhale a steadying breath. *I'm in control.*

"Miss Autumn." Isaac steps up, nodding his head, eyes flashing to my vest. I want to hug him but notice others at the doorway and pause. Julio flicks a worried look between us. "He's inside with the others."

"Anyone else know?"

"No."

"Paperwork?" He nods. I swallow hard. "The rest?"

Isaac gestures to Julio, who holds out a briefcase. Julio murmurs, not quite at me. "Qué estás planeando, hermana?"

"Saving Leo's ass," I answer in English, Julio blinks at me, shocked while Isaac opens the briefcase towards me. Carefully, I check that he got every single item. I pull out a folder, closing it and meet his blue gaze. "I'm sorry."

"Madder I didn't figure it out, Miss Autumn." A smile tugs at his mouth. "On *every* account, better at my job than me."

We share a smile, some of my anxiety washing away. "I just know how to hide in plain sight."

"No more hiding."

"No more hiding," I repeat.

"Wearing that in?" He juts his head toward my attire.

"For now," I answer, heading for the door. "Give that to Chesty, explain everything. Whatever I say in there is law, are we clear?"

"Yes, boss." Isaac, Drew, and Waylon all answer. Julio chokes out a sound, whispering to them as they follow me into the building. It's dimly lit, two guards stand at the next doorway. They look to the four men behind me, and then to me.

"No one's allowed—"

"Let her through," Isaac interrupts. "She owns your asses."

The guards exchange a look, and I recognize one. A semblance of reprieve hits me. "Mike, isn't?"

His eyes flash, widening. "Yes, Ma'am."

"You learned. Good." He steps aside as I pass.

Beyond the door is a small tech center, tables covered with monitors and computers. On the other side, stands Owen and Rudolph gaping at me. I stop, dripping water onto the concrete floor as I glance around the space. There's a handful of others standing off to the side. Mila stands near the back, beside a wall with a metal door. I ignore the hairs standing on my skin, feeling everyone's eyes on me.

"That door?" I ask, nodding toward Mila.

"Yeah," Drew answers.

Rudolph and Owen approach, while I head for Mila. The two reach us before I can get to her. Owen starts, "Autumn, what the hell are—"

"Gonna want to read this," Isaac interrupts, handing another folder to him.

"Everything's legal," I add.

"*Barchën,* what are you doing?" Rudolph asks.

"Giving you orders." My chest squeezes as I clear my throat. Stay calm. Come on, Autumn.

Rudolph stares at me, eyes flicking over my vest then down to the ring on my hand and a slow grin grows on his face. Realization clicking in place. He murmurs something in German as Jameson approaches out of seemingly nowhere.

"What the hell is she doing here?" He questions, stalking towards me with a rage. He tries to argue with Drew. "I told you —"

"He did everything *I* said," I interject. "And *you* don't order me around."

Jameson steps closer, fuming under his breath, "What the actual fuck you think you're doing? You can't be here. You have no right—"

"Yeah, she does," Owen interjects next, holding up the folder. Jameson's face contorts from fury to shock. "She co-owns everything of his, equally, including assets tied to the mafia. They're married."

"She's in charge," Isaac says.

Jameson sputters, "Leo never—"

"You can take it up with my husband later." Jameson glares at me. "Where is he?"

He comes closer, bringing us within inches of the other. "How long?"

"Does it matter?"

"How...*long*?"

"November."

"Day you disappeared."

"Yes."

"You lied to us. *All* of us," he grinds out.

Some reason my heart doesn't thunder in my chest. I feel calm as I stare up as Leo's best friend and second in command.

"I'm sorry," I say with a leveled tone. "You said at a diner once you'd do anything to help your best friend. So, know that I'm willing to *anything* to protect my husband. That's what I'm doing. Step aside or I force you."

He glances back at the others, and then back to me. "I won't chance him losing you, which may happen if you walk through that door. So...force me to move."

A very chilling, quiet possessiveness runs through my veins. It trickles down through my core, wanting through this last barrier to Leo. No one, not even Jameson, is going to stop me. He wants to play dirty? Fine.

"Stop me," I state, tilting my head in an arrogant manner. "Put your hands on me."

Jameson's eyes widen.

No one moves, including Mila who watches with a neutral expression, only delight dances over her gaze.

There's suddenly a muffled scream through the metal door. And another. I flick my gaze to the sounds, then back to a seething Jameson. They can attempt to stop me, but touching me? I know they won't, not when their boss is torturing others beyond that door, after *months* of killing those who've touched me. And then the other reason flashes over Jameson's face, taking in the vest I wear. Biker trumps mob; no touching Old Ladies.

Jameson steps back, voice suddenly shaky, "Autumn, there'll be no unseeing hell."

"I'd rather go back to hell *with* him, than an empty heaven. He's not who I'm scared of."

In that moment, Jameson averts his gaze, staring at the concrete floor. Slowly, I strip the vest off and hand it to Animal. They all remain in their spot as I stalk towards Mila. Abruptly, she moves in my way, speaking low when I'm close, "They'll barely be alive. He's been in there for hours."

"Alone?" She nods once. I look over my shoulder at the others. They left him *alone*. My hands fist, wanting to scream.

"It's him saving us *from* him," Mila murmurs. "I warned you. Don't blame them."

"Give me your gun."

She raises a brow, pulls it out, and unlocks the door. "I'll do *my* job, ma'am. Just remind him I didn't touch you."

Mila opens the door. A few bulbs hang in the middle to illuminate two tables filled with tools—chains, ropes, knives, and guns. Blood is streaked everywhere, glistening from the hazy light. I follow her into the darkened room. Three men are strapped to chairs. Two lay on the ground. Leo's back is turned to us, standing in front of one with a large knife. He's covered in blood. His boots squelch in the puddling crimson as he takes a few steps back.

"*No one* comes in," Leo warns in a hollowed icy voice. Mila flinches. One of the men stirs, limbs barely attached.

"Orders, sir," Mila responds in a steady voice.

My insides scream at me, wanting to hurl and run screaming. Another man groans. Leo turns, slamming the knife into their leg, while another whimpers with blood dripping down his face.

Enough.

"I didn't—"

"Kill them," I order, struggling to keep my voice from shaking. Leo freezes. Mila moves forward, aiming. A swift headshot to each before their bodies slump against their chairs. "All of them."

She does as she's told, sending bullets into the ones on the floor. My stomach wants to revolt, release whatever contents are left in it. I breathe deep, ignoring the stench of blood and death. I swallow back the bile. Leo remains frozen as Mila walks back to me.

"Leave, lock the door, and no one enters." She nods, slamming the door with a heavy thud and lock.

I remain out of the light, keeping my gaze on Leo as his hands twitch. Minutes drag by in silence. Leo's breaths are heavy as he stares at the dead men.

"Get out," he finally speaks, but all command in his voice is gone.

"No."

"Leave."

"No." I step into the light.

"You weren't supposed to see this...*any* of it."

"I'm not afraid of you." My boot hits blood. Leo flinches at the small sound.

His head shakes as his body begins to tremble, clenching his fists repeatedly. He holds them up, and rasps, "I couldn't stop...I couldn't after they admitted what they...get out. *Get out.*"

Leo begins to plead. His words tumbling into the next. I take another step into the light, seeing more of what he's done. My heart clenches as I recognize two. What's left. A waiter I've seen multiple times, Nick I think, but it's the other with his familiar scruff, whom I sat with that cuts deep. Carl.

"You can't see this, you can't—"

"Look at me." He stops. His breathing erratic almost broken like his voice, body vibrating uncontrollably. I soften my voice. "Look at me, baby."

Finally, he does, turning towards me. Blood soaks through his clothes, his tattoos appearing more frightening than ever. There's a hollowness in his gaze, not quite focusing as he tries to bring them to mine. His brows are furrowed while the rest of his face contorts in agony.

I know that look.

Faraway eyes, searching for relief. Uncontrollable shaking, his throat working like he can't swallow. Quick, heavy breaths as if he can't find enough air. My chest constricts as it feels like I'm staring into a mirror.

Panic attack. Leo's having a panic attack.

"Come here," I demand in a gentle tone, stepping forward to grab his trembling hands. The shaking worsens as he chokes out a sound. I place a hand against his jaw, and he flinches. He *flinches*. *My* Leo.

"Don't leave me," he rasps.

"I've got you, Leo."

"No, no…you were gone."

"I've got you," I repeat, heart cracking. "You're safe, baby. I'm here, Leo. I'm here."

Abruptly, his knees buckle, and he falls hard upon them as he clutches my legs. He violently trembles as he buries his face against my stomach as I cradle his head against me. My other hand rubs down his neck, trying to comfort him. Screams tear at my throat to escape as he starts to sob against my wet clothes.

"Autumn…my wife, not my wife," he cries.

"You're not alone, baby," I whisper, stroking his head. "I'm here, Leo."

Tears fall from my eyes as Leo, my husband, my rock shatters before me. His own screams are almost silent against my body.

Hands gripping harshly to the back of my thighs. It hurts, but I don't move. I can't. I won't.

He was left alone, isolated while having a mental breakdown.

I stare at the bloodied mess, rage coursing through me warped in grief. He never wanted this life to begin with, he'd fought and left. Leo survived his family, made a new life to be proud of, only for it to be blackmailed and twisted out of his hands. Did he ever truly have a choice? To help his brother or bury him like his parents? Even the dead men before me had more of choice. They could've said no. What consequences would *they* have gotten if they said no?

And now, Leo's been betrayed by the one he gave up his freedom for.

I clutch Leo, knowing that destructive anguish. After giving *everything* to just be used, what good you had thrown against you. Pieces of yourself dying. Humanity to be damned. Those you loved turned against you, taken from you, and then faced with horrible decisions that can drown you.

My gaze sweeps to Carl. Whatever pity was left in my heart is gone. Mercy obliterated.

Leo listened to what those men had planned. What they were going to do to me. After months getting rid of those who *had* already done abysmal things to me and others. How would that *not* fuck you up and drive you insane?

All of them had brought Leo to his knees.

They *broke* my husband. And then he was left *secluded* to deal with the shadows on his own. His own demons. Monsters.

Cold.

Suddenly, I want to take those words back from so long ago.

I close my eyes. Not again. I won't let the man who's held me in my darkest moments be utterly alone. Never let those hazel eyes become dead inside. To lock himself away, trying to protect what's left of his heart.

Heavy is the crown one wears, but bloody is the soul for those who twist the spikes within.

"Leo?" His sobs subside as I stroke his hair. He grasps me harder. "I'm right here, baby. I love you, my dear husband, more than you may know."

"I love you," he whispers. "I'm sorry…I'm sorry."

I hush him gently, keeping his head cradled against me. "Do you trust me, Leo?"

"Yes," he rasps.

"If I order you to do something, will you follow it?" My voice comes out stricter, but still trying to remain gentle. He inhales sharply, but nods. "Words, Leo."

"Yes, whatever you want."

I sink slowly to my knees, landing in the blood alongside him. His eyes find mine, less hollow but filled with confusion and pain. I cup his face, smiling faintly before placing a tender kiss upon his lips. His breath hitches, trembling hands trailing up to my shoulders as he whimpers against the contact. I pull away and some of the shaking subsides.

"You're going to clean up," I instruct, rubbing my thumb over his stubbled chin. "Listen to Drew and Waylon. They'll explain everything. I will love you no matter what, it is *your* decision."

His brows pinch. "What are you talking about?"

"I can't tell you because I have to go soon." Panic flashes over him. "I'm not going far, but I have to do this. I'm not leaving you, but I can't take you with me. You've taken care of me through my darker days, let me take care of you now. It needs to be your decision, not mine. So…for once Leo, *you* be selfish." Eyes search mine, and I clutch him harder. "It's my turn to protect you."

His face falls, but he nods. He breathes easier, appearing less shaken. I kiss him again, standing as I bring him up with me. He strokes my face gently and I lean into the touch. Blood sticks to my skin. The worry and nausea have vanished, replaced by wrath. His hand drops as I feel my expression darken, falling into an old part of myself I'd convinced myself had died.

She's coming back with a burning vengeance.

"I'll be waiting for you, mister," I whisper. "No matter what, I love you."

Agonizing pain hits me as I turn, heading for the door. It takes everything not to run back to him. Leo's sobs replay in my head as my anger simmers. The door slams open as I storm out and start giving orders.

"Sombra, Bond, and Iron Buffalo, you're with me. Animal and Chesty make sure you have everything from Bond. Chesty, do *not* leave him completely alone." I nod to Isaac, who does what I say without a word. "Enigma, contact Chiari when he's decided. Ringer and Mila be sure my husband gets to his destination safely."

"That is?" Mila asks as I pass.

"He'll tell you." I walk out with others close behind. I'm about to pass the next set of doors but stop and glance back at Mike. "I need trusted security with me, you one of them?"

He stares at me in shock, clearing his throat.

"Answer her," Owen warns.

"Yes, Ma'am."

"Mike, right?"

"Yes, Ma'am."

"Follow." I start walking again. "You're Michael from now on, I'm not giving you a chance to sully a good friend's name."

"Yes, Ma'am."

"What are you doing?" Jameson asks as we come outside.

Clouds cover the sky, damning grey everywhere as storms roll in. I prowl past the bikes to the SUVs.

"Crew in the car with me," I order. "Michael, you and the others follow. Oh, and Michael?" I ask before they step away. "Fuck me over, and I'll make you wish Mr. Luciano got to you first. Clear?"

Fear sweeps over Michael and the two behind him. He nods.

I climb into the vehicle, quickly noticing my face in the rearview mirror smeared in blood. Jameson gets in beside me as the other two sit in front.

Jameson starts again, "Autumn—"

"I'm giving him what he gave me months ago," I say, suddenly seeing *her* staring back at me. "A choice."

Chapter 43

Toss the Match

"How you not CIA?" Owen asks.

"I turned them down," I answer.

Isaac and Owen exchange a glance, Jameson exasperatingly sighs beside me.

"I hate that I can't tell if you're serious," Owen mumbles. "But I'm telling Julio."

"Now you know why Roger wanted me back," I retort. "To the point of keeping me in confinement."

Jameson huffs, shaking his head. "Leo's gonna be pissed with your involvement."

"It's *my* choice." Jameson scowls at me. "I'm not being coerced into this, it's my decision. I had everything before any of you came around, might as well finally use it. Even if I'm rusty."

"If this is you rusty, every government agency should be scared," Owen comments.

"Speaking of, even after your surgeries, why didn't they relocate you?" Jameson asks. "You're a liability being this close. Not to mention your skills."

"Cause I'm no one."

"They would've—" I give him a look. Realization flashes over him. "They don't know."

"So, *no* CIA then?" Owen asks.

"They think I'm dead, too." All three men swear under their breath. "Roger made the FBI believe it all came from him, that was our deal. I never wanted fanfare; I wanted out. I was an 'informant' that's it. At the time, it felt like a good idea. I do my good deed and he gets his merits. Feds only allowed my identity change because Roger told them I'd been a good asset, and he didn't want any traces of Sarah Marie to anyone. I just didn't realize how deep his lies went until after the interrogation."

"Fucking cunt, he really did use you," Isaac mutters.

"Sarah was a computer forensic MBA drop out druggie, who ran away from home. No family. Nothing. Creating Autumn Watson was the easiest thing I did. The FBI didn't create her and wipe away Sarah's existence, I did."

"Because you thought they knew about you, but in reality they didn't," Owen mentions.

"Yup."

"That's why the entire police force took the credit for the bust," Jameson says. "Why no one knew it was you."

"Cause I knew what it meant to be a rat, I saw what happened to them," I say. "I worked for Roger, in return go back to a peaceful life."

"Right *now*, it makes sense why you didn't hand him everything," Jameson mentions, watching me carefully. "Why didn't you back then?"

"I was naïve and desperate, not stupid." A flash of memory of Roger yelling at me over the phone. "He put me through torture, not caring what happened to me. I knew I needed something in case he left me for dead again. I believed the assault was *because* they realized what I was doing, and mobsters abuse hackers, too. I wanted leverage if they came for me. Buy my way out. But alas, no, Roger lied about that, too. I thought *some* knew the truth, but they didn't."

"Fuck," Owen mumbles. "Unless someone recognizes you, connects the dots…he made you a ghost."

"Again…I'm no one," I mutter.

"How the fuck did you not notice what she was doing?" Jameson questions Isaac suddenly. "You were practically with her every day."

Isaac glares at him through the mirror. "I'm her bodyguard, not her fucking keeper."

"Play nice and no punching," Owen warns. "How about we be grateful that we finally have an upper hand? Including if Gabriel comes back?"

"Exactly…if," Jameson grunts.

"He will," I say.

"Autumn—"

"You honestly think Matteo did this on his own? I won't believe it until I see otherwise. Gabriel knows Leo's weaknesses. *He* wants that position back, cause he's the only one with balls to put a hit on me *and* Leo."

"We already told you who targeted—"

"And *he's* not smart enough to pull strings on his own, I've seen his ledgers," I practically growl. "Until we figure out how to handle Leo's brothers, the other bosses need to know their place."

Owen whistles low as we come up to the back of the hotel.

"And if they do recognize you? Connect the dots?" Jameson counters.

The car stops at the loading dock. Outside, Chiari and Logan wait as I unbuckle and leave the car. The men get out with me as I stop, tilting my head back to stare up at the hotel.

Anger pressed deep for years flourishes under my skin. My entire being remembers the pain. It silences even the faint prick at the back of my mind to run.

"Good," I reply, turning towards them. Whatever expression is on my face, makes all three step back. "They can remember it was a roofied *whore* who grips them by their throats."

I spin on my heel, stalking towards the hotel as I meet Chiari's serious expression. We head into the building, her beside me unflinchingly, speaking, "Paperwork is in the office, including clothes as requested."

I glance over at her as we pass employees, who freeze as we pass. Isaac comes up beside me, holding out a handkerchief. I take it, whispering, "Thank you."

I wipe at my face, although it's not going to help the blood covering the rest of me.

"Charlotte retrieved everything you requested," Chiari continues.

"I'll thank her later."

"Notice was sent to the bosses and underbosses, they'll be arriving soon and assemble in the main conference room on the top floor."

"*All* of them?" Jameson asks.

"Mrs. Luciano specified *all*, so I did," Chiari replies, smiling ruefully.

"Logan?" I ask as we approach the elevators.

"Last of the footage is being pulled," he answers. "I'll have it ready with external hard drives in fifteen."

"Backups?"

"Mikey's taking care of it. Ready to push the button."

The elevator doors open, and I walk in followed by everyone but Logan. I give him a nod and smile; he returns it before leaving for the security room. I wipe my face again, glimpsing at the blood that isn't mine. Although my heart pounds in my chest, my anger drowns out the worry as we leave the elevator when the doors open.

"Chiari, give them all the plan details while I change, please," I say, heading toward Leo's first floor office.

"Of course, there's washcloths and makeup in there as well."

I walk into the office, closing the door and lock it. My hands shake as I lean against the door, releasing a shuddering breath. "You can do this. You *have* to do this."

After reciting parts of *The Raven,* I begin stripping out of my damp and bloody clothes. I toss them aside, wiping myself down with what Chiari provided. There's a knock at the door when I unzip the garment bag. I tug on the robe, unlocking the door for Chiari to enter and lock it behind her.

"They know the plan," she says, flicking her gaze to the garment bag. "And I thought you could use some help." A dryness forms in my throat. I nod. She half smiles, ushering me over to the desk. "You missed a spot."

She wipes the underside of my jaw, removing the last of the blood. "Thank you."

"You're already playing your role well."

"Who says I'm playing?" I whisper.

Her smile grows. "Hell hath no fury, right? Remember that when you go into that room."

I nod as I begin changing.

Long billowy pants, high-waisted, which will hide my heeled boots. A deep forest green silk blouse with a high collar and cuffed sleeves, accompanied with an underbust corset made of black velvet. Chiari helps lace me up, pulling the ribbon tight enough to have the compression give me that sense of security as the rope harness did. Today, it'd do the job of helping keep me steadfast in a room filled with dangerous men.

My hands smooth over the velvet. I go to grab my engagement ring when Chiari stops me. "Wedding band goes on first."

I blink at her. She moves us over to the desk, pulling out an envelope with the rest of the stacked folders. I stare at the envelope Leo and I sealed months ago. There's a lump in my throat.

"We were supposed to do it together," I whisper.

"He'll understand." She pulls out a piece of paper.

A copy of our marriage certificate with my legal name—Autumn Watson Luciano.

"They'll want something physical to know who you truly are, and the visual will help," she murmurs.

I open the envelope, my wedding band tumbling out. It's encrusted with pieces of emerald. I slide it on first and then my engagement ring. My throat tightens when Leo's wedding band falls into my palm. Titanium with a line of green slicing through the middle. My hand tips, allowing it to fall upon the envelope.

My gaze goes to the rings on my left hand. "To know who you truly are," I repeat.

I am the wife of a hotel mogul.

The wife of *the* Mafia Don of New York City.

Leonardo Durante Luciano's wife and partner.

"Teams are in place?" I ask. She nods. "Plans B and C?"

"All set, they don't know it's there, just sit in his chair," she reassures me. "I'll be in the hall when you're ready."

She begins to step out, but I stop her. "Chiari. Thank you…for whatever happens next."

"It was and always will be a pleasure working for you, Mrs. Luciano. You'll win this time."

Chiari walks out, leaving me alone as I stare down at his ring. Other paperwork sits beside it, ready for him. I flash my gaze to the small mirror, walking over, and push my hair back.

"*…don't forget the box we buried was empty.*"

My breath catches, inhaling sharply as Nan's words ring in my ears.

The shaking in my hands slowly stops as I glide my hand over my heart, knowing I'm about to face those who helped break me. Killed me—

"You didn't die," I state, tears forming in my eyes. "I'm sorry. I shouldn't have believed they killed you…me. Sarah."

I take another shaky breath, stepping closer to the mirror, pressing my hand against the glass. "You brought them to their to knees, while beaten and half-dead…this time…" I grit my teeth, something shifting over my eyes, "*…keep them there.*"

One more steadying breath, I turn on my heel and grab what I need and walk out. Chiari meets me at the door, handing over another thick folder.

"More coming if you need it. Choices in damning evidence."

I smirk darkly. "Thank you. Be prepared if Leo shows, and if he doesn't…"

"Everything's set." She gestures down the hall. "On your command, boss."

Emotions drain from me as my heels click on the marble. Isaac, Owen, and Jameson step behind me as I lead them through the lobby to the private elevator. The ambiance becomes quiet as I stride through the space, noticing several staff who've stopped to stare. Some look in confusion, others with relief. We come to the elevators, stepping on after I've entered the code for the top floor.

"Time?" I ask once the doors shut.

"Almost five," Owen answers.

"Start the timer when I reach the door. If he doesn't show, Chiari will take care of the rest."

"Are you sure about this?" Jameson asks. "If he doesn't show, you'll be left with *them*. After what happened, he may not—"

"It's his decision," I state, staring ahead at the elevator doors. Warped worried expressions reflect behind me. "Whatever he decides, I'll finish what I started. So…you have until the top floor to decide if *you* are in or out. I won't blame you if you walk away, but I assure you after today these men, in any capacity, will *never* be an issue again."

Silence. It ticks like the pricks along my spine.

Isaac adjusts his jacket, Owen his cuffs. Both become more relaxed, while Jameson seems to tense behind me.

The elevator ride seems like forever as my heart pounds within my ears. I adjust my stance, focusing on the compression of the corset to keep me present. The elevator halts, but just before they fully open, Jameson says, "Got your six, boss."

Michael and quite a few other guards stand with solemn expressions. I step out, flicking my gaze to the guards for the other crime bosses lined near the conference room. My gaze meets Michael's, who doesn't flinch away, nodding once.

"Very good," I whisper, making his eyes widen.

All the men follow me as I stride for the heavy doors, ignoring the confused, condescending stares of the guards who aren't mine. I stop before the wooden doors.

"Now?" Isaac asks.

The trembling stops. The prick vanishes. Calm.

I am Autumn Luciano, and I will defend my husband until my final breath.

"Now."

Chapter 44

Howard the Duck

Leo

The steel wall of the shower presses against his hands as hot water streams down his back. Brain fog consumes him with the last of the unstable emotions. Confusion. Ache.

What the fuck had he done? She walked in and saw *them*. What he'd done. She stared right at the devastation he created.

There was no fear in her eyes. No flinching. No cowering. Then again, maybe he didn't notice. It was as if someone tightened their grip around his windpipe, hauling him under. He'd fought it in the past, kept this terrible part of him buried. Years of pushing it further down, the ache into that damned dark well. Hiding it.

"You're safe, baby."

Her voice was a blast of fresh air, music roaring through his head. It was all that he needed to fall to his knees; wanting…no, *needing* her praise and peace.

Leo stares at his hands.

The horrid thoughts of before are replaced by memories of her.

Ecstasy on her face, flushed as her body bowed to his touch. The shivers of her skin. Yearning in her eyes. She watched him as if he was an angel, not some monster. Peace had been in her gaze, loving him. Perhaps…

Leo shakes his head, turning the water off. What they had was enough. It had to be. After everything, he couldn't ask more from her. He knew what she needed, and it would be enough for him. His ability to be gentle.

Stepping out of the shower, he grabs a rough towel. The showers of the warehouse were bare bones, enough to clean up any blood to disappear down the drains. He dries himself, pausing at the fogged mirror. Leo wipes the steam off the surface to stare at his reflection.

"If I order you to do something, will you follow it?"

"Words, Leo."

Only once did he ever give up full control, and it almost cost him.

There'd been no one to change his trust. It wasn't worth the risk. Except Autumn. She'd been everything he needed. But this?

Leo shakes his head, exhaustion pulling in every direction. There were other things more important right now.

There's a knock. Leo grumbles, shoving the thoughts away as he pulls his pants on. They knock again as he grabs a shirt and heads for the door. He slams it open, glaring at Waylon.

"I didn't fucking drown," Leo mutters, pulling his shirt on.

"We're on a tight schedule, clock started," Waylon says, walking over to a table near the security monitors. A briefcase, stacks of folders, a laptop, and two folders sit, one marked *Option One* and the other *Option Two*.

"What's going on?" Leo asks, glancing between the folders.

Julio and Drew stand on the other side of the table, no one else around in the eerily quiet warehouse. He thought he'd heard orders being given, perhaps Autumn, but she wouldn't. That wasn't like her.

"She wanted to give you more time but given circumstances

we've got…" Drew looks down at his watch, sighing, "…about an hour. Give or take a few minutes."

"What the fuck you talking about?" Leo questions.

"You need to listen, Spartan," Waylon speaks solemnly. "Listen good. And know she did all this for you."

Leo furrows his brows, moving his gaze to each man. "Again, what the *fuck* is going on?"

Drew starts explaining, "In January, after Autumn started working with Chiari, she began collecting data on mafia members outside our organization. Then she started collecting intel on high-profile guests on *your* payroll, going through everything management kept on them. Didn't matter if they're a manager or maid, she went to all of them for their notes as part of her 'job' in helping Chiari. She targeted politicians, bankers, realtors, investors…and whoever else."

"Most her nights with security, that's what she was doing," Waylon adds. "They were helping her collect it, using her program to, well…"

"Hack into other hotels and businesses," Julio finishes, grinning slightly. "Outside ours."

"Outside?" Leo asks.

"Anything owned by the other crime bosses," Julio continues. "She used her program from years ago to hack computer mainframes to get into bank accounts, security footage, and business accounts. Almost three months, she's been collecting evidence of a *shit ton* of people conducting illegal activities."

Julio opens the *Option Two* folder, revealing spreadsheets. He pulls out another folder, flipping open to photos.

"She was assembling blackmail at the highest degree," Drew says in a somewhat worried voice. "With Chiari's help and few others at the *Italian Lily*, she was curating a master list, like she did four years ago."

"Quite enough to scare some folks," Waylon mutters.

"How?" Leo breathes out, staring at the folders as he trails a finger down the list of accounts and companies.

"She never sold the feds the *real* software she created. Instead, she sold them *Castor,* an inferior prototype," Julio says, pulling forward a laptop and Leo recognizes it as the one Owen and Julio gave her. Julio opens it, bringing up a coding program. "She made good use of the laptop, and with all the precautions Owen and I put on it…we made it easier for her to protect the real software, *Eleanor,* and upgrade it to handle new technological advances. This thing mirrors and imitates other software to hack into systems seamlessly, basically hiding in—"

"Plain sight," Leo finishes. "How did the feds not know she duped them with a fake?"

"Cause *Castor* works, but crashes hardware regularly and infuses viruses," Julio explains. "*Eleanor* doesn't. It's practically invisible, and then wipes away any sign of existence after you're done."

"Autumn didn't give Caltz everything," Drew murmurs, causing Leo to look at him. "And, well, *Castor* was only if she got caught. Bargaining chip. She thought her cover was blown and that the mob would come for her again, she didn't trust *anybody*. Even with the promise of an identity change, she wasn't going to chance fate, so she gave him half of what she found, enough to take out Gabriel. Make Caltz leave her alone. That was her only goal."

"Half? Wait, how'd she even remember any of this? It's been years since she's touched a computer, she's smart but that—"

"Oh, *Eleanor* wasn't the only thing she kept to herself," Julio says.

Leo furrows his brows. "Kept?"

Waylon opens the briefcase, pulling out a dozen of Autumn's movies. He opens a case, *The Thing,* and puts it into their computer. The monitor pulls up bank accounts and shell companies from across seas. All of them Rossi's. Julio takes out another, *Howard the Duck.* This time, it's photos of drug deals with police, federal agents, and a judge commissioner. Another movie, *Donnie Darko,* with bank accounts that the IRS would love to find.

"She should be on track to being one of the most sought-after cyber analysts or programmers for the CIA or FBI," Julio speaks low. "What she created makes what I do look like a Nintendo Gameboy system."

"Probably why she freaked about the movies being moved to the estate," Waylon says, holding up *Mommie Dearest*.

"And called Nancy to protect them," Julio adds.

Leo's silent, staring at the mountain of information that's been hiding in his own home. She could've taken him out. Easily. There was enough here to control the mafia families, *him*, and anyone in New York as puppets. One small leak. She *knew* the power of the software she created, not giving it over. *Eleanor* would be worth millions outside the mafia, and she refused to sell it. Governments would've been after her.

Memory flicks back to Autumn and Caltz's arguments in the interrogation room. Was that why he was so intent in getting her back? Did he know what she was capable of? Leo then remembers how still Autumn became when he mentioned coming to *Blue Java* before. A sinking feeling gnaws at his chest, realizing that Autumn's actions may have been manipulated from the very beginning.

"She never planned to actually use *Eleanor* again," Drew murmurs.

"We agreed she'd step back," Leo whispers, pressing his hand against the paperwork. "I refused to use her. But why now? To help Matteo?"

"She's saving yours." Waylon opens the *Option One* folder.

Leo's face goes slack. An itinerary to fly out to California. Leo picks up the folder and reads through the details. A plane has been chartered *not* under his name, along with letters typed up and ready to be signed. Documents to sell and liquidate every business owned by the Marchetti and Luciano family lines. Every tie to his family would be cut, and Gabriel, Matteo, even Renato would be left with *nothing* of his. Autumn, his wife's signature, on everything.

They're contracts to sell to the US government.

"Got a choice, Spartan," Waylon says, and Leo looks into his old friend's eyes. "Choose to stay, we use all this to control these fuckers, keep them in line, and hopefully your brothers. Keep the feds out of it, handle it ourselves. We got the ammo now. Other choice is to leave, go back to Cali and leave it all behind. Let'em burn." Leo's eyes widen. "She'll meet you in California when it's done."

"What?"

"She's meeting the big fish now, that's why there's a time limit."

Leo drops the folder. "*What?*"

Julio folds his arms, saying, "You don't show, she knows what you chose. Feds get called, everything you see is handed over to them. She buys you and her out with *Castor 2.0*, while *you* take the real deal." Julio holds up a movie case, *Fast Times at Ridgemont High*. "This is *Eleanor*. She doctored things to make it seem like you were coerced into all this by Gabriel and Matteo. She burns them for you."

"She's covered every scenario, boss," Drew comments.

"Until they figure out it was her years ago," Leo argues.

"Nah, she isn't going to be caught again." Julio pulls out a photo, pushing it toward Leo as he explains the last pieces of Autumn's multi-layered plan. "She tells the feds that if Caltz ever disappeared, all belongings of Sarah Marie Mitchell goes to the FBI. Every movie case is labeled as Sarah's. And she has in writing, signed witnesses by Nancy, Trix, and Dr. Wilson that it was Sarah's dying wish for Autumn to do this for her. To *finally* tell the truth."

In the photo is a woman with long blonde hair, wired glasses, and thin frame. Her face is blank, half smiling as she holds herself close standing in front of Nan's bookstore. All Leo can truly recognize are her eyes, those light brown eyes which are hollow and empty.

She knew. Autumn knew they were going to take everything from her. She's been playing the long game ever since. Survive.

"Your choice, stay or go," Waylon says. "We'll follow wherever."

Leo's gaze flicks between the folders.

He'd be free. Those left would be scrambling for power, even his own family. They'd be going after the mess Autumn left behind in attempt to regain control. She even included Renato, checking every box to spite them all. There's still a possibility of people coming after them or the feds, but it'd be his choice finally.

Then again, he could stay. Control them far easier than before. To not lose what he and the Crew built. He glances down at where *Eleanor* rests. Or what she built.

All Leo sees are those light brown eyes which have always calmed him. *Be selfish*, she'd told him. He glimpses toward his left hand where the wedding band should be.

Independence. That's what she was offering.

As each second ticked by, staring at the stacks of information she's collected, he could finally see whom he married.

This was Sarah Marie Mitchell.

Autumn Watson—a woman scorned with everything to lose. She was giving it all to him.

"Boss, what you choosing?"

Leo grabs the folder, heading for the exit.

"My wife."

Autumn and Leo's Story

Will finally conclude in...

My Dear Leo

Take heed against a man willing to bleed for love…

…but beware the wife whose mercy has been siphoned by false incompetent men.

Books Also By Elm Jed

<u>**Paranormal Mafia**</u>

Mafia, Murder, and Mayhem Series

Vinny the Vampire & Me

Sweet Cheeks & Her Mob Boss

The Wolf Boss & His Darling

Prequel: Memories of the Underground - Volume One

<u>**Suspense Romance**</u>

My Dear Watson Series (In Order)

My Dear Watson

My Forgotten Demons

My Emerald Fire

My Dear Leo

About the Author

Elm Jed is a Marine Corps veteran, who's been writing since they were ten years old with a degree in Theatre. They live with their husband, who is their biggest supporter from making sure they're caffeinated to listening to them ramble for hours about chaotic ideas. They spend most of their time jotting down chaotic ideas, reading monster or mafia novellas that make them laugh, or going to the gym to "lift away the sads". (Sometimes it works)

www.ingramcontent.com/pod-product-compliance
Lightning Source LLC
Chambersburg PA
CBHW062101290726
48975CB00001B/68